# Hearts That Survive

# Hearts That Survive

## Survive

### A Novel of the Titanic

Yvonne Lehman

Abingdon Press fiction
a novel approach to faith

Nashville, Tennessee

Library of Congress Cataloging-in-Publication Data

Lehman, Yvonne.
    Hearts that survive : a novel of the Titanic / Yvonne Lehman.
        p. cm.
    ISBN 978-1-4267-4488-4 (trade pbk. : alk. paper) 1. Titanic (Steamship)—Fiction. I.
Title.
    PS3562.E43H43    2012
    813'.54—dc23
                                                                    2011039138

Printed in the United States of America

1 2 3 4 5 6 7 8 9 10 / 17 16 15 14 13 12

To my dear friend Peggy Darty, a novelist who, several years ago, presented to me the idea of writing a story about the *Titanic*, enlightening me on Nova Scotia's importance and involvement in the aftermath of the great ship's sinking. She encouraged my present efforts, although it seemed *The Titanic* had already been written.
But . . . my story had not been . . . until now.

To my readers, who may want to compare my story with the book and award-winning movie, as I did when beginning this project. There is no comparison, however. That is their story. This is mine, and it is my desire, hope, and prayer that my readers enjoy this book, find it entertaining and filled with events and characters that come alive in their hearts and minds, and know what it means for a heart to survive.

## Acknowledgments

First and foremost, I must mention Dr. Donn Taylor, who wrote the poem that my character John Ancell writes in the book. Donn, accompanied by his lovely wife, Mildred, participated in my writers conferences as the poetry faculty member. You simply haven't lived until you've heard him read a poem. He is poetry personified. I am deeply grateful to him.

While my story was being developed, before I had a publisher for it, I contacted Donn and gave him a brief description of my character and what I had in mind. The following are his suggestions, which helped considerably in the development of John and gave me a lesson on poetry.

This is the English adaptation of the Italian sonnet form: an eight-line octave, rhyming ABBAABBA, followed by a six-line sestet. The pure Italian form usually rhymed CDECDE or a similar pattern. The English varied the sestet by ending with a couplet that either summarized or climaxed what went before.

I'd suggest that John start out to write a simple love poem, choosing quatrains (four-line stanzas) as his form because he can develop as many of those as his developing idea requires. So he gets one quatrain, the first four lines of the poem as a simple love poem. Then maybe you should take the story somewhere else for a while. Then he finds out that Lydia is pregnant and writes the next quatrain to attest the genuineness of his love. Again, take the story somewhere else.

After the ship hits the iceberg, he converts the poem into an Italian sonnet by dashing off the last six lines.

To be completely honest, it isn't a very good poem outside the context of your novel. Just competent, at best.

Personally, I think it's wonderful. Donn even gave this bit of instruction: "For a poem written in the early twentieth century, the poet would capitalize the first letter of each line. The change to normal sentence punctuation doesn't arrive until the final decades of the century."

In serious moments of contemplation influenced by my husband's suffering with cancer, my son-in-law, Steve Wilson, wrote a poem titled "Life as a Boat." Steve doesn't claim to be a poet. The poem fits in perfectly with my character, Beau, who doesn't claim to be a poet. Nor does Steve claim to be a singer or a guitarist or a photographer, but he does all those things well. He is a graphic designer holding the position of Advertising Director at the company where he works. His greatest accomplishment (according to me) is being a wonderful husband to my lovely fun daughter Cindy (who is also my friend and reads every word I write and likes my books) and being father to Simon, who is learning to be a tennis pro.

To my wonderful editor at Abingdon, Ramona Richards, who said after reading my book proposal, "I like it." I am deeply grateful to Abingdon for being receptive to the late inquiry and working with me on this and having confidence in my ability to write a T-I-T-A-N-I-C novel.

Thanks to agent Steve Laube for his invaluable advice. He's the one who handles the business side of writing, freeing me for the creative side. He also found the answer to my question of whether a corked champagne bottle could be in the ocean for many years, *decades* in fact, and still be intact.

Among several accounts that Steve found, this is a "sweet" one. In 1914, British World War I soldier Private Thomas Hughes tossed a green ginger beer bottle containing a letter to his wife into the English Channel. He was killed two days later fighting in France. In 1999, fisherman Steve Gowan dredged up the bottle in the River Thames. Although the intended recipient of the letter had died in 1979, it was delivered in 1999 to Private Hughes's eighty-six-year-old daughter living in New Zealand.

Many thanks to Elma Schemenauer and Janet Sketchley, who led me to Janet Burrill. Janet B and I shared e-mails almost daily due to my questions about Nova Scotia. She found where my character might live and sent pictures. She offered information, answered difficult questions—even the seemingly trite one-word ones, such as my characters' Bedford Basin home—would they live "in, at, on, by, around, or near" Bedford Basin? She told me where my characters should honeymoon, suggested I mention Rappie Pie, and sent the recipe. She said my book would not be authentic without my mentioning the 1917 Halifax Explosion that so devastated the city. Her book, *Dark Clouds of the Morning*, is set around the Halifax Explosion, which was caused by two ships colliding in the harbor. One of the ships carried tons of munitions, setting off the worst man-made explosion prior to the atom bomb. Thousands were killed or injured. She is working on a sequel, *Sunrise Over the Harbour*, covering the recovery period following the disaster.

Anyone traveling to Halifax might be interested in staying at her daughter's Blue Forest Lane Bed and Breakfast, situated in the country in a beautiful neighborhood tucked into a forested area (www.blueforest.ca.)

Janet provided much more material than I have used. I am sorry if I made mistakes about Nova Scotia. If so, it's not Janet's fault but my own.

I would be remiss if I did not acknowledge Dr. Dennis Hensley, writer, teacher, editor, director of the professional writing major at Taylor University, for his friendship and writing expertise and his participation in my writers conferences for more than twenty-five years. But here, I will confine it to his offering his opinions and suggestions. Thanks to him for putting me in touch with Kate Gutierrez, who graduated from Taylor University Fort Wayne with a B.A. in Professional Writing and a Minor in Christian Education. I appreciate her organizing ability and her outline of the fifty years of Nova Scotia history that corresponds with the time span of my novel.

## Acknowledgments

Eva Marie Everson suggested Ramona Richards as a good editor for my work. Thanks to others for their comments, prayers, advice, listening ears; and thanks particularly to my son, David Lehman, for sharing his invaluable insights. The experience of my character David is based on my David's witnessing to his schoolroom class at age six, after having accepted Jesus into his heart. And when I was on a tight deadline, my writer/friend Debbie Presnell brought me a dinner of her homemade lasagna, breadsticks, and an amazing cake, so I could write without having to cook or starve.

Thanks to my writers group and friends for their encouragement and prayers.

# Part 1
# Before

When anyone asks me how I can best describe my experience in nearly forty years at sea, I merely say, uneventful. Of course there have been winter gales, and storms and fog and the like. But in all my experience, I have never been in any accident . . . or any sort worth speaking about. I have seen but one vessel in distress in all my years at sea. I never saw a wreck and never have been wrecked nor was I ever in any predicament that threatened to end in disaster of any sort.

Edward J. Smith, 1907
Captain, RMS Titanic

"Isn't that an iceberg on the horizon, Captain?"
"Yes, Madam."
"What if we get in a collision with it?"
"The iceberg, Madam, will move right along as though nothing had happened."

Carl Sandburg, *The People, Yes*, 1936

# 1

Friday evening, April 12, 1912

$\mathcal{C}$lothed in her shame, Lydia Beaumont stood on the deck of the *Titanic*, waiting for John. Each evening since they departed two days ago from Southampton, she and John strolled here after dining. Other first-class passengers found their own special spots, like congregants in a church sanctuary.

Oh, the church analogy brought thoughts of condemnation she'd rather not entertain. The grandeur of the greatest ship ever built had pushed aside her personal feelings, any doubts or guilt that had so beset her in previous weeks. She'd tried to forget her fears by planning the trip, convincing her father to allow her to go, and helping her maid pack the trunks.

She thought back to the day before sailing while she was staying at the South Western Hotel. She'd made the acquaintance of several passengers, her favorite being Caroline Chadwick, in her mid-twenties. She and her husband, Sir William, had arrived from London and were awaiting the ship's maiden voyage to America.

Staring out the hotel suite window at the magnificent structure, four city blocks long and ten stories high, had accelerated her heartbeat. However, walking up the gangplank to board the ship and seeing the grand staircase took her breath away. Even Craven Dowd, the president of her father's company and accustomed to the best, commented on the luxury as they were led to their suite rooms.

John Ancell glanced her way, his deep blue eyes shining with excitement beneath raised eyebrows and lips turning into a mischievous grin. Had Craven not been entering the room between hers and John's, her beloved would likely say aloud what he only mouthed, "This is no toy ship."

Lydia saw Caroline and Sir William entering their stateroom. Caroline halted at her doorway and called, "Are you going on deck to wave goodbye?"

"Ah, we must do that," Craven answered for them as if the matter were settled.

"Yes," Lydia echoed, "I'll be along shortly."

"Just peek in when you're ready," Caroline said. "The door will be open."

Stepping from the private promenade deck to explore the sitting room, and then the bedrooms, Lydia was amazed. Her father, Cyril Beaumont, had endowed their home with the finest furnishings, but her personal knowledge and university studies in art and design made her realize she'd stepped into a world of unmatched luxury.

She entered John's and Craven's rooms. The furnishings represented various countries. "Reminds me of the Ritz in Paris," she said of Craven's bedroom. He gestured to the furnishings around the room. "Chippendale. Adams. French Empire."

She returned to her bedroom, where Marcella was hanging gowns in the wardrobe. Craven walked through the adjoining door that she must remember to keep locked. "The White Star Line has actually outdone their advertising." He glanced around. "Not only were they correct in saying it's one hundred feet longer than the *Mauretania* and bigger than the *Olympic*, but the other ships are like . . . toys."

His pause was so brief one who didn't know him well wouldn't suspect it was deliberate. But she knew, then reprimanded herself for being overly sensitive. Craven's adding, "toys," could mean the word slipped out before he thought about what he was saying. However, Craven always thought before speaking.

But there was a certain amount of truth to it. Further exploration could wait. After peeking in for John, then Caroline, the two women walked ahead of Craven, John, and Sir William.

"I've been to Windsor." Caroline grinned, indicating she wasn't bragging. "But, from what little I've seen already, I feel like the Queen of England without the responsibility."

Even the men chuckled. Lydia knew John couldn't make comparisons, because he hadn't traveled extensively. But Craven and William talked of the ship's design and of its opulence with no expense spared. She felt rather like a princess as she ascended the grand staircase beneath the glass dome that allowed the noonday sun to anoint them with a golden glow. She glanced back at the staircase as they moved along the deck and to the railing.

Passengers waved and people on the dock did the same. They must be feeling sheer envy.

She jumped when a sound like a pistol shot rang out.

Another.

And another.

Happy goodbyes changed to gasps and questioning.

"Nothing to fear," a man called out. "The lines tying the *New York* are giving way." That sounded rather fearsome to her.

Another said the suction from the *Titanic*'s gigantic propellers were pulling the other ship away from its berth.

The ship headed for the side of the *Titanic*. However, deck-hands stopped the *New York*'s drift and the *Titanic* steamed out of the harbor.

A man said playfully, "You don't christen a ship like the *Titanic* with a bottle of champagne, but with another ship." Several passengers laughed.

A woman warned, "It's an omen."

Lydia didn't live by omens. But the word made her think of signs. Robins were a sign of spring. Snow was a sign of winter. There were . . . personal signs. She swallowed hard and shook away the thought.

That woman was wrong about the *New York*'s breaking away being a sign. It hadn't rammed into the *Titanic*.

Maybe she was wrong about her . . . signs.

For two and a half days, she'd allowed herself the privilege of denial and had enjoyed John, her new friends, and the grandeur all around her. She'd explored the ship's grand shops, the restaurants, the women's library, and the Parisian sidewalk café.

Now as she stood looking out to sea, visualizing their destination of New York, she had to face reality.

Her long fur coat covered her silk dress. Her kid-gloved hands held onto the steel railing. The bitter-cold air burned her face, and her warm breath created gray wisps, reminiscent of Craven's cigar smoke, when he wasn't making entertaining smoke circles.

Only a moment ago she'd said to John, "Finish your dessert. I don't want any tonight. I need a breath of fresh air." That uneasiness in her stomach had nothing to do with seasickness.

John and Craven slid back their chairs and stood when she pushed away from the table. She felt Craven's gaze but met John's eyes that questioned. Usually after dining, Craven joined other men in the smoking lounge. She and John would walk onto the deck, They would stand shoulder to shoulder. With his arm around her waist, he'd speak of the aesthetic beauty of the ocean and sky. She'd dream of her future life with him.

She shivered now, looking out to where the sun had sunk into the horizon, analogous of her having sunk into the depth of yielding to temptation. A mistake seemed much worse when one was . . . *caught*. Only four weeks had passed. But she knew.

She would be an outcast if others knew. The night they'd expressed their love physically, she'd never felt so fulfilled. But with passion sated, guilt entered. She felt violated. Not by John, but by her own weakness. A decent woman should say no, keep the relationship pure until marriage.

Oh, she knew they both were at fault. But had she, more deliberately than she wanted to admit, lured him into the physical relationship because she was afraid of losing him? He wanted her father's blessing before marrying her. She doubted he would ever have it.

It was a wondrous thing to be loved, but a fearsome thing to be tainted.

For now, only she and John knew about their tainted love.

She had thought she and John could face anything together.

But anyone?

Craven?

Her father?

Her father said she was all he had after they were both devastated by her mother's death from a deadly lung disease and a stillbirth. However, Lydia had had the best of tutors and nannies. She had been accompanied to the appropriate outings by Lady Grace Frazier, a middle-aged widow. Her father and Lady

Grace became close companions, although he vowed he had neither time nor inclination to marry. His heart attack last year so frightened and weakened him, he'd made it clear that although Lydia would inherit the business, he was grooming Craven to run it.

She'd surprised him by expressing a desire to learn more about the business and win the respect of the company's American executives. She suggested that John accompany them on the trip, since he could explain his designs better than Craven. Beaumont Company wanted his designs, and John wanted to be sure that he wanted to divulged those secrets to the company. The matter would be discussed and any agreements drawn up in a legal contract.

"You may have a business head on you after all," her father said at her suggestion about John. He'd meant that as praise, so she smiled and thanked him.

Although he and others often complimented her on having inherited her mother's beauty, Lydia thought her looks paled in comparison with her mother's loveliness and grace. She'd inherited her father's ambition and strong-mindedness rather than her mother's submissive attitudes, but he never acknowledged this. He did, however, occasionally admonish her to behave in a more ladylike fashion.

Her father and Craven cultivated identical goals. One was ensuring that Beaumont Railroad Company continued to be number one in the world. Two was that Lydia become Mrs. Craven Dowd. And in that order.

At one time she'd felt that marriage to Craven was her destiny. Her friends proclaimed it her good fortune. To be honest, however, rather than sitting in the plush coach of a noisy, smelly, smoke-puffing Beaumont train, she preferred flipping a switch, watching a little Ancell toy train huff and puff, its wheels turn, and its engine chug-chug along, as she laughed delightedly with John.

Hearing footsteps, Lydia took a deep breath. The cold air in her throat made her feel as though she'd swallowed too large a bite of the French ice cream served at dinner.

Before feeling his touch on her exposed wrist, she knew this wasn't John, but Craven. Like many women, she liked the aroma of his after-dinner cigars, offset by a slight fragrance of cologne. But she preferred John's light, fresh, faintly musky scent.

"Lydia?"

Turning her head, she glanced at him. "Where's John?"

Craven's deep breath didn't seem to affect his throat. Likely, it was heated, as his face had been when she told him she couldn't see him anymore. "He's sitting at the table." His eyebrows lifted. "Writing."

"That's what poets do." She glanced beyond his shoulder, hoping John would appear.

"Lydia, there's something I want to make clear."

Facing the ocean that reflected the star-spangled night, she was reminded of the spark in Craven's eyes earlier, when he'd kissed the back of her hand and said she looked lovely. John had smiled, as if he agreed.

She'd requested they not sit with other passengers this night, but at a smaller, more intimate table. She'd planned to tell John after Craven left. But then she'd experienced that queasiness. She felt it now.

"I want you to know," Craven said. "I understand why you wanted to take this trip."

*He couldn't.*

He mustn't. John would be ruined and in the process they both would face a worse fate than if she'd stayed in London.

## 2

*L*ydia faced Craven. "Well, I'm sure you do." She hoped he thought her voice shook from the cold and not from his intimidating manner, particularly since he'd voiced his adamant disapproval of her seeing John, and had kept saying, "What if your father knew?" as if he might tell him.

"Aren't you the one who's been shouting the praises of this—" she looked out at the vast gray sea rather than into his eyes of the same color, that had a way of piercing her soul, "greatest ship ever built?"

He lifted his hand and shook his head as if she should hush. She would not. "I told you and Father I need to make this trip. After all, he is ill."

"I know." His words halted her. "You claimed it's a business matter." His tone was condescending. "But I know you wanted to be with John." He looked around, but unfortunately John wasn't approaching. "I understand that. You're young. He's different."

"Different?" Her voice squeaked. For a long time she'd been in awe of Craven. Somewhere along the line, she'd grown up.

Now he was trying to make her feel young. But, compared to his thirty-five years, twenty-one *was* young.

She shifted her gaze to the silver hair at his temples, below the darker brown. He had a handsome face. Mischievous eyes that women said were flirtatious, in a complimentary way. He certainly fit the picture of a distinguished gentleman.

"What I mean is, he's a nice boy."

*Boy?*

"And likeable. But he's a dreamer."

Before Lydia could retort that they were on an acclaimed *ship of dreams*, he added, "And he's a toy-maker."

Lydia refused to conceal her indignation. "That toy-making is what brought him to your attention, Craven. You brought it to my father and the board and gave John a place in the company so he could learn about it. Have you forgotten that?"

"Of course not. We all recognize his ingenious designs and hope we can incorporate them into real trains."

She knew Craven did not hold in high regard those who didn't come from old money, name, and prestige. She'd held some of that attitude before meeting John.

She sighed. "You're telling me what I already know."

"I guess what I'm trying to say, Lydia, is that you have every right to find out what and who you want in your life. In case this is just a phase, I want you to know I still care for you. I wish that, by the end of this voyage, you would know who is the better man."

She gasped and glared at him, open-mouthed. He held up both hands and grinned, as if she were having a childish temper tantrum. He remained calm. "I know I'm not a better man than John in many ways. But keep in mind I'm, what, ten, twelve years older than he is? Who knows what kind of man he might be in ten years? What I'm saying is, I think long term, and I'm the better man for *you*."

Lydia turned from him and looked down at her gloved hands grasping the railing, needing to hold onto something. "Thank you," she said softly. She'd enjoyed being escorted by Craven the last two years. They'd been noted in the society pages, the heiress and the president of the Beaumont Railroad Company. He'd been married and divorced and had had many women friends before her. But she could not condemn or judge, considering . . .

And she knew he cared for her. But he'd never said "love" the way John had.

"You will think about what I said?"

Alienating a powerful man like Craven wouldn't be wise. She was the heiress, but he ran the business. She smiled at him. "I was just doing that."

He gave a quick nod, lifted his regal chin, straightened his shoulders, turned, and strolled off in his confident way. Her father thought Craven the better man too. But the two of them judged a person more by his financial holdings than by his heart.

She'd never known a dreamer before, nor a man who made her dream about just being near him. John had done well to come from so-called nothing to designing a popular line of toy trains. But she didn't care if he hadn't a penny to his name.

Looking around, she nodded and spoke to those who strolled by. But where was John? Had he lost some of his eagerness to be with her?

As much as she dreaded it, she must tell John about the lie, and the truth.

Would he still love her?

Instantly everything changed. She heard his steps, sensed his presence, breathed in his essence. Felt his warmth when his fingertips touched her cold cheek.

*John.*

Before she could find the words, he spoke in that delightfully excited, energetic way of his. Probably the way a child would react upon playing with the train John had designed. John was delighted with *her*.

She'd loved it when she and John, along with her friends Elsie and Edward, had dressed like commoners and acted young and free. But being on this ship was life too. Although she had fallen in love with John when he wasn't dressed in a formal suit and white tie, her heart beat faster at the picture of male perfection. He was tall, dark-haired, lean, and quite elegant. She, in her silk and fur, felt they went right well together.

"I'm sorry I took so long," he said. "I got caught up in writing a poem to you. May I read the beginning to see if you like it?"

She nodded but dared not look into his deep blue eyes that made her feel as if the rest of the world had receded and only the two of them mattered.

He read:

> *As sunflowers turn to contemplate the sun,*
> *I turned to view your golden loveliness*
> *And loved, desired to care for, not possess:*
> *To cherish till our earthly days are done.*

His words halted. His hands moved to her shoulders as he turned her to face him. "Lydia. You're crying? Please forgive me."

She could hardly see him through her tears. How could she respond to something as beautiful as having a poem written to her? Not now. Not this way.

"I was so caught up in wanting you to know how much I love you. I know things haven't been right since—"

She could stand it no longer.

"John. I lied about making this trip for business reasons." She didn't know if it was only her head that shook or if she was trembling all over. "I am," her voice became a frigid whisper, "with child."

His mouth opened, but no warm breath came out. His eyes stared. His hands fastened like a vise on her shoulders. John looked frozen.

# 3

*J*ohn could hardly believe what Lydia had just said. He'd been thinking about the words he'd penned on paper. He'd begun the poem that first night after they boarded the *Titanic*, and had worked long and hard on the quatrain. Four lines.

Now he tried to decipher the four words she spoke. *I am with child.*

Nothing he might say or write could match that. There could be no higher honor for a man than to have the woman he loved carrying their baby.

He looked at the paper he held in his hand. He might as well toss that so-called poem into the ocean. She held inside her . . . the world. A life. His offspring.

He needed to say something. But he was not adept at speaking his deepest thoughts. They came from his mind to his fingers holding a pencil or pen, and onto paper. Orally, his sentences were like the tip of an iceberg, while in writing they expressed his depth. Even then, he felt lacking.

She was turning from him. Physically, emotionally.

What did she need from him? Joy? Apology? Should he blurt out he'd marry her now when he'd already said he wanted to win her father's blessing first?

He must find a way to make her believe her father's blessing was now a concept that might as well be buried at the bottom of the sea. He and Lydia needed the blessing of their heavenly Father. And he needed to be a blessing to Lydia and their child.

He grasped the cold, hard steel railing. "You know I love you."

"Yes, John."

His beloved stood as calm as the sea's surface. But beneath she teemed with life. The life of his child. His intake of breath was audible and brought her head around to look at him. He could hardly bear the wonder of it.

His eyes closed for a long moment. When he opened them, he barely saw her.

"John?" she whispered.

"I'm so full of feeling. I must think."

A sound, seeming to express displeasure, escaped her throat. "Can't you say anything about this? Something?" Her words were strangled. "You hate it? It's all right? Say . . . anything?"

After a moment, he shook his head, dissatisfied with himself. "There's so much to say. In my own thoughts I'm a blundering idiot. Please. Will you give me time?"

She turned from him again. "This takes time, you know."

"Just tonight. Let's talk in the morning. We might break-fast together on our promenade deck."

She nodded.

"And, Lydia. Will you do something for me? Will you read Psalm 51 tonight?"

"I can't."

He groaned. Apparently that wasn't an acceptable request when the woman you love has just told you she's carrying your child.

She glanced over. A hint of a grin tugged at her mouth. "I don't have a Bible with me."

He dared a smile. "After we retire to our cabins, I'll knock on the door of your suite and lend you my Bible."

She shook her head. "I'll have Marcella retrieve it from you."

So much was said in a simple sentence. Their eyes met for less than an instant before they looked away, as if having to confirm that neither would behave improperly. They were careful with their words, with their actions. They planned their moves. That other night, they had not planned, otherwise it wouldn't have happened.

"Shall we retire for the night?" It was early. But they had played at life too long, pretended all was well.

She nodded and they strolled along the polished teak deck. He did not put his arm around her waist. They spoke casually to others standing by the railing or walking past them.

Upon reaching their private promenade deck, neither offered the usual tender kiss. She opened the door to her sitting room. Marcella, in her white cap and apron over a black dress, walked into the sitting room and gave a brief nod.

John said, "Good night." He went to his bedroom on the other side of Craven's. He hoped Craven would follow his normal routine and not seek him out. Since he'd locked his door it had remained so and he supposed Craven had locked it on the other side to ensure privacy. He picked up his Bible from the nightstand. When the light tap-tap sounded, he opened the door and handed the book to Marcella.

Marcella took it, then made a small gesture of a curtsey. She turned away and John's focus fell upon the steward, who served several of the nearby suites.

"Anything I can get for you, sir?" the steward asked.

"No, thank you, George. I'm fine." John had not been accustomed to having anyone curtsey, nod, or constantly refer to him as "sir" before coming into the good graces of Cyril Beaumont. Such gestures made him uncomfortable. That was Lydia's world. The company's interest lay in the design of his toy trains. He could manage without the deference, and without first-class accommodations, fine as they were, but could not imagine life without Lydia.

Reminding himself he had other matters to think about, he closed the door and sat at the desk. He took his notebook from the top drawer of the nightstand, and the fountain pen and poem from his pocket.

He prefaced his intentions with closed eyes and a prayer. At the "amen" his eyes opened and his gaze moved to the window that would have been a porthole in a lesser ship. All ships were lesser to this hotel on water. Or perhaps a better description was a palace afloat.

John could imagine how one might become overwhelmed by such luxury. He shook aside those thoughts. Despite the lighted cabin, the medium blue sky was visibly aglow with brilliant starlight. That disappeared as he stared into the distance where his creativity existed.

His fountain pen became an instrument of emotion and feeling. Words poured from his heart and soul. He prayed for God to give him the proper way to make his poem a work of skill and beauty, not just idle thoughts, so that it would express exactly what he meant. He continued with the English adaptation of the Italian sonnet form. This too would be a quatrain to attest the genuineness of his love for Lydia and their child.

After a couple hours spent composing several drafts, he had the next four lines. He opened the desk drawer and took out a piece of White Star stationery and meticulously copied the first quatrain he'd read to Lydia on the promenade deck and added the second quatrain.

Perhaps morning would bring fresh thoughts, but this was his best for the moment. He tucked the sonnet into the note-book and closed it. He couldn't follow his routine of reading the scripture before turning off the light. His intent to lie in the dark and think of Psalm 51 was halted by an unbidden verse.

"Faith without works is dead."

Words too, without works, were dead.

A burden swept through him. He needed to bring this work of poetry to life. He must not only tell Lydia about the depth of his love.

He must not only avow his love, he must show it.

With a start, he rose from the chair. His mind formed a plan as clear as sunlight. He hastened from the room, praying it wasn't too late.

# 4

**Saturday morning, April 13, 1912**

$\mathscr{L}$ydia was dressed long before the ship's bugler passed along the deck announcing meal call. She'd had Marcella ask the steward to bring breakfast for two to her private deck.

John had told the steward to have Lydia order for him. Not knowing what he liked for breakfast, she smiled, thinking of all the things she would learn about him. Looking at the menu gave her a ravenous appetite. She ordered baked apples, grilled sausage, tomato omelets, Vienna rolls, buckwheat cakes, and Narbonne honey. "Oh," she said, "get the grilled ham too. He may not like sausage."

Feeling a chill, she considered turning on the heater in the sitting room and opening the door. But that would be much too cozy. She longed to return to the carefree days when she and John sneaked away to enjoy each other's company. Everything was light and gay and they laughed at the most minute happening.

They'd only meant to talk more seriously the night she had pulled the fur-trimmed hood close around her face lest she be seen. She'd reveled in being so naughty as to visit a man's apartment. Since then, she had been a person divided. Now she was a person responsible for another life, and she trembled at the thought.

Marcella had not been able to keep a sly little smile from her lips ever since Lydia mentioned breakfast for two on the deck. Now, while her maid set the table and the steward placed the food on the sideboard, Lydia looked out the windows and faced another beautiful day.

"The air is cooler this morning than last, miss, but quite pleasant." The steward's weather report mimicked yesterday's.

"Marcella," Lydia said, "I need the Bible brought in from the bedroom."

"Yes, miss." She headed for the bedroom.

Lydia glanced at George. Was she trying too hard to make others think everything was fine and she was simply going to have a Bible study with someone? My goodness, would she ever be able to think properly again? Marcella and George were the hired help.

But already John had an influence on her. John was the dearest, smartest, most creative, kindest person she'd ever known. Money and background had not made him so. And what had money and background done for her? She'd begun to see even the hired help as people. Of course, she'd known that, but now she knew it in a different way.

"Anything else I can do for you, miss?" George said.

"No, that will be all. Thank you."

He nodded, put his hands on the handle of the food cart, and rolled it from the room. Marcella brought the Bible, and Lydia placed it on the corner of the breakfast table. When the light tap sounded, Marcella opened the door and John walked in.

Last night she'd been anxious over what John's reaction might be, so confused by learning that love was not only simple and beautiful but could also be filled with problems. Now all she wanted to do was throw herself into his arms and tell him never to let her go, and to make her believe everything was fine and they would live like the ending of a fairy tale, happily ever after.

Ach! If she were such a vixen, she would not be so troubled by it all. And John had not shown much of a reaction last night. In fact, he'd been speechless. Now, he looked at her with loving eyes, then walked over to the sideboard. He lifted a couple of silver covers. "My, this is quite a spread."

Lydia joined him, deciding she could serve herself. "It all looks so good."

They filled their plates and took them to the table. John sat opposite her. Marcella poured their coffee.

Lydia glanced up at her. "You may leave, Marcella. Take as long as you like."

"Thank you, miss." Her glance moved from Lydia to John, and pink tinged her cheeks. She turned, placed the coffeepot on the sidebar, and hastily left, closing the door softly behind her.

"I hope Craven doesn't pop in," Lydia said.

John shook his head. "I already informed him we wouldn't be joining him this morning. He said he intended to take a turn in the gym."

Lydia sat with her back to the windows and the ocean view, but she could see the soft blue of the sky in John's eyes.

He offered a brief prayer of thanks for the food and asked that it give them health.

After the "amen" Lydia buttered a Vienna roll, wondering if the uneasiness she felt was a touch of seasickness, or the dreaded morning sickness she'd heard about, or her concern over how John would express what was on his mind. The aroma of the breakfast however, became overwhelmingly appetizing. She had eaten little dinner last night, had no snack later, felt tired after reading Psalm 51, and fell asleep contemplating its meaning. Now she felt quite ravenous. She must try the buck-wheat cake with a tad of honey.

John took a couple gulps of coffee and returned the cup to its saucer. He told her about his past and the events of the Prodigal Son sermon that had caused him to confront his sins of having yielded to a less than exemplary kind of life during his college years. He'd asked the Lord's forgiveness and had learned of God's great love. "Something like that is what I thought you might find in Psalm 51."

She nodded, now trying the tomato omelet. Surely she had heard the psalm read before. She supposed it hadn't concerned her, because she had never before felt she had sinned or gone against her upbringing or dishonored her father or herself.

"We need to get this behind us, Lydia. Get rid of the negative and focus on the positive."

*Get rid?* Oh, what did he mean? They could not change what was. Or is. Closing her eyes, she shook her head and swallowed her bite of food.

"Lydia." His voice was soft. "Give me your hands."

She opened her eyes and looked at the outstretched palms of his hands on the table. "Let's ask God's forgiveness."

"Let me take a sip of coffee first."

He sighed. "Maybe my idea of combining breakfast and talk wasn't a good idea."

"Oh, yes," she said. "Otherwise, I would faint from starvation."

His gaze turned thoughtful but patient while she took a couple sips of coffee. "I'm ready now. I really am." She set down her cup and placed her hands in his.

His gentle pressure was like a sweet caress. "Forgive me, Lydia, for disrespecting you."

"You didn't disrespect me, John. There was no coercion."

He appeared to accept that. "But I did disrespect God's law." He bowed his head. "Almighty God, who sees our hearts, who knows our every thought, our every breath. We have brought a blight upon our love. Forgive us." He paused.

"Thank you that you forgive us the moment we ask. You really forgave us when Jesus died on the cross. We only need to repent and ask. We are starting over now, with you as our guide, and we ask Thy blessing upon our lives. Amen."

"Amen," Lydia said tentatively and barely managed not to grab her fork and behave like some hungry little urchin who'd never had a speck of learning.

"Look out there," he said. "The ocean and sky have met and the horizon reaches into infinity. That's where our sin is now."

She turned, squinted, and put her hands over her eyes as if she couldn't see that far.

"That's right. We'll never be able to see it again. God said he would cast our sins into the deepest sea and remember them no more. We're clean, Lydia. We start anew now."

She nodded. She wanted to believe that. If she did not have every indication a child was growing in her, if she hadn't missed her monthly time, if she didn't have that churning in her stomach even before shipping out to sea, then guilt likely would not have lain upon her so heavily. "I don't want you to think we have to get married."

They were talking about this so calmly. And how could she be eating at a time like this? But the aroma beckoned and that's what breakfast was for, even if John hadn't touched his.

As if reading her mind, he laid his napkin on his lap, lifted his fork and took a bite of eggs. Oh, the aroma wafted right to her. If he didn't hurry and eat his wonderfully seasoned sausage, she would.

He swallowed and shook his head. That loving look came into his eyes, bluer than the ocean, bluer than the sky. "I don't want you to think I'd marry you because I have to." He glanced toward the deck beyond the private one. "I'm well aware there's a man out there who wants you as his wife. He's made that clear to you, me, your father, and possibly anyone with whom he comes in contact."

A terrible dread settled over her. "Are you saying—?"

"Oh, my, no," he almost shouted. His eyes and voice held distress. "Maybe this will speak for me." He reached into his pocket and brought out the poem. "I need to read it myself because—"

"Quit explaining and read it, John."

She let her teeth toy with her lower lip to keep from smiling—maybe laughing. In showing his trains, he became an excited child and confident man. When showing his poetry, which was his heart, he became self-conscious. She loved that about him.

He took a deep breath. "You remember the first lines?"

She'd been so concerned about how to tell him she hadn't really absorbed the poem but thought it was something about her hair being like sunshine.

"Of course you don't." Color rose to his face.

"Read it all, John."

He read:

> As sunflowers turn to contemplate the sun,
> I turned to view your golden loveliness
> And loved, desired to care for, not possess:
> To cherish 'til our earthly days are done.

He glanced at her and she nodded for him to continue. "It isn't finished, but these are the new lines."

*But then desire for pleasure we should shun*
*Crept in: Brief bliss brought shame with each*
*caress.*
*Though we have sinned, I love you none the less,*
*But more, yet more, 'til life's last thread is spun.*

She could only whisper through her closed throat, "Again."

With shaky breath he read it again.

Finally she found her voice. "I've never heard anything so beautiful. I don't know of anything you could ever give me that would mean more."

"Except . . ." He held up a finger, and his lips turned into a grin.

She did not feel the guilt—she felt the joy. She nodded and placed her hand on her stomach. "Yes, except."

## 5

Now I have two of you to love," John said, grateful they could focus less on the sin and more on the miracle of life. They could sit and eat breakfast together and have a conversation about the most important things in life. She took a forkful of baked apples and, while chewing, began buttering her second roll.

He washed down his sausage with a gulp of coffee. "I'm glad you like the poem." Realizing he was pointing the fork at her, he lowered it and focused on the Bible. "But I certainly cannot hold a candle to King David. He's the greatest poet that ever put pen to paper."

"Greater than Shakespeare?" She bit into the roll.

"Shakespeare's pen was indeed mightier than the sword, as the saying goes, but not greater than the pen of David, whose writings have God at the center."

Chewing, she gave him a tolerant glance and laid the roll on the bread plate. "John, I'm not completely ignorant of the scriptures. I believe in forgiveness and in God's love." She looked down, then up again. "But there are also consequences.

David and Bathsheba's child— Oh, John. You know what happened to it."

For a moment, John could not draw in a breath. The child had died because of their sin. Such a thought was horrifying. He and Lydia wished the events hadn't happened as they had. Now he thought she felt as he did. Both wanted this child of theirs.

He took a swallow of coffee to dislodge what was stuck in his throat. "Yes, King David sinned. He was a human being who yielded to temptation."

"And he paid the price."

"But he was forgiven. And good came from it. He penned Psalm 51. If David had not sinned, we would not have the words that have reached the world since they were written and will continue as long as there is life on earth. I daresay his words are sung in heaven."

Sensing her uncertainty, he hastened to add, "Fortunately, I'm not a warrior king whom God has called to be an example to the world. I'm just a poor poet."

"You're not poor, John. But I don't care if you don't have a cent."

"If I hadn't a cent, you'd never have known me. But anyway, I'm poor compared with the other first-class passengers. I only have these accommodations because your father's company made the reservations."

"But you don't care."

He toyed with a spoon for a moment, then clasped his hands on his lap. "I care in the sense that my having had some success with my trains brought me to your father's attention. More importantly, to yours. And I want to be a success. Frankly, I'd rather be a success as a poet than a toy-train maker. My trains and I are considered minor compared with the first-class passengers, and with your father's real trains."

"Considered," she said. "But real trains only take people from one destination to another. Your trains bring joy and happiness and dreams of going to all sorts of places. And my father is impressed with your designs."

"Thank you. That's your opinion because you love me."

"Yes, I do, John. When I am around you, it's like the rest of the world goes away. And that's fine with me."

He leaned toward her. "Someone mentioned that our relationship might well be a passing fancy for you. I'm a different kind of person from what you're accustomed to."

Seeing her sigh, turn her head, and tighten her lips, he knew she thought Craven would have been the one with that bit of wisdom. And she would be right. Craven made no secret of wanting Lydia for himself. In the meantime, he tolerated John, although trying to brainwash him into thinking he was not worthy or not mature enough for Lydia. John often thought so himself.

Lydia was remarkable. She hadn't given in to Craven but had been determined to continue her education. She'd followed her heart about John instead of society's unwritten rule that she choose someone of equal background. Few had the wealth of Cyril Beaumont.

But he'd lingered too long. What more could he say? He might quote Othello from Shakespeare's tragedy. *When . . . you shall . . . speak of me . . . speak of one that lov'd not wisely but too well.*

Pushing his plate away from him, he reminded himself he must not quote others. He should adhere to the advice in Longfellow's poem "The Courtship of Miles Standish," that said, *"Speak for yourself, John."*

First, he couldn't resist saying, "I do believe you are eating for two."

Her mouth opened, her gaze fell upon the third roll she held in her hand. She covered her mouth with the other hand and laughed. Ah, it was good to hear that laughter. At least he was learning how to make her happy. Keep her pregnant and give her food.

"I'm a pig this morning," she said.

Good. The mood was lighter. Now was the time not just for words but for action, to show Lydia his love.

# 6

*O*h."

Lydia laid down her fork and placed her hand against her heart. John pushed away from the table and stood. Her ravenous appetite must have disgusted him. She started to question, but he said the strangest thing.

"Don't move." He knelt on one knee in front of her and took her hands in his.

"Lydia. Love of my life. Will you do me the honor of becoming my wife?"

He reached into the pocket of his morning coat and brought out a small black box, which he opened to expose a diamond ring sparkling in a bed of lush blue velvet. "I love you with all my heart. Will you marry me?"

She stared and finally stuttered. "Where . . . when . . . did you get this?"

"Last night. There's an American jeweler aboard. You know, Mr. Claude Deeman."

Of course she knew. Every woman should have a Deeman jewel. "I couldn't ask for anything better. But the size? How?" Her gaze darted from the ring to his face, which had paled.

"We have a few mutual friends."

"Elsie?"

His raised eyebrows indicated she'd guessed.

"The night we went to the carnival with her and Edward." She gasped, remembering. John and Edward had insisted they get those cheap little rings and pretend the two couples were engaged. How silly they had been, making Lydia and Elsie swap rings while the men decided which one they should wear.

"You and she wore the same size," he said. "She was in on it, too, and gave me her ring so I would know your size. I've kept it with me, waiting for the right moment."

The carnival night preceded the night they had spent together. "You wanted to marry me way back then?"

"From the moment I met you."

He removed the ring from the blue velvet and held the yellow gold band between his fingers.

A question hung in the air. Not when, or how, or what, or why. But, will you?

She extended her trembling hand. "Yes, John. I'll marry you. I love you."

He slipped the ring on her finger. She stared at the ring, remembering the times she'd looked at her mother's ring, the one her father said would be hers when she married, either to wear or to keep.

But she knew her father would not give it to her if she didn't marry a man of his choice. John was here, and a manifestation of his love was on her finger. If a choice had to be made, she'd rather have John's ring, even if it were the carnival one in her jewelry box. Someday perhaps she could give her mother's ring to her daughter, or to her son for the woman of his choice.

Welling up inside her were contrasting emotions: sadness at not being able to share this with her mother alongside excited anticipation of spending her lifetime with the man who touched her heart.

He took her fingers, brought them to his lips, and kissed them.

"May I?" He glanced at her stomach.

She nodded. Wet emotion spilled from her eyes and she could not suppress a small laugh of happiness as he gently touched where his child grew. He looked so wonderful kneeling before her and even reached out to the table and steadied himself.

She laughed. "John, you might want to get up now."

The color in his face deepened. "Oh." He rose from his kneeling position and pulled his chair over in front of her. "Of course, you will want to plan the wedding. Whatever you want, wherever you want. New York. England. France." John grinned. "But I have a thought."

"Uh-oh." She lifted her gaze to the ornate ceiling and back to him again. She would love to look at him forever.

"I know. I'm the dreamer."

"I love that about you."

"Well, what do you think about our getting married right here on the *Titanic*? Not wait any longer?"

"Would that be legal?"

"I'm sure it would be. I'll ask. I know captains and chaplains can perform ceremonies. So the captain should have legal papers on board. All licenses have to be signed and filed, but once a man and woman are pronounced husband and wife, the preacher says they're married." He stared at her with hopeful eyes.

When she didn't answer immediately, John began to reassure her. "We can later be married in a church and invite our friends. Your father can walk you down the aisle."

He shook his head and spoke apologetically. "I've never put great value on money, but since I've achieved some success, I know the possibilities that lie before me, and I have to admit I am impressed with what wealth can do. Seeing this ship in particular, I understand how one might get caught up in it, be dazzled by it."

This seemed so foreign to how John usually spoke. But his next words thrilled her. "I would love to see you, the most beautiful girl in the world, at the top of that grand staircase while becoming my wife."

"Oh, my." She saw it in her mind. If anyone overheard John's words, they might think he had become caught up in the opulence around him. She knew better. When they'd explored the impressive ship, many had spoken of, "What money can do."

John said, "It also shows what the creative mind can conceive and do, with God's permission." She'd never really thought of God as being so personal. He'd perhaps brought John to her for a reason.

For now, however, she put her hand on her chest to still her drumming heart.

Her breath came fast. "Married on the most glamorous ship in the world." She laughed lightly. "Now who's a dreamer?"

"No," he said. "I'm sure that can happen. I want you to have the best."

He returned her smile. "I'll talk to the captain and see what can be done. We'll invite—" He waved his hands to encompass the earth. "Everyone."

"Everyone," she repeated. He must know *everyone* meant those in first class.

"Ohhhh," she moaned. "I don't have a wedding dress."

"You're wearing a lovely white one right now."

"It's a morning dress."

He shrugged. "Morning. Night."

She sighed. "Men." She waved her hand and wiggled her ring finger. "Go, John. Find out what we can do."

He stood. He wanted to grab her and hold her and kiss those sweet lips. Soon they would be husband and wife. The thought was overwhelming.

The look in her eyes reflected the longing he felt. He lifted her hand, gave it a proper gentleman's kiss.

"I love you, Lydia."

"I love you, John." She raised her hands to his face and pressed her lips against his, and they shared a deep, meaningful kiss. In his mind, in the mind of God, the sin was no more. Theirs was now a new love, a pure love.

He moved away, and she clasped her hands on her lap.

"We will soon be a family," he said.

She nodded. Her eyes were moist. Or was he seeing her through the mist he felt in his own? With overwhelming love in his heart, he hastened from the room.

# 7

**Saturday mid-morning, April 13, 1912**

*J*ohn thought he should tell Craven first. He'd get the negative out of the way so he could concentrate on the positive. He found him on the promenade deck sitting in a chair next to a gentleman Lydia had pointed out in Southampton. He was a steel tycoon with whom both the Beaumont Railroad and the White Star Line had done business.

Craven introduced them as A. T. Fortone of Fortone Steel and John Ancell of toy trains.

"Ah, yes." Fortone vigorously shook John's hand. "Actually, several of my grandchildren have been entertained for hours with your trains." He chuckled. "I admit I've had my turn at them."

After the brief exchange of polite conversation, John addressed Craven. "I don't mean to intrude or interrupt. But when you have a free moment, I'd like to speak with you."

"Of course," Craven said and rose. "Always business," he said to Fortone, who gave a knowing nod.

Craven walked with John a few feet away, to a secluded spot at the railing and held out a cigarette case. John shook his head. He'd never seen Craven with a cigarette, only a cigar.

"Is Lydia all right?" he asked, the cigarette held between his lips.

John both appreciated and resented Craven's first thought being of Lydia. "This isn't anything negative. Quite the contrary, in fact."

Craven took his lighter from his suit pocket, snapped it open, moved his thumb over the ragged wheel, then peered at John over the flame. He dragged on the cigarette and exhaled the smoke, which mingled with the aroma of fresh air and sea water. His raised eyebrows questioned John with a condescending tone, *Well?*

John coughed lightly at the smoke in his throat. Or was it inhibition? He might as well come out with it. "Actually, Lydia and I are engaged to be married."

He was not unprepared for the momentary silence during which Craven's nostrils flared minutely, and despite the intensity of those steel-gray eyes, this was one time John didn't avoid the stare.

Craven's heavy drag on the cigarette turned the end into a smoldering red mass that burned along the white paper covering, leaving a black line and turning the tip to ash. Craven raised his chin and blew a ring of smoke that drifted out over the sea. Likely, he'd named it "John."

John breathed in the fresh sea air. "We want to marry here on the ship."

With a flick of his wrist, Craven tossed the cigarette into the ocean. He faced John squarely, with the stance, the gaze, and the aplomb of a man who accepted only his own opinions.

"That's ridiculous, John. It shows your immaturity," he scoffed. "Do you know what you're saying? A spur-of-the-moment wedding? Lydia's wedding should be the social event of the season. With her friends present. And her father."

Arguing would serve no purpose. "Tell me this, Craven. What church aisle or even palace steps are more impressive than the grand staircase?"

Craven's inability to name one spurred John on. "You speak of friends. How could there be a more splendid event than the gathering of these first-class passengers on the greatest ship in the world? Where else would she be more acclaimed? What more could you want for Lydia?"

John knew. Craven's expression and eyes seemed to say *myself*.

"You've made your point," Craven allowed. "But Lydia sees with you a kind of life that is different from the one to which she is accustomed. And this ship? I daresay even a woman older and more experienced than Lydia would be impressed with romantic thoughts of a wedding on this ship. Do you really think this is the time and place for deciding something that will affect your entire life? You haven't even known each other long."

"Long enough," John said.

"I'm older than you, John. Perhaps I could give you a little advice."

*Yes, he could use some advice—where to find the captain.*

"Lydia is somewhat sheltered. And she's impressionable."

Circumstances now ruled out whatever opinion, advice, or lack of blessing that might come from Craven or Lydia's father. But John would like their approval. "We love each other, Craven."

Craven scoffed, "I cannot imagine a man who wouldn't love her."

John understood the implication. Lydia was everything a man could desire. Aside from that, she was heiress to a vast fortune and would likely come into it at a young age, since she was an only child of her parents' middle-aged years.

"You know her father would be highly displeased to hear of your plans. Such a move could affect her entire future."

As much as John didn't like to admit it, he felt inhibited around men like Craven, who gave such a vivid impression that they owned the world that one could almost believe it.

Nevertheless, he said, "I wanted you to be one of the first to know."

"To be sure," Craven said stiffly.

The conversation—or was it a confrontation?—unnerved John. Just as he turned to try to stroll confidently along the deck, he almost tripped over a little boy, who sprinted away from a man shouting after him, "Henry." John caught hold of the railing and forced himself against it rather than fall over and crush the boy.

The man and John said, "Sorry," at the same time. The little boy had stopped and looked up at them as if he had no idea what might be their problem.

The man, whom John recognized, touched the boy's head. "You need to watch where you're going, son." He extended his hand to John. "Henry Stanton-Jones."

John shook his hand. "John Ancell. Pleased to meet you."

Henry introduced the boy as Henry George and the pretty young girl near him as Phoebe. An elegant middle-aged woman John had seen with them before walked up and was introduced as Lady Stanton-Jones, his mother. The gracious lady extended her gloved hand, and John bent his head and touched it with his lips.

"Come along, children, let's get to the dining room. Henry George, don't run ahead."

The woman and two children walked on. John wasn't sure what he should say. He'd never say to Cyril Beaumont, *I've ridden on your trains.* But he might as well plunge in. "Mr.

Stanton-Jones, I've read your books. And I was particularly intrigued with *Once Upon an English Country Garden*."

The author smiled. "Thank you. I appreciate that." He paused, as if weighing his thoughts. "I've seen you with Miss Beaumont and Mr. Dowd."

John wasn't surprised that he knew Lydia. And Craven, who was well known in the right circles, just as were Stanton-Jones and his mother. Elation swept through John at the thought this would be his first real announcement. The one to Craven had been an informing of intentions. "This morning," he said, "Lydia Beaumont and I decided we'd like to get married aboard this ship." He shrugged. "I need to track down the captain to ask if that's a possibility."

"What a marvelous idea." The author's eyes brightened. "A wedding on the *Titanic* would be a wonderful memory. The first wedding on the *Titanic* will be an event to interest the world."

John nodded. Maybe his idea wasn't so far-fetched. "If I can pull this off, you're invited. And your—" John knew the novelist noticed the catch in his breath before he quickly finished his sentence by saying, "your mother."

John felt terrible. He'd been caught up in his own good news and quite forgot that he had read that the novelist's wife had suffered a long illness before finally succumbing to it. He didn't know if Stanton-Jones had remarried, so he had no idea if he should offer condolences or congratulations.

Stanton-Jones began to walk along the deck, and John fell in step with him, hoping to redeem his *faux pas* of rattling on about his own good fortune. "Judging from your book, you're apparently a man of great faith."

Stanton-Jones glanced his way. He must have sensed the misery John was feeling. He smiled. "I came to faith through the worst struggle of my life. The *Once Upon* book is a tribute to my wife. It's based on our personal story."

"I'm so sorry. Please forgive me—"

"No, no." He stopped to look straight into John's eyes. "Writing about it was my healing. That, and the fact God forgave my years of ranting and questioning. I was angry and turned my back on him. But he wouldn't let me go and has blessed me tremendously."

John nodded, now remembering that the book's male character had had a similar experience.

"You see, the purpose of the book is to let readers know there is still life after death, on earth and in heaven."

John wondered if his own faith could be that strong. But he'd never experienced the kind of loss this man had faced.

"I refuse to live in grief," the novelist said. "I keep alive my wife's memory within myself and alive to our children." As if fearing John would again apologize, he added quickly. "But I fully expect to marry someday if I can fall in love again."

A brief pause ensued as if each must respect a moment of acknowledging the late wife of this famous novelist. Then Stanton-Jones continued the conversation, "If you can join us in the reception room before lunch, I'd like us to become better acquainted." His smile lit up his face, reminding John of an interview he'd read, proclaiming the novelist as most fortunate, being a stereotypical tall, dark, handsome man with alluring dimples.

John wasn't one to compare one man's looks with another, but Stanton-Jones made a striking appearance. John was most impressed, however, with his friendly manner.

"And too," Stanton-Jones leaned closer as if confessing a conspiracy, "perhaps we shall discuss this floating plot of a novel that might have a main character who marries on a ship of dreams. Believe me," he added, "James Abington, whom

Yvonne Lehman

you may know is a fellow-passenger, has made it clear he is interested in publishing my books in America. I can almost see the wheels in his mind turning as fast as those propellers at the bottom of this ship."

"I dare say," John said and joined his good humor with a laugh.

"Sorry." Stanton-Jones sobered. "I'm monopolizing what should be a two-way conversation. It's just that I'm so over-whelmed with my surroundings and—"

John interrupted, "Not at all. I understand how all this grandeur whets the creative appetite."

Stanton-Jones stared for a moment, before realization struck his eyes. "You wouldn't be the poet, John Ancell?"

John nodded.

"You had a reading at the Library in London."

"You were there?"

"No, sorry. I was deep into research at the time. But I've read of you in the Art sections of newspapers. I confess, although I admire a poet's ability to capture so succinctly what takes me an entire book to say, I was never good at getting a clear grasp of poems without some instruction."

John appreciated his honesty and smiled. "Such sentiments are not uncommon."

"But I'd love to hear how a poet's mind works. You must already have numerous possible themes about something on this ship."

"To be sure." John thought of the poem he was writing to Lydia. "And thank you for the invitation. I would like to join you in the reception room."

"Bring Miss Beaumont, of course." As he turned to walk away, he said, "By the way, I'm known informally as S. J." He paused. "Ah, there's a steward. Perhaps he can assist you in locating the captain."

That was handy. Within a short while John's emotions had gone from the extreme elation of becoming an engaged man to the distress of having to abide Craven's disapproval and finally to an easy camaraderie with S. J. He'd not thought through how to reach the captain.

The man in charge of this floating city wouldn't be sitting around awaiting his presence. "A moment, please." He lifted a finger.

The steward stopped. "How may I assist you, sir?"

He asked how he might speak with the captain. "There's no problem," John hastened to say. "Just a request to speak with him about a personal matter."

"You might write a note," the steward said. "Then it will be passed along to the master-at-arms who will ensure it gets to the captain."

"Yes. Of course."

"Anything else, sir?"

"No. That's quite all. Thank you."

Embarrassment wafted through John. The steward would know he wasn't accustomed to the protocol of first-class.

Then he felt discomfiture for having such a thought. He was of no more worth than the steward or anyone else. How easily one might fall into the trap of illusion. In the sight of God, all men are equal.

He knew that, of course. But as he'd reveled in the opulence and luxury surrounding him, and the reported worth of first-class passengers on this ship described in newspapers as *The Millionaire's Special*, the words of the poet, Alfred Lord Tennyson, came to mind.

> *Equal-born? O yes, if yonder hill be level with the flat.*
> *Charm us, Orator, till the Lion look no larger than the Cat.*

# 8

Marcella opened Lydia's sitting room door after John's knock, and he stepped into the lion's den. Craven and Lydia stood facing each other, he with a heated face and she with a determined one.

The air became thick with silence, and Marcella's eyes doubled in size with her obvious concern.

Lydia stepped toward John. "Have you spoken with the captain?"

"I've sent a note by the steward, requesting a conversation with the captain." Since a quick glance revealed that Craven neither sneered nor balked, that had been the proper procedure. However, the man's expression reminded John again that he likely wished it had been John he had flipped over the ship railing rather than his cigarette.

But John felt it time that Craven stepped away from his role of Lydia's guardian, protector, advisor, and wishful fiancé. All these roles were John's responsibility, and he intended to fill them.

Strange, what had happened as a result of his weakness was giving him newfound courage. He was no longer oppressed by whether Craven, Cyril Beaumont, or anyone else thought him worthy. His thoughts were on Lydia and their child.

With God in their hearts and lives, they need not cower before anyone's disapproval. Their love would see them through. To deny that would be an ultimate transgression.

John felt confident as his thought blocked any negative ones from Craven. "I bumped into the novelist, Henry Stanton-Jones. He has invited us—" he made a quick motion with his finger at Lydia and back to himself, despite pointing being considered undignified, and did not look at Craven, "to visit with him and his family in the reception room before lunch."

"How delightful," Lydia said. "I've read his books and my parents were acquainted with the Stanton-Joneses, but I've never formally met them."

Lydia's shining blue eyes darkened with doubt. "Oh, I hope we hear something soon from the captain. My trunks will need to be brought up. I must find something suitable for the—" her glance moved to Craven as her chin lifted, "the wedding."

He scoffed, "Is that not getting the cart before the horse?"

Lydia's euphoria wasn't daunted. "Like John, I am a dreamer."

John wondered, if they were not expecting a child, could they resist Craven's displeasure? Having this secret, however, emboldened them. He would try to have a civil relationship with Craven. "Would you stand up with us, Craven? Be my best man?"

Craven's dark eyes were steel beneath raised eyebrows. "I would not displease nor dishonor Lydia's father by agreeing to something that would be expressly against his wishes and my better judgment."

"I understand. But you are invited."

John had often heard his father say, *Keep a stiff upper lip, ol' chap*, but it didn't apply here. Craven was wearing his quite well.

Craven turned without another word. Marcella had the door open by the time he reached it, and she closed it after him.

"Congratulations," Marcella said softly, her eyes dark as the dress she wore but the twinkle in them as bright as her white apron and cap. She put a finger on her lips as if keeping them mum.

Lydia laughed, apparently knowing her maid well. "You may tell, Marcella." She smiled and John nodded. He felt that made at least three on the ship who were pleased about a possible wedding.

"Go, John." Lydia pushed him from the room. "I must dress for lunch in anticipation of speaking with the distinguished captain, who just might be as excited about a wedding as we are."

"Impossible." John drew her to him for a tender touching of their lips. Although many people spoke as if servants couldn't hear, he mimed, "I love you."

"I love you too," she said aloud. "Now go."

He went, and within the half-hour rang her room. "The steward has delivered a message from a most important person aboard this ship." He laughed at his own words. "Perhaps in this case I should say *the* most important person, since he is the one in charge of this ship of dreams."

# 9

Saturday, April 13, 1912

Caroline, who apparently waited on the promenade deck for Lydia to appear, exclaimed, "I heard a juicy bit of gossip."

That's what Lydia had expected. The night they were in Southampton, Marcella had become friends with Caroline's maid, Bess. And Lydia had said Marcella could tell.

Lydia brought her hand up to the throat of her lace-trimmed dress, displaying her ring finger.

Caroline's delighted squeal pleased Lydia. Her eyes questioned. "John?"

Confused by the question, Lydia simply nodded.

Caroline grinned. "I wondered which one you would choose, your being pursued by two such eligible men."

Lydia wouldn't exactly call it "pursued." Craven suffocated her. John liberated her. "I love John."

The wistfulness in Caroline's reply of, "I know," took Lydia aback for a moment. But only a moment. Choices weren't always made according to one's heart. Many conformed to the expected, or what one's family had decided long ago, or what or who was acceptable. The wrong choice could result in the loss of position and favor.

Lydia wondered about Caroline's reason for marrying Sir William. She hoped they'd become good friends. Caroline seemed the kind in whom she could confide and trust.

"It's lovely." Her soft hazel eyes held warmth. Lydia had the impression Caroline wouldn't sneer even if she were wearing the carnival ring.

Soon John joined her, and William joined Caroline. They walked onto the deck that surrounded the ship, then down the staircase to the reception room.

"The band's ragtime was especially enjoyable last night," Caroline said. "Did you hear them?"

Lydia replied that she hadn't but looked forward to it. She thought of how differently her late evenings had been spent. That's when she'd been so troubled by what to do, what to say to John, how to tell him.

Amazing how one's anxiety could be dispelled in a short time. Her glance kept returning to the ring, glistening on her finger, and she felt her heart must surely be shining too.

Reaching the entrance, Lydia's gaze scanned the assembled passengers. She recognized Stanton-Jones from the picture on his book covers. He wasn't difficult to see, being half a head taller than most of the men. Lady Stanton-Jones looked like her photos in newspaper society pages.

John took the envelope from his pocket and said to a steward, "The captain said I might speak with him."

He ignored the envelope. "Mr. Ancell. This way please."

Caroline held up crossed fingers and the tilt of her head meant *Go with my good wishes*.

Lydia and John followed the steward, who reported to the captain, "Mr. Ancell has arrived."

The captain excused himself from Lady Stanton-Jones and the friendly Mr. and Mrs. Straus. Lydia thought how grand if she and John would have a long life together and be obviously in love like that older couple.

John introduced her to the captain.

"Miss Beaumont. I've looked forward to meeting you. I'm sorry your father is ill and couldn't make this trip."

After a brief discussion of her father's health, Lydia told him what he likely already knew, and which was true of many travelers: "My father wouldn't cross any ocean without you at the helm of the ship."

His smile enhanced his handsome, white-bearded face. "Cyril and I have had many a good conversation." He looked at John. "I believe your note mentioned a personal matter."

"Yes, sir," John said. "Miss Beaumont and I are engaged to be married."

He appeared genuinely pleased. "Congratulations."

Seeing John's discomfort at how to ask, Lydia took over. "Would you consider performing the marriage ceremony?"

His great white eyebrows rose, and his eyes twinkled from both the light of the chandeliers and his obvious pleasure. "You mean have a wedding on this maiden voyage of the *Titanic*?"

"Exactly. Imagine the publicity," she said, as if there hadn't been a sufficient amount already.

His fingers touched his bearded chin. "Ah, decisions. But Cyril would never forgive me if I refused a request from his daughter."

She refrained from saying her father might never forgive him if he agreed to the request.

"How about this?" he mused. "There are some who would want to have a deciding vote on such an event taking place. I mean, unless it were to be small and private."

"I was thinking the grand staircase."

He didn't seem surprised. "Barring any unforeseen circum-stance I will be honored to perform the ceremony, privately or including the—" he grinned and his eyes danced merrily, "the grand staircase."

He cautioned, "I don't make the plans, however, I just ensure they're carried out."

He waited until the bugler wandered farther down the deck, announcing lunch with the blasts of his trumpet, and then spoke again. "Shall we discuss this further at dinner?"

"Yes, thank you," Lydia said as John thanked him too.

Captain Smith glanced at the steward standing a few feet away appearing to be deaf, but his nod indicated that he had received the silent message from the captain about dinner and would comply.

# *10*

*J*ohn watched Captain Smith walk over to a group of passengers. He'd never personally met the managing director of the White Star Line, J. Bruce Ismay, or Thomas Andrews, the ship's builder, but he had seen their pictures in the newspapers and in the *Titanic's* advertisements.

He'd heard it mentioned that John Jacob Astor was the richest man on the ship. Lady Stanton-Jones engaged in conversation with Mrs. Astor, whom Lydia said was in the family way and in her teens; although Mr. Astor was forty.

Seeing Andrews glance his way, John quickly averted his eyes. He didn't want to think they might be as condescending about him or his toy trains as was Craven. However, he must remember that Craven had brought his designs to Cyril Beaumont. To think it had all started many years ago with a little train John's father had carved from a slab of wood, useless except for burning.

The room of people began to stir. After having visited with others, they began leaving the reception room. Stanton-Jones walked up to Captain Smith's group, spoke briefly, then he and his mother headed John's way. Lady Stanton-Jones spoke to Caroline and William, who had joined them. A stewardess brought S. J.'s children.

The Chadwicks and Lavinia, the name Lady Stanton-Jones insisted upon being called, had met on other occasions. John appreciated the informality but knew he'd never say "Lavinia" without prefacing her name with "Lady."

"Henry told me the exciting news," Lady Lavinia said after introductions were made. "Let me see that ring more closely."

Lydia offered her hand.

"I can hardly wait to hear all about it," Lady Lavinia said. "Nothing I like better than a good romance story."

"I want to hear it too," Phoebe said.

Henry laughed. "John and I have already commented on the novel plot possibilities."

"What isn't a novel idea to you?" Lady Lavinia said, with a fondness in her tone. As they entered the saloon, she said in invitation, "This is our table."

John had noticed that most of the passengers seemed to congregate at the same table and with the same set of friends at dinner, although not at lunch. As he and Lydia had done one day, many lunched in the sidewalk café.

"If you'll pardon me," William said, "I promised to lunch with Craven." Caroline smiled. He excused himself and headed for a table in a far corner where Craven and two other men were seated.

Stewards pulled out chairs for the ladies. Master Henry, looking bored, played with the silverware. He used a spoon to tap every object within reach. He was discreet about it. Phoebe glanced at him and then away as if that were an ordinary occurrence.

That reminded John of the writing of another Henry. Thoreau, to be exact. *If a man does not keep pace with his com-*

panions, perhaps it is because he hears a different drummer. Let
him step to the music which he hears, however measured or far
away.

He couldn't help being intrigued with the young boy's
intensity in seeming to concentrate on the varying tones as
he lightly tapped the objects with the spoon.

As if thinking about different drummers, Lady Lavinia
began a discussion about her son's novels, particularly *Once
Upon an English Country Garden*, and Lydia and Caroline
joined in.

S. J. turned the conversation to John's poetry. John admitted he was not widely acclaimed outside his university and
possibly London. "My recognition has come through my toy
trains."

"The Ancell trains. Of course." S. J. showed interest. "I've
looked at those. Undoubtedly, jolly ol' Saint Nick will make a
delivery of one under our Christmas tree this year."

A clatter sounded as a spoon dropped onto little Henry's
bread plate. His face became animated. "Is it Christmas?"

They all laughed while his father leaned over to speak
past Phoebe. "Not yet, Son. First is your birthday." He looked
around at the others. "Henry will be three the day we arrive in
New York." He spoke loudly enough for his son to hear. "And
there will be a present."

"A train?"

"No. Santa considers bringing trains for good boys at
Christmastime."

Gentle laughter sounded, but Lady Lavinia said, "Henry is
always a good boy."

Henry tightened his lips and continued playing with the
silverware while Phoebe gazed from one person to another as
they talked, as if every word were interesting.

John marveled at how different the conversation seemed. Lydia's engagement was the exciting news, of course. But to his surprise, those at the table discussed his toys as though they were as noteworthy as Cyril Beaumont's passenger trains.

As if that were not enough, a steward appeared and held out an envelope. "Mr. Ancell, sir. The captain requested I give you this."

John nodded, unable to catch his breath for a moment.

The captain's regrets would be easier to deliver in a note than face-to-face with Cyril Beaumont's daughter.

Or, he wondered, taking out a folded piece of fine quality paper . . .

*Is it Christmas?*

## 11

*E*veryone at the table, except little Henry, turned their faces toward John, awaiting his response about the note. Lydia shot eye arrows at him, but he stared at the note, and after heaving a heavy sigh, he passed it to her.

"Iiieee," Lydia squealed, then grimaced. Phoebe giggled.

"Oh, I know what that is," Caroline said, "but what does it say? I'm assuming it's about your wedding."

Lydia pretended to be nonchalant. "It's only a formal invitation to dine at Captain Smith's table this evening in the À la Carte Restaurant." But she felt euphoric and read it aloud.

*To*
*Mr. John Ancell and Miss Lydia Beaumont*
*It would be my distinct honor*
*If you would dine at my table*
*in the À la Carte Restaurant*
*RMS Titanic*
*Saturday, April 13, 1912*
*From*
*Edward J. Smith, Captain*
*P.S.*
*Mr. Craven Dowd will be welcome,*
*along with a few friends of your choice*

Her first thought was *Why Craven?* But of course, Craven had sailed with her father many times. He'd been with her and John during most meals. The three of them were obviously traveling together.

"You know what that must mean?" said Lady Lavinia.

"Let's see," Lydia said innocently, "it means he admires my father, who will sail with no other captain?"

Lady Lavinia clicked her tongue. "As long as nothing interferes with whatever makes the passengers happy, it will be done."

Caroline scoffed, "What on earth, I mean what on the sea, could be more important than a wedding on this grand ship?"

Lydia appreciated their playfulness. She'd witnessed the excitement and the nerves of friends anticipating their wedding, the plans that had to be made, the wondering daily if all was going to fall through. Some threatened to elope. "In case we can do this," she said tentatively, "I'll need help."

Before the words left her mouth, Lady Lavinia said, "Done." Caroline touched her arm. "Of course."

Lydia held up the invitation. "The captain said for us to invite friends of our choice. Would you join us?"

"Already on my agenda, dear," Lady Lavinia said.

"On mine now," Caroline added.

"I would be honored," Phoebe said, like a confident young lady.

All eyes turned to her.

"Weren't you planning to be with some of the young girls in the sidewalk café this evening?" her father asked.

Her dark curls bounced with the shake of her head. She looked at her crystal water glass, demurely picked it up, and took a sip.

Unsure of what to say, Lydia smiled at Phoebe, then noticed a steward nearby. "Should we order?"

While others were discussing who had eaten what, she perused the menu and noticed there were twice as many delectable items in the buffet column than for the luncheon and grill combined. "It all looks so good."

Sensing a movement, she looked over at John. He discreetly placed two fingers against his cheek. The mischievous twinkle in his eyes seemed to say they had their own private joke.

It was no joke, but she felt a delighted tickle in her throat. Yes, she was eating for two. She decided on the fillets of brill.

After ordering, Caroline asked Phoebe if she had a favorite part of the ship.

"The French sidewalk restaurant," Phoebe said immediately. "It's nicer here than in Paris." She paused. "And I like the band."

"Our Phoebe is quite an accomplished pianist," Lady Lavinia said proudly. "Little Henry, on the other hand, is much like his father at that age, still trying to figure out what makes things work."

"Henry, do you have anything favorite on the ship?" Lydia asked.

He nodded. "The camel."

"Oh, you've ridden a real camel?"

He nodded.

"No, he hasn't," Phoebe corrected. "Only the jumping one in the gym."

Henry continued playing with the utensils, unperturbed.

"I haven't ridden the camel," Lydia said, "but I looked in the window of the gym and saw it. The mechanical horses too."

S. J. began to tell John about the gym. Lydia noticed Caroline and Lady Lavinia often spoke in soft tones as if the conversation were not for the entire table.

Soon their lunch came, and while enjoying the sumptuous food Lydia tried not to be too obvious in observing Phoebe and Henry. She liked children just fine, but generally gave them little thought. Now she wondered if her child would be a girl like pretty Phoebe or a boy like the adorable Henry.

While eating, she noticed Caroline and Lady Lavinia still engaged in private conversation. However, any uneasiness vanished when lunch ended and Lady Lavinia addressed Lydia. "Caroline and I have been scheming," she said. "We should meet for tea this afternoon with some of the other ladies and get this wedding event under way."

As Craven had warned, she shouldn't put the cart before the horse. "The invitation is only for dinner. The captain didn't mention a wedding."

"Well, if Caroline and I aren't convincing enough," Lavinia said, "we'll sic Molly on him."

They laughed, knowing the flamboyant Molly Brown's charm and personal stories delighted and impressed everyone.

John spoke up, "With you ladies ganging up on the captain, what can he say?"

"What else?" Lydia said, finding John's playful mood contagious, "but, 'Ahoy mates'?"

# *12*

*E*ach time Lydia thought of becoming John's wife in this romantic setting, shivers of excitement washed through her like an ocean wave about to overwhelm. The wedding bells seemed to be ringing, and she'd had little time to freshen up since lunch and be ready for tea with heaven only knew who.

The girl in the mirror looked at her with shining eyes, glowing skin and a smile on her lips. "Sorry, Lady Grace Frazier," who would have looked forward to planning her wedding, "I'm off to plan my own wedding."

She hardly had time to even miss John. But he was off on important errands after lunch. Caroline reminded him he'd need to respond to the captain's invitation. And John said he would show the invitation to Craven, since he was included.

A few minutes before two o'clock, Lydia left her suite and almost floated up the grand staircase to the boulevard leading to Café Parisien. She entered the sunlit veranda decorated with ivy and other plants scaling the trellises. Yes, this really was a boulevard and as Phoebe had said, even more like Paris than Paris itself. The other ladies were already seated.

Caroline saw her first and lifted her hand in greeting. Three tables had been moved together. Around them were seated Caroline, Lady Lavinia, and Phoebe. Three others she'd seen but had not met formally were Molly Brown, Madeleine Astor, and Harriett Sylverson.

Introductions were made, congratulations extended, questions and answers exchanged between Harriett and the French waiter, and tea and scones ordered by everyone, except Phoebe, who preferred hot lemonade.

The discussion turned immediately to the wedding.

"But," Lydia cautioned. "shouldn't we wait until the captain tells us for sure?"

"Oh, he knows already," Lady Lavinia said with a dainty sweep of her thin, lace-gloved hand. Madeleine smiled sweetly as if agreeing with her statement.

"Of course he knows," Molly said, "but before telling us women—" the roll of her eyes brought chuckles and nods, understanding exactly what she meant by that sarcastic tone of voice, "he will make certain the right men are present. They will make their plans about how the publicity is to be handled. Just you watch who's at the dinner table tonight and be prepared for all the photos being snapped."

Conversation quieted while the waiter served the delicacies.

Lady Lavinia took a sip of tea, lowered her cup, and addressed Molly, "You'll be with us at the captain's table tonight, I assume."

Molly's china cup clinked against the saucer as she set it down. "Been there every night so far." She laughed. "The men will make the decisions, but they need some outspoken women to tell them which ones to make."

Lydia had loved her before she formally met her. Some who were considered among the "new money" class weren't really accepted by some who had name, background, and wealth reaching as far back as Methuselah. But Molly accepted herself, and from the expressions of the women around the tables, including Lydia, they admired her spunk and forwardness, a quality that proper ladies were expected to keep in strict abeyance.

"You see," Lady Lavinia explained further, "this is an event to be publicized. The *Titanic* has already received wide acclaim. Simply sailing into New York harbor is anticlimactic. But a new bride, being the first to be married on this floating pal—"

"City!" Molly broke in. "This is no palace. It's a world. There's nothing like this in all Europe. And I've seen it all."

"Quite true," Lady Lavinia agreed. Others nodded. "Grander even than Windsor."

"Well, let's get on with the plans," Molly said. "We'll have ourselves a wedding, and if Edward can't perform the ceremony, I'll do it myself."

"Then it's settled," Caroline said in her calm way. "We'll tell that to Captain Smith, and he won't dare back down. He doesn't allow chaos on his ships."

With the what-ifs and maybe-nots out of the way, the real plans began.

"You'll need something borrowed, something blue, and a sixpence for your shoe," Caroline said.

Lydia laughed. "You don't suppose a coin in my shoe would cause me to trip and fall? That would be the ultimate disgrace."

"Oh, but you'll have someone to escort you, won't you?" Madeleine asked. "Like walking someone down the aisle of the church?"

"My father isn't here, and I don't have anyone to do that."

"What about that nice Mr. Dowd?" Lavinia said. "He seems to hover over you and John like a chaperone."

Lydia began shaking her head and glanced at Caroline, who smiled knowingly. "Um . . . nooo."

"Enough said," Molly put in, getting the point that Craven's role had not been to chaperone. "You don't need an escort. The attention should be on you only."

Phoebe spoke up. "I could be the flower girl."

"Indeed! Yes!" came from several of the women, and they all looked pleased.

Phoebe looked ready to pop with pleasure. "I get pink roses in my room every morning. And I have a really pretty pink gown that Grandmother got for me."

"Oh, it's gorgeous," Lavinia said. "I hope it won't outshine the bride."

Phoebe shook her head and spoke wistfully, "She's so pretty."

"Well, that settles that," Molly said. "The prettiest bride and the prettiest flower girl on the ship."

Phoebe looked so grandly happy, Lydia supposed she didn't realize they would be the only bride and flower girl on the ship.

"Henry could be a ring bearer. He'll be good if we tell him he won't get a train for Christmas if he misbehaves."

"Holy Mackerel!" Molly came unglued. "I was lucky to get a whistle for Christmas. Not the whole train."

Finally, the group settled down from the kind of boisterous laughter Lydia had only experienced with her young friends. When she could get her breath, she explained John's toy trains to Molly.

"But," Lydia announced, "this was not preplanned. I don't have a wedding band."

"Let's see if you could use mine." Caroline removed her wedding band, and Lydia easily slid it onto her finger with only a slight tug over her knuckle. She returned it to Caroline, who said, "John wouldn't really need one. Many men don't wear them, you know."

"I have the perfect cushion in my suite for the ring," Madeleine offered. "And now that you have a flower girl and ring bearer, what about a maid or matron of honor and best man?"

Lydia slipped her hand over Caroline's and lightly tapped it. Her friend smiled, turned her hand over, and gave Lydia's a little squeeze.

"Since Lydia and Caroline are holding hands under the table, maybe matron of honor has been decided." At Molly's words, they returned their hands to their laps and leaned away from each other, again bringing frivolity to the group.

Oh, planning was fun, even if something happened to prevent the wedding from materializing.

"I'd be delighted," Caroline said. "If that's what the hand-holding meant."

"It is." Lydia looked around at the happy faces of the women. "John will have to decide on best man." She looked at Molly. "Won't he?"

Molly lifted her shoulders. "Yeah. Then we'll see if it's the right one."

They could hardly drink their tea or keep a straight face when the waiter came to attend any further refreshment inclinations.

Lydia recalled that Craven had already refused to be best man, only an objecting *better man*. John's new friend S. J. would be perfect. Especially since his children would be taking part.

"I could wear my pink and rose gown," Caroline said. "If those colors suit you."

"That sounds grand. And something old should be no problem. A corset. A comb," Lydia mused.

"The engagement ring is new," Caroline said, "and the wedding band is borrowed."

"I have a blue garter," Madeleine offered.

"I'll give the gold coin," Molly said. "Heaven knows I have more than I know what to do with."

"Might I say something?"

The talking ceased, and they became as tranquil as the ocean. Although Harriett had joined in the frivolity, she hadn't said much. Judging by the intense look on her face, Lydia had a feeling Harriett might throw a splash of reality on their sea of plans. A few cups made a tinkling sound, returning to their saucers as if teatime had ended.

"*Ma chère*," Harriett said, "do you have a wedding gown?"

"No, I—"

She stood. "Never mind. If we're to dress for dinner, we'd best adjourn this little tête-à-tête and continue the discussion later."

Not even Molly made a comment, but studied Harriett with curiosity. Others looked as uncertain as Lydia felt about Harriett's abrupt dismissal when she had not really been much of a participant.

Nevertheless, they deferred to her and adjourned the . . . tête-à-tête.

## 13

**Saturday dinner in the À la Carte Restaurant, April 13, 1912**

$\mathcal{T}$he air on the exposed promenade deck felt decidedly colder, and Lydia shivered beneath her fur. However, her heart was warmed by excitement, anticipation, and the women being so eager to make this the grandest event ever. It had clearly sparked the romantic imagination of the women.

She finally had a moment to let John know about the plans made during teatime. He nodded. "I believe I've been congratulated by half the people on the ship. And I suppose this means I need to find a best man."

"At least we know that man isn't Craven," she said as they descended the staircase.

"Don't be so hard on him, Lydia. I can't blame him for wanting you."

She looked into his beloved face. "John, he cares for me. He thinks the world of me. He finds me lovely. He enjoys my company. He—"

"I get the point."

"Get this one too," she said. "I admire and respect him. And find him attractive. But," she said, dispelling the mock grimace on his face. "I love you."

"You know I love you."

She nodded, feeling a tightness in her throat and a warmth in her heart. "I know."

"We should go in," John said. They entered the reception room, where Caroline and William greeted them.

"Did you find out about printing invitations?" Caroline asked.

"It turns out," John said, "there's a printing room here on the ship with a printer and an assistant. As soon as we get official approval, the presses can print invitations as easily as they print daily embossed menus for the restaurants."

The bugle sounded, and they were escorted into the À la Carte. While they were being seated at their assigned places, Lydia realized anew that this room was even more elegant than the dining saloon. The crystal chandeliers reflected the sparkle of the ladies' jewels making them shine and seem to dance. The French fawn panels on the walls were a perfect companion to the rose-colored carpet. Little pink silk shades covered softly glowing lights on the tables. Silk curtains graced the large bay windows.

Lydia was seated beside John, and next to him at the end of the table was Craven, looking stiffly distinguished. On her left were Caroline, William, Henry, and Conrad Daley, the American owner of several newspapers. Mr. Ismay was across from Craven. Captain Smith sat directly across from John. Lydia thought that might be a good sign. On the captain's right were Molly, Harriett, S. J., Lady Lavinia, Madeleine Astor, and John Astor.

Everyone at the table seemed to be holding their breath as they waited for the words of the captain, who wore a smug expression. He gave a brief blessing, "Thank you, Lord, for the bounty, for it is in Thy name we pray, amen."

Following the "amen's" around the table, they placed their orders from the À la Carte menu.

"Now," the captain said, "I believe there has been some mention of a wedding aboard ship."

Molly poked him with her elbow. "What everybody wants to know, Ed, is are you going to do this or do I have Ismay fire you, and take over this operation myself?"

"Why, Mrs. Brown," he turned his head toward her with a dignified look on his face but a playfulness in his tone, "surely you know my passengers' wishes are my command."

Ismay lifted his glass. "I believe we'll go with Captain Smith on this one."

"This is an occasion," Daley said from down the table. "A front-page article, to be sure. With pictures."

His glance started the photographers snapping and flashing.

Men chorused, "Hear, Hear." Women made sounds of agreement. They all toasted with their glasses of wine. Passengers at other tables turned to observe the joviality.

Lydia thought of her father's photos of him sitting at the captain's table. Daley had said a picture would be delivered the following day, along with a copy of the menu and a note of thanks from the captain.

That was possible because on the *Titanic* there were several photographers.

"There will be chapel in the morning," Captain Smith reminded them. "But I will be able to perform the ceremony following dinner tomorrow evening. Just inform me of your plans."

Lydia felt overwhelmed. "Oh, this is too wonderful. You're all invited, of course. The whole room. The whole ship." She looked at John.

He laughed. "Whatever you want."

She wanted him as her husband. That would have been enough. But this would be wonderful for the passengers, and the kind of publicity that would be good for all the business-people involved. Perhaps her father would be pleased with news that would be worldwide. She dared not look past John at Craven. She could imagine the tolerant expression on his face. She knew about his lingering gazes, reminding her of his saying she and John were impulsive, young, and foolish.

She wished he could read her thought: *And just what in the world is wrong with that?*

Lydia saw Madeleine discreetly put her hand to her mouth, turn to her husband, and whisper. Mr. Astor nodded, picked up his glass, and announced, "The reception will be my and Madeleine's gift to the bride and groom, one befitting the first couple to be married aboard the ship of dreams." He lifted his glass higher. "Invite the entire first class, if you wish."

The "hear, hears" sounded again, the toast made, and the wine sipped.

The captain raised his hand for attention. "We must give time for diners to finish a leisurely dinner, and allow the staff time for setting up the reception."

He knew a reception given by the Astors would be no small affair.

Glasses were lifted again in agreement. "Settled," the captain said. "A wedding at 10:00 p.m."

"I have something to say," Harriett began and everyone quieted. She looked directly at Lydia. "You didn't bring your wedding dress, is that correct?"

Lydia controlled the urge to bristle. "I do have suitable gowns and—"

"Oh, *chère*, you misunderstand. There's no question of your wardrobe."

Lydia should hope not. After all, she was Cyril Beaumont's daughter.

"What I've been thinking is, I have trunks full of wedding dresses. They have never been shown anywhere. New York will be their debut."

Aware that her jaw had dropped, Lydia closed her mouth, took a deep breath, and tried to speak. Harriett Sylverson was the most famous dress designer in the world. "But wouldn't that take away from your showing?"

"Oh, Lydia. There is no place for a fashion parade to compare with the grand staircase nor a couture salon floor more exquisite than these polished teak decks, or rooms more luxurious." She paused, wearing a sly smile. "You appear to be about the size of the model I've chosen to wear the wedding dress."

She shrugged as if no problem existed. "If something needs attention, my staff can handle it. No one ever sees my final creation other than the model who wears it. But where would I find a more distinguished group gathered in one place to view my creations? Surely," she continued, "you would not deny me this privilege. The wedding dress, of course, is the showstopper. I would be honored if you would wear the dress."

Lydia could hardly breathe. She was accustomed to the best, but being on this ship was outdoing it all. She was on the greatest ship ever built, might wear the most famous gown the world would know to this point, and marry the most wonderful man in the universe. Of course, she knew Harriett would gain more publicity and a more worthy audience here than at several showings in New York, but that didn't take away from her and John's wedding.

They would all benefit for their own particular reasons.

Molly spoke up. "Think you could suffer through all that, hon?"

Lydia picked up her glass. "I believe I could."

They all lifted their glasses.

Dinner began to be served.

"Tomorrow evening," the designer said. "Then you lovely young people can honeymoon aboard the *Titanic*. Oh, what stories you will have to tell." She glanced at the newspaperman. "And you."

"Sounds like it's settled," the captain said.

"Hear, hear," said the men.

Molly laughed. "We haven't finished by any means, but only just begun."

This time the women echoed, "Hear, hear."

"Perhaps we should dine," William said, "then retreat to the smoking room and allow these ladies to plan all they want."

That cue to change the subject led to mention of the temperature seeming colder. "I've heard mention of icebergs," Daley said. "Any chance of our getting into something like that?"

"Perhaps." The captain spoke confidently. "If any icebergs are spotted, the ship will simply take appropriate action."

"I've crossed many times," Lady Lavinia said. "But I'm not fond of deep water."

"Are you finding everything to your liking?" the captain asked.

"Oh, yes," she said. "Being on the *Titanic* is more like walking on land than any ship on which I've sailed."

The conversation turned to men's topics: the world being on the threshold of prosperity, autos, flying machines, faster transportation.

"Speaking of fast," Ismay said, "as you know, White Star has always outshined the Cunard Line in luxury. Now, with this ship, we can outrace them in speed."

The men were clearly impressed. Later, as most of them left the table to retire to the smoking room, John laid his hand on Lydia's shoulder.

She looked up at him. "I miss you."

He leaned closer, and she longed to be in his embrace. His tender words indicated he felt the same. "Soon, we'll have a lifetime."

"I know we don't need all this—"

"No, we don't," he said softly. "But it's the best. And I want that for you."

She reached up and put her hand over his. "I have that, in you."

Lost in his gaze, with his face so close to hers, the whole world seemed perfect. Nothing could mar this moment, until she heard a familiar voice say, "Pardon me," She felt John stiffen, as did she.

John turned and faced Craven, who said, "Might I have a word with you?"

"Certainly," John replied.

"In private."

*Now what?* Lydia wondered. John glanced at her, gave her a tender look, stopped to speak briefly with S. J., and walked out of the room with Craven.

# 14

If you don't mind my speaking personally," John said when he joined S. J. in the library, where they had agreed to meet after dinner.

"I consider us friends, John." His cheeks dimpled. "And judging from dinner conversation, along with my mother's comments this afternoon, my children will be involved in your wedding."

John sat in the armchair near his new friend. "S. J., I fully intended to ask if you would be my best man."

S. J. must have judged by his face that something had changed. "But?"

"That's what Craven wanted. You see, when Lydia and I became engaged I asked him. He was furious, said it was against his and her father's best judgment."

"But he changed his mind?"

John nodded. "He has reconsidered. And his going along with this will help me and Lydia remain in her father's good graces. He's willing—" John couldn't help his sarcastic tone, "willing to suffer through being the best man if I'm still so inclined."

"And are you?"

John's fingers toyed with the soft material covering the chair arm. "I am and I'm not. Since he's realized Lydia and I are really serious about each other, his attitude has been contrary to what I'd consider the attitude of a man wanting the best for a woman he loves, even if it isn't him. If I believed Lydia loved Craven, I would want her to be with him. Mind you, it would break my heart."

S. J.'s demeanor was serious. "I might understand him better than you."

"What do you mean?"

"Craven had everything to gain until you came into the picture. Now he has everything to lose."

John scoffed, "I'm not taking anything from him. Lydia chose me."

"There's more at stake. When her name is talked about in *our*—" his face dimpled, "our circles, she's spoken of as the Beaumont Railroad heiress. Who is John Ancell when he becomes the husband of the heiress?"

"Are you talking down to me, S. J.?"

"Not at all. I'll share this with you. I've proved myself as a novelist, but I might never have had my first book published were it not for my mother's name and my father's background. This is the world we live in."

"I don't care about that."

"I believe you. That's one thing I admire about you. But you see, once you become Cyril Beaumont's son-in-law, he will ensure your status is elevated."

John was doubtful. "He says I have ingenious ideas. But I know when he says 'toy maker,' he means a nobody."

"You're right. But with the publicity you'll get from this wedding, Cyril Beaumont will hold his lapels, throw back his shoulders, and proudly proclaim you as his son-in-law. Then you're like Molly, accepted among the *nouveau riche*."

John laughed. "I rather think he'd disinherit her and disown me."

"And how would that make him look, after the romantic wedding of the century?"

John got his point. "I do believe you think like a novelist."

S. J. nodded and a sadness crossed his face. "Yes. And like a man who married the most wonderful woman in the world who was considered beneath his station."

John hadn't known that part. He remembered the novel. It had had an impact on him. He felt regret for S. J.'s loss, but returned to the subject at hand.

"Perhaps I will be accepted publicly, but as I've been reminded many times, my trains are just toys."

S. J. nodded. "Can't you imagine that Ismay's and Andrews's first ships were little wooden boats with a paper sail, perhaps in a rain puddle? Incidentally, my first novel was written when I was five years old, and it consisted of three lines. *Once upon a time there was a boy. He didn't like his tutor. He shot him.*"

S. J. laughed. "Been eliminating my characters ever since. And the public loves it."

John knew that was true, considering his wide acclaim.

"Getting back to the toys," S. J. said, "If Cyril Beaumont and Craven Dowd weren't aware of what can come of toys, you wouldn't be near their company, nor I daresay, eating at the captain's table."

John scoffed, "I'd be in steerage, perhaps."

"Mmm, maybe second class. For your information, I've been down to—" He glanced around and said "second class" as if saying a dirty word. John knew he was kidding, and yet they were both aware even second class was a dirty word to some of the more elite.

"Seriously, John. There are quite a few writers and artists down there. I doubt you'd have time to join me there since you'll be honeymooning for the rest of the trip."

"Perhaps in New York."

"That's possible," S. J. replied. "Negotiations have already taken place over the wireless between Abington and my London publisher. However," he said congenially, "let's get together in New York if at all possible. Perhaps with some of the writers on the ship. Incidentally, many second-class passengers would be first class on another ship, such as the *Mauretania* or the *Olympic*."

That was interesting. "I didn't know that. But I haven't crossed before and didn't pay my own passage."

S. J. showed no surprise. He likely assumed Beaumont would have done that. "You must really be a genius."

"No," John said. "Just a dreamer."

"And sometimes," S. J. replied, "dreams come true."

*Sometimes*, crossed John's mind. A short while ago at dinner remarks were made about the wonders of the ship never ceasing to amaze even those accustomed to the world's best. He thought it was Daley who quipped, "This is almost too good to be true."

But it was true. John had found his dream wife. S. J. had lost his. He had her forever in a book, but that wouldn't keep him warm at night, wouldn't both hasten and still the beat of his heart.

Now, without questioning, John would savor the reality of love and happiness with the one who would make him complete, on this ship of dreams.

## 15

*L*ydia didn't want to offend anyone by hurrying away from the À la Carte, and showed her ring to all who approached her. But there was so much to do.

Before Caroline left the À la Carte, she'd said, "Do you want help with anything? Like the invitation, music, order of the ceremony, anything particular in the vows, rice thrown at you?"

Lydia laughed. "I'll forego the rice." She sobered quickly. "I'd love your help."

Caroline nodded and said she wanted to get a breath of air and hoped her lungs didn't freeze in the process, and that she would then be on the promenade deck or in her room.

William had walked over. He nodded to Lydia and spoke to Caroline, "Let's take that walk, my dear. Seems many of the fellows are occupied with plans for an upcoming wedding."

"Oh, but you will have your brandy and cigars?" Caroline asked.

"To be sure," William said. "What's the end of a great evening without a visit to the smoking lounge?"

Caroline rolled her eyes for Lydia only, and they grinned. William offered his arm, and they left the À La Carte.

Lydia sought the Astors to thank them.

They were delighted about the wedding. "Lydia, you have made this crossing anything but boring." Madeleine's lips pursed slightly as she glanced coyly at her husband. "Rather wish I'd thought of it."

They laughed lightly, and after casting an adoring glance at his wife, John Jacob said, "Our staff and the ship's staff will handle everything about the reception. So don't give that a thought."

"Unless," Madeleine added, "you want anything in particular."

"I'm sure I couldn't think of anything more delightful than what you will do. Thank you so much."

"Our pleasure," the two said together.

Soon, Lydia rushed out to meet Caroline. She and William stood at the railing. Slowing her steps, Lydia viewed the calm sea and thought how smooth the surface looked, reminding her of how things were working out for her and John—so much better than they could have imagined.

She became aware of William's resonant voice. "Perhaps we should renew our vows on this ship. Astor might throw in a substantial gift."

He laughed, as though it was a joke.

Caroline did not laugh. "We have more than we need, William."

"But you've never minded the extras, I daresay."

Lydia wondered if she should continue her approach. She sensed contention, not jesting, in his tone.

"Did you see how they looked at each other?" Caroline's words barely reached Lydia. "Have we ever had that kind of expression in our eyes, William?"

He turned to Caroline, but she turned her face away. Was she afraid of what she might see in his eyes? Surely they had been in love.

"Have I not been a good husband to you, Caroline?"

Caroline's focus fell on Lydia, who hoped it might appear she had just walked up.

Caroline's gaze moved to her husband, and she smiled. "Of course, William. You are the perfect husband. Oh, here's Lydia." She reached out her hand. "We were just talking about you. So impressed with young love." She glanced at William as she moved away from him. "Lydia and I are off to plan the most exciting event this ship could offer. And you might be thinking about a wedding gift, William."

As they walked away, Lydia insisted, "No gifts for us, Caroline."

"I was just ribbing William about something."

Lydia smiled. Yes, ribbing him about wanting to receive a gift instead of give. Caroline was a woman after her own heart.

"Brrrr." Caroline shivered. "It's much cooler tonight than last."

"Decidedly," Lydia agreed. "I'll turn on the heater in my sitting room."

Caroline paused at the door of her stateroom. "Let me get out of this corset so I can breathe." She shook her head. "Men want their women to look as trim as the day they married them. But do they give a thought to their own—" She made a curved motion at her stomach. They both laughed.

"Some men do wear corsets, Caroline."

"Yes, you're right. William doesn't." She opened her door. "I'll be right over."

"I'll get more comfortable too. A change of shoes wouldn't hurt, either."

"Exactly!" Caroline's finger gestured to her pointed-toe shoes.

Soon they were in comfortable dresses, and designing invitations. Along with them were a couple of notes formally inviting Phoebe and Henry to be attendants.

"I think Phoebe would like such a note as a memento," Lydia said.

"What about me? Don't you think I want a keepsake?"

"Of course," Lydia said playfully. "You took the words right out of my mouth."

"Mmmhmm," Caroline murmured as Lydia wrote the note. Soon Marcella had all the notes, which she would give to a steward, who would deliver them to the printing office.

"I'll also need thank-you notes for after the wedding."

Caroline thought a moment. "Let me do that. It could be to all who attended, just as the invitation is to everyone. After you arrive in New York, you could send notes to those who were a part of this in a special way, such as the Astors."

"Yes," Lydia said. "I would like to give a token of my appreciation. Not even free passage on a Beaumont train would be impressive after having sailed on this ship."

Caroline lifted a dainty finger. "What about a toy train?"

"Perfect!"

They laughed together at the irony of how such a gift would be something most wouldn't have and that it might serve as an intriguing conversation piece. And it would represent John's expertise, not her father's money.

Marcella returned and poured tea for them.

"You do know," Caroline said, stirring sugar into her tea, "you and John are going to be the toast of New York." Her eyes widened. "All of America, in fact."

"Oh, you're being fanciful."

Caroline shook her head. "Not at all. This will be greater news than John Astor stepping off the ship in New York. Or even Ismay and Andrews."

Lydia couldn't hold back her giggle.

"A bride. What sparks the imagination like a wedding?" She answered her own question, "Nothing. The whole world loves romance."

Lydia heaved a sigh as her eyes roamed the sitting room, admiring its elegant furnishings, fireplace, and original paintings. "This is like a fairy tale."

"Better," Caroline said. "Better even than royalty."

"Oh, I think not. Your wedding must have been grand."

It was common knowledge the Chadwicks were royalty and their fortunes had been handed down over many generations. Lydia heard that King Edward had attended their wedding.

"Yes, the wedding was grand," Caroline said softly. She toyed with the huge diamond on her finger. "I never had to make a choice. We've always accepted that we are well-matched. And of course, I love him. He's my husband. William was simply the one for me."

Lydia nodded. "My father and family acquaintances, with the exception of a couple of young friends, feel Craven is the one for me." She described him, as if Caroline didn't know: "A great catch. The right background. Compatible with me in every way. And I like Craven's looks."

Caroline's nod and grin seemed to say she did too.

Lydia added, "His ability to run the company, the way he impresses my father, his impeccable manners, his gentlemanly attributes, his intelligence."

"Oh, my," Caroline said. "Perhaps we should cancel the wedding or change the groom."

"Not a chance."

"All right." Caroline set her cup and saucer on the side table, then folded her hands on her lap. "Now tell me, how does John compare?"

*What was it about John?* He wasn't as highly educated as Craven or other possible suitors, nor as up on politics or world events, and owned no stock at all, although he was being advised to consider such now that he was in negotiation with Beaumont.

"I'm not completely delusional," she said. "I don't want to live poorly. I can't imagine anyone would. But John isn't poor. Compared to my father and Craven and others here, yes." Caroline and William would be among that group.

"So," she said with a tilt of her chin, "can John compare with Craven?" She answered her own question, "Not at all."

Caroline touched her lips with her fingers as if to stifle a laugh.

"Oh, in looks he can. Of course, he doesn't have that mature look of Craven. But he's so handsome. Did you ever see such vivid blue eyes?"

"Only on you, when you speak of him or look at him," Caroline said.

Seeing Caroline's enjoyment, she took it further. "So why do I want John?"

She felt the joy, the shiver of warmth, the feeling that swept over her. John, without any worldly possessions to speak of, touched her heart. "John thrills me. Excites me, makes me feel more loved than ever in my life." She added tentatively, "He quotes poetry to me."

Caroline's eyebrows moved up, and the smile remained on her lips.

"All I know is, it's a feeling, a knowing, that you want to be part of that person, share a life with them, raise a family."

Realizing she should have asked this sooner, Lydia said, "Do you have children?"

"Not of my own." Caroline looked at her tea cup. Then she focused on Lydia again. "I've had three miscarriages. William decided not to put me through that again."

Caroline took a sip of tea, then smiled with her lips, if not her eyes. But as she talked, her hazel eyes softened, as did her voice, "I have children in orphanages where I've volunteered. I dearly love children. But—"

She seemed to change her mind about what she might say and nodded to Marcella, who brought over the teapot. "We can talk after you're an old married woman. For now, let's concentrate on your wedding."

Her being childless seemed a difficult subject for Caroline to discuss. Lydia had considered mentioning her condition to Caroline, thinking she'd understand and even be happy for her. Now she knew that might only make Caroline sad.

"Are you just visiting America, or will you and John make your home there?"

"That's not been decided yet."

"Oh, Lydia," Caroline said. "I'm so glad we met. Let's make a point to remain friends."

"I'd love that," Lydia said sincerely.

"Now, let's make sure we have everything planned." She lifted her tea cup. "To love."

With a delighted laugh, Lydia touched Caroline's cup with her own.

# *16*

*C*aroline wondered at her strange thought when William stepped into the bedroom where Bess was brushing her hair. He looked into the reflection of her eyes. "Bess may leave for the night unless you have further need of her."

"No, that will be all. Good night, Bess."

"Good night, ma'am, sir." She laid the ivory brush on the dressing table, and William picked it up.

Caroline pondered her thought.

*They all smell the same. Like smoke and brandy.*

Not that she minded. That was among the least of the facts of life she'd accepted. But here on this ship, her senses seemed keener. Everything was so new.

No other woman, besides servants and workers, would have looked into that mirror. And they, not to groom themselves. Now she and William were there, like a moving photograph. His fingers played gently with her hair as he smoothed it with strokes of the brush. He enjoyed doing that, so she kept it shoulder length.

"I especially wanted to bring you on this trip," he said. "This is living, Caroline. We're in a new age. Lights and autos. My autos will be known throughout the world."

*Yours?*

Yes, of course they were his, and had proved to be profitable. Her main goal had been to have a family. But not being able to, she'd sought to be useful.

But she must stop thinking about what she couldn't have. Right here, right now, she had all the opulence the world had to offer. There could be nothing grander. And she said so.

William smiled and laid the brush down. His hand moved to her shoulders, which he gently massaged. She thought he was in an amorous mood.

"Even the stars of heaven fade when we're under the light of those great chandeliers," he said appreciatively. She smiled, though a little shiver ran through her. But she understood. He wasn't criticizing the spectacular beauty of the sky, but praising what man had made.

Yes, she would not fret about whether or not she was a productive person. There was still time. The doctors all gave encouragement. She had conceived, and they found no reason that she couldn't go full term at some point. But too much hope only made the disappointment greater.

But tonight, with Lydia having asked about children, a renewed hope rose. They were on a miracle ship. Lydia's and John's falling so deeply in love and being willing to defy convention was somewhat miraculous. Her gaze moved to the reflection of the bed where no one other than she and William had slept. They had been exhausted from the excitement of these past nights. And William had access to more people of his liking than ever before in his life and came in late, often rather inebriated, whether with brandy or the sheer awe of his surroundings.

Now she looked away from the bed and into his eyes as he stood behind her, his hand warm and gentle on her shoulders.

Caroline looked at the silk gown she wore, which William had included among his favorites. Touching her midsection, she thought of his many compliments on her girlish figure, as he called it. She'd much rather have the figure that many women complained about after bearing children.

In an occasional moment she allowed herself regrets. But just a look around the room renewed her gratitude for the blessings she had. She was accustomed to the finest.

"Oh, William. This ship is grander than anything I've ever seen. I dearly love it. But should we be so proud of it? There are so many who—"

He interrupted with a raised palm, "My dear." His smile was tender. "We each have our place in this world. And without those who build and progress, we'd have no electric lights. We'd still be astride horses. And," he said with warm regard, "without wealth, how would you have the purpose of helping the needy?"

"You're right, of course." She wanted to end the discussion immediately. He would never intentionally insult her. But she felt the sting, brought about surely by her own sense of insecurity, of having no real purpose but reaching out indirectly to children.

She shook that thought away as deliberately as she shook his hand from her shoulder when she rose and moved away from the mirror. She would not wallow in pity. No one else pitied her. They expressed admiration for her. The wife of Sir William Chadwick. A few even went so far as to envy her for having the free time to give to others.

William took off his jacket, hung it in the wardrobe, and turned toward the bathroom.

"William," she said, and he stopped, resting his hand on the door casing. "Tomorrow we women will be planning a wedding. You will need to occupy yourself without me."

"That will not be a problem. A few of us want to check out every nook and cranny of this ship. Do you know there are no handrails in the walkways because the ship won't even feel the push of a wave?" He added in light jest, "The sea is silent in deference to this floating city."

"And to think I had wondered if I'd have seasickness."

He shook his head. "We walk as if on land." His voice held awe. "This is truly a wonder of the world." He disappeared into the bathroom and closed the door.

Yes, he'd had an amorous ember in his eyes.

But it was about the ship.

Not her.

Caroline smoothed her hand across the edge of the satin counterpane and slipped between the sheets that had never wrapped anyone else in their comfort and warmth. She concentrated on the steady hum of the engines, which lulled her into thoughts of a wedding and how she might be of service to a couple so much in love.

# 17

**Wedding day, Sunday morning, April 14, 1912**

*L*ydia stretched and moaned deliciously upon awakening. This was her wedding day. Looking at the canopy, she thought this a breakfast-in-bed kind of day. However, she decided to feast in her dressing gown near the fireplace. Her lips kept spreading into a smile with the thought that before this day was over she'd be a married woman.

When Marcella brought breakfast, she also brought a note from John.

*Let's attend church this morning and thank the Lord for his goodness.*

Lydia was tempted to say she was too busy for church. She was supposed to look at Harriett's wedding gowns. But one of the things she respected about John was his faith. And she did want to see him. Be near him.

She wrote back, *Yes, we'll do that.*

She and John met outside their rooms. He took her hands in his. "I've missed you."

"Me too." She welcomed the touch of his lips on hers.

The service was held in the dining room. She hardly heard Captain Smith's sermon, nor could she concentrate on the meaning of "O God, Our Help in Ages Past," although she joined in singing. She even peeked at her husband-to-be during the closing prayer.

As soon as the service ended, Caroline came to them, followed by Lady Lavinia and Phoebe.

Caroline took her arm. "I must steal her away. Important business not for your eyes."

John nodded and walked over to where S. J. stood holding a sleepy little boy, who rested his head on S. J.'s shoulder.

"The wedding party members are probably waiting," Lavinia said.

Indeed they were. Molly and Madeleine were already ooo-hing and aaahing over the models parading through Harriett's room and the adjoining one, likely belonging to the top model and the seamstress.

They gathered at one end of the room. This was their own private showing of more than wedding gowns. The beautiful models entered and exited the bathrooms and glided through the rooms as if in a fashion parade.

Harriett explained that she was breaking the tradition of the rigid Edwardian styles. "No corsets. These are for comfort and casual elegance."

They all gasped when a model appeared wearing silk trousers. Spontaneous applause sounded along with exclamations of delight.

"I could not begin a showing with wedding gowns," Harriett said. "Now for the finale."

The model appeared, dressed in a gown grander than one could imagine.

"I've never seen anything like that one," Lady Lavinia said. "Is that crochet?"

"Every inch." Harriett swelled with well-deserved pride.

They were all amazed. Long sleeves, puffed above the elbows, frills, high neck, tight bodice, layers of form-fitting crochet bordered by more crochet in a different direction, and flared below the knees to the feet.

"That is so dramatic." Lydia had attended fashion showings in more than one country, her favorite being Paris. "I've never seen anything like it."

"There is nothing like it." Harriett's expression held mild censure. "These are originals. Is that the one you want?"

"I adore it. It's fit for a queen. But John and I aren't quite so flamboyant."

"Difficult to please, are you? Fine. Less flamboyance, Celeste!"

The bathroom door opened at the far end of the stateroom. That gown was worthy of any princess.

As the graceful model floated toward them, Harriett explained, "White silk." She circled her finger, and the model slowly turned. "Formfitting with simple lines. Wide back sash that gathers at the center with a bow."

"This," Harriett said, "may be worn as a wedding gown, formal dress, or dinner dress. It is tea length in front and comes just to the top of the ankles, which is of course shameless."

They all laughed. This garment was modest compared with her popular line of lingerie that raised many eyebrows.

"And," Harriett pointed out, "it's a couple of inches longer in back. The front bodice has a hand-decorated section of lawn material. The three layers of material hang in tiers to the floor. For a wedding there will be the addition of a veil."

Lydia could not imagine a gown more beautiful. "It's perfect."

"Try it on for fit," Harriett encouraged. Afterward, she examined it for any needed alteration. "Only a slight tuck in the waist is needed," she said with a glance at the seamstress.

They all agreed this was the one.

"Oh, I'm delighted," Harriett said. "And you're right, Lydia. You're more genteel than flamboyant. Besides, I could not part with the crocheted one. That's my showstopper." She grinned. "But I couldn't resist getting your reactions."

Judging from the awe on the women's faces, there would be purchases made here before these new fashions ever arrived in New York.

"And this is a wedding present," Harriett said, handing Lydia something wrapped in soft tissue.

Lydia moved the panels of the tissue and held up the garment.

"Oh, naughty," chided Caroline playfully.

Lady Lavinia said, "Don't look, Phoebe," and the young girl put her hands on her face, then peeked through her fingers.

Others reacted with mock consternation but followed with demands of when and where they might purchase her latest fashions.

"Well, I could be persuaded to have a showing for the passengers," she said. "Why wait for New York?"

"Lovely idea," Madeleine said, and they all agreed.

"You invite the men and you'll make a mint selling things like that." She pointed to the lingerie. "But let's get this wedding done first."

The wedding party, as Lydia had begun to think of them, ate lunch on Lydia's deck. They had to ensure everything would be as perfect as that wedding dress. Trunks would have to be brought up for the entire first class because as Molly said in a joking way that held truth, "The ladies can't wear their dinner attire to a wedding like this."

Lady Lavinia reminded them, "Every lady on the ship will have to get her hair done before dinner."

That afternoon Lydia's hair would not behave. She'd never seen Marcella so nervous. She burst into tears and could not tame Lydia's curls.

There was only one thing to do. "Get Caroline."

Caroline and Bess came in. Among the three of them, they accomplished a miracle. "Your curls shouldn't be tamed," Caroline said. "Let them fall across your forehead and these longer ones along your face."

She did like the effect, and Marcella stopped crying.

They would put the jeweled combs in later, making sure to leave room for fastening the veil.

*✒*

Caroline felt she had plenty of time. Her hair was wavy. Bess never had any trouble sweeping it back into a roll above her ears or piled high on her head.

"The usual style, Bess. I'll just wear more jewels for the wedding."

"Yes, ma'am. Everything you will need is right in the top of your jewelry box. Rubies and diamonds for the dress. Emeralds for your eyes."

"My eyes are brownish."

"With a touch of green when you're happy."

Caroline glanced at her quickly through the mirror, but Bess kept looking at her hair, wearing her characteristic impassive expression. She recalled that in her young years she'd been told she had green eyes. They'd changed to hazel. She never really gave them much thought.

At the moment, she gave Bess some thought. Bess was a twenty-nine-year-old spinster. She'd been a governess in early days and that's the reason Caroline chose her among the household staff after her marriage to William. She wanted someone who would become familiar with her and the household. And Caroline would decide if she thought Bess would be good with children.

She did think so. But the children never came.

And Bess became more like a mother to Caroline. Gently patting the roll, Bess said, "There." She looked into the mirror. "You're a very beautiful woman, Mrs. Chadwick."

"Thank you." Caroline thought she looked like a proper, matronly woman.

She'd never asked if Bess had wanted to marry and have children. Maybe someday they could simply talk like one woman to another. But for now, there wasn't time.

That's what Lydia said when Caroline went to her room and told her it was time for dinner.

"I don't have time for dinner," Lydia wailed even as they headed for the dining saloon.

"But you must make an appearance," Caroline said needlessly. "The guests consider this your pre-wedding dinner."

"Oh, I'm glad I have you to think for me," Lydia said. "This is the most splendid wedding any girl could have."

"You'll be a prime target for the photographers the moment you step out onto the deck, and next week you'll be famous throughout the world."

Lydia raised her hand to her brow. "Was it only yesterday all I wanted was to marry John?"

Caroline shrugged. "This is the price you pay for being rich, beautiful, and on the most magnificent ship in the world."

Lydia grimaced. "Oh, the burdens we bear."

"Yes," Caroline agreed playfully. "Now we enter through those doors for your last dinner as a single woman."

At the table for the wedding party only, Caroline looked over the menu.

*Hearts That Survive*

R.M.S. TITANIC
*

APRIL 14, 1912

*First Course*

HORS D'OEUVRE VARIES
OYSTERS

*Second Course*

CONSOMMÉ OLGA
CREAM OF BARLEY

*Third Course*

POACHED SALMON with MOUSSELINE SAUCE
CUCUMBERS

*Fourth Course*

FILET MIGNONS LILI
SAUTÉ OF CHICKEN LYONNAISE
VEGETABLE MARROW FARCIS

*Fifth Course*

LAMB, MINT SAUCE
ROAST DUCKLING, APPLE SAUCE
SIRLOIN OF BEEF, CHATEAU POTATOES
GREEN PEAS
CREAMED CARROTS
BOILED RICE
PARMENTIER & BOILED NEW POTATOES

*Sixth Course*

PUNCH ROMAINE

*Seventh Course*

ROAST SQUAB & CRESS

*Eighth Course*

## COLD ASPARAGUS VINAIGRETTE

*Ninth Course*

## PATÉ DE FOIE GRAS
## CELERY

*Tenth Course*

## WALDORF PUDDING
## PEACHES IN CHARTREUSE JELLY
## CHOCOLATE & VANILLA ÉCLAIRS
## FRENCH ICE CREAM

She slipped a copy of the menu into her purse. Lydia might like that as a keepsake but seemed too excited now to think of anything.

They went through the usual number of courses, which seemed to go more quickly than usual. No one bothered their table, and after the men left, no one lingered.

Lydia worried, "It's so late and getting colder on the outside deck. I wonder if some will simply go to their rooms and turn on their heaters or get beneath the covers."

"Not a chance," Caroline rebutted. "Anybody who is anybody wouldn't miss this for the world."

Lydia laughed. "I've been a bridesmaid a couple of times. This hardly compares. I hope I won't fall down the staircase."

"Don't worry. There's not a chance of that."

Seeing the astonishment on Lydia's face, she laughed. "We have everything under control. We'll tell you every move to make, and all you need do is obey. After all, tonight you'll promise to love and cherish for the rest of your life and," she emphasized, "obey."

Lydia laughed with her and said, "I could manage a couple of those."

## *18*

**The wedding, Sunday evening, 10:00 p.m., April 14, 1912**

*S*hortly before 10:00 p.m. Lydia, in the white wedding dress and veil, wondered if she would ever breathe normally again as she rode up in the elevator with Caroline.

"Stay close," Caroline instructed as they stepped onto the upper deck. The band played a tune Lydia didn't recognize.

"Stand behind me," Caroline said, "and you can peek around."

The sight was unbelievable. Below the staircase, more than three hundred people—it seemed the entire first-class—were adorned more elaborately than at the formal dinners. Jewels glistened more brightly than the chandeliers. Men stood in formal wear, gloves, white shirts, vests, and white bow ties.

Across the way, beyond the staircase, several people stood in a doorway facing her, and she knew John was there. Collette, a beautiful, widely acclaimed singer who had been pointed out to Lydia, walked to the edge of the railing near the clock.

The band played "Let Me Call You Sweetheart." Collette's beautiful voice seemed to rise up to the glass dome, over the guests on the deck, and out across the sea.

Even from a distance Lydia's gaze at John in the doorway said, *I'm in love with you*. He answered the words, *Say you love me too*, with an ever-so-slight dip of his head, and a smile curved his beautiful lips.

When Collette finished the song, Harriett appeared and quietly described the singer's gown to Lydia. Then she did the same for the captain, who walked from the opposite room to stand on the landing in front of the clock. He wore a white Edwardian tuxedo with miniature medals on his jacket and rank braid on the cuffs.

The band played "Be My Love," and Craven strolled across the deck and stood to the left of the captain. Craven looked perfect in his formal wear, but Lydia allowed him only a glance. John was the object of her attention.

Lydia's eyes did not veer from John as he took his place on the landing, in front of the space between the captain and Craven. He stood with his side to the staircase, waiting for her.

The onlookers seemed to fade away as if the only reality were she and John. She thought her heart might burst.

But reality made an appearance in the form of young Henry, when he caused a slight commotion. Lady Lavinia tapped his shoulder, and he moved forward. He looked adorable in his formal suit, tails, and white bow tie, and holding a white satin cushion with tassels at each corner.

Lavinia coughed lightly. Henry stopped, looked back, then walked backwards and took his place beside Craven.

A few amused murmurs sounded. Caroline whispered, "That's what an audience looks for. That moment when a child delights them with a light moment amid the seriousness. Reminds us we're human."

Lydia needed that. She was feeling like a princess.

"Now it's my turn," Caroline said. The band played, and she leisurely moved across the deck in her elegant pink and rose gown and gleaming jewels. She took her place near the right side of the captain. Lydia saw the look of delight on her face.

Lydia knew this wasn't the usual order of wedding procession. But, as many said, nothing on the *Titanic* was like anything in that other world out there.

"Now you, beautiful girl," Harriett prompted, and Phoebe began her slow steps along the deck, holding a white basket and dropping an occasional pink rose petal, the color of her satin and lace dress. The blush of youth adorned her cheeks. Her every gesture was perfect, and not a single shiny black curl moved.

A moment of silence followed. Glancing down, past the elaborate railing of iron scrollwork, Lydia glimpsed the happy, smiling faces of those who wanted to celebrate with her and John. Farther back were staff members and ship officers.

She ordered her tears not to fall.

Harriett handed her a bouquet of pink, red, and white roses tied with a satin bow and said, "Breathe, dear." The band began to play "The Bridal Chorus."

She hardly saw anyone, but kept her eyes on John, facing her. She reached him and took his outstretched hand. They stood for a moment looking at each other with their sides to the audience.

"The bouquet," Caroline whispered, and she handed it to her. She and John faced the captain.

"Who gives this woman to be wed?"

"We do," sounded a few feminine and a couple of masculine voices in unison. Lydia suppressed a nervous giggle. They'd rehearsed a few things without her knowledge.

"Dearly beloved," Captain Smith said solemnly. Lydia felt the light squeeze of John's fingers.

The only other time she held her breath was during the part about objections being stated or one should forever hold his peace.

He . . . did.

At the appropriate time, little Henry held out the cushion on which gleamed two golden wedding bands. One was Caroline's. John must have gotten the other one from the jeweler.

She could hardly believe the words, "I now pronounce you husband and wife."

There was a pause.

No applause?

The captain couldn't keep the humor from his face. "You may now kiss the bride."

John leaned toward her.

That's when the applause sounded. And the cheers.

For a moment she detected restraint in them both, but then she felt the touch of his hand behind her neck. She raised her face to his and closed her eyes and felt his warm, soft lips touch hers. They did not demand but rested gently, and she felt the overwhelming feeling of passion rising within her, so strong, so beautiful, so knowing they belonged together.

Their lips did not seem to move, and it was as if the life flowed from each and they truly became one. Like a first kiss. Like a first time.

The other time was forgiven and—

Well . . . forgiven.

John drew away and looked into her face with moist eyes, reflecting what she felt. Well-brought up men didn't cry in public, perhaps not at all. Ah, let them not. Her man did, because he loved her. And those were the first words he said to her as her husband.

"I love you."

"I love you right back."

As the applause receded, Caroline told her to stay there for a moment. "The photographers must have their day."

While she and John held hands and faced the guests, Lady Lavinia took Henry's hand. They descended the staircase amid applause.

Phoebe descended like a princess. Lydia knew that girl would never forget this night. She wouldn't be content to have an ordinary wedding after being a part of this.

With what Lydia called his practiced smile, Craven stepped up and offered his arm to Caroline. She handed the bouquet to Lydia and placed her hand on his arm, and they descended together.

The captain stepped up and put a hand on their shoulders. "Before I formally present the bride and groom, I believe they have a chore to perform. All the single ladies gather to my right and the single gentlemen to my left, please."

Several gathered, even some divorcees and widows. Phoebe was the youngest. When Lydia leaned over the railing and threw her bouquet, the older ones didn't attempt to catch it. It was caught by a young lady who looked to be about seventeen.

The captain smiled. "One more little chore." He gestured to a chair someone had set against the wall.

"Do the honors," said a voice that sounded like Molly's.

Lydia looked at John, and he shrugged. She walked over and sat in the chair, turning away from the crowd. John knelt in front of her.

Her ankles had been exposed for all to see, but the location of the garter was for John's eyes only. She'd placed it right above her knee. John discreetly removed it, stood, and held it up amid applause and a couple "Hear, hear's."

They walked to the railing.

"Come on, men," John said. "Chance of a lifetime."

Lydia was not surprised that only a few males gathered near where Craven had stopped at the landing, along with Caroline, now accompanied by William. They moved back, and S. J. walked up to stand beside Craven.

A couple of mature gentlemen and a couple of teens joined the group with sly glances toward the girl holding the bouquet.

Just as Craven stepped back to abandon the gathering, John tossed the blue garter. It sailed right to Craven's chest, and his automatic instinct was to raise his hand and catch it. Although he shook his head as if this was totally unexpected and unwanted, he nevertheless had the garter and was applauded.

"Now if the bride and groom will step this way, please."

Finally, she could descend that staircase. The photographers had been primed and snapping from the outset. She felt as though she was in a perpetual pose, and she was loving every minute.

"Right here, please," the captain said. She and John walked over and stood in front of him at the top of the staircase. He spoke firmly, "May I present the first couple to exchange vows on the greatest ship ever built. Mr. and Mrs. John Mark Ancell."

Oh, my, she'd never heard such a rowdy-sounding crowd of refined ladies and gentlemen. But as many had said, this was a once-in-a-lifetime event, worthy of celebration.

John offered his arm. While the band played, they slowly made their way down the grand staircase, while the guests clapped hands in time with the rhythm of the band. She

looked up once at the great glass dome and remembered someone had called this the stairway to heaven.

She had ascended and descended the staircase as a single girl. But this was different. Another first. She and John
descended as husband and wife, and with a blessing only he
and she were privileged to know.

She was happier than at any moment in her life. She, on
a ship of dreams, walked down the grand staircase with the
man she loved, and they would spend the rest of their lives
together.

# *19*

All these first-class passengers had taken time and effort to give her the best day of her life. The least she could do was stay around to thank them and let them have their pictures taken. These pictures would be in newspapers throughout the world.

She couldn't wish her father were here, knowing he'd never have allowed this, but when he learned of this event, and saw the photos, he would accept John.

Would she stay in John's room tonight or he in hers? She had a sitting room, and he did not. She didn't like the thought that Craven was in the room that adjoined both hers and John's.

She must stop thinking about Craven. They both might need time to get over the sparring between them. But they could never be that familiar again. He worked for her father. He had no hold on her. No control whatsoever.

Those days were over, and she'd have to recondition her mind. It would be a pleasure. No longer her escort. No longer able to advise her or correct her or condemn her about anything.

With John's arm around her waist, the two of them walked into the reception room aglow with light from the crystal chandeliers.

"Oh, John," she said, "no one could ask for a more perfect wedding."

"And to think," he said with a smile, "S. J. reminded me that all this probably started with a wooden boat and a paper sail."

"Speaking of a boat!" She gasped at the table in the center of the room. On it was the largest wedding cake she'd ever seen, a replica of the ship, on a sea of blue. The huge silver tray it rested on was surrounded by red, pink, and white roses accented with green leaves. On each side of the edible ship were great platters of individual frosted cakes with roses on top.

"How could anyone do this on such short notice?" Lydia said.

Captain Smith wore a pleased expression. "By having the finest chefs in the world." He motioned and the chefs entered the room. The guests applauded. The chefs nodded and returned to their kitchen.

Molly called out, "I think it's time you stuffed some of that cake in each other's mouth so we can eat, and drink that champagne."

They all laughed. Photographs were snapped. John picked up the pearl-handled cake knife and glanced at her as he moved it toward the smokestack. She nodded. He cut off the top, laid it on a china plate, and looked for a utensil.

"This is the way." Lydia pinched off a bite of the white cake. They fed each other the cake while everyone cheered again.

"By the way," she said amid the applause. "Did you get your wedding band from the jeweler?"

"No," he said with a small grimace. "I didn't want to go back to him again. So I tore up a train for this."

He held out his hand. It did look a tad loose.

She laughed. He was so delightful. She couldn't help thinking that her dad and Craven would be willing to tear up their lives, and hers, for the sake of their trains. But John would tear up his trains for her. She gazed into his loving eyes. "Thank you."

By that time the individual cakes were gone. Waiters came and cut the wedding cake. Champagne flowed. The guests, some three hundred of them, came around to congratulate them. No, that would be two-hundred-ninety-nine. The best man had other things to do.

Mrs. Straus, holding her husband's hand, came up to her. "You look absolutely radiant, my dear. The glow of love suits you. But please excuse us, it's past our bedtime."

Lydia could imagine their curling up together on this night that seemed to be getting colder. She'd like to do that with John. But she owed these people their time after they'd given her the most wonderful night of her life.

Harriett came by to tell Lydia that she could keep the dress. "By the time we make it to New York it will already be the talk of the fashion industry. Besides," a sly look touched her eyes, "I still have my showstopper with which to wow the world."

Lydia smiled at her. "I believe you have already wowed the world, Harriett."

She murmured, "I do admit at least half the ladies here are clothed in my creations. The one-of-a-kind, of course." She spoke in an appreciative tone, "For example, the one you wore to dinner this evening."

"Of course," Lydia said. "A special dress for my pre-wedding dinner."

"*Oui*. But I'm holding up others who want to congratulate you."

S. J. walked up with Phoebe. "Mother has already taken Henry to the suite. It's time Phoebe and I do the same."

Phoebe's face crumbled.

"After our dance," he said, and her face lit up.

Just then Lydia realized the band had arrived. Soon, there'd be dancing, and she'd be in the arms of her husband.

## 20

Sunday, approximately 11:30 p.m., reception room,
April 14, 1912

*L*ydia thought everyone in the room had finally completed their congratulations and compliments, more than enough photos had been taken, too much cake eaten, champagne enjoyed, and women's pointed-toe-shoe-clad feet weary from dancing. But it was a lovely scene. Better than anyone could really capture in a picture or in words.

"I must sit for a moment," she said to John. He led her to a small table against the wall, and a waiter brought champagne and cake.

The Astors joined them. "I know how you must feel," the lovely girl said. Lydia smiled, her thoughts speeding to what she hadn't thought about in a while.

"Perhaps we should call an end to this," Madeleine said. "Otherwise, I might cause a scandal, take off these shoes and go barefoot."

They all laughed. John Astor gestured toward the cake table. "Our *Titanic* has been devoured. So, if it's all right with you, I'll make an announcement."

Lydia and John assured him it was all right and thanked the Astors for their generosity and thoughtfulness.

"Least we could do," Astor replied with a smile.

"Our pleasure," Madeleine added.

Yes, they knew how to throw a party.

Mr. Astor held up his hand. The band stopped playing, and the guests ceased dancing.

"May I have your attention, please." He graciously thanked everyone, expressed the bride and groom's delight, and suggested that the newlyweds should share a final dance while others made their departure.

The group extended polite applause and began to leave as the band resumed their playing.

"You're wonderful," Lydia said to the Astors. The two Johns shook hands and said good night.

Lydia and John danced, waltzing ever so slowly to "Der Rosenkavalier," the popular waltz by Strauss that Lydia and her friends had enjoyed at many gatherings. It was one of her father's favorites, to which he'd sit and listen with closed eyes. Lydia liked to think he was fondly remembering his wife.

As John held her, she trembled.

Or was it John?

Both?

The band played a discordant note?

Was it their swaying while dancing that upset her equilibrium? It was only slight, but enough to draw her attention. Many had said this trip was as if the ship were on land. However, it was not. They were on the sea. Surely, although they'd seen none, there would be at least an occasional wave.

Maybe it was the champagne.

Or her condition.

Or her imagination.

She wasn't sure if the guests had gone, but she raised her face to John's and their lips met. "I love you," he whispered, his lips against hers.

"Never let me go."

"Never," he promised. "Even when you're not in my arms, you'll forever be in my heart."

# *Part 2*
# *During*

It was the best of times,
it was the worst of times . . .
we had everything before us,
we had nothing before us . . .

Charles Dickens, *A Tale of Two Cities*

## 21

The collision, Sunday, 11:40 p.m., April 14, 1912

*W*illiam engaged Caroline in conversation about the wedding. "Craven did the right thing standing up for Ancell." They walked along the promenade deck, heading for their stateroom.

That was a strange way to put it. "What do you mean, William?"

"Although Craven pointed out he understood the young couple wanting to do this, he knew Cyril Beaumont would not approve. They don't know the boy that well. He's promising but still just an up-and-coming young man. Quite likeable, I do say."

He chuckled. "Had I known the wedding would turn out to be such an event, I might have been more conciliatory toward John myself."

She hadn't observed him being rude to John, just indifferent. And she knew what he meant by being more conciliatory. The event of the decade, perhaps century. All the publicity. A romantic, fairy-tale event, instead of Cinderella marrying the prince, the up-and-coming young man married the princess.

This would be talked about, written about, and approved by the general public.

"I was thinking," he mused, "when you walked across that deck, I would like to have been in Craven's shoes, with that lovely woman in this exquisite gown walking toward me." His glance roamed over her approvingly.

"Why, thank you, William," she said, not bothering to add she had walked down the aisle toward him six years ago. They had just forgotten some of the magic of that day and had settled into being an established married couple. Tonight, however, Lydia and John's love story touched even him.

Having witnessed the love exhibited between Lydia and John, Caroline decided, *I think I will stop evaluating mine and William's relationship and just love him, not question.*

Her resolve to show more love pushed aside the doubt trying to resurface. If others had not been strolling along, she might have stopped and kissed him right there.

But they had reached their stateroom. William opened the door and stepped aside for Caroline to enter. She felt a faint shudder beneath her feet and glanced over her shoulder. William shut the door, giving no indication anything was amiss.

Mentally shrugging it away, she walked on into the room, telling herself that it had not been a shudder but rather a shiver. Others had noticed the colder air. This warmth she was feeling for William likely caused a physical reaction. She smiled at that. She'd almost forgotten what it was like to be young and giddy like Lydia and John.

She almost laughed. She'd been young, but never giddy. Just accepting.

William asked her to excuse him. "I want to freshen up a bit. I'm either not used to all that dancing or I'm getting old."

"Oh, it's the dancing, to be sure." How nice to joke with William. She sat on the edge of the bed and took off one of her shoes.

She was leaning over with her hand on the heel of the other shoe when he surprised her further by saying, "We will have to do it more often."

The shoe slid off. "Yes, let's." She straightened and looked at him. He was staring oddly.

"William?"

A curious expression crossed his face. "Do you hear anything?"

She listened. Her glance moved around the room as if to see what might be making a sound. Water running in the lavatory? The curling iron? The electric heater? Maybe it had to work harder since the temperature had fallen. Or he could have heard something or someone outside. She disregarded what might have been a door opening or closing because the partiers would be heading for bed. With a slight shrug, she said, "Nothing."

"That's just it." He looked thoughtful. "There's no noise."

He was right. She'd become accustomed to the hum that was as familiar as breathing. One didn't think about it. It made the ship move. Her mouth felt dry, and she needed to swallow. Had the ship stopped?

William dismissed the uncomfortable moment with a lift of his hand. "Nothing to be concerned about." He headed for the door. "But I'll check it out."

Caroline sat for a moment, listening to the silence. She could get undressed. However, she walked barefoot to the window and looked out, but saw nothing. And for lack of anything else to do, she slipped her feet into her shoes.

She clasped her hands, felt her ring, and remembered Lydia had her wedding band. She and John were still in the reception room when Caroline left. They likely hadn't returned yet, but she might spy them in the hallway.

On second thought, she wouldn't ask for the ring. Lydia could give it to her in the morning. There was no rush. But she might peek out and see if they were heading for their room. Or if William was returning.

She mentally reprimanded herself for this indecision. What was wrong with her?

She opened the door and saw a few passengers in the hallway, speaking in soft tones or not at all. Likely, they had left the reception and were just talking. Or they might have felt the vibration and were waiting for an explanation. Where was William? She didn't see him, but Bess hurried to her.

Caroline stepped back, and Bess entered. Her maid's face was pale, and her voice thin. "I came to see if you needed anything?"

*Or know anything?* First-class passengers would be informed of anything before other classes or servants. Earlier that evening, Caroline had told Bess she wouldn't need her after she'd dressed for the wedding. "But you could come on deck and see the wedding," she'd said.

"No, ma'am. I won't be allowed," Bess had said flatly.

"I'm allowing you." But she knew Bess wouldn't chance being shooed away like a moth coming to the light, considered a nuisance.

Now that she was here, however, Caroline felt the sense of comfort she often felt around Bess. "I would like you to stay with me until William returns."

Bess looked relieved. And as if she wanted to say something. Caroline decided to make it easier for her. "Is everything all right, Bess?"

"I just wondered why the ship stopped. I overheard passengers say they're just changing course. Or something." She unclasped her hand. "Shall I lay out your night clothes?"

"Not yet. Let's just sit."

"Sit?"

"The dressing table chair," Caroline said with a wave of her hand. She sat on the edge of the bed.

Bess looked like she'd been sentenced to a jail cell. She wouldn't mind chatting with Bess the way she did with Lydia. But Bess had never been able to reciprocate. In spite of Caroline's attempts at being friendly, Bess remembered her place, and strictly kept it.

"I know what," Bess said, standing, "let's see what you might wear tomorrow." She was heading for the wardrobe when the door opened and William entered.

He and Caroline stared at each other. Finally he spoke. "Nothing to be alarmed about. The stewards said the ship struck a little ice." His laugh seemed forced. "Third-class passengers are out on their recreation area having snowball fights with the pieces." He shook his head as if he disapproved and took his timepiece from his vest pocket. "My word, it's almost midnight. Let's call it a night."

He began to shed his formal coat, and Bess waited to hang it in the wardrobe when a knock sounded.

William shrugged into the coat again and answered the door. A steward spoke in a level voice. "Everyone should put on life vests and come on deck."

"Why?" William said. "I was just up there and nothing's happening. What's this about?"

"The captain's orders, sir. Please hurry." The steward wasn't asking, he was demanding. He turned and almost collided with Craven, but quickly stepped aside.

Craven entered the stateroom, holding his life vest. "Checking to make sure you were informed."

"Did you check on Lydia and John?" Caroline asked.

"Oh, yes," he said. "No answer to my knock." His shoulders rose, as did a speck of color in his face. Caroline knew he didn't like the idea of the two being in there and not answering. An instant passed, and he said lightly, "They're apparently still dancing the night away." He held up his life vest. "Maybe we can help each other into these things. A fine time to have a drill."

"Is that what it is?" Caroline felt an easing of the twinge of fear that had begun to twist her insides.

"Must be. Nobody's concerned about a problem. I didn't see Ismay or the captain on deck. On Sunday mornings, there's been a drill on every ship I've sailed on. But on this one," he scoffed, "they wait until midnight."

"Why a practice drill for a ship that can't sink?" William said, and ordered Bess to get the life vests.

She already had them in her arms.

"Oh," he said. "Caroline will need her fur."

Bess laid the vests on a chair and opened the wardrobe.

"A drill," Caroline said. "That might take some time. Get a coat for yourself, Bess." Caroline stepped into the bathroom. Fortunately, she was still in her evening clothes, but she should at least, as William had said earlier, freshen up.

# 22

**Shortly after midnight, Monday morning, April 15, 1912**

*J*ohn never wanted to take his eyes from Lydia or his arm from around her as they walked along the deck. But Lydia stopped in her tracks. "John, look." He looked at the surprise on her face and could hardly believe the shocking sight even as she described it. "They're uncovering lifeboats."

Immobilized, he searched for some explanation. The captain, Ismay, and Andrews appeared rather grim while talking to an abundance of officers. Passengers were questioning each other. Crew members seemed as uncomprehending as they.

People were coming on deck wearing life vests. A steward spoke to him and Lydia rather harshly, "You need to put your life vests on. Captain's orders."

"What's the problem?" he called as the steward passed, but he received no reply. John turned to Lydia. "I'll get our vests. Stay near the lifeboats and get in if they tell you."

"No." She grasped his arm. "Not without you."

Indecision wafted through John. Was this serious? Should he stay? Should he take her with him? In a crisis, one doesn't leave his loved one. Unless it's for her own good.

Looking around as if the answer lay elsewhere, he spied Caroline and William. A passenger he hadn't met stayed near them. Then he saw that was not a bauble in her hair but a maid's cap.

"What's happening?" Lydia looked from one to the other.

"We're thinking it's a drill," Caroline said in a hopeful tone. "Ships always have them."

"They would tell us if it were anything serious." William's voice sounded more hopeful than confident. "If there were a real emergency, we'd hear sirens, or whistles, or bells, or something."

"I heard something earlier, faint but like—" Lydia searched for the proper words. "Like a muffled foghorn, I'd say." Her words sounded like a failed effort at bravery. "I've never really heard a fog horn."

"Oh, that," William said. "It would have been when they hit a small iceberg. And like the captain said at dinner, the bergs would simply move out of the way." As if trying to console all who were staring at him, William said steerage passengers were playing with chunks of ice that had fallen on their deck.

The Strauses made an appearance, looking fatigued, as if they'd just been awakened, and sat in chairs against the wall. The Astors went immediately to the captain.

Craven approached, wearing a life vest, and John thought it a good time to make his exit. Craven had sailed many times and would understand the situation better than he. John wanted Lydia safe, regardless of who kept her that way.

"I'll be right back," he said.

Lydia's eyes pleaded. "Hurry."

He sprinted away. On the way down the steps, he passed a passenger who said to another, "There doesn't seem to be a problem except the ship has stopped moving."

John thought so too, until he stumbled and reached for the railing to steady himself. Something about the stairs felt off. Perhaps it was his imagination and his hurry to get back to Lydia.

Stewards and stewardesses were knocking on doors, and unlocking them when no one answered. Lydia's was unlocked. He entered her sitting room and on into the bedroom. He took her fur from the wardrobe and picked up her life vest, and the Bible from the bedside table.

On the way back, the hall was blocked. A woman lay stretched out on the floor. A man knelt nearby and a stewardess was feeling the woman's neck. A young girl stood nearby holding a life vest. Then he realized that it was Phoebe.

He hurried to them.

S. J. looked up. "Mother," he said. "She fainted."

"She's breathing," the stewardess said. "Let's see if she can sit up. Sir," she said to John, "could you wet a cloth with cold water?" She pointed to the stateroom next to them.

*What an upside-down world* crossed John's mind. He didn't have time to think but was aware that before he was involved with the Beaumonts, he would comply with a request to get a cloth, or get one without being asked and think nothing of it.

His life had changed to having others wait on him, particularly on this ship, when many times a day some worker asked if he or she could do anything for him. Now it was reversed again, and a crew member was asking a first-class passenger to perform a chore. He would find it amusing were things not so serious. Perhaps later he'd write a poem about how precarious life is.

He returned quickly with the wet cloth.

The stewardess propped Lady Lavinia against her, took the cloth, and pressed it against Lady Lavinia's face.

"Should we take her to the hospital?" S. J. asked.

"I'm sorry, none of the facilities are available now. Compartments have been shut off." She sounded distressed. "Everyone is ordered on deck, sir."

S. J. scoffed helplessly, "She's in no condition to go on deck." He looked around. "Where's her maid?"

Phoebe made no response when he glanced at her.

"Should we take her back to her stateroom?"

"No," the stewardess said. "We'll take her to the nearest room. I'll stay with her. She'll be fine soon."

S. J. mumbled something like this being unheard of.

John watched him look around helplessly. "Where's Henry?"

Phoebe, in her nightclothes, began to cry. "I don't know. I was trying to help Grandmother." She looked petrified. "He had a fit about getting up and said he wanted to sleep. Nanny had to force the pillow away from him, and he . . . he was very cross."

John touched S. J.'s shoulder. "I can go for him if you'd like."

S. J. shook his head and talked it over aloud. "We'll get Mother into the stateroom, then I'll get Henry." He looked at his trembling, crying daughter, who was holding her life vest. "I would appreciate your taking Phoebe to the deck. We'll be along soon."

"Yes," John thought that a good idea, if there were any good ideas in this mysterious situation. "I'll take her to Lydia. We'll keep her with us until you join us."

"Thank you." His quick glance meant much more, something akin to hope in a confusing situation. This reminded John of the novel S. J. had talked about. He had an idea for a plot, but didn't yet know the ending.

John found it difficult to fathom what was happening. He needed to be with Lydia. But S. J.'s difficulty was greater. His mother could not be treated in the ship's hospital. A doctor apparently couldn't be summoned. His son was missing, and now he had to put his daughter into the hands of someone she hardly knew.

He liked children, but this wasn't exactly a time for everyday conversation. In the reception room he'd complimented her and thanked her for attending as flower girl.

"Have you seen the Ancell trains?" he asked, hoping to divert her attention from passengers heading for the deck, some with heavy coats over nightclothes that showed beneath them. Some in slippers. That was a foolish thought. This young girl was quite astute. Aside from that, she wasn't blind.

"I don't know if it was yours," she said, "but I did see one that puffs smoke and runs on a track."

Her eyes lit up a little when she glanced up. Perhaps she too wanted anything to keep her mind from the quiet chaos around them. "What does Miss Lydia—?" She stopped her words. "I mean," and she actually wore a little playful look, "what does Mrs. Ancell like about your trains, since her father has real ones and yours are toys?" Likely this child had heard a comparison spoken of before.

Mrs. Ancell. The name thrilled him. It was the first time anyone had said it since the captain had proclaimed it. In the reception room friends called her Lydia.

He smiled down at Phoebe. Her question was similar to the one he'd asked himself when Craven Dowd approached him about the Beaumont Company having an interest in his toys.

The child made no mention of the now-slanted staircase, but held onto the rail and ascended them awkwardly rather than in the graceful way she'd descended after the wedding. He tried to concentrate on her question. But he could hardly tell a child about his designs that he hadn't yet fully explained to the Beaumont Company. Finally, they stepped onto the promenade deck.

Phoebe pointed. "There she is."

## 23

*T*he band came on deck and began playing ragtime. Lydia could not imagine anything more ridiculous. Ragtime accompanying the chaos? Perhaps it was meant to assure the passengers this was nothing serious. She was trying to be brave. Some of the crew were having trouble with the boats. Passengers had been told to get into one, then told to get out again. Something about ropes being tangled.

She tried to believe that Caroline was right, and this was only a drill. She tried to deny hearing Craven and William repeating what they heard others saying. The voices carried on the still cold night like some eerie foreboding.

Surely she hadn't heard correctly when William rebutted someone's remark. "What?" he shouted. "Those compartments are watertight. You can't mean five of them are flooded."

"No worry," someone replied. "The ship will stay afloat."

Further down the deck an officer allowed a man to climb into a boat with a child while the officers at a boat near her group announced, "Women and children only."

An officer took hold of Lydia's arm. She wrenched it away. "I can't go without my husband."

Craven stepped up. "She's the one who had the big wedding and reception. She mustn't go alone."

"You're the husband?"

As if talking down to one beneath his station, Craven scoffed, "Not if I don't get on that boat with her."

Molly, who had joined them and was talking to Caroline, spoke loudly, "I could go speechless on that one."

The officer and crew must have heard. Or maybe it didn't matter. They were having to threaten some men who tried to get into the boats. One boat was being lowered to the water, and a man jumped into it. A woman screamed when he fell on her.

"Look," Molly said. "There goes the president of the line. Brave man."

Lydia understood Molly's cynical tone. Mr. Ismay walked past crew members and stepped into a boat without a glance at anyone.

Craven had stepped back at the officer's warning. Now he was walking further down the deck. No one seemed to know where to focus or what to watch. But then a woman two boats away, holding a crying baby, pleaded, "My daughter. She's with the maid. I can't go without her."

A little girl came running up the deck crying and calling for her mother.

Craven stopped the child. Lydia and her group watched. Perhaps they were as surprised as she when he knelt in front of her and began to talk. He gestured toward the boat. The little girl quieted and nodded.

Lydia was rather mesmerized with Craven's being so thoughtful as to notice a child in distress. He picked her up and walked to the boat. Accompanying the band were shouts and goodbyes and questions and talk and difficulty with boats.

Craven approached the boat and told the officer, "I can help row."

The officer nodded. Craven stepped into the boat with the child, handed her to her mother, proceeded to keep everyone calm, and took hold of the oars. Lydia had heard officers ordering crew members into boats to help with rowing. But none had called to a first-class male passenger who likely had never rowed anything other than a canoe in his life.

The boat began to be lowered. It moved down, out of sight, and the last glimpse she had of Craven was the determined set of his chin when he glanced her way, with a look of steel in his eyes that seemed to say he was indomitable.

"There's John," Molly said, "and Phoebe."

Phoebe came to Lydia and put her arms around her waist. Lydia held her close.

"Come over here, and let's get you warm," Molly said. She wrapped Phoebe in the warmth of her coat.

Caroline held Lydia's fur while John fastened the vest on her. Then he took the fur and placed it around her shoulders. Realizing she wasn't wearing gloves and her hands were freezing, she slipped them into the pockets. In one was her little beaded purse.

She looked down as she started to bring the object out of the other pocket.

"It's the Bible," John said. "It was on your nightstand, so I picked it up and slipped it in there."

Ah, the irony. Some passengers had pieces of luggage with them. William held a briefcase. They probably were thinking it possible they'd be transferred to another ship while this one underwent repairs, if that were necessary.

But this was John's way. It wouldn't occur to him to pick up her jewelry box.

"You must get into the boat, ma'am," the officer commanded.

Looking over, she saw that it held women and children only. But earlier he had asked Craven if he were her husband. She caught hold of John's sleeve. "He's my husband."

He spoke sternly. "Women and children only."

"Please, Lydia," John said. "I'll wait until the men are allowed into boats. This is only right."

No, it wasn't right. "The boat's not full. There's room." Her legs were rubber. Her body frozen. That tiny boat was small and the ocean so big and cold. She was wearing a wedding dress. She'd muss it up. Harriett's dress. Where was Harriett?

Astor brought his young wife over. "I think we'd be safer on this ship than in those boats."

"Orders," the officer said, taking Madeleine's arm. He held his hand up, indicating Mr. Astor wasn't welcome. Lydia thought of the many times the word "first" was used synonymously with *Titanic*. That was probably a first too, someone indicating Mr. Astor wasn't allowed to do something.

He kissed his wife, told her he'd be along soon, and began helping other women.

"Let me help you, miss," an officer said to Phoebe.

She was more adamant about not getting into the boat than Lydia. "I have to wait for my daddy and Henry." Her voice trembled, as many voices did in the extreme cold. "And Grandmother."

"They'll be along soon, I'm sure." Caroline looked at Phoebe, wrapped in Molly's coat. "You go on, Lydia." She gestured down the deck. "There's a boat with only a few people in it. We'll take that one."

They said quick goodbyes. Lydia glanced at Madeleine, looking so brave, having to leave her husband, carrying his child.

John's hand dropped to his waist. His nod told her that his thoughts had turned to the life growing inside her. His life. Their life.

They both knew there was only one answer. Her lips trembled. Then he covered them with his own. Warmed them with all the warmth within him. They shared the long kiss before he moved away, and her arms were bereft of him.

Unfamiliar hands grasped her arms. "I love you," she said, feeling herself being forcefully moved away from him. "You will come."

"Yes. Please go." She saw his face about to crumble. "Now."

"John," she whispered, willing but unwilling to get into the boat. She held out her hand to him. He kissed his fingers and sent the kiss to her.

She kept telling herself this was temporary. Things weren't as dire as they seemed. They would be together again. Whether he got into a boat, or her boat returned after the drill.

After all, she'd heard many times, *The ship is unsinkable.*

## 24

"Not even God can sink this ship."

"William." Caroline's warm breath mingled with his and condensed in the cold air. She knew the *Titanic* had been labeled unsinkable. But upon hearing her husband say that, at a time such as this, Caroline felt a chill colder than the frigid night. His words seemed as stiff and frozen as the chunks of ice that the ship had scraped off the iceberg, and which now lay on the listing deck.

She looked into his eyes, which held a vacant expression, bleak and drear. "I'm only repeating what the ship's officer said." His tone had become bland, calm as the glassy sea surrounding them. Her gaze followed his as it lifted to the starry sky, glittering with a magnificence with which the ship's chandeliers could not compete. William had said the opposite.

She'd never seen such a vacant expression on his face. Her movement to pull the fur closer around her shoulders as a protection from the icy air brought his gaze to her. His eyes widened. "Caroline. The life vests." Neither was wearing one.

His eyes searched for Bess and found her a few feet away talking to another maid. "Bess." He glared. "Where are the life vests? I distinctly told you to get them."

She stepped closer, dread on her face. "I put them on the chair for you to take. I thought you just stepped out a moment with Mr. Dowd." She began to cry and spoke with effort. "I put mine on and waited for Mrs. Chadwick. I had the coats."

"You should have made sure Caroline had what she needed. She is your responsibility."

Bess was unfastening hers.

"No," Caroline protested. "Everyone is saying this is only a formality. I'll be fine."

"Wait," Molly said. "There's a stewardess over there handing out vests."

"I'll get them," Bess scurried away. Within seconds, she reappeared.

While William strapped her into the vest, Caroline looked around, seeing men making sure that women and children had vests. William might have remembered such a thing, but he had been busy making sure he had important papers in his black bag. Caroline excused that by reminding herself this ship couldn't sink. It was only a drill.

But Caroline began to fear this was no drill. But some were saying they would fix the problem. The boats would return before breakfast. This was a precaution.

A precaution—for what?

The ship leaned. Caroline grasped William's arm. He clutched the railing. Some passengers seemed unnaturally quiet, talking in whispers, while others conversed and even laughed in an eerie sort of way. Through it all, the band kept playing.

The Strauses remained in their deck chairs. Many efforts were made to persuade Mrs. Straus to get into a boat. She refused. "I've been with my husband for forty-one years and I'm not leaving him now. Where he goes, I go."

"You ladies may get in," the officer said.

"I can't. Daddy hasn't come." Then Phoebe jumped out of Molly's coat and ran, yelling, "Daddy! Daddy!"

Her father rushed to them, carrying Henry. He set the boy down, then glanced around. "Don't let him get away. He'd rather sleep."

*Hadn't they all?* Caroline mused silently.

Phoebe rushed to her father. He held her closely for a long moment. He moved back and said, "I have something for you." He motioned to a stewardess, who handed him a blue teddy bear that he then gave to Phoebe. "You hold onto that, now."

She nodded and hugged it close.

S. J. knelt in front of Henry. He stared long into the small boy's big brown eyes. It seemed to take all his strength to do no more than hold him tightly, then kiss both cheeks and say he loved him.

He let him go and glanced around at the stewardess, who handed him a package wrapped in colorful paper. "This is your birthday present. Tomorrow you may open it. Hold it tight." His voice caught. "I love you both with all my heart."

"I love you, Daddy," Phoebe said, and Henry repeated the words, looking confused. A short while ago these children had been the highlight of a wedding, happy and smiling, and now their father was leading them to a tiny lifeboat that would drop, with them aboard, into the sea.

"Ladies, you must get in with the children," the officer said.

Caroline looked at Bess standing back, watching. "Bess," she called.

Bess came, tears in her eyes. "Anything I can do for you?"

"Yes. Take off that cap."

Bess looked bewildered. But she obeyed, whispering, "Remember me."

"Remember you, nothing. Now pull that coat close around you, take Henry's hand, and get into the boat."

Too shocked not to obey, Bess went to the side of the boat and took Henry's hand, and the crew helped them in.

Caroline turned to William. His arm tightened around her shoulder. His face was ashen. He wouldn't turn loose. "I have to go with her. She . . . I'm all she has."

"I'm sorry, sir," the offer said sternly. "Women and children only."

"I must go. She needs me." Caroline felt him shaking and knew it wasn't just from the cold. Then he lied. "She's ill."

He struggled to get into the boat, but two officers held him back.

"Sir, please," a man said. "We can help the women and children, then find our own lifeboats or stay with the ship until they get the problem solved."

The officer beside Caroline was pushing her into the lifeboat. William again grasped her arm and wouldn't let go.

An officer forced William's hand off her arm. As the lifeboat was lowered, William screamed, "I have to go. You have to let me go. Caroline, don't leave me. Don't leave me."

Someone said, "Just tell your wife you love her and you'll see her again."

William obeyed. His voice was strained and fearful, but he called, "I love you, Caroline. I will see you again." This did not have the ring of truth.

As the lifeboat took on more passengers, Caroline reminded herself he wasn't the only man to be pulled away. Some even plunged into the freezing water trying to get into the boats.

Some men were going to other lifeboats, helping women and children. She wondered what made the difference between William's cowardice and the other men's bravery, and reprimanded herself for the thought. Suppose she had been made to stay on the ship. What would her reaction be?

Lydia had wanted to stay with John.

If she had not felt this responsibility for Phoebe and Henry, would she have attempted to stay with William?

Perhaps he didn't know it, but he needed her.

Finally, she turned from his stricken face and looked into the dumbfounded one of Bess, who seemed not to comprehend how she managed to get into this boat with first-class passengers.

But Caroline knew. Wearing her white apron and cap she was a servant with quarters in second class. Without the job as maid, she could have been in steerage. Wearing Caroline's coat and without the cap, Bess was simply a woman.

Caroline looked at Phoebe. Just a little girl. Brave as any woman. Terrified as any woman.

They all gasped and jumped when a blast sounded and a flash flew high into the night sky. The rocket burst into tiny, distant stars, much smaller than those that were stationary, high above them. They twinkled down like fireflies.

"Fireworks," someone said with a tone of irony.

"Ohh." Henry, holding tight to his package, lifted his sweet face and stared with an awed look in his eyes.

But no one celebrated.

No one applauded.

Rockets.

Rockets at sea meant only one thing.

## 25

*J*ohn stared at Lydia as long as he could. Panic and chaos were taking place on deck. No one spoke of a drill anymore. Passengers crowded to the railing, throwing kisses, waving.

Surely he hadn't heard that. Nobody would shoot a third-class passenger who just wanted to live. No one would lock them behind iron gates because—what did they say? Not enough lifeboats? John watched his wife and unborn child move away from him.

Peering down the deck, he spied S. J. waving to his children being rowed away from the ship, out to sea.

S. J. had lost his wife several years ago. Now he wouldn't know if he'd ever see his children again. His mother was ill somewhere below deck, perhaps alone. John made his way down to him. This was not a time to say they might not make it. "How is your mother?"

Without looking at John, S. J. spoke, sounding like a suffering man, "Not well at all." He stopped waving and grasped the railing. The ship listed noticeably. "She's in a stateroom, lying on a bed." His shaky breath was like icy mist. "Part of her face wasn't working right. Her ramblings were incoherent, but I pieced together the story."

S. J. looked out at the tiny boat, moving farther away on an empty ocean. He related the incident, as if trying to convince himself it was real.

"Mother and the children were asleep when a steward awakened them," he began.

John pictured the events as S. J. told them. The steward demanded they put on life vests and go on deck. The nanny and maid were overcome with fear, saying water was flooding the ship. They couldn't get the vests fastened properly. The vest was too big for little Henry.

People passed by, telling them to hurry. Henry fought them, wanting to sleep. The nanny popped Henry on the backside. When his mother reproached her, the nanny and maid ran from the room. Phoebe cried. Henry clung to a pillow. A steward entered and picked Henry up, and they went on into the hallway with their vests. When the steward moved on, Henry ran back to the room.

"At the first sign of trouble, I hurried from second class and found Phoebe trying to pull Mother along." S. J.'s voice faltered, "Mother kept saying there was no hope. She fainted. She has an innate fear of water. She would not be able to leave this ship in a small boat. And she's terrified of water coming up into the ship and drowning her."

He waved again. The children were too far away to see. "She was breathing, but she was just staring. I'm going down to be with her."

The ship was slanting eerily now. John blew a kiss toward Lydia's boat. She wouldn't see that. Maybe she would feel it. He turned to S. J. "I'll go with you."

They pushed through the crowd. "You should find a boat," S. J. said.

"We should." John grieved for S. J., who should do every-thing in his power to be with his children, all the while knowing that the woman who gave him life lay, probably alone, in a room where water was rising, and she was terrified.

They no longer needed to ask about boats. Officers and crew kept repeating loudly, "There are no more boats. And no more life vests. We can do nothing."

The deck slanted further. The band stopped playing. The horror became more pronounced. People screamed, begged, pushed, shoved, tried to find something to hold onto. Then the band resumed playing "Autumn Dreams." The beauty of the music was a decided contrast with the cries of the panicked, pleading humanity facing the reality of their helplessness.

"Strange, what one thinks," S. J. said as the two of them hurried as best they could, like salmon swimming upstream. "I was with some writers. We heard a strange sound and felt a shudder. We stopped talking, trying to comprehend what had happened. Then the ship stopped." He shook his head. "It reminded me of when I'm editing my work and come across a line that doesn't belong. I visualized a giant pen scraping along the side of the ship as if a hand directing the pen said, *Let's just cross this one out.*"

S. J. glanced over at him. "That must sound fool—"

"No." John grabbed his arm. "It reminds me. There's some-thing I must do. I must go to my stateroom."

S. J. nodded. "If either of us make it . . ."

"I know," John said. "We will. I promise."

"Glad I met you," S. J. said as John ran. The ship was list-ing even more, but he mustn't dwell on that. He rushed inside and went immediately to the writing desk. He had to finish the poem.

Taking the paper from the notebook where he'd tucked it, and a pen, he hurried from the room. He stopped to look where others were leaning over the deck and pointing. Far below, about five decks down, was seawater, deep green from the lights and noticeably creeping higher.

Forcing himself from the hypnotic scene, he made his way to the reception room, fighting through the throng trying to go somewhere, anywhere. He reached the room. It had not been cleaned. There hadn't been time. Three waiters sat around a table, tipping bottles of champagne to their mouths. No one spoke. There was nothing to say.

John had something to say to Lydia. But there was so little time for one's last words to the one he loved.

His life must not end with his work left undone. There wasn't time to follow his initial intent. The first quatrain was a simple love poem. The second was more serious, assuring her of the depth of his love. Now he must quickly write. Yes, he would convert it into an Italian sonnet.

Form was not the important thing here but rather the words. He wrote quickly, from his heart. He signed it "John," and added a scripture reference. He folded it, ready to put it into his pocket as if water would not wash away the ink, the thoughts, the love, the words.

He stood, having finished.

Water entered and rolled across the floor.

The icy flow crept into his shoes.

A line from Emily Dickinson crossed his mind.

> *A word is dead when it is said, some say.*
> *I say it just begins to live that day.*

Her poetry had begun to live posthumously. Could his words, his love, his message live on and somehow reach his beloved wife, who had captured his heart? Could it reach Lydia?

Stifled groans sounded from the table. Water rose to their ankles. These were brave men. John understood their wanting the oblivion of excessive drink instead of feeling frozen water that would invade their throats.

"I'm John." He waded over to them. "I need a bottle."

"Paul. Patrick. John-same-as-you," they said in unison. They each picked up their bottles and held them out to John as if pushing back the inevitable and attending to their duties. One last request of those committed to serving a first-class passenger. Perhaps to feel one last deed would make some kind of difference.

John had witnessed unselfish acts on deck. Men being brave, facing death while encouraging their loved ones and others, praying. Older women giving their places in a boat to younger ones. Women refusing to leave their husbands. Telling others to be ready to meet their God.

"No. I need an empty bottle. And a cork." John took the poem from his pocket. Paul emptied his bottle's contents down his throat, making sure he got every drop, while John rolled the paper. He took the bottle and inserted the poem. Patrick gripped the bottle while John-same-as-he forced the cork into the opening, making it airtight.

The water rose to John's knees, and kept pouring in. It rose to the seats of the chairs, but the men didn't try to stand. There was nowhere to go. Patrick swallowed hard. "It'll find its way. Don't worry."

John felt strangely calm. Maybe because everything was completely out of his control. If there was something to which he could swim, he'd try. But already his tingling legs were going numb, and he sat in the fourth chair at the table. All four held onto it. There was only one thing to say. "Do you believe in Jesus?"

"Yes."

"I hope so."

A nod.

With icy water up to his waist, John began to quote, and the men joined in. *God so loved the world, that he gave his only begotten Son that whosoever believeth in him should not perish, but have everlasting life.*

The "amen's" sounded.

Tables and chairs floated. Something bumped into Paul. He lost his grip on the table that had begun to slide. He and the chair fell away. John-same-as-he, with eyes wide and mouth opened, seemed deliberately to let go. Patrick called on God to help him just as the water covered him.

John tightened his grip on the bottle. His chair slid out from under him. He tried to stand but tottered like a child unable to walk.

A child.

Oh, Lydia.

The water pierced him like icicles. He held his breath. Chairs, tables, bottles beat his body. A pink rose floated by.

That's when he lost his grip on the bottle. Frozen eyes watched it wobble into a corner of the ceiling. It would be trapped. Lost forever. Please, God.

Life did indeed flash across one's mind at the end.

His life was Lydia, their child, and God.

He had to let go. He could not bear the pressure.

Liquid breath froze his throat.

The water turned dark.

With complete abandon he let go with a last thought, *Though I walk through the valley of the shadow of death . . .*

Painful darkness . . .

*To be absent from the body is to be present with the Lord.*

. . . turned to serene light.

The joy of the Lord flooded his soul.

## 26

The rowers moved away as fast as they could. The ship slanted, like a big toe testing to see if the water were too cold, or if the temperature were suitable for a dip. The decision came from somewhere far below. The explosion burst into the silent night. A great red light flashed and disappeared below the surface. The ship cracked, snapping right in two.

Half the ship was going down. Pianos and furniture and deck chairs and objects of all kinds, even parts of the ship, were flying through the air and falling into the sea. People sought a handhold but found none. The water passed through their naked fingers, and their arms were heavy in the icy gelatin. They had nowhere to go.

Thousands and thousands of desperate screams pierced the cold night air. Surely, surely a ship somewhere would hear.

But only—

Only half the ship went down. The other half settled back on the water. Lydia knew John had to be on the floating half. She screamed. Others in the boats screamed. Lydia's voice joined with those of other women, pleading that their husbands were out there and to go back, go back. The boat's not full.

The rowers kept moving farther out to sea, saying the ship would pull them under. How could half a ship do that? She wished John had been a coward. Had forced his way into the boat.

But she knew he wouldn't as long as there was a woman or child, even another man, left on the ship. He might even try to save third class. She knew, just as she'd known she was carrying his child, before there was conclusive evidence.

On deck he had placed his hands on his midsection, reminding her they had a child. That was no solace now. She was in a worse predicament than the night she'd stood at the railing wondering how to tell him. She couldn't survive this without John. If he wouldn't come to her, she would go to him. She stood but was pulled down.

"Let me go. Someone else can take my place."

"Hold her. She's delirious."

"We have enough to do without your making it worse," said the man rowing.

That was disrespectful. Didn't he know who she was?

No.

What and who they were on the ship was a lifetime away from who and what they were in a lifeboat in the North Atlantic with an iceberg looming and a ship sinking.

They didn't even know she wanted to exchange her place with those wailing the chorus of death groans in the freezing water.

Hundreds and hundreds of passengers were packed on the floating part of the ship, and some of the screaming abated. Only the struggling, freezing ones were pleading. John would be on the floating part of the ship, safe.

Of all the unbelievable things that occurred, the strangest was what next took place. Silence replaced the screams. Only helpless groans accompanied the event. The floating half of the ship began to melt like a dollop of butter on a hot roll. It just melted smoothly into the ocean and the hoard of people were in the water. Their hair didn't get wet. No water splashed on their faces. For an instant they didn't scream. They couldn't. A communal gasp went out over the sea, produced by hundreds and hundreds of terrified people who unexpectedly stepped into icy water up to their necks.

No one even cared that she didn't want to live if John didn't.

Looking out at the vast, still water, she told herself it was all right. She hadn't been put out here to live, but to die a slow, agonizing, freezing death.

Was that her punishment? A silent sea? A silent sky. The stars weren't even twinkling. Just there. Like eyes. Watching. She stopped screaming.

Death groans came from the throats of others in the boat, one louder than the others. Then she realized it was her own.

She wasn't imploring, pleading for God and Jesus to save her, like those trying to swim to safety but who had nowhere to go, or who were beaten back from the boats lest they pile in and capsize and kill them all. One of the rowing crew members said the captain told them it was every man for himself.

That's what it had become. For man and woman.

Save me? For what, without John?

She felt . . . already dead.

Her eyes hurt from trying to see what wasn't there. She'd seen the lights of the ship underwater, exposing green sea water. Then black. Then nothing.

The ship of dreams had vanished, disappeared completely, as it sank into the sea.

In its place emerged a nightmare.

# 27

Caroline could not take her eyes from the sight. From out in a small boat, the ship had not looked so big. Not invincible, not unsinkable. It seemed like a giant hand had taken it and snapped it, breaking it in two, like a human hand might snap a little twig.

Half of it fell into the ocean, and anything not fastened down cluttered the sea. Half the ship leveled off. It would float. They wouldn't sink. There was an eerie quiet. All would be well.

And then it sank.

Her world became a tiny boat on a vast sea. The life she'd questioned was gone. There was nothing she could now be sure about. One wave, one shark, or freezing to death. Would they freeze or starve or die of thirst? Should they hasten the inevitable by slipping into the water? William?

Too late for her resolve about William. He was out there among the frozen. How strange, when and where one sees one's self most clearly.

When it's too late?

Just when she'd decided to love him unconditionally, it was over.

Oh, if I had to do it over, William, I'd put you first instead of efforts to bear a child. Did that help freeze our relationship?

The last hymn she heard the band playing was "Nearer My God to Thee." To whom did that apply?

Where was God in this? Did he see?

She saw. Ice. Toy boats on a cold ocean. Heard hundreds. Hundreds! of voices pleading God. Jesus. Save me.

In vain. The ship didn't. The life vests didn't. The boats didn't return to pick them up, although there was room for more. God didn't.

Nobody and nothing helped those screaming, pleading, freezing human beings packed in ice. Not drowning, but being frozen alive.

Too late.

Did life really matter? Could hopes and dreams and plans and life end so quickly, so terribly? She looked at the sky. Was anything there besides stars? What did it all mean? What was God? Who was God?

Why was she here, vulnerable, with no assurance of anything?

Did life mean anything?

If it didn't, she might as well slip off the side as easily as the man being rolled over the edge of the boat because he froze to death. She almost laughed. This was not real. You can't see this, hear it, believe it, and . . . survive.

Little Henry cried. She'd rather hear that than the crying of hundreds dying.

Her gaze moved to Phoebe, whose huge, unblinking eyes saw it all. Heard it all. She hugged her only possession, a blue teddy bear. Little Henry cried and screamed until his weary eyes closed. Caroline willed her attention to the children.

Was their daddy out there trying to swim to them while the rowers moved farther away? Where was their grandmother? William?

How long does it take to freeze? Later, she knew.

It took an eternity before the voices became fainter. They were a roar at first, like a crowd at a polo game or a horse race. Then they became a bad musical where voices couldn't hit the right notes but only screeched in terror.

The silence sounded worse. Hundreds. Thousands? Out there floating. Dead. They no longer screamed.

Just in her head. And in her heart.

Even in this ridiculously impossible situation she still had one thing.

Choice.

And so she drew little Henry closer beneath her coat. She forced her trembling, freezing mind to think of the little warm body next to hers. He dozed, then awakened to cry for Phoebe, and she would pet him and say, "I'm here, Henry. Be quiet and go to sleep."

He'd doze, awaken again, terrified, and Caroline soothed him, as she'd done in orphanages, in volunteering in baby wards at the hospital, with friends' children when their mothers were at their wit's end and Caroline knew, believed she could be a better mother than they.

The silence stopped her thoughts.

She saw bodies floating like ice.

She no longer wondered how many were crying for help, raising their hands, wailing, pleading, screaming, God help, Jesus save me.

How many were crying now?

None.

How many were in these boats? A few hundred.

Which meant that out there, floating, silent, freezing, frozen, were over two thousand.

Spread out for miles were hundreds.

She tried counting how many hundreds on her icy fingers. One hundred, two, three, four, five, six, seven, eight, nine, ten.

She didn't have enough fingers for them all.

She'd have to count twice.

And then each hundred was made up of one person at a time.

One, two—

William was just one.

The losses were how many Williams?

And as the seconds, the minutes, the hours droned on with only the sound of oars rippling the water, she counted how many were losing someone and didn't even know it.

She was one.

She had parents. William had parents. There were distant relatives. Business associates. Friends. Acquaintances. They all lost tonight. And how many of those could she count? No, not enough fingers or toes. Perhaps she'd count them by the brilliant sequins in the sky.

And dear Bess, who leaned against her to give any warmth if there happened to be any. There wasn't. But it gave comfort. Who would miss Bess?

Did she have anyone to care one way or another?

Yes. She had one. She had her.

Caroline looked up.

Were there even enough of those stars?

Yes. There were enough for all the losses, and more.

Someone intruded on her contemplation. "We should pray."

Those able to speak, agreed. They debated how and settled upon the Lord's Prayer.

They all knew the words and spoke them in unison.

That was a ritual in the church she'd often attended.

*Our Father which art in heaven.*

Had that ever been an assurance? or a hope? or was it just words?

She kept her eyes on the stars. Was He above, beyond that?

*Give us this day our daily bread.*

They had none. Nor water.

But this wasn't really asking for anything. It was a eulogy.

*Amen.*

Nothing changed. The passengers on the way to nowhere remained silent. The men and women took turns rowing to stay warm, as if there were a destination. The sea remained calm. The air still. Caroline thought of them as freezing figures suspended in a twilight of uncertainty.

Until there appeared the first gray light of dawn. She felt no elation when the thought came.

She thought she wasn't going to die.

But she didn't know why.

## 28

Monday, April 15, 1912—Nova Scotia

Armand Bettencourt awoke to an aggravating buzzing that disturbed his warm, comfortable state of being. Unwilling to open his eyes, he turned on his side and pulled the covers over his head. Ah, that stopped it. Then it started again.

Groaning, he lowered the covers and peered out at the dim room. Gray, foggy mist dared not enter through the open window out of respect for his sleep.

Squinting at the black hands on the white-faced clock, he thought it too early in the morning for anybody to call. Not here, anyway. This country home in Bedford was his haven. His office knew he was taking today off, and nobody but close associates and friends knew where to find him. That's why he kept only one phone in the house, and it was downstairs in the kitchen, near where he liked to cook.

Tomorrow he'd have one installed upstairs so he could pick up the receiver, put it back down, turn over, and go to sleep again. It was probably a wrong number or somebody who hadn't learned how to operate the relatively new contraptions.

"All right, all right." He sat up, switched on the lamp, and made his way out the door, across the hall, down the stairs, past another hall, and into the kitchen. He could have done it with his eyes closed. Just follow the persistent ringing.

He reached into the small nook in the wall and lifted the receiver. "Yes?"

"Mr. Bettencourt?"

Resisting the urge to ask if that's who the caller wanted, he replied blandly. "Speaking."

"This is Jarvis."

Jarvis. Yes, one of his young interns, who came to the office early to bring the mail and to be ready to run errands by the time the others arrived. Didn't that boy know the sun might be coming up in the city, but here in the country things moved more slowly? Looking at the fog-laden window, he thought about the cool mist that would be rising from the lake. A light breeze would be blowing through the trees, and he liked to walk in it. A little later in the morning, however.

"I took today off," he reminded Jarvis, in case he hadn't gotten the word. He'd had a long day on Saturday, with several of his neighbors having a dispute with a railway company over a property line. Then Sunday had been church and rest and fishing. Well, rest and fishing were just about one word. Certainly one activity. He'd stayed up late reading and had looked forward to sleeping in this morning.

He heard Jarvis's deep breath. "Have you heard about the *Titanic?*"

Now *that* penetrated Armand's sleep-laden mind. "Everybody in the world has heard about the *Titanic*, Jarvis."

"I mean, there's been an accident."

Armand turned from the window and lifted the candlestick base of the phone from the nook, then set it on the small table in front of the window. He pulled out a chair and sat.

"Accident?"

"The radio says the *Titanic* hit an iceberg. She got a little banged up. Since Halifax is closer to them than New York, the ship's coming here."

Wondering if he were dreaming, Armand ran his fingers through the curls that fell across his forehead and which felt as disheveled as his emotions. "The passengers are going to disembark here?"

"I guess so. Otherwise they wouldn't need to send the report, would they?"

Armand supposed not, unless they needed to wait until the ship was repaired or they could get on another one. He tried to calculate. The *Titanic* was due in New York on Thursday. It would arrive here maybe late Tuesday or Wednesday. There was time to find out more and help where needed.

"Let me know if you learn any more. Thanks, Jarvis."

"Yes, sir."

By the time Armand had his coffeemaker perking on the stove, the phone rang again.

"Me again," Jarvis said. "Now the word is that White Star chartered trains for friends and family of passengers to come here. They'd expected to meet them in New York."

Armand could hardly comprehend this. Almost three-thousand passengers were coming to Halifax by ship. Who knew how many by train? Maybe Jarvis had taken up drinking. "Why are you calling about this, Jarvis?"

"I was told to. The other attorneys in the office are trying to find out what they need to do. People will need places to stay."

Armand spoke his mind. "This is not making a lot of sense."

"Nothing is. Some reports are that everything's fine. Another says the *Titanic* is badly damaged."

Armand sighed. "I'll come in. Maybe I can make some sense of it."

Before he had finished the cup of coffee he took upstairs to drink while dressing, the phone rang again. He didn't go down to answer, but instead listened to the radio broadcasts. They were as mixed as Jarvis had said.

Armand called the pastor of the little country church and then proceeded to dress in his business suit. He was the attorney for the Marstons, a couple of church members traveling on the *Titanic*.

The Marstons had been friends of Armand's parents and were a great comfort to him after his parents were killed several years ago in a train wreck. As difficult as that had been, it had conditioned him for a worse catastrophe. But this wasn't the time to be thinking of that.

Shortly, Rev. Oliveera arrived in his carriage. "What you've heard is all they're reporting on the radio." The man's tone of voice revealed his own effort to comprehend such news.

They rode in the carriage, with the horse driven at racing speed, to the Bedford station and boarded the train to Halifax. The pastor was as befuddled as other passengers, passing information back and forth, finding it difficult to believe a great ship like the *Titanic* could be in trouble. "If it is, the people will need us. Sounds like we might be getting about three thousand people coming into Halifax Harbor."

Armand nodded. That was among the more heartening of the reports.

Others on the train seemed equally hopeful, saying if people couldn't be safe on a great ship like the *Titanic*, who'd be safe on any ship at all?

As soon as they arrived in Halifax, they heard other reports from people gathered at the station and in the streets. Armand and the pastor hurried to Barrington Street and into a two-story building much like others on the block that had been turned into offices. Bettencourt Law Firm took up the entire first floor. Armand's town residence was on the second. He stayed in the office, where he could receive telephone and wireless messages.

Armand had a direct connection with the Cunard Line, which wired that White Star had sent the message that the *Titanic* had hit an iceberg but all was well. As he conveyed the message to the pastor, both breathed a sigh of relief. The damage wasn't as bad as some reports made it out to be.

He began making and receiving calls immediately. Halifax would need to take care of the ship's passengers until they could be transported by another ship or by train to New York. He didn't know what he could do, but he'd be available.

Nobody believed that there was any real trouble. The *Titanic* was the greatest, grandest mode of transportation ever built.

Other than the one Noah built, Armand thought with a trace of humor. But God had directed that one down to the kind of wood and the size. He'd have to look into it and see which was larger, the Ark or the *Titanic*.

But he wasn't trying to make a point. For all he knew, God had instructed Andrews and Ismay and each worker about how to build that ship. Noah's problem was rain. The *Titanic*'s was an iceberg.

Both floated, apparently, because the next message came that all the passengers were safe on the *Parisian* and the *Carpathia*. Because of ice encountered on the way to Nova Scotia, they would be taken directly to New York.

The train trips were cancelled.

It looked like their initial scare was unfounded. They wouldn't have to find available space for thousands of ship and train passengers.

But the crew would need their help. The *Titanic* was being towed by the *Virginian* to Halifax.

## 29

Time didn't mean anything anymore, and Lydia wondered if they were all dead and this was a forever place. There was nothing to scream about now. A stillness lay in the air and across the smooth sea.

All of a sudden someone found a voice. And another.

"We're saved. We're saved," rang out over the ocean. She couldn't imagine that that boom and light on the horizon represented safety. An irrational crewman lit a piece of paper and a woman's hat to wave above his head as a signal. That would make no difference.

Did anything?

Nevertheless, an object came into view. Something inside warned she might be hallucinating. "Careful. Be still," someone cautioned.

But hope stirred in the little boat as the bigger object drew nearer. Where the rowers found strength, she didn't know. They wanted to get on that ship, for it to take them somewhere, for some reason unknown to her.

The ship stopped. People in the boats climbed up rope ladders. Some were taken up in chairs dropped for them. Officers quietly gave orders. Crew members acted in a professional manner, as if this took place every day.

Lydia was fastened into a chair, and she began to rise. Looking up, she saw passengers lining the railings, silent, staring with the kind of concern and disbelief she'd seen on that other ship.

Maybe John was here. Had been in another boat. When she was brought to the deck and taken from the chair, someone wrapped a blanket around her and held her around the shoulders while she shivered. They were asked if they were first-, second-, or third-class passengers. She opened her mouth to speak, but nothing came out. She was led to the wall, and she slumped against it and slid to the floor, exhausted.

People were around but it was like a—no, not a dream. A vague awareness. So tired, so cold. "Let's take the coat off and wrap you in another warm blanket."

After a while she was able to reach out and take the cup offered. It was warm. She could swallow, but it hurt going down her aching throat. That didn't matter. Finally she could lean her head back.

Someone mentioned the lovely sunrise.

Nothing was lovely. She should have let the sea swallow her up. But not as long as there was a chance, for John. She was wearing a wedding dress. Harriett's wedding dress.

"Harriett," scraped across her throat and onto her tongue.

"She wouldn't leave without her models and staff and dresses."

Lydia wasn't sure she had uttered the name aloud. Nor had she known Molly was next to her. Then she saw Caroline and the children.

Molly added to her statement, "That was her life."

Was.

John was her life. When feeling returned to her frozen limbs, she went to the railing and stood looking out to sea with the others, ignoring those who said soup and sandwiches were available in the dining room. She couldn't eat.

She stared at the hundreds of people who were being brought aboard from the lifeboats, more slowly than the sun rising above the horizon. Then someone said there were no more boats.

No more?

There had to be.

One more.

"Nothing more out there but ice." That was said so quietly. So matter-of-factly. She looked to her right. And left. Sympathetic expressions were on every face. So different from those below that grand staircase, in that other life she had lived. These people were divided into classes too.

Passengers wore stylish clothing.

Survivors wore blankets.

"Beautiful sunrise," someone said, as if it hadn't been said before, and a response was, "Yes."

What was wrong with them? That must be a *Carpathia* passenger saying such a ridiculous thing. She would never have a sunrise without John.

She didn't know the blanket had slipped from her shoulder until it was put back on and held with an arm across her shoulders. After another forever moment she allowed her eyes to slide to the side. Was it John?

Her head turned quickly.

Craven.

It started to come. It rose in her throat. She put her hands on her stomach. Nothing came up but the taste of bile. The sound from her throat was foreign. She'd heard it somewhere. Yes, now she knew. She'd heard it on the ocean. From those helpless, freezing to death. It was a death groan. A hundred, a thousand death groans.

She was freezing to death without John.

He would not leave her. Like this. With her hand on her stomach, she remembered. His look had said *Take care of our child.* She couldn't. Without him. Her stomach seemed to know that.

What little sense her mind had, knew that.

So she stared at Craven, saw his mouth move with incoherent words like *come away from the rail, let's get you something, you need to sit, eat, drink something, sleep,* foolish meaningless things like that. What good would any of it do?

She tried to give voice to her thoughts. *What are you doing here? Why didn't you put John in the boat instead of yourself? If you cared about me why didn't you make sure John was with me? You could have picked him up instead of that child.*

That's when she knew she was an evil person. Oh, she wanted that child to be safe. Her thought was not against that child. She wanted the thought to go away. She looked toward the sun, and it hurt her eyes. They were filled with dry tears, and the sun baked her eyes, hurting.

She wanted everyone to be safe. But for herself, she wanted John. She turned, and the announcement was made that everyone should meet in the main lounge. There would be a service.

As if they were the walking dead, they obeyed. They crowded in and sat or leaned against walls and each other. A minister thanked God for those who were saved and spoke a few respectful words for those lost at sea. Many murmured prayers.

A woman became hysterical. A few others joined. Captain Rostron fought back tears, and when the short service ended, he announced that names would be taken. Survival lists would be wired to New York. A doctor would examine each person. Then they could go to the dining saloon for brandy, coffee, breakfast, and then be told where they might bunk.

Like sheep, first-class passengers followed stewards and stewardesses to the dining saloon, and Lydia sat at a table.

"Your name, please?"

How could she speak? She had not spoken all night after yelling herself hoarse calling for John. She could only make a rough sound. She didn't know how she'd managed to say "Harriett" earlier.

She would try. With effort she began. "Mrs. Jo—"

"Her name is Miss Lydia Beaumont," the familiar voice said.

She didn't bother to look up. "No."

"I need to let her know that a wire is being sent to her father."

A wire? Her father?

She managed to turn her head then and saw a wrinkled tuxedo and knew who wore it. Craven again.

Struggling, she found her voice, although it sounded and felt like an enflamed throat. "He has to know I'm here. I'm not—"

"Lydia, save your voice. Sip your tea, it will help." He sat in front of her. "You are listed as a passenger of the *Titanic* under the name Miss Lydia Beaumont. Do you want to give a different name, have everyone including your father think you're lost at sea? What do you think that would do to him?"

What was she doing?

What others had done during that awful night. Anything. Hope. Find just a bit of warmth. A bite of food. A swallow of fresh water. A reason to be floating for hours and hours, a lifetime in a . . . toy boat.

What they were doing was called survival. That's why they refused to go back for those pleading and freezing in the ocean. Their boats might capsize.

She took a sip of tea, and the swallowing wasn't quite so difficult. She looked over at him, handsome, calm. "How can you be so calm?"

"Somebody has to."

She stared at her cup. That was what the rower in her boat had said. "Stop your bickering, complaining, moving around, making demands. We have to keep our heads about us." He'd been quite adamant and had said even more harsh things and had used strong language. He'd done it through the night when people lost hope, wailed they might as well get into the ocean—he'd said go ahead. They didn't.

Yes, someone had to keep their sanity.

It would be easy to lose.

## 30

**Monday, April 15, 1912, Halifax, Nova Scotia**

Since Armand had been awakened by that piercing telephone call early in the morning, chaos rose in his mind, spread
to his office, moved over the entire city of Halifax, and, like
a thick fog impossible to see through, was settling throughout
the world.

He considered himself an organized man. He chose to be an
attorney who tried to make things right when there was a con-
flict. He liked to settle disputes, or questions of what was right
and wrong, and to help solve problems, sometimes legally and
sometimes with common sense, and always with God's help.

But he was struggling to grasp the truth in what was being
reported. He wouldn't go as far as some who said the *Titanic*
couldn't have gone under because it was unsinkable. But it
was . . . unthinkable.

Another article came through.

> The gravity of the damage to the *Titanic* is
> apparent, but the important point is that she
> did not sink. . . . Man is the weakest and most
> formidable creature on the earth. . . . His
> brain has within it the spirit of the divine and

he overcomes natural obstacles by thought, which is incomparably the greatest force in the universe.

*Wall Street Journal*

He didn't exactly care for the way the *Journal* reported the event, but at the moment he wanted to know what was happening, and what might be expected of Halifax. They could hardly prepare without proper information.

However, headlines and articles in the New York papers were contradictory, as Jarvis had said. So were radio reports. It seemed reporters were trying to get a story and didn't care about accuracy.

Another came.

## ALL SAVED FROM TITANIC AFTER COLLISON

*The Evening Sun*

## THE NEW TITANIC STRIKES ICEBERG AND CALLS FOR AID

## VESSELS RUSH TO HER SIDE

*The Herald*

As the day grew brighter, the news became darker. Radio messages were delivered, not in professional voices, but in fearful ones, as if reporters couldn't believe what they were saying. Reports of a number of lives having been lost changed to reports of a great loss, and finally, a horrible loss.

By mid-morning, the grim news was no longer rumor and speculation.

The *Virginian* would not tow the *Titanic* to Halifax.

"I regret to say that the *Titanic* sank at 2:20 this morning," came the official announcement from the White Star office in New York.

A survivor list was posted on the front window of the White Star office and a copy relayed to Halifax. Several passengers from Nova Scotia, including the Marstons, were not on the list.

The *Carpathia* was taking 675 survivors to New York.

If the unthinkable were true, and only 675 had survived, then more than fifteen-hundred souls had perished.

Reports were that thirty-thousand people lined the streets of New York. Many in Halifax gathered in respect and sympathy for them. Almost everyone knew someone who knew someone on that ship. They certainly knew about them, since many of the most prominent people of Halifax were, or had been, aboard that ship.

The *Carpathia* reported no other information, except a revision when another name was removed from the survivor list.

The *Carpathia* would steam toward New York for three more days. Survivors would be in great sorrow. Have great needs.

Was there nothing Halifax could do?

Rev. Oliveera isolated himself in an office to phone other pastors, wanting to make sure those in the U. S. knew Halifax would assist in any way. Prayer meetings would be set up throughout the city.

Armand didn't know which was whiter, the face of Jarvis or the paper he handed to him. When Armand read it, he understood.

There was something Halifax could do, after all.

The request put the face of reality on the nightmare. This was not something anyone was going to forget soon, if ever.

The request had been made and confirmed. The words had been printed and accepted. The chore that lay ahead of those fulfilling the request involved an unspeakable horror.

## 31

Captain Rostron had first-aid sections set up with doctors and nurses. Some survivors had obvious cuts and bruises. Lydia passed the examination within a few moments. Her limbs had thawed and now moved adequately. She answered a few questions and was apparently deemed normal.

Normal?

So many things made her want to laugh. Not that anything was funny. Just ironic.

Madeleine and two other women were assigned to the captain's quarters. Many first-class passengers gave up their rooms and suites. When Lydia was taken to the room, she saw an adjoining door and didn't have to ask who would be on the other side.

A knock sounded. The stewardess stepped aside to allow a young woman to enter. A maid accompanying her held an armload of clothes.

The young woman introduced herself as Kathryn, on the way to New York with her parents to visit relatives. "You look about my size, Miss Beaumont. Choose any you like."

Lydia sat on the bed. "Just anything. I appreciate this."

"Oh. I want to help." Kathryn looked tearful and turned to show another dress. "They don't compare with what you're wearing."

"They're lovely." How different this was from when Harriett presented her originals.

She reached out to take the blue day dress but drew back her hand. She might be wearing it for a couple of days and should take one that wouldn't as easily show wear. "The brown one, if you don't mind."

The girl nodded. "I'll leave the blue one too." The maid put them in the empty closet. Lydia didn't ask where the girl and her parents were staying. They would know that if they'd been so fortunate as to have traveled on the *Titanic*, they could be on this side of things.

"Do you want my maid?" the girl asked tentatively.

"No. I'll be fine. Thank you."

"Bye. Oh, here's a nightdress."

Lydia bathed, aware that she'd washed her hair only yesterday. Less than twenty-four hours ago. And yet, a lifetime.

Soon, she stared into the mirror at the brown dress with delicate fawn lace designed to enhance one's feminine charms. But she was wearing a stranger's dress and Caroline's wedding band. She couldn't use the name of the man who'd given her the happiest day of her life. And inside her, she carried the child of her husband, who was . . . where?

She faced . . . what?

She didn't know what to do. But a meal was announced. Which one?

She left the room and saw Caroline, Bess, and the children coming from their suite. Immediately they were joined by her . . . escort?

There was hushed conversation at dinner. She was glad to return to the room, get into the nightdress, and take one of the sedatives the doctor had given her.

She crawled between the sheets that had probably been slept in before and then laundered. The ones on the *Titanic* had been slept on by only her. Now they were wet.

These would be too, because she cried herself to sleep.

She awoke in the night, freezing and terrified, and repeated the cycle.

## 32

*H*enry wanted to sleep with his sister. He wanted to hold the package in bed, but there wasn't room.

"We can put it on the table, and you can watch it," Phoebe said. "Hold my teddy bear."

He lay on his side with eyes wide until he could keep them open no longer. He clutched the teddy bear while Phoebe kept her arms around him and soothed him in the night when he awakened screaming for her.

Caroline knew his little ears had heard it all. His little heart beat with as much fear as a grownup's. She could not grasp the immensity of what had happened. How could a child's tender mind even know what to ask?

Finally the children slept, and so did Caroline. But they were all awake before breakfast was announced. She and Bess dressed the children in clothes other passengers had given them.

Caroline saved Lydia and Craven a seat in the dining room. When Craven ushered her in, she noticed how delicate and young Lydia looked. Last night—was it only last night?—she had been gorgeous. Now, she wore the brown dress, no makeup, and her hair stuck out in unruly curls. She was undoubtedly the most beautiful creature in that natural state that Caroline had ever seen.

No wonder Craven hovered nearby. Caroline noticed Lydia's turning from him several times. At least Lydia had someone to . . . resent.

She wouldn't ask for her ring. Lydia might feel she was giving up another part of John if she removed it.

Children were much easier to approach than adults. Many spoke to Phoebe and Henry. Even Lydia joined in, "What's in your box, Henry?"

"My birthday."

"When's your birthday?"

He put the box on his lap. "Tomorrow."

"Today," Phoebe corrected. "Grandmother planned for us to have a party in the French restaurant."

Glad to get her mind onto something cheerful, Caroline assured Henry he would have a party. Right after breakfast she spotted the captain, who delighted in the idea of their making up a small cake. He even had a little toy put on top.

Word was passed around, and in the afternoon they gathered in the dining saloon for the party. Five *Carpathia* children sat at the table with Henry and Phoebe.

Molly led in singing "Happy Birthday." Then the children ate cake and drank cocoa, but kept eyeing the package. Finally Henry tore the paper away and exclaimed, "Oooooh."

Phoebe held up the box for others to see. "He had one like this but lost most of the parts."

"Those are great for children," a man said.

"And their dads," another said, and a discussion followed about the Meccano construction toys.

Henry joined in eagerly, "I can make a frog. With biiiiiig eyes."

Soon the children became occupied, taking turns making funny animals and shapes, even laughing.

Caroline noticed Craven looking at the bulletin board and walked toward him. He had taken over for the first-class passengers. He relayed messages from the captain, gave messages to stewards, and was consulted about sending wires to families and friends. He took control, made decisions, and gave information.

She stood beside him, looking at the list, and thanked him.

"Could I be of assistance to you, Caroline? I'll be glad to handle any matters for you, personal or financial."

She had no reason to resent Craven Dowd. "I would appreciate that. I'll write down the information for you."

He nodded.

"I'm sure," she said, "Mr. Beaumont will be proud of how you're taking care of his daughter."

"As I am the president of her father's company, she is among my responsibilities." He said that in a formal, businesslike tone. But she thought a little grin hovered about his mouth before he bade her a good day.

Watching him walk away, she thought of his dignified manner of acting and speaking. Not only did he have a commanding, controlling way about him, which was very much needed in this situation, but he was one incredibly good-looking man.

## 33

Halifax, Nova Scotia, April 17, 1912

*M*uch of the time, Armand stood alongside throngs of others on the dock, watching in horror what was taking place. To return to the safety of their homes except when absolutely necessary seemed a sacrilege.

He and the pastor had stayed in Armand's home above his offices. One or the other would get up in the night to listen to radio reports and read any wires coming through.

They spent the days with other people as they all became united in disbelief, horror, uncertainty, hope, despair, waiting.

The passenger list reported not only the names of survivors but their class. The *Titanic* had carried more third- than first- and second-class passengers; these were making their way to America, considered the greatest nation, the land of opportunity.

Many working on the docks and in other jobs available to immigrants had been expecting relatives and friends from many countries. Reportedly, therein lay the greatest number of victims.

The *Titanic* had carried some of the richest men and women in the world. Those considered most important. But the survivor list didn't include the names of the most prosperous, prestigious, and successful. They were out there beneath the sea or floating on the water like chunks of ice.

"If this could happen to the world's most technologically advanced ship," those standing around said, the wires said, the radios said, "then where is mankind's hope?"

There was mention that God went down with the ship. He was dead.

Armand scoffed inwardly.

The only way God was dead was when his son died on that cross. But he rose again so man could have life.

Then he reprimanded himself. Hadn't he, himself, asked at times, where was God?

But right now, the world was trying to find someone or something to blame, and God was closest. He was right down there in their hearts, even if they didn't know it.

On Wednesday Armand went down to the dock and saw a doctor friend standing there with the pastor.

"What's all that?" Armand asked.

"Embalming fluid," the doctor replied.

The pastor expelled a deep breath. "They've asked for tons of ice, more than one hundred coffins, canvas bags, weights for burial at sea, and," his voice lowered further, "supplies for embalming."

Armand felt as sick as the pastor looked.

He hated being helpless, unsure, ill at ease. If there was anything he could do, even though he knew there were times you couldn't do anything to ease another's pain. Just do something.

He watched in awe at the cargo being loaded. When two men boarded together, the doctor said, "That's the minister and the mortician."

There was only one other time when Armand had felt totally helpless. With the Lord's help he'd been able to get past it, even though he still struggled when the memory and the feelings threatened to overwhelm him again.

A lot of people needed to know that someone else knew and understood loss and grief. He was one of those. Strange, his own loss was little compared with all this; at the same time, he felt his loss even more keenly, as if it were happening all over again.

Just when he thought he couldn't feel worse, Jarvis hurried up to them. "I thought you'd want to know."

Armand really didn't want to know.

But Jarvis was trying to be efficient, even if his eyes had doubled in size during the past days. Perhaps it was true of them all. "The Mayflower Curling Rink is being turned into a morgue."

He gestured toward Agricola Street, a few blocks from the dockyard.

Armand couldn't find it within himself to say thank you for the information.

He and the horrified throng on the dock watched the *Mackay-Bennett* sail out from the harbor into the miasma of an ice-laden sea.

There weren't any passengers, or survivors, coming to Halifax.

Just bodies.

# Part 3
## After

No man is an island, entire of itself; every man is a piece of the continent, a part of the main; if a clod be washed away by the sea, Europe is the less, as well as if a promontory were, as well as if a manor of thy friend's or of thine own were; any man's death diminishes me, because I am involved in mankind, and therefore never send to know for whom the bell tolls; it tolls for thee.

John Donne, *Meditation XVII*

# 34

*L*ydia didn't try to keep track of the time or the day. The important thing was getting to New York. Craven relayed her options of where to stay. He had friends in New York. Executives of Beaumont had wired assurance that they were welcome to stay in their homes or guesthouses.

She would feel even colder staying with people she didn't know. "I'll go to a hotel. Or where Caroline goes."

"Caroline will stay in the hotel until she knows what will happen with Phoebe and Henry," Craven said. "Lady Stanton-Jones had made contact with distant relatives she planned to visit while in America."

"Oh, the children and Caroline have become so close. I know she would take very good care of them."

"Not if the relatives want the children," Craven said. "The Stanton-Jones attorney is on this. Someone will control the Stanton-Jones's assets, and the children's trust."

Lydia hurt for her friend. "Caroline will be devastated."

"Blood and money speak louder than love."

Later that day, Craven said that suites were reserved for them at the Waldorf Astoria.

The closer they came to New York, the more Craven stuck to her like glue, reporting everything from another survivor marked off the list to Caroline's finances being wired to New York to when and what to eat. Perhaps that was his way of making her face reality. But she had all the reality she wanted. She wanted John. She cradled their child deep under the blanket at night to keep it warm. But her heart remained cold.

He said they'd soon be in New York, so she stood at the railing, wanting to see that first sight of land. She vowed never to set foot off land again.

"We'll be bombarded with photographers and reporters, asking questions."

She flashed him her best exasperated glance. "I won't answer any questions. Out there on the *Virginian*, or in a lifeboat, is my husband," she ground out.

"You mean your fairy tale."

She stared. Oh, she could kill him. For the first time since the nightmare began, it wasn't herself she wanted to drown. It was Craven. She had an idea. With an energy that surprised her, she headed down the deck. She would get her face and hair made up for the pictures. The brown dress would be suitable for what she had in mind.

She would tell the reporters—the world—about her marriage. Just because Craven thought he knew everything didn't make it so. John would be there waiting. He would confirm their marriage. Yes, she was a married woman.

Later that afternoon she saw the Statue of Liberty and something else. A boat was coming their way. They were being met. By loved ones?

Then she saw it was a press boat. Reporters and photographers yelling, asking questions, offering money to any who would jump off the ship and swim to them.

They wanted a story.

Revulsion welled up inside. She thought she couldn't stand it. Like others, they moved from the railing, but not before she saw thousands upon thousands of people gathered as if the passengers, the so-called survivors, were pigeons in a park and the spectators were luring them with crumbs.

She was not . . . hungry.

The waiting seemed interminable. She just wanted to put her feet on solid ground.

Finally, the *Carpathia* arrived at Pier 54. Announcements were made that assistance awaited them. The Council of Jewish Women, the Traveler's Aid Society, Women's Relief Organization, churches. There was clothing and transportation to shelters.

Lydia knew all this didn't apply to her. She had Craven.

He held her arm and shielded her from reporters and photographers screaming for pictures and a story. In all that throng, John did not appear.

Several cars and a few limousines lined the road. The drivers stood with signs. "Beaumont vehicles will be assisting some passengers," Craven said. He and a driver outside a limousine recognized each other.

She and Craven climbed into a limousine. Caroline, Bess, and the children into another. The drivers chauffeured them to the Waldorf Astoria, where they were expected, and they were escorted to their rooms.

"You and Bess have adjoining rooms," he said to Caroline when the elevator reached her floor. Lydia and Craven rode up to another floor where they shared a two-bedroom suite.

She removed her fur and tossed it over a chair in the living room while he called room service. Chefs would prepare meals as long as the new arrivals wanted them. Craven asked what she wanted.

Shrugging, she said, "A sandwich."

He ordered chicken sandwiches and wine. "Be back in a moment." He walked from the living room, through her bedroom, and into the adjoining room. She thought it a good time to find her own bathroom.

He was in the living room looking out the window when she returned. She sat on the couch and looked around. It didn't matter that the room would normally seem perfectly wonderful and elegant, as had the bedroom and bathroom.

Her gaze fell upon her hands, which clapsed each other on her lap. She untwined them and pinched a fold of the brown dress.

"I have nothing but the fur, the Bible, and my evening bag, and—"

He turned. "Stop it, Lydia." He walked over to her. "All you lost can be replaced."

She refused to honor that statement with even a glance.

"Get a good night's sleep and go shopping in the morning."

"Shopping?" she squeaked. "I have no money. I don't even have a decent dress to wear. This one needs to be cleaned."

Clearly exasperated, he said, "Don't you even know who you are?"

Fortunately, the tap on the door halted the scream she felt rise in her throat. She used to know who she was. But now, feeling faint, she raised her hand to her forehead.

"Open the wine," Craven ordered, and the employee complied. He poured a little for Craven to taste. "I'm sure it's fine. More."

The waiter poured more, and Craven handed it to Lydia.

She sipped. Yes. She needed . . . something.

The next thing she knew, the waiter was gone, and a small table with the sandwich was in front of her. "Eat," Craven said. "You're pale. Sometimes it takes a while to adjust after being on the water for a while."

She began to feel better after eating and drinking a little. He settled across from her and ate. After a moment he said, "In the morning I'll have cash for you and a Beaumont card. Caroline's finances will take a little longer, but she may use the charge card. If anyone balks, they may call the Beaumont offices and the person calling will be fired."

Lydia managed a small laugh, even though she knew this could easily happen. "I doubt Caroline will leave the children."

"Whatever you two want to do. The wives of Beaumont board members and friends are eager to be of assistance. They can provide anything. From homes to children watching."

For an instant she felt grateful for all Craven was doing. But she shook away the thought. She wasn't completely helpless. Beaumont executives would have contacted her and personally offered their assistance. But he should be doing this. He worked for her father. Someday, if he was lucky, he might work for her. "Thank you," she said.

He finished his sandwich. After a sip of wine he said, "One more important thing. Do not talk to anyone. I will do the talking to reporters for you."

She set down her glass, shaking her head. "What are they wanting?"

"Every little morsel available."

She chewed the last morsel of her sandwich.

"This is the biggest story ever. They're not going to let it go even if they have to make things up. No," he said pointedly. "Not a word." He took a sip of wine, set his glass down, and waited until she looked at him. "Your name is already out there. Among the 675 survivors. And in New York, Beaumont is right up there close to Astor."

He had to say the word, of course. The word "survivor" brings to mind the opposite.

Victim.

"I'm all right now. You can leave."

"You have a little color now." He looked closely at her face. "If you need anything—"

"I'm fine."

He stood and reached for the bottle.

"Get your own," she said.

He looked down at her with that faint turn of his lips as if he were thinking of a grin. "Maybe a little wine will help you sleep. Good night."

She didn't need him to explain that. She watched him walk through her bedroom, heard a door open, then close. She called the front desk and asked about cleaning service. Almost immediately, a woman came to get her dress.

She went to the bedroom and changed into the nightdress and then returned to the door and handed over the brown dress.

The woman's lips trembled. "I'm so sorry."

"Thank you," Lydia said quickly, and the woman turned just as quickly.

She closed the door, and forgoing the glass, took the bottle into the bedroom.

After she got into bed, she sat for a while. His words *Don't you even know who you are* came to mind. To him she was Cyril Beaumont's daughter, heir to a fortune.

But that's who she used to be. Now she was a married woman. She would claim it. Shout it. Her life and John's child were something to live for, not to be ashamed of. And so what if her father disowned her.

She could not keep her father alive by obeying his every wish or preventing a scandal.

She was more than his daughter.

She was John's wife.

With that resolve, she reached for the bottle and lifted it to her mouth. Empty.

The light switch was her next chore.

That done, darkness enveloped her, as if it hadn't already. Her hand moved over the other side of the bed.

Empty.

Only her eyes were full.

Her heart was empty.

## 35

Caroline was glad Craven had called and said he would wait until morning to let her know what was transpiring concerning her finances and the children. A difference in time zones meant some people were at work while others attempted to sleep. She felt, however, the entire world was probably existing on adrenaline.

Exhausted, she slept most of the night and was amazed that the children also slept soundly. She knew Bess checked on them all during the night. They awoke early and were getting ready for breakfast when Craven called.

"You might like to breakfast with Lydia in the living room," he said. "You shouldn't go to the dining room. Even the children would be hounded by reporters." He asked of her what she had no intention of doing. "Don't speak to anyone about the *Titanic*. We're working on having affairs settled and questions answered in an orderly manner."

"Do you know any more—?"

Obviously knowing she was thinking about the children, he said, "I will let you know."

How anyone could be organized in such chaos, Caroline didn't know. But Craven was taking care of legal matters with wires and telephone calls and the myriad assistants he knew in New York.

On second thought, when one managed a worldwide railroad company, he could certainly handle the affairs of a few people. Just as William had, on a lesser scale, in the auto industry.

She needed Craven handling the legal aspects and Bess the personal. But she so wanted to learn how to take care of at least one person. Herself.

Maybe that's why she wasn't allowed children. No, she mustn't start taking blame for something that had a reason, apparently a physical one.

By the time they had the children dressed and decisions made about breakfast, the morning was speeding by. Fortunately, they had the children to focus on. Phoebe was pleased to see Lydia and wanted to sit by her at the breakfast table. She seemed tickled that Lydia was still in her nightdress because the brown one hadn't yet been returned.

However, before they finished the meal, a maid delivered Lydia's brown dress, and she went to the bedroom as soon as she finished breakfast.

While Bess sopped up orange juice that had spilled onto the table, she told Henry about the time she dropped an entire cake on the floor. The children liked that.

Henry held out his Meccano set and wanted Bess to make a dragon, with biiiiig eyes. "Oh, I am not good with dragons. But Miss Caroline makes wonderful dragons." Bess smiled. "With biiiiig eyes."

Just as Caroline settled on the couch with a hopeful little boy and a box between them, a knock sounded on the door.

The fear of certainty stabbed Caroline's heart when Bess opened the door and she saw Craven standing there with that horrible look of purpose in his gray eyes.

She knew. Of course she'd known all along.

Bess knew. "Here," she said, reaching for the Meccano box and touching Henry on the shoulder. "Let's go back into our rooms while Mr. Dowd talks with the ladies. I can make a dog."

He shook his head. "I want a dragon."

"Well, I'll bet Miss Phoebe and I can make a dragon with the biggest eyes in the whole world."

He looked doubtful, but of course he'd been taught to obey those in charge of him. "I can make a dragon," Phoebe said. Following Bess and Henry, she exited the room. What would happen with these children?

Craven would know. That's why he stood there, reminding her of a dragon with eyes of steel, able to spit fire from his nostrils. She sat on the couch, feeling hot, knowing what was coming.

He was there as a businessman bearing official information, so she said, "Morning, Craven," without it being preceded by "good."

He presented the *good* news first, if it could be called that. Perhaps "necessary" was the word. He held out an envelope. "Here is cash. You may charge anything to the Beaumont account until your financial situation is settled. There's no problem, but right now everything is slow and temporary."

She thought things were moving rather fast, but nodded and took the envelope. She was temporarily existing. Rather like a bird that could be made from the Meccano set. Where would she alight?

Bracing herself, she sat at attention. Then he said the words, "They've arrived."

He handed her a copy of an official report. She read it twice, to make sure.

"Are they—?" Should she say, *nice?*

She tried again. "Do you—?" *Like them?*

Ah, she was being ridiculous. "They have the legal right to them?"

"They do. The attorneys have confirmed it. Lady Stanton-Jones left information in London concerning where and who she might visit while in America. This young couple's parents, on both sides, were listed. The young couple, Mary and Bobby Freeman, took the train from California days ago, as soon as they were assured Henry George and Lady Stanton-Jones were not on the survivor list."

While taking a deep breath, she had to remind herself that Craven was not sitting. This was not personal. It was business. "May I meet them?"

"They're in the lobby. I can have them brought up."

She nodded, and he made the call.

Lydia came in wearing the brown dress. Craven handed her an envelope identical to the one Caroline had received. She had probably overheard the conversation. "I'll be in the bedroom," she said.

Caroline nodded, and sat, and waited. She didn't like to deliberately think of class, but she'd always been identified by it. When Craven opened the door, the young couple stepped inside, uncertainty all over their faces and in their eyes. Judging by the suitable clothes they wore, Caroline judged them as being second class. The young woman clasped her fingers in front of her and then unclasped them, letting her hands fall to her side.

Craven introduced them, nodded, and made his exit. His business on this was concluded. There was no room for debate.

Caroline was just a woman who had offered kindness to a couple of children until their relatives arrived.

She must be gracious.

She'd had experience in that.

"I'm Caroline." She stood, offering them the couch. She
sat near them in an armchair. They were Mary and Bobby
Freeman. Nice names. Yes, their train trip was fine. The
weather was good. They'd had breakfast. They looked forward
to meeting the children. Their conversation stopped there.
Who wanted to say anything about the tragedy? That wasn't
necessary. It was simply there, having taken precedence over
all other thoughts or events. The word "sorry" wasn't adequate.
Everyone knew that.

They were nice. And she liked them. Ordinary, they
seemed, with rather common names, self-conscious, perhaps
because they might think she was somebody.

"I think they would like to ride on a train. That should be
interesting, especially to little Henry. Do you have children?"

"Not yet," Mary said. "We've only been married a year. But
we plan to. My parents and Bobby's parents will help us. And
we have other family."

"That's wonderful. You're fortunate to have a big family."

Mary nodded and smiled. She seemed like a sweet girl.

Caroline opened her envelope. "Here is some cash. I would
like for you to buy what you and the children need or want, as
a gift from me."

Relief touched their faces. She had the feeling they didn't
have extra. "If you're sure," Bobby said.

"I am. I've—" She stopped and cleared her throat. She
mustn't say she'd grown fond of them. Her voice would never
get the words out. "I've learned a good bit about them over
the past days," she said. "I'll be glad to tell you all I know."

She did. After a while, Bobby assured her, "We'll take good care of them, ma'am." That wasn't necessary. She had no hold on the children.

It must appear that she did. After an uncomfortable silence, Mary said softly, "Where are they?"

"Oh. They're with my maid in another room. I'll call."

She would call? How did these telephones work? Neither Mary nor Bobby offered to call, so she rose and went to the telephone. She stared for a moment, then lifted the receiver. The front desk answered. She asked for her rooms and was connected.

"Bess, bring the children, please."

Caroline had tried to prepare them for this. Phoebe said her grandmother had told her they might meet their American relatives. Bess came in with them, and the children related well with the young couple.

Bess stood near the door.

"Bess has been so good with them," Caroline said.

Mary's and Bobby's eyes moved to Bess, their faces questioning.

"Does she go with us?" Mary said, uncomfortably.

Bess stiffened like a mannequin in a department store window. If Caroline said yes, she would go. She would obey. She was her maid.

But she was Caroline's friend, whether she knew it or not. There were no legal papers to take Bess from her.

She would keep Bess.

"No. Bess stays. But the children are accustomed to maids and nannies and tutors."

Mary's and Bobby's eyes opened wide. Then they nodded, perhaps remembering from whom the children were descended.

When there seemed nothing more to say, Caroline asked, "When do you leave?"

"Now," Mary said. "Mr. Dowd said a car is waiting to take us to the station."

"I have two rooms if you want to stay for a while."

"We have our tickets."

All right. What more was there to say, to do? She beckoned Henry and he came to her. "These nice relatives are going to take you shopping. And take you for a ride on a big train."

Henry looked pleased. Phoebe looked reticent.

Caroline didn't say you may never see me again. No one had told them they'd never see their daddy or their grandmother again. And maybe they would.

She took a piece of stationery from the desk and wrote her name. She had no address. A sense of panic started to rise, then she quickly wrote Caroline Chadwick, c/o Craven Dowd, Beaumont Railroad Company, New York, USA.

Then she remembered that the attorneys had information. They had found relatives, all too quickly. They could keep in touch.

She and the children hugged the way Henry hugged his toy box and Phoebe her blue bear. They said goodbye as if they'd be back before breakfast the next morning. Someone had said that when they were getting into the little lifeboats.

Then the door closed. Bess kept her back to Caroline. Maybe she was guarding the door lest Caroline make a break for it and drag them back in. Bess's shoulders rose and fell.

"All right now," a welcome voice said, and Lydia appeared from the bedroom. "We have shopping to do."

Yes, they did. Lydia must get makeup. Her eyes were much too puffy and red.

"And you," Caroline said to Bess, "will come along. I don't want to see anything that looks like an apron or cap."

"Yes, ma'am."

Caroline heaved a sigh. "You're my companion. You will dress like it."

Bess hesitated. "I have no money, ma'am."

"Of course you do. You're my employee, remember?"

Bess said, "Yes, ma'am," again, a slight tinge of rebellion in her tone. But if Bess insisted on class distinction, Caroline would make her demands.

"I'll call down about the car," Lydia said.

After she made the call and was told at what time the car would arrive, they planned the shopping trip. "No talk about anything except clothes and jewelry and maybe a hair salon."

"We wouldn't have to worry about that if we wore caps," Bess quipped.

Caroline and Lydia stared at her a moment, then all three laughed. Maybe Bess was coming around after all.

Caroline refused to think of what she could do nothing about. She and Lydia knew how to shop. Simply go through the motions.

She counted her blessing of having two friends. Even if she had had to buy one of them.

## 36

*C*raven came to the door of Lydia's suite and introduced Lawrence, a man in a business suit, who would accompany them on their shopping trip. Lawrence said, "Your car is here, ma'am."

He led her, Caroline, and Bess to the limousine out front, waving aside reporters still shouting their questions and photographers snapping pictures. Then she was reminded they had arrived only last night. Somehow it seemed like another lifetime.

The chauffeur knew where to take them. Lydia was not surprised when Lawrence accompanied them into the department store.

Caroline leaned close. "He sure takes good care of you."

Lydia did not think she meant Lawrence.

Their purchases were chic but sensible. They didn't need evening gowns or elaborate jewelry. They did buy pretty hats.

Lydia enjoyed helping Caroline pick out clothes for Bess, who balked all the way but looked pleased when viewing herself in the mirror, dressed like a lady.

They returned in the afternoon from the most unusual shopping trip Lydia had ever experienced, it being one of necessity. Lawrence helped deliver their packages and made it known he was as near as a telephone call.

After unpacking and placing her clothes in the closet and drawers, Lydia dozed for a while, until Craven called and asked that they have dinner together.

"In the dining room?"

"No, that's not safe yet. We can have dinner brought up."

"Caroline and Bess could join us."

"Not tonight. We have business to discuss."

"Business?"

"Personal business. Yours."

She scoffed. She had no personal business. But at least this would give her a reason to dress in her new clothes. "Order for me," she said. She hadn't eaten since having the late breakfast.

She wore the medium blue silk gown and fastened a string of pearls around her neck. A little makeup helped take away that haggard look.

Being in no mood to fight with her hair, she brushed it, twisted it into a roll at the back and let the curls at her face do what they would.

When she opened the door to Craven, his glance moved over the dress in a casual way. Something about his eyes made her feel them. "I see you went shopping."

She bristled. He knew she went shopping. He was the one who had given her the money, had sent the car and the driver and the bodyguard or whatever he was.

Apparently, he had gone shopping too. The fact that a man could be blessed with a face that needed no makeup just wasn't fair.

"Does much more for your eyes than the brown one."

But not what a Beaumont should wear in the evening at dinner? He might as well ask again if she knew who she was. She did, and she would tell him when the moment was right.

While they waited, she peeked out the window at the streets below, which were still crowded with people, coming and going, even as the sun vanished and darkness crept in. "Phoebe and Henry may be on the train now."

"They were to leave several hours ago."

"Caroline will miss them. She's naturally drawn to children."

So was John. He built toy trains for children.

She turned quickly to the window again and pretended to look out. Ahead of her was some vast nothing, like a sea with no land in sight, and she found she was twisting the rings on her fingers. She looked down. Caroline's ring. She kept forgetting to give it back. The thought of taking it off was too—

"I think dinner's here," Craven said even before the knock sounded.

She looked up and saw their reflection in the glass.

He stood in the center of the room, but she knew he'd been watching her. He had a habit of that.

Filet mignon, baked potato, and vegetables. Nothing fancy, but it looked wonderful and the aroma whetted her appetite. "I'm famished," she said.

He passed her the breadbasket, and she quickly buttered a roll and bit into it while he poured the wine. "The hearing will begin in the morning," he said. "So I will be tied up with that most of the day."

She cut into the filet and savored the taste of it. Tender, warm, delicious. How she could enjoy eating when everything else seemed a burden, she didn't know, but welcomed having an enjoyable activity.

"What's that about?" She took a bite of vegetable and smothered her potato with butter and sour cream.

"An investigation. And they want your story. I've told them you're in seclusion and I am the spokesman for Beaumont. I will let them know when you have something to say."

"I will talk to them. I will tell them I married John Ancell on that ship."

"No."

Her mouth opened, and she didn't care if there was food in it. "This is not up for debate. I am making a statement. To you, before I make it to the rest of the world."

He swallowed the steak and took a bite of potato, calmly, unperturbed, waiting, not blinking, just looking.

"I can speak for myself. I will report that I am Mrs. John Ancell."

His expression didn't change. After a moment, he reached for his wine glass, lifted it to his lips, and drank from it.

She picked up her glass, just as calmly as he.

He returned his to the table, keeping that bland expression. "Just in case anything should come up about that night, you need to get your nonexistent marriage annulled."

Lydia gasped, and not having fully swallowed the wine, she began to cough as the glass fell from her hand, spilled on the table, and crashed to the floor.

"I'll call for someone to clean it up."

She looked around. "Marcella. Where's Marcella?"

His face grim, he didn't answer. He didn't need to.

She tried to collect herself while he got a towel and covered the mess. Marcella's name wasn't on the survivor's list.

Neither was John's.

Could this really be true?

She could not eat any more. How could she ever eat again? But when he poured wine into his glass and handed it to her, she drank. She didn't need to make a spectacle of herself.

He must have thought she'd calmed down, because he lost his mind again. "The papers have been drawn up," he said. "All you need do is sign them."

Obviously he was not as smart as he was made out to be. That was too ridiculous to even discuss. However, finally, as she nibbled absently on a roll, she managed to say, "Why would I do something so inane as to get an annulment?"

# 37

Lydia," he said calmly, having returned to the table and taking an occasional bite. She would too, and she lifted a forkful of potato. "It's the only sensible thing to do because you're not married to John Ancell."

She chewed furiously and glared at him.

"There was no license. No papers officially filed. Did you sign anything?"

"We were going to the next morning."

"It wasn't done. You're not married. If your father doesn't make it, God forbid, and you claim to be Mrs. Ancell, then as your husband he inherits part of Beaumont Company."

She felt so angry, she spouted what she didn't want to face. "He isn't here."

"He has relatives. He has parents in a small town outside London. His father is a carpenter. He has a nice business and his family is comfortable. He was very handy with wood and liked to whittle and—"

"I know. He made little wooden trains. Why are you telling me this?"

"If you insist upon being Mrs. Ancell, then they are legally entitled to some of your inheritance."

"They wouldn't."

He raised his eyebrows. He didn't have to tell her what people did for money and what it could do to them. It made them think they ruled the world and could look down on dear people like John simply because of a lack of it.

Relentless, Craven continued. "Can you imagine a middle-class family being asked to sign papers, giving up any rights to the biggest railroad company in the world?"

She didn't know about the legalities. She remembered John saying his family was proud of him.

"Another thing," he said, interrupting her thoughts, which made no sense anyway. "As his wife you would be rightful owner of Ancell Toy Trains."

Her jaw dropped. That had never occurred to her.

"But, I expect he had a will making family members his beneficiaries."

She got up from the table and paced. She didn't want to think of all that. She wanted to think of John, her husband, their lovely short life together, their wedding. She put her hands over her ears.

She heard him anyway. "Even if he had a will, leaving everything to his family, you as his legal wife would be entitled. It will involve the courts, and attorneys they probably can't afford."

She sneered. "I have no need or desire to take anything from his family. As you've said many times, they make toy trains. I have real ones."

"It's out of your hands, Lydia. It's business. Your father will not have the privilege of favorable publicity about that pseudo-wedding now that the *Titanic* has sunk. Quite the contrary. It will be a shame and a disgrace."

She stopped pacing and opened her mouth to deliver a reprimand, but he spoke quickly. "If you had received the publicity, and the *Titanic* hadn't sunk, he might have accepted John because John's toy company would have become a part of his own business, and John would be your husband. But," he said pointedly, "the *Titanic* did sink."

She walked faster about the room as if she were going somewhere. She knew the *Titanic* sank. But she didn't want to think about it. She wanted to say she was married to John and to go off somewhere and find some kind of peace.

"What might have been, has changed now." He glanced at her and then at the floor as if she might wear a hole in it. She wished it would swallow her up. "If your father thinks you married John Ancell, the only way he can save face, in his opinion, will be to demand you take control of Ancell Trains." He shrugged. "I mean, how else can we incorporate John's designs?"

"No." She sat on the couch. "I will relinquish any control over Ancell Trains. His family can have the business and Beaumont cannot."

"This kind of business does not work like that. Your father owns Beaumont. Beaumont has a board. They can make decisions that don't necessarily go along with your father." He shook his head. "We might talk Cyril out of any legal action, but the Board in London wants John's designs. The board in America will want them. How can they get them?"

Lydia was getting the point. Likely, not from his family. Beaumont would take legal action.

"And it only takes one Ancell or one member of his company to put a bug in the ear of an attorney about John having been married to a Beaumont." He shrugged as if it were a hopeless situation. "There's a court case. The Ancells want a piece of Beaumont."

She scoffed, "They would know that's a losing battle."

"Right," he agreed. "But the attorneys would know Beaumont would settle rather than go through a scandal of whether or not a marriage occurred, and who is entitled to what."

She shook her head and walked over to the table. She took a bite of roll and said confidently. "There's the other side of it. The Ancell family might not want a scandal either."

"Lydia." He looked at her as if she were a foolish child. "For the Ancells, his marrying a Beaumont would not be a scandal. It would be like winning the lottery."

"Did John's company have a board?"

"He had business dealings with other companies. But John was owner and president. His company had the usual things an ordinary business has." His shrug meant they were inconsequential. "Assistant. Secretary. Financial Advisor. John had vision," he acknowledged. "Not big-business sense."

She looked down at him. "Really?" He met her gaze for a moment, then simply turned to his glass for another sip of wine. She didn't have to say the obvious.

John had enough sense to cause Beaumont Railroad Company to pursue him, have the board consult with him, have him inspect their designs for the possibility of incorporating his, and pay his passage to America to talk with the board in New York. "Maybe I should sue Beaumont for—for—"

He gave a small laugh. "You can't sue Beaumont. You own it."

She returned to the table and sat across from him. "Even if I said there was no wedding, there were over three hundred people who witnessed it."

His glance meant *were*, just as she thought it.

The sound of his voice was quiet and might even be mistaken for reverent. But the words were tearing down all her lovely memories. "There are no pictures, no stories about the wedding to prove it ever took place. The publicity is all about the tragedy. When women lose their husbands, I think they will be mourning instead of talking about another woman's wedding."

Mourning? Didn't he know that's what she was doing?

He handed her the glass, and she sipped.

"Besides," he said, "they didn't know John. Yes, there were a few introductions and his name was said at the end of the ceremony, but at times like this, who is going to remember him? Did anyone connect John with his trains? And his trains aren't that widely known outside London. It wasn't his train success that brought him to our attention, but his designs."

She wasn't sure she had even mentioned the trains to Caroline. It was mentioned one night at dinner. But as Craven said, at a time like this, who will remember? A three-year-old thinking about a Christmas present?

"But if just one person remembers and tries to make a story of it, then comes the scandal and the courts. An official annulment will put it all behind us before it can begin. Let's hope nobody mentions it."

She dropped her hand to her lap. "Like you said, who knows?"

He shrugged. "I have no idea who might have wired someone between the time of your engagement and your wedding. I wired your father every day, sometimes more than once. John could have wired someone."

Yes, he might have. But she didn't think Craven had had time to wire her father after the wedding. "Did you mention anything to father about the wedding?"

"Of course not. I didn't want to kill him." He paused for a sip of wine. "And I wanted to wait until I felt you could handle this, but—" He paused, then said quickly, "Your father is under constant care right now. He's worried about how you're handling everything."

She scoffed. "Did you tell him I'm not handling anything?"

No, Craven was handling everything.

"You can," he said calmly. "The decisions are yours to make. You have two options. One, you can say you're John Ancell's wife and take possession of his toy train company and have them try getting a part of Beaumont. Or you can have the marriage annulled and protect his family, your father, and keep Beaumont out of any litigation."

She remembered he had stopped being condescending after he realized she and John would be married despite his misgivings. He'd been . . . best man.

Best man?

Even a good man didn't go around destroying someone's dreams.

"Sometimes, Craven, you can be so cruel."

"Not cruel," he said blandly. "Realistic."

# 38

Shortly after Craven left the living room, he knocked on the adjoining door. Lydia opened it, and he held out a manila envelope. Her paralyzed hand could not take it. "I'll just leave it here on the dresser." He did, then stepped back into his room and closed the door.

She could not stay in the room with it, so she returned to the living room and called room service to come for the dishes and the broken glass. She called Caroline, who said she and Bess had had a nice dinner, had read newspaper articles aloud to each other, and were working a crossword puzzle.

They all were about ready to turn in, but yes, they'd breakfast together in her suite. After the phone call and the mess was cleaned up, Lydia got into the nightdress she'd bought that day and wondered what to do.

She did not want to read a paper. The headlines were enough to turn her world upside-down, as if it weren't already. She looked at the Bible but didn't want to touch that either. Listening to the radio might be worse. Perhaps she could find some music. She found a program that said "Sweet Dreams Music." That sounded perfect.

Feeling drained, she thought she might sleep and turned out the light. It was a restless night, but one without nightmares. She awoke to another day without purpose and wondered why she should live it.

But, of course, to have breakfast with her friends. So she readied herself and was in a little better state of mind when Caroline and Bess entered.

Fortunately, they had finished eating before Craven came. Surely he would not ask for those papers. He didn't, but held another envelope.

"I thought you'd be at the hearing," she said.

"This was delivered." He took a deep breath. "Identifications are coming in from the *Mackay-Bennett*."

"*Mackay* . . . ?"

"Let's sit on the couch," Caroline said. The three women left the breakfast table and settled on the couch, but Craven remained standing.

"Not for you, Caroline," he said.

She nodded and reached for Lydia's hand.

"We can do this alone if you prefer, Lydia."

She didn't know what the envelope held but had the feeling she shouldn't be alone. "Identifications? *Mackay-Bennett?*"

"The *Mackay-Bennett* is the ship that left Nova Scotia to find survivors before we even reached New York," he explained, and she nodded.

"John has been identified."

She drew in a breath but could not expel it.

He opened the envelope. "You can read it, or I will. Or I can leave it."

She'd never known him to be so unforthcoming.

She motioned at it, and he looked at the paper.

"The *Mackay* received a passenger list from White Star. There weren't many first-class passengers his age. His stateroom key was in his pocket."

He glanced at her, but she said, "I want to hear it all."

"A small black mole at the jaw below—"

"The right ear," she finished for him.

She was nodding when he read the description of the suit and the clothing label. She had helped John pick out his formal clothes. Not as expensive as those Craven wore. But certainly acceptable. John wasn't competing with anyone. John didn't need to. He had his youth, and his nice face, and excited blue eyes, and . . . his woman.

"Wearing an unusual kind of gold wedding band. Shaped more like a small wheel than the usual bands that lie flat against the finger. There were a couple of almost imperceptible nicks as if it had been cut by a sharp object."

She looked over at Caroline and gave a self-conscious laugh. Caroline smiled but wouldn't know what that was about. That would be the toy train wheel. It could be checked against other wheels. Lydia knew they would match.

"There will be additional fingerprinting and—"

She shook her head and held up her hand.

He replaced the paper. "Do you want this?"

"No." She had enough, in that envelope on the dresser.

"Caroline, there's no word yet on William." He paused and said, "I'm sorry."

Lydia wasn't looking at him but at her hand in Caroline's. Was he sorry William hadn't been found or that John had? Maybe both.

She was glad. He wasn't out there on that cold, icy ocean anymore. She looked up. "Where is he?"

"On the ship."

That didn't tell her much, but before she could think of anything else to ask, anything that would make a difference, he said he needed to get back to the hearing and left with the envelope.

The door closed.

The three of them sat in silence, as though in a boat on a vast sea. It felt cold. Except for Caroline's hand.

Lydia looked down and noticed the ring. Her hand moved to it.

"No," Caroline said. "Not now. Do you want to be alone?"

Her breath was still hung in her throat, so she nodded.

The two women stood, and Lydia was glad they didn't try to hug her. Caroline seemed to understand. "We will come back later."

"Oh, one more thing," Lydia said and went into the bedroom. She returned with the paper bag containing Harriett's wedding dress. It didn't mean anything to anyone now. The designer wasn't on the survivor list. All those lovely creations would never be shown. The models would never wear them. It would never be in the newspapers throughout the world. "Do whatever you like with this, will you?"

Without asking what it was, Caroline took the bag and left.

Lydia picked up a pen from the desk in the living room and returned to the bedroom. She opened the envelope, signed on the appropriate line, and wrote the date. She laid the pen down.

Everything seemed so unreal. The wonderful fairy-tale wedding. Then the disaster. Her gaze moved to her finger. John's engagement ring that would never be paid for. The wedding band that belonged to Caroline Chadwick. Who ever heard of such a thing? She took off the rings and laid them beside the envelope.

What kind of marriage was that for the heiress to the Beaumont fortune?

Her signature on that paper meant there was no marriage. John's family would receive the identification about him. They would never know of her nor she of them. It all began with his father whittling on a piece of wood until he had made a little wooden train.

John said the *Titanic* probably started with a little wooden boat and a paper sail. That idea became a ship made of steel. Now it lay on the bottom of the ocean.

Like her dreams.

She was no longer married to John.

With one more glance at the envelope, she felt she needed to change that thought.

The marriage was annulled.

She was never married to John.

She began to laugh.

And laugh.

And laugh.

Until she fell across the bed and thought she'd surely drown from the liquid laughter that filled her eyes and spilled onto the pillow she clutched to her heart.

# 39

*L*ydia awoke late in the afternoon and sat up with a start. The clock on the bedside table indicated she had slept for a couple of hours. Her eyes moved to the dresser. The rings were there. The envelope wasn't. When had he slipped into the room and taken it?

Had he heard her cry?

Or laugh?

He'd done his duty. He had protected her father's heart and Beaumont Railroad Company from threats of a scandal or litigation or making a settlement. That's what he was paid to do.

And Lydia, don't you know who you are?

To find out, she pushed the pillow aside, stood, smoothed her dress, and went over and looked in the mirror. You are heiress to the Beaumont fortune, she told the reflection. And should not have those puffy, red eyes or a red blotch on your previously acclaimed, beautiful face or a wrinkled dress or be sobbing into hotel pillows.

She would hold her head high. And she did, all the way to the telephone. "Shall we put on a new frock and find a place to lunch?" she asked Caroline when she answered her phone.

"Yes, let's do."

"Hats and all," Lydia said.

"Indeed," Caroline said with enthusiasm. "We will hurry. I'm famished."

*We*, Lydia was thinking as she hung up and hurried to the closet. How amazing that Caroline treated Bess like a friend. Lydia didn't mind, but she could not imagine having done that with Marcella.

Determined not to let her mind stay there, she opened the closet door with a little more force than she'd intended. This was a new day. A new beginning. She chose the conservative dove-gray suit she had purchased yesterday. The light pink blouse with the high neckline bordered by fine lace complimented it perfectly. It would match the red blotch on her face, she thought with a hint of flippancy.

However, after washing her face and applying makeup, the spot had faded. She brushed her hair back from her face, holding the curls down with jeweled clips, and turned it into a roll at the back of her neck and fastened it with pins.

After donning the clothes, she stepped into rather tight, new, pointed-toe black shoes, and perched the gray hat on her head, tilted it slightly to one side, and flicked the little black and pink feathers with her fingers.

Observing herself in the mirror, she nodded. One final touch, fastening the strand of pearls, and she was ready. Pleased with herself for having managed all this by lunchtime, she picked up Caroline's wedding band, and grabbed her black purse and gloves.

She was not surprised when she stepped into the hallway and the next door opened.

"Good afternoon," Craven said. "Might I ask where you are going?"

"Out." She continued on, then realized she hadn't been to Caroline's room, although she thought it was on a lower floor. She stopped and looked over her shoulder. "Where might I find Caroline Chadwick's room?"

"Take the elevator down to the next floor, get off, and her room is two doors down on the right."

With her head high, she marched to the elevator, resenting his grin. This was no occasion for a grin.

Lydia thought both Caroline and Bess looked equally smart, but not so much so that they might attract undo attention. Just three ladies going out. The desk clerk recommended a little restaurant nearby, since they didn't want to eat inside the hotel. It was lunchtime, and everything would be crowded.

"Especially with the hearings going on," Caroline said. "The reporters will be hounding them and maybe not notice us."

They walked out onto the sidewalk. Never in her life before had Lydia appreciated the feel of a sidewalk beneath her feet. Had never given it a thought unless it were a negative one, like it had a crack in it or a chunk torn out. "Sunshine," she said appreciatively.

Caroline smiled and mentioned how caring the people of New York were. "The newspaper and radio are still reporting how survivors might get help. So many are volunteering out of compassion."

"You always see the good in people, Caroline."

"Not really. But I try to concentrate on the good. Sometimes we have to look for it, but it's around us."

Lydia nodded. She must try working on seeing the good.

"I believe this is it," Bess said.

They entered the restaurant on the corner, and Lydia asked if they might have a table near a window. The waitress led them to one where they could look out onto the street. She laughed when they sat down. "I've never before thought of myself as a people watcher."

"Even the horses are a welcome sight," Caroline added.

They ordered coffee and sandwiches and talked about ordinary things like the smell of the food, the taste of the coffee when the waitress brought it, if they'd get dessert or try to find a chocolate shop, whether they'd make a trek through Central Park later, and how nice Bess looked, particularly in that cute little hat.

"Blame her for that." Bess directed her glance at Caroline. Lydia wondered if she called her Caroline or Mrs. Chadwick.

The waitress brought the sandwiches, and they discussed lettuce, tomato, mayonnaise or mustard. Incidentals now seemed important, or at least a worthy topic of conversation.

They found a chocolate shop, delighted in the delectable morsels, then took a carriage ride to Central Park. Lydia felt they might be able to talk about that other life now.

She opened her purse and took out the wedding band. "Thank you," she said.

Caroline took it and slipped it on her finger, then just looked at it for a while.

"How do you do it, Caroline? How do you stand it? Losing William?"

Caroline took a breath of the fresh, cool air and looked out before her. "I don't know that I've really faced it yet, Lydia. I can't really analyze myself. But I know that people behave differently in the same situation. Just as they did on that ship."

Lydia felt the possibility of an overwhelming wave stirring in her stomach. But she could do this. It had to be done, faced. She nodded, remembering some had been brave, strong, helpful, while others were panicked, fearful, jumping, pushing.

"You see, we even behave differently in love."

Lydia wasn't sure she could handle this, but listened. "You react differently about John because you loved him differently. You were fortunate to love like that, against what you were raised to do, to have, to be."

She liked hearing John's name connected with love. He would always be in her heart.

"I loved William in my way. He loved me in his way. I was younger, pretty, he said, and would be a perfect wife."

She made a little sound. "Perfect," she repeated. "Neither of us knew I could not carry a child to term. But I tried to be what he wanted and needed. I don't think he ever knew how much having a child meant to me."

Caroline's eyelids closed for a moment.

Lydia touched her hand. "We don't have to talk about this."

"I want to, if you don't mind listening. We need to accept the facts of life and try to move on."

That sounded like good advice.

"But to answer your question of how I do it," Caroline said, "the hardest part of my life has been in losing my children. Others call it a miscarriage. But he, or she, was part of my body as much as any other part."

She gestured toward a woman pushing a baby carriage. "I see babies, and I see perfection. We may turn into something else, but we start out so wonderfully made."

Lydia breathed deeply. She and John had begun to see their baby that way. Had just begun. He said it was the most wonderful miracle.

"So you see, I blamed myself. William could give me a child, so he was all right. I have some defect, some problem within me. And how I handle it is to go directly to the ones who break my heart. The little ones. Instead of turning from them, I go to other people's children, and I love them as if they're my own."

"You're so wise and unselfish."

"Not so much," she said with a sadness in her tone. "I wanted to help Phoebe and Henry. But I also clung to them because of my need. In that little boat on that huge sea, I comforted them, which comforted me."

"That's not wrong, Caroline."

"No. I know that. But I'm not entirely unselfish. I discovered what I need to be fulfilled. And it's to care for children. And if relatives hadn't come for Phoebe and Henry, I would have tried to adopt them."

"I would love to have had a mother like you."

Caroline looked over at her. "So would I."

They were able to share a small laugh because they could be honest with each other, expose their hearts. Bess hadn't said a word, but Lydia noticed when she took a handkerchief from her pocket and wiped her eyes.

"You see," Caroline said, "out there on the sea, I suppose I expected to lose William. Even Phoebe and Henry. I'm accustomed to losing children."

She did not say it like one who was bitter at life, but bravely, like one who tried to face reality.

The idea seemed to ride on the breeze at first, just a hint of possibility, when the thought came. Anyone who cared that much about children who were not her own, would be the world's greatest mother. Better than she, herself, could ever be.

That's when it came as clear to Lydia as that blue sky overhead. She knew. She would claim to be in seclusion over the tragedy. She and Caroline would find a place somewhere away from prying eyes. Bess would be there to help.

She would give her friend something no one else could.

She would give her baby to Caroline.

# 40

Lydia knew she had made the right decision. Knowing also that she could be impulsive, she would wait for the right moment. Perhaps at dinner. No, after dinner. Caroline would be overcome with shock. The joyful kind. They could plan together how to work this out.

Caroline would give a child her undivided attention and raise him or her just right. And Lydia could be a part of the child's life. Perhaps, Aunt Lydia. There would be some kind of legal paper drawn up so that at the right time the child would be heir or heiress to the Beaumont fortune.

They'd have to do that secretly. Get an attorney from some obscure place. Craven must never know. Not for eighteen or so years, anyway.

At the same time she was facing reality, her heart felt heavy. She must ask herself what John would think. She was not married. He would not want her or his child labeled. He would want the best. Caroline was the best.

As they left the park, Caroline said, "Lydia, it's so good to see you smiling again. This was good for us. I'm glad you suggested it."

"Well, there's more," she teased. "Let's have dinner in my suite." She looked at Bess. "The three of us. I have something special planned." She had another thought. "It goes perfectly with champagne for the celebration."

Caroline looked skeptical. "You're going to make a dessert?"

Lydia scoffed, "Never. But you'll see."

They became like children. Even Bess managed a laugh. Lydia thought Bess would be in her element again as a nurse-maid or nanny. They would be . . . all right.

After arriving back at the hotel, the expected knock sounded on her door. "I trust you had an enjoyable day," Craven said.

Without him, he might have added.

"Very," she said, "facing reality."

"I'm glad. Would you like to have dinner with me and tell me all about it?"

"I have other plans." Indeed she did! And she didn't have to explain. "Thank you."

Observing his studied appraisal, she stepped back to close the door and held her breath, half expecting him to yank her into his room and demand to know where she had gone and what she had done.

However, he said, "I'm having dinner in the hotel dining room with several men." He turned, and she watched him walk purposefully, heading toward the elevator.

By dinnertime she, Caroline, and Bess had each changed into comfortable dresses and now sat at the table, where dinner was brought up. "And what did you two do for the rest of the afternoon?" Lydia asked.

Caroline was hesitant. "You may not want to hear this, but we read the newspapers again. The hearing is being reported. There's a big article about Craven in the afternoon paper."

Lydia started to say Caroline was right. She didn't want to hear it. But this was a new day. A new beginning. She would face things like a mature woman. "Yes, I'd like to hear it."

While they ate, Caroline talked about the articles. "Most men who survived are portrayed as villains, like Ismay. However, Craven is seen as a hero, complete with great acclaim from the mother who credits him with saving her daughter."

"Sounds like he almost walked on water."

Bess choked on that one, and Caroline patted her back. Soon they were finished, and Lydia's hand shook when she set her coffee cup on the saucer. "It's time."

Her voice sounded rather shaky. She needed to be calm for this. "All right, you two get settled in the living room. Bring out the glasses. Roll the champagne cart near, and I'll be right back with the surprise."

As she walked into the bedroom, she laughed, hearing Bess say to Caroline, "It's in the bathroom?"

No, she went to the bathroom because nerves made her do so. And she'd brush her teeth for the clean, clear announcement. I mean, how often does one say, "Guess what, you're going to be a mother?"

After coming out of the bathroom, Lydia glanced into the bedroom mirror at her smiling reflection. That proved she could. She would.

With that resolve, her gaze moved to the engagement ring lying on the dresser. She would not need to wear it. She picked up the ring and opened her black purse. The beaded evening bag was inside. That's where the ring belonged. She would save it and think about it someday, but not now. She unfastened the top and something caught her eye.

Something gleamed in the corner of the purse.

She reached in and brought out the carnival ring, grasped it in her hand, gave a cry, and held the ring to her heart.

She had kept that ring for months. It represented the fun times she and John had. The playfulness. He'd said it was an engagement ring until he could get her the real thing. They'd laughed like it was a joke. But he'd meant it. She'd wanted it.

She'd valued and kept a cheap, worthless little ring.

She couldn't bear to throw it away or to give it away.

But she would give away John's child.

What kind of person was she?

Was John's child worth less to her than a cheap carnival ring?

# 41

$\mathscr{L}$ydia's hand covered her mouth as she slumped to the bed and gave a muffled cry. Oh, she was going to throw up. She rushed to the bathroom and lost all her dinner. She heaved until her stomach hurt.

She didn't know what worried her most. That she might lose her baby like Caroline had lost hers. Or that she wouldn't.

"Lydia?" Caroline's arm came around Lydia's shoulders. Bess wet a washcloth and pressed it against her forehead.

Following much heaving and gagging, she nodded. "I'm okay."

They led her to the bed and she sat on the edge. Bess wiped her face with the cool cloth. "It's not going to work." No, the surprise was on her. "I . . . I . . . please go."

"I don't think we should leave you."

"Please."

"All right. We'll check on you later."

She nodded and stood to prove she could and walked behind them to the door. Seeing the champagne cart, she rolled it into the hallway. There would be no celebration.

She closed the door and locked it. Maybe she wouldn't go out that door ever again. For what? Where? Why?

She slumped into the nearest armchair. Her head throbbed.

What would she do now? Moaning, she leaned her head back and closed her eyes. She felt every rap on the door in her head. Caroline must have found him or called him. She would not let him in.

He came through the bedroom.

"Lydia?"

She would not answer. She would not look.

"Caroline said you're sick."

"Just a headache."

He opened the door and brought in the cart. She heard pouring. "Here, have a sip of champagne."

She waved it away. The champagne had been meant for a celebration.

"You need something. Water? Caroline said you lost your dinner."

What might have been a laugh was a heave. "I lost something?" Her mouth tasted rank. She squinted, saw the glass, and took a small sip. "Order coffee, please."

He did, and a sandwich.

"You think it was something you ate?"

She moaned. "That's what came up."

"You seemed to be doing so well."

"I was." She moaned again. "I am." A sigh. "I will." She wanted to be left alone.

Maybe instead of being frightened by the idea of sailing, she should get on a ship and disappear like John did. She felt as numb as if she were still on that cold ocean. But she couldn't destroy herself because then she would be destroying a part of John too.

"How is Father?"

"About the same. I wired him today that you were well and went out with friends. He was pleased, but he needs to hear from you. This is hard on him."

On *him*?

She moaned again. Suppose she did go to see him. And suppose her father died. She would need to stand in front of the board as the new owner.

Pregnant!

The wives would have great fun with that. All of London, in fact.

She lifted her hands, but they returned helplessly to her lap. "I don't know anything about running a business."

"I do," he said abruptly.

She shrugged.

"Lydia."

"I don't even have a home," she cried.

"I'm working on that."

The food came. As soon as the waiter left, she sighed. "All I do is eat and sleep and eat and try to sleep and eat."

"Don't throw it up, and you won't have to eat again tonight."

She didn't find the humor in that. But after a few bites of food and a few sips of coffee, the headache lessened and she began to feel human again.

"You've only been here two days."

That surprised her. "It seems like forever. I feel trapped. I don't know what to do."

"I do," he said.

She thought she'd heard that before. Yes, he did. But that wasn't her.

"And I know what you can do."

Go shopping again? She picked up her cup of hot coffee and brought it to her lips.

"Lydia."

Oh, she wanted him to go away. Everyone to go away. She wanted to go away. *What?* her exasperated breath said.

"We can get things set up for you the way they should be."

She took a sip and swallowed.

"Marry me."

That took a moment to absorb. She hadn't believed she could ever hear anything more shocking than she'd heard on that ship, from that deck, in that water, in those little boats. Amazing. But of course she had heard wrong. This was somehow mixed up with John and his proposal. All the worry and problems were causing her to lose her mind.

But this . . . person brought the desk chair over and sat in front of her. He said again, "Marry me."

No, that wasn't John. John had a tender voice, hopeful eyes, loving face, gentle touch, the look of one who needed her for his completion.

This one had the look of one who thought he was her hope, her answer, and the sound of his voice was somehow demanding. As though he was the answer to whatever beset her. But, most assuredly, she had misunderstood.

She'd better set her cup down before it ended up on the floor, broken. She did.

"Mar—?" Her voice failed.

She tried again, "How could you want to marry me? I just married John. When—three days ago?"

"I told you when I found out you were seeing him secretly that this was not the proper relationship for you. I warned you he wasn't right for you. I told him. Even up to the day he gave you that ring. You wouldn't listen."

"I love him."

The nodding of his head was not condescending, but more like agreement. "I know. Remember, I said he was different and that appealed to you. I understand you, Lydia. You're strong-willed. You're young and foolish."

The lift of her head seemed to change his attitude slightly. He shook his head and sighed. "That's not an insult. It's the way of things. I've been there. I've had my dalliances in my day. I found someone I thought was the woman for me, and that led to divorce. So I understand how everything can look like a fairy tale that leads to happily ever after."

Yes, she had thought that. It would have. With John.

"You and I. We could be like—" He shrugged then. "Caroline and William."

And what would that be? Caroline had seemed submissive to the more controlling and rather aloof William.

"I did catch the blue garter."

The garter that John took from her leg. She remembered his gentle touch. His tossing of the garter. And the applause when it struck Craven and he grabbed it. He'd been appalled.

Now he used it as a sign of what should happen.

She saw it as a sign of—

She needed to chew on that as well as on the sandwich.

Her thoughts went to why he would want to marry her. It would be to his personal advantage. Ensure his position. He could never face the fact that he was not the better man for her. It all had to do with position and pride.

And why might she marry him?

To keep her father alive. To keep the company from failing. To avoid scandal, although there might be talk initially. But that would end when someone else came along with a juicy topic whispered in drawing rooms and smoking rooms.

Marry him?

That could save her temporarily.

And when he knew she carried another man's child, what would happen?

Divorce.

But would he dare tell anyone he was not the father of his wife's baby?

Never in a million years.

And who really cared when she conceived? She would be a married woman when she gave birth to the child.

She and her child might be labeled by some. But not nearly the way they would if she were an unmarried mother, no matter how much money she had.

Marry him?

In the eyes of the world Craven was all and more than one should want. Handsome, wealthy, successful. She had sat there with vomit in her mouth and makeup washed off and her eyes swollen with tears. But he proposed.

That just proved it. He was very much in love—

—with the Beaumont Railroad Company.

She looked him in the eyes. "You say my marrying John was fantasy?" Her head moved from side to side. "I say this is insanity."

As if a string suddenly pulled him up, he stood, towering over her. His steel-gray eyes stared down at her as if to say so much for that. He'd been thoroughly rebuffed. The nostrils of his exquisite nose flared ever so slightly. He was miffed. One of the world's most eligible bachelors, even a *Titanic* hero now, had proposed and was told he was insane. Where were the reporters when you needed them?

Just as his face and foot appeared to favor the door, she said, "Craven."

He stood still but continued to stare at the door as if he, too, were wooden. Polished wood, mind you.

"A girl likes to think things over. Do you suppose it might be more fitting if you were to ask, rather than demand?"

Was that a flash of disbelief when his glance swept her way? Maybe he would learn she could use shock tactics as well as he.

She saw it then, because she'd learned to look for it. That little twitch right at the corner of his mouth. His nod was as slight as the breath that lifted his shoulders.

Without another word or glance he walked out the door.

She needed a sip of champagne for this. It felt rather celebratory on her tongue and in her throat.

# 42

The *Titanic* tragedy for Lydia was like the stroke of midnight for Cinderella who lost her glass slipper and her coach turned into a pumpkin. She had danced with her prince before that midnight hour. But her prince would not arrive on his white horse.

The following day, Lydia began her new life. He wasn't the same prince. But he was charming. And this one came with a black limousine.

Craven suggested they begin the proceeding to acquire a marriage license just in case a proposal was accepted. Wearing the dove-gray suit, shortly after complying with his suggestion, she rode with him to the station. Earlier, he'd informed Caroline that Lydia wouldn't be available and casually mentioned to Lydia that she might bring along her blue silk dress. "Or there are places where you might shop, if you prefer."

They boarded a Beaumont train, she with her bag holding the blue dress, a small makeup kit, and a few personal items. His was a much larger bag.

She was the only passenger in the private coach. Looking past the burgundy velvet curtain fastened with gold cord, she saw people for a moment, and then they were left behind. The train whizzed through the countryside.

She only had to sit and enjoy the ride. But unlike her fantasy of thinking something could last ever after, she knew there could be a wreck at any moment. In the meantime, the soot had been washed away, and she would not return to the fireplace with a scarf on her head and a broom in her hand. Do you know who you are, Lydia? Yes, a princess on the way to becoming queen.

The picturesque landscape of crops and green countryside and farmhouses changed. "The Gold Coast," Craven said, as mansions emerged.

She became interested in the picture of the history of America he painted as he talked about the King's Highway and the route George Washington had traveled more than a century ago in a horse-drawn carriage. "The president," Craven said, "had the intention of thanking the Long Island supporters for helping win the American Revolution."

"I know so little about American history," she said. "It's fascinating."

He nodded, looking pleased, and she was aware they had a civil conversation going on. "Those early founders started something that has grown to be recognized as the greatest nation in the world. The land of opportunity. And beauty."

Large estates and wonderful views came into sight. Some homes looked like castles, but they were not as stuffy as the big stone mansion where she'd lived with her father.

They were met at the station by a car and driven to a large estate. "Craven, I'm not up to visiting." This was the only objectionable thing so far.

"I'm aware of that, Lydia."

A servant took their bags inside. Craven gestured toward the perfectly groomed lawn, which stretched to a lake. "There are forty acres here. Trails that can be walked, stables, servants' quarters."

At her glance at him, he grimaced. "I know it's not half the size of your father's. And not as opulent as those you're accustomed to visiting. It has only thirty rooms, but I'd like you to see it."

He really didn't need to apologize for someone else's home. She could honestly say, "No, and it's not as large as that castle you pointed out."

"That was the Gould Castle, the design influenced by the Kilkenny Castle in Ireland. This one," he had a doubtful look, "is a Tudor Manor."

She recognized the style. "It's lovely."

"Shall we?" They walked to the entry.

A butler stood at the door and a maid inside the foyer. "Good to see you again, Mr. Dowd."

"And you, Conners."

Before Craven could introduce her, Conners said, "Welcome, Miss Beaumont." He turned his head toward the maid. "This is Regina. She can attend to your every need."

"Thank you." Lydia knew the servants wouldn't ask questions other than how they might be of service.

"I've visited here a few times," Craven said as they walked through the foyer, decorated quite nicely, airy, with fresh flowers in a tall urn beneath an oil painting near the staircase. "It belongs to the Grahams, parents of Hoyt Graham, a friend of mine, a board member."

She looked around. "Where are they?"

"In the Greek Isles for the summer." He led her through the living room, the music room, the spacious formal dining room, and an informal dining room that could serve as a romantic setting for two people just enjoying dinner and each other.

"I could live in this room," she said when they walked into the library, where books lined the walls. There was a comfortable-looking couch and chairs, particularly the big chair one might crawl into and feel protected. "What a place to sit and read all about American history. Or romance novels."

He was trying to please her. And she was as pleased as she could be, under the circumstances. They ascended the less than grand but nice staircase to the landing. Regina stood at a bedroom door. "This is your room, miss. Yours is the usual, Mr. Dowd."

She looked around at Craven, standing as if awaiting her assessment of the elegantly furnished room. "How long are we staying?"

The indentation appeared at his mouth. "You'll see."

He was very good at planning what to do and where to go, as she had discovered when he'd escorted her in London and Paris. He may not be *different* in the manner of some people, but she was getting the impression he might have in mind a honeymoon before the wedding proposal.

For now, however, she was along for the ride. And that's what they did after selecting riding clothes kept on hand for guests. They rode the trails through the woods, where a squirrel ran up a tree and birds chirped from treetops, and over the land, and by the lake. The fresh air, and the wind blowing her hair out of its restricting pins, felt liberating.

Rather than exhaustion she felt exhilaration and a mild sense of anticipation about what might follow his saying, "Time is flying. Perhaps we should dress for dinner."

When she descended the stairs in the blue dress, her hair pinned back except for the few impossible curls, he was waiting, dressed in a formal dark-blue suit that made his eyes look almost the same color instead of their natural gray. He extended his arm and led her into the dining room. The romantic one.

A lace tablecloth covered the round table, and a crystal chandelier glowed with just enough light for an intimate setting, enhanced with candlelight throughout the room. Music was piped in from somewhere. He seated her and then sat across from her.

The entrée George served on gold-trimmed china plates was fish topped with roasted almonds. Craven was very familiar with George. He was old enough to be her father, but obviously capable in his position. When she complimented the food, he credited his wife, Ethel, who was in the kitchen.

This was all so perfect. Was Craven trying to tell her what life would be like with him? She already knew what that would be. She'd heard the phrase, money can't buy happiness. No, but it could help keep one's mind off the unhappiness. Give the impression all is well. But you never know when out of the darkness . . . when . . . an iceberg . . .

With a shake of her head, she looked at her fork and saw it stranded halfway between the plate and her mouth. The music played on. The band had played on the ship.

She laid down her fork, touched the side of the plate, and George came. "Anything else, Miss Beaumont?"

"No. Thank you. It was delicious." She was glad she'd eaten most of it.

She didn't have to do this. Occasionally, she thought she might know who she was. Not only her father, but she too, had hundreds of people to do her bidding.

And Craven Dowd was one of them.

At that thought she lifted her chin, and her gaze, from the empty spot where her plate had been. Her eyes met his. As if he had received the thought, he lowered his eyelids to half-mast, glanced over at George, and made a gesture of pushing the plate aside. George came over for it.

Craven gazed at her again, seeming a tad uncomfortable as if he thought she might say no.

Might she?

## 43

*G*eorge poured champagne into flutes. Afraid to lift the glass lest it shatter, she thought of other flutes raised in celebration. An orchestra had played in a reception room. Hundreds had danced. She'd laughed and smiled and joked and kissed her husband, and she'd been young and gay.

Now she sat demurely, while elderly George poured champagne. She was no longer a girl, but a woman old enough for the man across from her. He was wise, intelligent, thoughtful, and knew how to treat a woman. He should, being thirty-five years old—a middle-aged man.

He nodded to George, who left the room. She knew Craven Dowd could woo her, placate her, indulge her, but no way under heaven would he kneel. Not even her father had enough money for that. She didn't want that. It would be a mockery. A mockery she would be unable to abide.

He took a small box, dark blue, from his pocket and opened the lid. Of course it wouldn't be a diamond. That would be too much like John's. The ring sat in light blue satin. Craven explained that the sapphire had half-moon-shaped diamonds around the jewel, as if she couldn't see that. It was set in platinum.

The ring was so beautiful it could be the envy of any woman. She remembered asking John how he knew her ring size. She almost scoffed now at her naiveté in questioning how Craven would know the size. Her ring size was on the records of many London, and at least one Paris jewelry store. Her father, or Craven, only needed to ask someone to find out the information, and it would be done.

Her throat felt scratchy, but she feared picking up the flute, so she cleared her throat. She didn't look to see if Craven took a sip, but she thought she heard him swallow.

"Lydia."

She heard herself swallow.

"Will you become my wife?" The voice was deep, resonant, serious, and perfectly modulated with the soft music in the dimly lit, romantic room. "Marry me?"

Her mind could not think of the words to say. I do? I don't? She looked at her naked finger but could not lift her hand. Her other hand was on her lap near her stomach. Not wanting to appear trembly, she let her hand slide over the fine lacy tablecloth and away from her.

His hands lifted hers, and the sapphire-diamond-platinum ring slipped so easily in place it seemed to give the impression it was the better ring. Should she say thank you? "It's . . . it's . . . breathtaking."

He gently squeezed her hand, and they both gazed at it as if wondering what it might do. He picked up his glass, so she did too. "To us," he said.

"Yes," she replied and touched the edge of his flute with hers.

They celebrated with a sip of champagne.

Then there was applause. Looking around, she saw George the waiter, Ethel the cook, Regina the maid, and Conners the butler. George held something. He came over with Craven's luggage.

Craven unfastened it and stood as he brought out a huge mass of white. She caught her breath when he took her hand, and she stood. He wrapped a long white fur coat around her shoulders. "Your engagement present." He motioned for George to take away the bag.

"I have nothing for you."

A minute shift of his eyes to hers—yes, his were a deep blue-gray tonight—sent a message of denial. She didn't know if it meant her, or the company, but he had refuted her statement.

"This is beautiful. Thank you." She moved her hands along the soft, luxurious fur.

"This will please your father. I know he would like a picture. Is that all right?"

She didn't have to glance at the doorway to know a photographer was there. He posed them against a blank wall with Craven's arm at the back of her waist. She knew what to do and held the fur close in front with her hand, exposing the ring. They smiled at the appropriate time.

Their engagement was not sealed with a kiss but a photograph. "I suppose this will be in the papers too?"

"As soon as the newspaper can print it but maybe not on the front page."

She nodded, knowing the reason. Headlines still jumped out from every newspaper about the tragedy. But the engagement would be reported, if only in the society columns. Somehow, that seemed important. It all had to be official.

"When do we leave?" she asked.

"Whenever you're ready."

Darkness shrouded the windows.

"When does the train leave?"

He looked surprised. "When you and I are aboard."

"Should we change?"

He shook his head. "No reason. And I like the feel of the fur." His hand moved along the side of the coat against her arm.

"I do too," she answered. "I truly love it."

Love.

She seemed to be taking up the habit of erratic breathing. But shouldn't "love" be mentioned at an engagement? She picked up the flute, lifted it, and said, "To the coat."

He laughed and joined in with the toast.

Later on the train, with darkness outside and no reason to have lighting inside, they sat with the fur between them, her arm on the inside, his on the outside. She made another statement that surprised him after he said they should have the ceremony as soon as possible.

One might think he was five weeks pregnant or something. "Why the rush?"

"I'm sorry I didn't explain," he said. "I thought you understood. The reason for this trip was to introduce the Ancell design to the American executives. I travel here several times a year, but my primary responsibilities are in Europe."

She shifted toward him. "I will not cross that ocean again."

"I know that. It's one of the reasons I took you to the Long Island house to discover if it suited you. They've offered us the house for the summer. That gives us time to make more permanent arrangements."

"When will you leave?"

"As soon as I know you'll be taken care of. The servants at the house will stay. You could begin making the acquaintance of the wives. Look at real estate. Have Caroline visit."

That was a good thought. Caroline would love such a pleasant place.

"I need to be in Europe. Your father's concern right now is his health. But of course, you could change your mind and go with me."

"No." That was out of the question. "So you will spend the majority of your time in Europe and I will live in America?"

Occasional light from somewhere outside silhouetted his fine profile. After a long moment he said, "That's the arrangement. For a while."

She relaxed against the plush seat. Of course. Her father, or she someday, could change his primary responsibilities and place of residence. No matter who might be let go.

When he took her back to the hotel suite and entered the living room and closed the door, she allowed his arms to go around her as he embraced the fur. When he lifted her chin with his finger, she remembered when the touch of his fingers on her lips made them feel as if they had been kissed.

But that was before John.

Now, John had left her.

Now, she lifted her face to her fiancé's handsome one. He had nice lips. They met hers, and she allowed their movement against hers.

He moved away. Looking deep into her eyes, he said, "I really want this, Lydia."

He said goodnight and left.

She stared at the door. He wanted . . . what?

While she readied for bed, she glanced at the adjoining door. As during the other nights, she had no need to lock it. He wouldn't come in. He would behave like a gentleman toward his intended.

And he had intended.

In the darkness she touched the ring.

She couldn't have the *ever after*.

And she cried about that.

But she could have the *now*.

And she cried about that.

This really was insane.

But it was also the only thing that made any sense.

He would give her everything he thought a woman should want. He would make her feel adored. She would be happy.

For a few weeks.

Until he returned from Europe and had a wife who had begun to show.

## 44

$\mathcal{C}$aroline screamed and meant to set her cup in the saucer on the bedside table. It leaned on the edge, causing some to slosh out before she righted it.

Bess quickly set her cup on the table, jumped up, and rushed over to her. "What?" She looked at the cup. "Did you burn yourself?"

"No." She looked to see if any had spilled on her clothes or the bed. It hadn't. "I've lost my mind. I'm reading and seeing something that isn't there."

Caroline shoved the paper over to Bess and tapped it.

Bess gasped. She read it aloud as if she could not believe it.

MISS LYDIA BEAUMONT, HEIRESS
TO THE RAILROAD FORTUNE, AND
MR. CRAVEN DOWD, PRESIDENT OF
THE COMPANY, ARE ENGAGED
TO BE MARRIED

Out of respect for those grieving over the tragic *Titanic* event, a private ceremony will be held.

An announcement of a marriage celebration
will be made at a more appropriate time.

"Let me see it again," Caroline said. She studied the picture
and squinted. "I can't quite make it out, but that looks like an
engagement ring on her finger."

Bess looked again. "But if it's true, didn't it have to happen
yesterday? How could it be in the paper so soon?"

"They do that, Bess. You know, we've seen some of the papers
that were printed before we were even on the *Carpathia*. Some
of the reporting was false, but it was still there. For events like
that, and this, they'd stop the presses to report it. And this is
the mid-morning paper."

Bess glanced at the clock. "It's almost noon, and she hasn't
called. You don't suppose—? Oh, shut my mouth!" She slapped
her hand over her mouth.

Caroline laughed. "It's true. Even in Southampton, I saw
the tension between the two men. I suspected something."

Bess nodded. "I suspected she was his prisoner."

"You can be funny, Bess." But Bess didn't laugh.

"Do you think she's on the rebound? I mean, isn't it a little
soon?"

Caroline thought for a moment. "Yes, but that's the kind
of marriage that would have happened if she hadn't met John.
And the *Titanic* tragedy can't be measured in days or hours or
minutes. It was another lifetime. We have to forget."

"I'd like to." Bess returned to her chair. "I'm glad she has
someone if that's what she really wants."

"Oh, I doubt it is right now." Caroline moved away from
pillows she'd propped herself against and swung her legs off
the side of the bed. "But she must wonder what else would be
in store for her. A love like hers and John's doesn't come along
every day."

"Maybe I shouldn't say this, but do you think a lot of it has to do with her being so *rich*?" She said "rich" as if it were a dirty word.

Caroline shrugged. "Who knows? But the likes of Craven Dowd could turn the head of any woman. I mean, a princess, a countess, a rich widow."

Bess seemed taken aback and Caroline laughed. "No, not me. In earlier days, perhaps. But I don't really care to be involved with a man again. If I were it would have to be for—"

"You can't mean for money. You have that," Bess teased. "You don't mean love?"

"I really don't know." Caroline realized the truth of that. "Oh, now, shut my mouth. Let's go find Lydia."

"Should we call first?"

"Nope." Caroline tapped the paper. "She surprised us. We'll surprise her."

They rode the elevator to the next floor, then traipsed purposefully down the hallway to Lydia's room. Caroline knocked hard on the door.

Lydia, dressed in her gray skirt and pink blouse, opened it. "Oh."

"May we come in?"

"I was just wondering if I should call you." She closed the door and clasped her hands behind her. "Have a seat."

They sat on the couch, and Lydia took the chair. Her hand was hidden beside her.

"Have you seen the morning paper?"

Lydia shook her head, a disturbed look coming into her eyes. Caroline began to think that she'd better not play around with this. "Your and Craven's picture is in the paper, Lydia. The engagement has been announced."

Lydia jumped up. "You think I'm awful. This is crazy."

Caroline stood. "No. I want to congratulate you."

Lydia looked doubtful but swallowed hard and held out her hand.

"Stunning," Caroline said. "Bess, come look."

Bess did and congratulated her.

"Now let me hug my friend." They embraced. Bess and Lydia looked at each other, not sure what to do, so Caroline gave Bess a little shove and the other two women hugged.

Lydia swiped at her tears.

"None of that. This is a wonderful occasion. What can we do?"

Lydia returned to her chair. "We're going to do this soon. I need to get a—" her voice squeaked, "wedding dress."

Caroline and Bess stared at each other. Neither could say they had one in a paper bag. Both returned to the couch. "Shall we go shopping?"

Lydia sniffed and nodded. "I can't wear another white one. I just couldn't."

"Maybe a fawn or cream," Caroline said. "Don't worry. We'll find the right one."

"There should be photos of that too. For the papers here and in London. For my father."

Caroline thought for a moment and had an idea. "The engagement photo looked wonderful. The weather is still cool. You could have the same coat but a different pose, perhaps coming out of the chapel."

"Perfect." She sighed. "Want to see my engagement present?"

Soon, the three of them took turns parading around like polar bears. And laughing.

Caroline thought there might be something else Lydia hadn't thought of. "If you want a witness or someone to stand up for you, I'm available."

"What did I ever do to deserve you?"

"Nothing," Caroline said. "And isn't that the beauty of it? When you're friends, you stand up for each other and stick by each other."

"I want to be a friend like that."

"Then you will be." Caroline smiled. "Now, when are we going to hear about how all this came about?" She gave her a sly look. "Every detail."

"I'll tell all. While we're shopping." She struck a pose and said saucily, "I must look perfect for Mr. Dowd."

"I don't think you'll have any problem with that." And she really didn't. Lydia was more fortunate than she knew.

Lydia told the story, and Caroline could visualize it all. Lydia invited her and Bess to come and stay while Craven was in Europe.

As tempting as the house on Long Island sounded, Caroline knew if she went she would only postpone getting on with her own life.

"Thank you, Lydia. But after we get you married and leave you in Mr. Dowd's capable hands, Bess and I are taking a trip of our own. Right, Bess?"

"Yes, ma'am," Bess said. Curiosity furrowed her brow as if to say she would accompany her, but she had no idea what Caroline was talking about.

## 45

*Y*ou're not thinking of returning to England?" Lydia said.

Caroline shuddered at the thought of going out to sea. "White Star has chartered a train to take any who wish to Nova Scotia. That's where identifying information of loved ones will be."

Lydia nodded, and Caroline knew then that the information about John had come from there. She quickly moved on, "Some, like I, have heard nothing. I'd like to go." She changed that. She wouldn't like it. "I need to go."

Lydia trembled. "You're much braver than I."

Caroline didn't feel brave. She might not have fathomed the reality of what had happened. Her mind knew it, of course. But she did not feel it. She'd shed no tears about losing William. She felt more the way she had when he went on a trip. Or when he hadn't felt the loss of a child the way she had and she smothered her feelings. But she'd excused that by telling herself he hadn't carried the baby in his body. Now a question occurred to her: Had she really carried William in her heart the way she should have?

Looking at Lydia she could almost cry, partly because she had not cried about William. But her emotions seemed to have lodged deep in her heart. They did not surface into tears that ran down her face as they did with Lydia. She wondered about Bess, but this wasn't the time to ask.

Lydia asked, "Will Bess go with you?"

"Yes, of course." Caroline glanced at Bess, again knowing how valuable this woman was to her. But who could say what one might do or not do? The roof could fall in at any moment. Or a person could be deeply in love and marry. A few days later she could marry someone else. Right? Wrong? Was there such a thing anymore?

She must concentrate on the subject at hand. "I'll let you know when we leave Nova Scotia and where we go."

Lydia nodded. "Do you know anyone there?"

"No."

"The Beaumont trains would be the ones taking you to Nova Scotia. Craven may know someone you could stay with."

"That would be nice." Caroline had thought Lydia might be too caught up in this wedding to remember that. Anyway, White Star would make some kind of arrangements or have someone available for advice. "But, we have to get you married before I go anyplace."

The rest of the day they made certain the bride looked lovely in her new fawn- colored silk gown with small seed pearls inlaid into the bodice. The upswept hairstyle that Bess knew how to arrange was fastened with jeweled combs. Across the top of her head Lydia wore a circlet of seed pearls interspersed with just enough diamonds to look unobtrusive yet fitting for a woman of her stature.

Caroline wondered if Craven would be able to keep that impassive look on his face and in his eyes when he viewed this vision of loveliness. Lydia seemed to have matured beyond the rather giddy girl she had been in that white gown. This was what Craven Dowd wanted. He was a very sharp-minded man.

This groom did not just dress in a tuxedo and show up for a wedding. He planned the ceremony, the place, the pastor, and the guests. Bess was invited. The clergyman's wife sat beside her. The photographer and reporter sat on the back row.

The lovely chapel that displayed a huge cross on one wall, stained-glass windows, and a discreet display of fresh flowers was a perfect place for such a wedding. Even in London she had heard the name of the prominent New York clergyman who would perform the ceremony.

Craven's friend, Hoyt Graham, had been introduced to her, and a brief review of the procedure was given by the clergyman's wife. The church organist played, and the pastor nodded at Caroline and Hoyt. They took their places at each side of the pastor. At another nod, Lydia, holding a white orchid corsage, and Craven rose from the front pew and stood before him.

The word "death" wasn't mentioned. *For the rest of our lives* was sufficient. He did not say kiss the bride, but when he pronounced them married, Craven touched his fingers to his lips and placed them gently on Lydia's.

Lydia didn't look into his eyes. They faced the photographer, who posed them. Grooms didn't have to smile. Brides did, and Lydia smiled modestly considering this was both a joyous and a solemn occasion.

The limousine was parked outside the church. The couple would go directly to Long Island. She and Bess and Lydia embraced again. Craven rather surprised Caroline when he stepped up to her and said, "Thank you."

Caroline wasn't sure what he thanked her for. Not objecting? That wouldn't have mattered. She gave him a brief hug and wished them well. She had been supportive in the marriage to John, and would be with this one to Craven, for her friend.

The last thing Lydia said, not as a bride anticipating a new life but as one rather dazed as if her world might fall in again, was, "You must come to see me."

Caroline took Lydia's hands in hers for a final moment. "The trains run both ways, you know."

✐

The following day around noon, after White Star provided transportation to the station, a Beaumont passenger train sped and rumbled along the rails until it stopped at the intended destination.

Caroline thought of it as a commencement. In London, her life was wrapped around William. She'd been a good, dutiful wife. If ever there was a time to find out who she was on her own, it was now.

As soon as she was a few feet from the train and her feet steady on Halifax ground, she stopped and turned to Bess. "Now we must find our luggage and ask about hotels."

"Mrs. Chadwick?"

She turned quickly, wondering who would say her name. She had a sinking feeling it might be a first-class passenger here for the same reason as she.

A man stepped up, removed his hat, and a flock of dark brown curls fell over his forehead. He attempted in vain to push them back. She was rather intrigued to notice the lighter reddish-gold highlights, which made her think of miniature halos.

He must spend time in the sun. His eyes, however, did not reflect the sun. They were wide, so dark brown she at first thought them black. She studied his face for any recognition but saw only the sympathetic expression in his eyes, and his full lips that turned up slightly at the corners, not in a smile, but perhaps in a grimace of sympathy.

For what seemed like an eternity she'd turned from suffering faces. Those of survivors, relatives, the population in general, and even her own reflection. Her defenses rose against it.

Although he wore proper clothing for a gentleman and his suit was quite nice, she thought he looked rather out of place in it, and she did not understand her thought at all. Glancing around, she saw the trainload of people and wondered how he had picked her out of the crowd.

"I don't believe I know you."

"No." Before he could say more, she asked, "How did you know me?"

"Mr. Craven Dowd described you, ma'am."

That gave her pause. Craven had not seen her in this outfit. What distinguishing characteristic did she bear that this stranger would recognize? She was a rather full-figured woman, with curves in all the right places and quite proud of it, but surely Craven hadn't said that. Or surely no man would mention such a thing.

Color came into the man's face, giving it a rather ruddy appearance. Perhaps Craven had said she had big ears. She felt inclined to touch them to make sure. But there wasn't much one could do about that.

"I'm Armand Bettencourt. Sorry to mention business at a time like this, but Mr. Dowd has transferred your information to my firm so that I might assist you in those matters. With your approval, of course. Also, I would like to offer my home, I mean my apartment, while you are here."

He seemed to stumble over the words "home" and "apartment." But if he had a record of William's finances, perhaps he thought that what was a home to him would be but an apartment to her. She wanted no more of that. "I could stay in a hotel."

"Yes, ma'am. But this would be more comfortable. At least, I find it so." He seemed a mite on the defensive. "And it's as close to everything as a hotel. It's located above my offices. I would be nearby to advise you."

She felt her eyebrows lift. Surely he wasn't saying he'd be in the apartment too. An apartment above offices didn't sound appealing.

His glance slid past Bess and around at others. "Mr. Dowd said you were traveling with your maid."

What a difference a cap could make. "My friend." She caught hold of Bess's arm. "Miss Bess Hotchkins."

"Please forgive me. I misunderstood—"

Bess interrupted, probably concerned with his embarrassment, "One can be a friend and a maid."

He nodded and gestured toward the only car in sight, into which someone was putting luggage looking very much like their tagged ones.

"Rooms at the hotels may already be taken." His glance indicated the throng of train passengers. "If the apartment isn't suitable, we might try and exchange. I should not have assumed—"

Bess interrupted. "Thank you, Mr. Bettencourt. We appreciate your generous offer." She began to walk forward. Mr. Bettencourt nodded and as if that maid had become his friend, they headed for the car and Caroline fell in step.

Since Craven had engaged a firm to handle her finances, she expected they were reputable. That was one thing.

But as for her personal life, she intended to begin taking care of herself. And now Bess was answering for her in the manner of a gracious lady. She'd developed a case of confidence all of a sudden. But Caroline could not allow a maid to make decisions for her.

And if she stayed in Mr. Bettencourt's apartment, where would that leave him?

Life, or existence, had become confusing, leaving her feeling adrift.

# 46

She'd tried to force herself not to think about John.

And now she had to think about him.

Everything about her was before and after John.

Before John, she'd been courted and wooed by Craven. He never tried to force his attentions on her. He had expected to marry her and did nothing to upset her or her father. She knew he was a passionate man. She had enjoyed his kisses, his caresses, and even the game of teasing him, knowing he would not philander with Cyril Beaumont's daughter.

She wasn't an experienced woman by any means. On their wedding night, she needed to convince an experienced man she was an innocent girl and knew nothing about moments of uncontrolled passion. She had to move from loving John to marrying Craven. And now they were at Long Island, on their honeymoon.

She became more distraught by the moment. Craven seemed the same as usual, knowing what to do. "You enjoyed the ride before. Shall we?"

"Yes."

Afterward she bathed, washed her hair and did not pin it back because he liked it curly, and dressed for dinner. They walked along the lake at dusk in the cool of the evening. She tried to think of this as being like old times. Except she did not tease. They did not kiss. He did not even hold her hand.

Later, he touched his fingers to his lips and then touched hers. He whispered, "You don't need to be concerned about anything. You can tell me to go away. Any time."

And so they kissed.

A lot.

Like . . . before . . .

Only . . . more.

For a long time.

And she forgot to pretend.

And then there was . . . after . . .

And not just because a preacher said so, she became Mrs. Craven Dowd.

He held her gently while she softly cried.

In the night he touched her curls, her cheek, her lips, her shoulder, and pulled the coverlet up and tucked it in, in case she was cold. When she opened her eyes in the morning, she met his gaze and felt as if he'd watched her all night long.

He looked pleased.

After a moment, he reached over and pulled the cord by the bedpost. That meant breakfast would soon be brought to them.

And so it went for three days.

But he had to go. Business would wait no longer. She asked if he were afraid to sail, and he said he had already had the scare of his life and he could handle it.

She had George and Ethel and Regina and Conners to take care of her, so she did as Craven said: Rest and enjoy the secluded estate on Long Island.

She was a married woman now, the honeymoon had been all a woman could want, and just when she thought she could endure this new beginning, she knew her marriage had ended.

She needed to think seriously about what she would do when Craven found out she was carrying John's child. He would return after a few weeks. She would be showing then.

He would hate her. And divorce her.

Nastily or quietly, she didn't know.

She remembered that ridiculous remark Craven had made, saying indirectly he had saved her and the company during that terrible tragedy. She had scoffed. But now, although he didn't know it yet, he had saved her and the company by marrying her.

Could she, as she had considered doing with John's baby, turn her back on him? What kind of friends would he have after this became known? What would his influence be in the world, with the board, with any company? Wouldn't she be exposing him to the scandal and ridicule he had saved her from?

She didn't know what to do.

A sound of irony escaped her throat. Every time she'd said to Craven, *I don't know what to do*, he had replied, *I do*.

They'd both said *I do* at the marriage ceremony.

But she wasn't *doing* very well. Never had, in fact.

She sat on one of the benches in the garden, sipping tea and telling herself she only needed to consider what *she* would do. Craven would decide what *he* would do.

He wired that he would stay a week longer in Europe than planned because of business matters. That meant he would be able to stay in America longer after his return. Now she had about two more weeks before her world caved in again. But this time it was better for her baby, for her reputation.

She had done all this, married John, married Craven, for the baby.

Now she must see a doctor, for the baby.

## 47

In the few days she had been in Nova Scotia, Caroline had developed a better opinion of Armand Bettencourt and a lesser one of herself. She wasn't sure what a cozy little home should be, but this so-called apartment gave her a much better impression than her initial concept of something over first-floor law offices. Any stuffy old hotel, or even an elegant new one, could not match the comfort and privacy of this dwelling. And it had its own inside or outside entry.

Nicely furnished, the decor was still definitely masculine, especially with that swordfish hanging over the fireplace. The colors were dark too, like the coloring of its owner, who gave her the impression of an outdoorsman instead of a man behind a desk, which was where he seemed to be whenever she and Bess decided to take a stroll or have a bite to eat in that little café.

Having just finished a cup of tea that Bess said they must have before leaving, she crossed the living room, which had been renovated from two bedrooms. Standing at the long row of windows with heavy burgundy drapes fastened at the sides, she looked down at the tree-lined street.

She preferred not to think about the chore ahead, and instead let her thoughts return to the day she'd been, if not rude, condescending to the kindly Armand Bettencourt.

When they'd left the train station that day, she and Bess rode in the back seat of the car. Mr. Bettencourt rode in front with the driver he introduced as Willard Oak, who seemed to think the road was curved instead of straight.

But his looking into the rearview mirror or turning his head could account for his erratic driving. Mr. Bettencourt kept his face forward, and since this was the only car on the road, he must be watching out for horse and carriage traffic. And the car did travel more slowly than a horse.

Willard Oak's mouth was anything but slow. Within a matter of minutes she knew almost nothing about Armand Bettencourt but a lot about Willard Oak. He was a fisherman by trade, didn't normally drive for people, the main reason being that Armand's was one of the few cars in Halifax. He was good at building and fixing things even if he did say so himself. In fact, he'd helped with Armand's apartment.

Armand?

His driver called him by his first name? She glanced at Armand, but he didn't react to anything. In her circles a driver wore a uniform, was basically ignored, and didn't start conversations. She had been informal much of the time with her servants, but at her instigation.

She found Willard rather entertaining. And if she was going to be an ordinary person, she might be getting her first lesson. She half expected he'd invite her to go fishing.

Looking over, she saw that Bess had an amused look on her face and seemed to be enjoying Willard's loquaciousness immensely.

"Just to let you know, Mrs. Chadwick." At least he didn't use her first name. She thought Armand hadn't told it to him.

"Anywhere you want to go, I'll take you. Any time Armand lets me use his car, that is. He said we could."

"Thank you, Willard."

"Yes, ma'am. We all want to do what we can."

She was accustomed to helping others with their needs. The tables had turned. This seemed strange, being on the receiving end of things.

Quite soon, the car stopped in front of a big, two-story brick building. Willard took one bag and Mr. Bettencourt the other, which indicated to her they assumed she would stay. She and Bess followed them inside, where a middle-aged woman, Mrs. Jessup, sat behind a desk and assured them she was there to help in any way.

Caroline and Bess followed the men up the staircase, and Willard set down the bag he carried and reminded them he was available. Armand or Mrs. Jessup knew how to reach him.

She said, "Thank you," and Bess said, "Thank you, Willard. You have been most helpful."

He smiled and sprinted down the steps.

Caroline looked at Bess, wondering what in the world had come over her. There was nothing wrong with her speaking to Willard, but she usually remained quiet as if in what she called "her place." Perhaps she considered herself and Willard in the same place.

On the landing was a table against the wall, where a vase of flowers sat beneath a painting she'd seen as a child in church. Little children gathered around the shepherd and one sat on his knee. She looked away quickly as Mr. Bettencourt pointed out the rooms on the left.

"There are guests in the rooms temporarily," he said and she quickened at the word "temporarily," knowing that meant they were here for the same reason as she, and it was not for independence.

"But this is the apartment where you can have privacy." He unlocked the door, opened it, stood aside, and invited them in. That's when she saw the spacious, inviting living room, which included a large table along one wall and a bookshelf along another as well as furniture on a large burgundy-patterned wool rug. She and Bess could even sleep on the couches facing each other. If she didn't look at the swordfish.

He took them across the room to a door. Outside was a small porch with a solid banister and steps leading down to the ground. "Another entrance," he said. "More private than going through the office lobby. If you stay, feel free to use either."

"And back here should be Lola," he said with a trace of a smile on his otherwise somber face. A wife? This would never do. She wanted to make new friends but wasn't quite ready to live with them.

As they entered the kitchen, she detected the scent of something chocolate and breathed more deeply of it, thinking she would prefer it on her tongue. A small table with two chairs sat to one side beneath a window that was next to the porch. At a window opposite them stood a gray-haired woman who turned from the kitchen sink and dried her hands on a towel. She wore a skirt the color of her hair and a white blouse, covered by a black apron.

"Lola Logan." She gave a smile in a pleasant face. "I'm the sometimes housekeeper and try to keep this place clean, but you know how men are." Then she said, "Sorry," and Caroline thought she probably knew she no longer had her man.

"I'm not a cook," Lola Logan said, "but I'm fixing a few things you might like."

Mr. Bettencourt introduced her and Bess, then said to Lola in a warning tone, "I'll be back." He proceeded to show them the bedrooms, which were joined by a bathroom.

These bedrooms didn't have the feminine touch either but appeared so inviting she would like to stretch out across one of the beds. She suddenly felt fatigued. But she had a little apology to make.

"Mr. Bettencourt. This is more than adequate. Much more inviting than a hotel room. Since we'll be staying in your home and working together, perhaps we should be on a first-name basis. I'm Caroline and she's Bess."

His smile replaced the concern on his face, and if she'd known that would happen she might have said her first name sooner.

"Armand," he said. "Please know I'm at your service. Many of us don't know what to do at a time like this." He gave her keys to the inside and outside entry.

"You're doing fine, Armand," she said in her sweetest tone.

His dark eyes seemed to grow a tad larger beneath those rather heavy eyebrows. He turned and walked back into the kitchen.

"Oh, no, you don't. Not without one of these brownies I slaved over all day." Lola held out the plate. He took a bite. "Good as yours?"

"Much better," he said.

"Ladies?" Lola said.

Caroline reached for one, so Bess did too.

"Delicious," she exclaimed, and Bess said, "Mmmm."

"I'll put your bags in the bedrooms," Armand said. She noticed a tiny chocolate crumb at the corner of his mouth and then wondered what in the world her brownie hand was doing in the air like that. She quickly stuck a bite into her mouth.

Armand left, and Lola said she'd be back in a couple days to see if anything needed to be cleaned, and she left.

Caroline looked at Bess. "I guess we're on our own?"

"Looks that way. Nice little apartment."

Caroline reached for another brownie. Looking into the cabinets and refrigerator, she saw an ample supply of basic food, but wouldn't know what to do with it. Bess would.

"You know," she mused, "Sometimes you can just be refreshed by other people's goodness."

"I was thinking that," Bess said, examining the knobs on the electric stove. "He would take time off from a job that probably doesn't pay much, just to drive us a few blocks from the station."

Caroline stared at her back. Friend or maid, she might just keep Bess around for the element of surprise.

For a couple of days they enjoyed the privacy of the cozy rooms, became familiar with the people in Armand's firm, and strolled around the area. One day Armand took them to a small restaurant and another time to Patriot's Point and gave them a little history lesson.

They were doing just fine, until the third day. The phone rang, and they both stared at it. Finally, Bess picked up the receiver.

"Hello, Miss Hotchkins speaking." She turned from Caroline. "Yes." A few seconds later she nodded as if the caller could see her. "I understand. We'll be there." She didn't say thank you. She must not have liked what the caller had to say.

Caroline braced herself.

Bess replaced the receiver and swallowed before saying, "Armand can take us to the—" she paused and moistened her lips. "To the Mayflower Curling Rink whenever we are ready."

Caroline's hands rose up and rubbed each other. She nodded. Bess said they should have a cup of tea first, turned, and hurried toward the kitchen, but not before Caroline saw the color drain from her face.

Closing her eyes for a moment, Caroline reprimanded herself for being insensitive. Whatever happened to the woman who tried to think of others? Anyone would be affected by that tragedy. But she'd been thinking of her own losses and did not think of Bess having lost anyone.

She went into the kitchen, where Bess was pouring the tea. They both sat at the table. Bess had said the curling rink, and they knew this was the morgue.

She realized that Bess had lost someone too. She'd been in the employ of William Chadwick for five years. People became attached, despite class differences. "You don't have to go," Caroline said.

She didn't know if Bess's reply was because she had lost William too, or because she was was Caroline's maid, or because she was her friend. Perhaps all. But she knew Bess meant it when she blinked her eyes and said resolutely, "Yes, I do have to go."

# 48

rmand had met Craven Dowd several years ago. The
Beaumont Railroad Company and the Bettencourt Shipping
Lines had business dealings, and Armand's father had hosted
a dinner for executives at his country estate. Armand joined
them for dinner and on his dad's yacht, but wasn't in on business discussions. He was acquainted with Dowd and found
him to be a congenial, interesting person.

His dad called Dowd the youngest but brightest executive
he'd ever come across. Said he was a no-nonsense kind of fellow, but fair. Armand hadn't thought much about him one
way or another, still being in law school at the time, and still
having Ami in his life.

Having seen the article about Dowd being a *Titanic* hero,
Armand called and asked how he and others in his area could
help. Armand was reminded of his father saying Craven Dowd
never forgot a thing when Dowd asked if he were pleased with
how his law practice had developed.

Armand got the impression Dowd already knew, maybe
because he had investigated whether he could ever use him if
a need arose in Halifax. They rang off on good terms. A few

days later Dowd called and asked if Armand would handle Mrs. Chadwick's finances while she was in Halifax.

"Can you tell me a little about her so I have an idea what to expect?"

He should have known Dowd wouldn't say anything as simple as someone being a brown-eyed brunette, short, tall, or middle-aged. He could visualize her as he described her.

"She's not the kind you'd notice in a crowd," he said. "But she grows on you. So don't expect her to stand out." He said she had a habit, when she was frustrated. Instead of raising her voice she gestured with her right hand as if making it speak for her.

"When you get to know her, you'll notice her eyes are a mystery, bluish, brownish, and when she's extremely happy there's a green cast to them."

Armand couldn't hold back his laughter on that. Dowd, joking?

He said, "She's pretty," in an offhand manner as if she wasn't extremely so. "But the main thing is she looks soft."

"Soft?"

"Yes. She has a soft way about her that makes you comfortable. Her voice is soft, which might be the reason she talks with her hand."

"Her age?"

"Mid-twenties."

He dared not ask any more and wondered how in the world that was supposed to help him recognize Mrs. Chadwick. Maybe Dowd's brilliant brain was too much for Armand's small one.

When passengers alighted from the train, everybody had a distinguishing look about them like short, tall, brunette, outlandish hat, no hat, and whoa!

Everything Dowd had said stood right there, wearing a dark gray suit with the edge of the skirt flirting with her ankles, and a pert little gray hat on her head, with her light brown hair rolled beneath it. She stood perfectly still, talking to another woman. He could not hear her voice but as her mouth moved, she gestured with her graceful right hand.

That meant she was frustrated.

He couldn't see her eyes but sincerely doubted there was a speck of green in them. And she looked soft.

He learned quickly that soft didn't mean acquiescent. She was trying very hard.

She and Bess had been in his apartment several days now, and he related well with them. Today was different.

He'd called and told Bess that Caroline might come and identify her husband.

As much as he had dreaded this day, he wanted—needed —to be of assistance. Telling someone you know how they feel is a caring thing to do, and perhaps you do know, but it doesn't take away the pain. So he didn't say it. He just kept driving the McKay Roadster until they arrived at the curling rink.

He supposed the news articles and reports about the terrible tragedy would never stop. They even reported how victims were identified, and some descriptions could make one ill. Hundreds and hundreds and hundreds of bodies floating on the ocean, while just one body, or two, could make you lose your reason for living. They became numbers and items in little bags. Rosary beads identified a person. Shoes, clothing labels, lapel pins, fountain pens, waiter's uniforms. On and on it went.

He accompanied the women into the room, where William Chadwick's identification was presented to Caroline. The cuff links had been a gift from her, and she named the store where they were purchased. The number on the key was the number of their stateroom. Yes, he had a scar on his right forearm that he'd received as a child, after a fall.

Yes, she needed to see him.

Armand remained outside while Caroline and Bess entered the back room. They returned looking like walking statues. They weren't speaking. They weren't touching. He understood that too. Sometimes you know that if you're touched, you'll break.

She still looked soft, and you wished you could hold her and take away the suffering. The two women looked brave, and when they stepped outside the building each took a deep breath as though the fresh air would make a difference. But he knew about tears being frozen inside, unable to fall, and a heart that could turn to stone.

What could one say? Caroline looked toward the sky. "It's a lovely day. I'll walk back."

"May I walk with you?"

"Do you want Bess to drive your—"

"Blimey!" Bess squealed. "The only way I'll drive a contraption like that is if you hook a horse up to it."

They actually laughed. All three of them.

As if they dared not look back at the curling rink, they ducked into a small café for coffee.

Armand watched Caroline remove her gloves as if they were soiled, although he didn't think she would have touched anything back there. But it had touched her, whether or not she let it show. She lowered her hands to her lap and ordered coffee with cream.

After a long moment she said, "They said I need to make arrangements." Her hand came up. "I hadn't thought of that."

He knew this had to be discussed and that the financial part of the arrangements would involve him. "Some are having their loved ones returned to their home. Others are being buried here. A place has been set aside for the *Titanic* victims, and later on there will be a memorial service."

"I suppose that's what I should do." She glanced at Bess, who nodded and said, "Since you don't want to return to London, it might be best to bury him here."

"Are there," Caroline began tentatively, "a lot to be buried here?"

"Yes. Plans for three cemeteries are already being made."

"So many," she mused.

"Yes, not only here, but in New York and Southampton." He stopped speaking. He should not say more than necessary.

The waitress came with the coffee. Caroline stirred in cream. "I thought seeing him would make it seem real." She gestured. "It didn't. I know it, but I didn't see only William just now. I could still see those hundreds on the ocean. All those who were not saved."

"What is worse," he said, "is if their souls were not saved."

She gasped. Her hand moved to the small, round gray buttons at the front of her jacket.

"I'm sorry. I didn't say that well."

She and Bess stared at the cups.

Armand could kick himself. Caroline had been through an unthinkable ordeal and had just identified her husband as a victim. Now he had made her think about the possibility of her husband being in a worse place than the morgue.

But another thought came. No, he should shoot himself if he made no mention of one's soul. And he knew, how well he knew, that in times of death one thinks more deeply about eternal matters. The number of church attendees had doubled since that tragedy. Special services were held, and not just on Sunday. When people realize they are not in ultimate control of their own lives, they seek someone who is.

After they had sipped their coffee in silence for a while, Armand thinking it best he not speak, Caroline said, "I've almost finished what I came here for. Now I need to start thinking about what to do, where to go."

Craven Dowd had been right in saying she grows on you. Sort of like an unexpected little lavender violet in a decayed bed of yesterday's flowers.

He picked up his cup and looked over the rim at her speckled eyes. He had an idea. He'd like to do it, but wasn't sure he could.

But he had a very strong feeling the time was now or never.

# 49

She was in a quandary again. No way could Mrs. Lydia Beaumont Dowd walk out that door alone and see a doctor. She couldn't ride the grounds without a groom or another servant keeping a respectable distance. If she said she needed to see a doctor for some other condition, Craven would be there the moment he returned home, wanting details. To let her go off alone, these servants would have to answer not only to Craven but also to the owners of this house. She liked them and they liked her, but they would not engage in some little game the way they might if she'd been a young girl going out with several friends, as she'd done with John.

She didn't know the area. Didn't know the doctors. And she couldn't just pop in somewhere and wait to be examined and told what she already knew.

And, too, it could be dangerous. She wasn't as well known in America, but her picture had been in all the papers twice already. She could be kidnapped.

Thinking it over, Lydia thought her only chance of any kind of obscurity in seeking medical attention would be to take a train to another city or state and use an assumed name.

But that wouldn't work. She knew about security measures, which could be taken so that you didn't see your protector.

She couldn't contact any of the wives because she was supposed to be in seclusion recovering from her ordeal. Craven Dowd and she would announce when they'd appear in public or at a private party.

She considered contacting the New York clergyman's wife and asking about a doctor. But she might consider it her Christian duty to contact Mr. Dowd because Mrs. Dowd had lost her mind since she could even have a house call from any doctor of her choosing.

She was in a lovely prison. By the time she thought of going to Nova Scotia, confiding in Caroline, and getting her help, the time had come for Craven to return.

By the time Conners picked Craven up and brought him to the house that afternoon, Lydia felt literally sick and later lost the dinner Ethel had prepared.

Since Craven had eaten the same as she, they couldn't attribute it to the food. "You're so pale," Craven said, concerned. As if a replay of a former time, except that the faces and the setting were different, she sat herself on the bed. Regina patted her face with a cold cloth. As if he were a doctor, Craven questioned, "Have you been having problems?"

She shrugged and replied as if her answer might be inconsequential. "I'm late."

"You mean?"

She nodded. "It happened once before when I had the flu. Maybe I've caught something."

"She has seemed a little pale." Ethel said. "If it's something she's eating, I'll never forgive myself."

Regina straightened. "I saw her holding her stomach a little as if it might be bothering her."

She'd held her stomach to try to push it in, is what. She could honestly say, "I have felt a little—," she needed the right word. There it was. "Queasy lately."

"Ike!"

They all looked at Ethel who put her hand over her mouth. Amazing what one little squeal of "ike" could convey. The silence was palpable. Lydia reached for another cloth and held it on her forehead, partly covering her eyes lest she meet anyone's gaze. She peeked through her lashes.

Ethel stood squeezing the front of her apron. Regina held the washcloth as if her hands had become bread for a sandwich. The possibility lit the room as if the sun had entered. But Lydia knew about storms that could obscure the sun. This one would likely have a lot of hail in it too.

Craven commanded, "Get her in bed and take care of her." He paid no mind to the late hour. "I'll call the doctor."

He called Hoyt Graham and mentioned a few symptoms. They rang off, and Craven stood by the phone as if willing it to ring. It did. He lifted the receiver. "Craven Dowd here. Yes, thank you, Doctor." Pause. He gave the symptoms. Throwing up. Nausea. Discomfort in stomach. Another pause, and she guessed what the question was. He turned to Lydia. "How late are you?"

She thought for a couple seconds. She could be honest about that. "Since you've been gone."

Into the phone, Craven said, "Almost a month." His eyebrows rose slightly as if listening to an interesting discourse. After a few more answers about her having more color now, looking better, feeling better, he thanked the doctor and said he'd call if there were any further developments. Yes, that would be satisfactory.

Craven hung up. He explained what the doctor had said. "This could be a case of land sickness, common for some people after being at sea. The symptoms and the treatment are the same as for seasickness. But he wants to see us first thing in the morning."

He didn't want her to be walking around and chance falling or being sick again. "Get a good night's sleep." He would not disturb her and would sleep in another room. The trip had been tiring, and he might be restless besides. Regina and Ethel would watch over her during the night and awaken him at the slightest concern.

She tried to assure them she was better, and said they should go to their rooms. Craven made no comment when they looked his way for any further directive. He gave none. They would take turns watching her. He touched her lips with his fingers before retiring, and she said, "Thank you."

"You're entirely welcome."

At least she would make the acquaintance of a doctor who could give her baby the best available treatment.

Exhausted from the throwing up and aware she became tired more quickly than she used to, she welcomed the bed and slept or dozed all night. Each time her eyes peeked open, she saw either Ethel or Regina in the rocking chair dozing. A couple of times she felt a large, strong hand gently touch her forehead.

Early the next morning she was pleased to meet the kind, courteous, dignified doctor. However, after being led into the little examination room, she could not imagine he had instructed the nurse to behave in such a manner. Some of Lydia's friends in London had talked about the humiliation of the examination, but she was appalled.

How dare he!

But she was helpless, and had to put her feet in stirrups as if going to ride a horse, but that wasn't at all the intention. Even with her reluctance, she was pried and prodded and coaxed.

When she was given no choice by the relentless twosome, she finally yielded and allowed the examination to begin. As he worked, the venerable doctor talked in a blasé tone about his grandchild learning to ride a bicycle.

The silly nurse pretended this was an everyday occurrence as he asked for an instrument and she handed it to him as casually as one might pass the time of day.

She did not scream much, and when he said, we'll just see what we have here, she could have said he already had. They left the room fully dressed while she lay draped in a stiff white sheet, her insides having been totally exposed as surely as if her brain had been examined and every thought revealed. After she dressed, the doctor returned, once again pretending to be a gentleman.

He smiled as if he'd discovered something that made him extremely happy and said that perhaps he should speak of his findings with her and Mr. Dowd together.

She thought not.

With renewed resolve, she decided that nothing she might say to him could be worse than what he did to her.

She smiled like a lady. "I want to hear it first."

"You appear quite healthy. Your symptoms are not unusual when this occurs," he said. "Mrs. Dowd, you are pregnant." He smiled but she felt it might be a tad forced. "I believe your and Mr. Dowd's picture was in the papers recently."

"Yes."

"Congratulations on your marriage." He pulled up a chair and sat at the small writing table, and then looked at his chart. He glanced at her. "Do you have any thoughts on when you might have conceived?"

The good doctor was most astute, and she began to feel considerably better. "Mr. Dowd and I were married a month ago. I might have conceived on my wedding night."

She knew that he knew she knew he knew better.

He also knew who she was, and when their gazes locked she was not the one to look away.

He nodded. After all, when one sees trains go by several times a day with the name Beaumont on them, one takes notice of a person bearing that name. She was heiress to a fortune, and married to Craven Dowd, who had friends who ran in the same circles as he. And he was among the most prominent of obstetricians. He would be thinking that unless he wanted to be boarded onto a coal car on a train of inferior quality with a destination unknown, her word would not be disputed.

He deserved this after what he had done to her.

"I'll just make a note on the chart," he said as if he were getting ready to go off and ride a bicycle. He summoned her and Craven into his office and gave his report.

He began with her health, which by all indications was excellent. Bouts of nausea were common with this condition. And when he saw that Craven understood, he said, "Congratulations, Mr. Dowd. You're going to be a father."

Craven's lips parted as if he might be forming a question, something like, *when can we expect this event?* but anybody knew it took nine months to form a baby and they'd been married about a month and had only spent three days together before he left for Europe.

No words, but the tip of his tongue moistened his lips, and then they closed. If he thought back to the other wedding, he knew she and John were in full view of others, she in a wedding gown, and they had not had time to consummate their marriage.

The doctor, being adept at seeing inside a person, and observing that she and Craven did not jump up, embrace, and shout at the happy news of their becoming parents, gave an answer to an unasked question. "At this early stage I'm reluctant to predict an exact date of delivery." He continued with advice about vitamins, the instructions that would be given them, and when he would like to see her again.

*Over my dead body* was her first thought.

But that's exactly the place she thought they were heading in that suffocating little room.

The doctor did not look into her eyes again. Craven thanked him, shook his hand, and when she glanced back over her shoulder the doctor sat with pursed lips and furrowed brow, staring at his desk. He might be wondering how to keep that baby inside her for an additional month. He might even be able to manage that, considering his expertise.

When they walked to the car, Conners's face expressed concern and curiosity, but he wouldn't ask. Neither she nor Craven said anything on the way back. Each stared out their respective window. She knew he'd think it through before saying or doing anything. And then he'd act. And it would be done.

When they arrived home, he suggested they walk in the gardens while it was still light.

At least the servants wouldn't hear. "Let me freshen up a bit." Later, she would try to wash away that doctor's grandson's entire bicycle episode.

He was waiting out back when she walked out in her skirt and blouse, having removed the jacket.

They walked a while through the flowers and the shrubs that bordered the path, and the aroma was sweet. The sun shining through the branches and leaves of the trees on this warm summer day made diamonds on the path. That would change when the sun set and darkness came, bringing shadows.

"Let's sit," he said. They settled on a bench amid the flowers and with a view of the lake. She sat stiffly upright. He turned toward her.

His face was a mask. "I don't think I've ever been at such a loss for words."

She remembered that John had said he didn't know what to say and so he had written her a poem. Craven wasn't the poetic type. Then he said what she never expected to hear.

"I'm sorry." He apologized. "I thought I was careful enough. We didn't plan this." He scoffed, "That is not what I should say at a time like this. But . . . we didn't plan this." Just as quickly, his mood changed. Lifting his chin and looking toward the horizon, he spoke as if remembering what might have become his motto, "We can handle this."

We?

No, not she. For the moment and for seven more months she was at the mercy of men. Always her father. Now Craven. And the doctor.

His head turned, and he again focused on her. He emitted a low groan. "I don't mean to be insensitive." He took her hands in his. "This calls for champagne. We must celebrate. Give out cigars."

She felt he might be repeating what he'd heard somewhere. "Maybe you'd better wait until after the birth to give out cigars."

"Yes, yes, I think that's the way it's done. I can at least smoke one, can't I?"

"Could I stop you?"

"With a word," he said. "I only puff on them because it once seemed the thing to do. Now, I have you."

"Oh? I'm as valuable to you as a cigar?"

"Well, almost. And maybe when there's an addition, I won't need them at all. Seriously, though." His demeanor changed from the attempt at playfulness. She knew he was trying not to sound insensitive. "You're pleased?"

She would be as honest as she could. "Yes. And no. Like you said, we didn't plan this."

He laughed lightly. "That makes me feel a little better. I'm just surprised. Didn't expect this. Well." He laughed. "I guess we are expecting."

His brain, never far away, began to click in. He'd considered building a house, but she would need something permanent sooner than construction could be completed.

That sounded like the perfect answer to one problem. She would be settled in her own home when he discovered he must divorce her. She and her baby would stay, and Craven would be the one to leave.

For now, he moved on to more current matters. They would plan their reception and announce the good news. He wanted her safe and secure, to have made the acquaintance of his friends, and to be free of worry before he returned to Europe.

He said quickly, "Am I being a good father?"

She opened her mouth. No, she mustn't say "the best."

She was a mother, good or not.

Feigning a playful mood, she managed her best coy expression. "Adequate."

He grinned.

At dinner, Craven announced the news to the servants. They exhibited exuberant delight. The lighted candles danced merrily as dinner was served and champagne poured, and they made a toast in celebration.

Later that night the subject turned to other matters. After all, he'd been gone for weeks. Although she feared he might think she looked rather like a small whale, he didn't really seem to give a lot of thought to her stomach.

## 50

"And what if I don't?" Caroline said with a saucy turn of her head as if she was not only stubborn but had an inborn wild streak.

*And what if I do?*

Forming the right answer was not an easy thing to do when Armand's feelings were taking off like a runaway horse. But his emotional carriage had smashed into a tree before, and he'd tried to pick up the pieces and identify something from the wreckage. Then Armand decided nothing was salvageable, so he let it lie, went about handling his work in an organized way, and spent his evenings in solace on the lake with the fish and his nights in distressing, and pleasant, memories.

Let things be. The Lord had given him peace, acceptance. The wounds had healed, but scars remained, and he didn't need to chance the hurt again.

The blame lay with her for being such a kind, helpful person, so caring about the plight of others. She wanted to help, and when she saw the statistics she put her hand to her mouth and closed her eyes. He didn't know if he'd know what to do with a crying woman. She didn't cry. She said she'd help.

She jumped right into the midst of the suffering and pain. They began to work in the office together as he helped her spend her money to meet the needs of others.

She was so involved in the work, she didn't ask how his plans were going with the idea of a rental place for her and Bess. Now the needs of victims needed to be met, the burials made, the memorials observed.

Sometimes Bess joined them and assisted Mrs. Jessup, who was teaching her a few secretarial skills.

One day in the midst of a difficult project, Caroline said they should stop for a spot of tea. He agreed and stood. "Café?"

As they strolled to the nearby café, she asked, "Where do you sleep nights?"

He laughed lightly. "I have a few rooms above my office." He missed his house, but he had an experiment under way in his mind.

"You can't rent them?"

"I could."

He felt her eyes on him. "You'd rather just," she gestured with her hand, "donate them to needy people?"

That was easy to answer. He reached for the door of the café. "Yes."

After they were seated and had ordered sweets and tea, hers with a little cream, she again mentioned her gratitude for his allowing them to stay in his apartment and that she knew it must be difficult for him to be confined to his office and a hotel bedroom.

"Not at all," he said.

The waitress brought the teas and sweets. She dawdled with the tea while it cooled and bit into the sweet, as did he. He was not surprised when she announced, "I will pay rent on the apartment until I find time to look at whatever places you find." She jested, "Or until you decide to evict us."

*Not a chance*, he might have said but swallowed it with his sweet and followed it with a drink of tea.

"But I will want to look at anything you find."

"Certainly."

She lifted the cup with her graceful hand. "I want to pay back rent."

"Good," he said. "And I'll donate it to the victims' families."

She gazed at him over the rim of her cup, and there seemed to be a little gleam of pleasure in her blue-speckled eyes, perhaps reflecting the color of her blouse.

The following morning, just as the sun rose and shone through the windows, she descended the stairs, walked across the lobby, and entered  his office. She came right up to the desk, braced both hands on the edge, and leaned toward him.

"Guess what?"

He couldn't begin to do that.

"I'm giving you the morning off." He contemplated that. Yes, he worked for her. His handling of her finances and what she did with them was a business matter. Perhaps she had an errand. "I've planned an outing."

"Bess will be going with you?"

"Bess is straightening up the apartment before Lola comes to clean. Said she wouldn't dare let anyone see the clutter. And then she's going to the market. She does all the cooking." She waved a hand. "I don't cook."

The thought of whether or not Bess were going along didn't seem to disturb him.

Then he realized she didn't say she was taking the morning off, but rather that she was giving him the morning off. He leaned back, away from the faint scent—akin to a fragrance forgotten, now remembered.

"You know I'm determined to be an ordinary, independent person."

"You've made that clear." He wondered what else she considered ordinary other than donating a fortune to the less fortunate and speaking about where she might be of help when this need ended.

"Since we have the morning off, I thought you might teach me to drive."

That brought him out of his chair. "The car?"

"That black contraption that goes honk-honk instead of neigh."

He didn't bother to say that this did not fit into the definition of ordinary. There were maybe six cars in the entire city, most driven by men. The rest of the population drove horses.

About that time the thirty-one-year-old man inside him, whom he'd forgotten about, paid a visit. He said, without thinking, what Bess had said quite effectively, "Blimey! Let's go."

*Why not?*

The question lent itself to positive and negative answers.

Because this was the first time he'd seen her hair fastened back from her pretty face and falling in soft waves around her shoulders, and he knew it wasn't light brown but sun caressed and turned to . . . he didn't think a lot about colors but had heard the phrase "burnished gold." It seemed to fit.

*Why not?*

Because when she was behind the wheel, paying little attention to brakes, he was scared out of his wits, not only by seeing the danger of a horse and carriage ahead, but because the attorney in him, who'd taken a short nap, had now awakened and returned with his common sense.

While the man and the attorney argued and debated, he thought of a garden. The flower bed of his heart began to show new growth. Daisies pushed up and let their yellow petals sway in the wind. Sunflowers appeared and some could grow to be ten feet tall.

*She grew on him.*

But if a garden wasn't tended, wasn't watered, weeds took over and would choke out the potential blooms. Then you could walk by and tell yourself you're not a gardener anyway, you're an attorney. And she is a recent widow who has gone through one of the most devastating experiences a person could have. Perhaps that's why he thought of such possibilities, because they were impossible. The thoughts must flee.

So the attorney said about her driving, "Why not? Why not drive faster? Because you're not in the country. You can get six months in jail if you go over ten miles an hour here. In some towns it's eight and others six. You have to obey the law."

She scrunched her face. "How fast in the country?"

"Fifteen."

Her eyes grew big. "What about there?"

She turned down Young Street, headed toward Patriot's Point at the end. He said no again. "Cars are prohibited in there. Don't!" He grabbed her hand just as she was about to honk the horn. "That could scare the horse, wreck the carriage, kill the people. Now get back over on the left side of the road."

Her hand was flying all over the place. "You can be bossy."

He took a deep breath. "We should stop. Let me give you some instructions."

"I can drive while you instruct."

She could kill them both. She slowed and moved up and down the roads. Fortunately, there was little traffic. "These machines aren't called devil-wagons for no reason." He tried to keep his voice calm. "They don't have horse sense. If you see anyone walking or standing in the streets, sound the horn while you approach. But not at a horse."

Fearful she might drive into the offices instead of around them to the carriage drive, he told her to park at the curb. Upon entering the lobby, she turned her excited eyes and flushed face to him. Before she could say whatever was on her mind, Mrs. Jessup called to her.

"Caroline. You have a telegram."

She looked concerned, so he stayed nearby. "My friend, Lydia." She looked at him. "Oh, you know Craven. They married shortly after the . . . incident. They've moved into a house in Manhattan and—"

Her voice trembled. "They're going to have a baby." Her expression looked pained. "That's so wonderful. She's getting on with her life." She turned from him quickly. "I must write to her right away."

He would contact Craven Dowd with his own congratulations, since Craven had asked him to handle the financial affairs of Caroline Chadwick. He would let him know he continued to be of service to her as needed. He almost laughed. Minus any information about the driving lesson.

Armand watched Caroline ascend the stairs with her hand to her face. Perhaps she thought she wasn't getting on with her life.

The following day he took her and Bess to see his plan.

The women seemed to enjoy the short train ride, particularly when they neared Bedford, and they praised the beautiful scenery. Many times he'd walked the several miles from the station to his home simply because he enjoyed it, and he would sing and praise the Lord and feel the peace and be thankful for his blessings.

Today, he rented a carriage and provided them with a view of the lake, stands of trees, and the rolling green landscape.

Upon seeing the house, Caroline said, "It reminds me of Lydia's description of the Long Island place."

They alighted at the front of the house. Caroline walked up the steps and onto the porch. She placed her hand on the banister and turned to him.

"This is the place you found to rent?"

She shook her head as if to say it wouldn't do, but she hadn't even seen the inside yet. He glanced at Bess, who looked as puzzled as he felt.

"It's one of the most peaceful-looking and beautiful places I've ever seen." But she reprimanded him, "I told you I wanted to live like an ordinary person."

"This belongs to an ordinary person."

Her eyes questioned. She looked at Bess, whose eyebrows rose.

They both stared at him. He felt color rise in his face, then took a set of keys from his pocket and held them up. Caroline said, "You don't mean . . . you?"

He must have looked guilty, so he gave a little nod. She said what she should not have ever, ever said, in a saucy tone, "Armand Bettencourt. There is nothing ordinary about you. I think you are quite extraordinary."

## 51

Caroline adored it. Every room, every nook, every cranny. It was peaceful, serene, and cozy, yet elegant and had everything one could desire. She could hardly fathom this being his home.

It occurred to her that if Armand were an ordinary person, Craven Dowd would probably never have heard of him. Who was this man? He led them into a kitchen that was a cook's dream and motioned for them to sit at the small table positioned beneath the window.

Bess looked as stunned as Caroline felt. They sat. He proceeded to pour water into a percolator.

"You rent this out?" She watched him reach into a cabinet and bring out a bag of coffee and then dip some out into a little metal holder.

"This is the first time." He put all the pieces into the pot, set it on the electric stove burner, and turned a knob. Was that ordinary? She didn't know how to make coffee. She only knew how to drink it.

He leaned against the island. "This is my main residence. The apartment is for convenience and bad weather." He lifted a shoulder. "Or whim."

Whim? Who was this man?

"My parents owned the home that is now my law office. They built this house several years ago." He brushed back the curls that had fallen over his forehead, and his dark eyes surveyed the kitchen. "Both were passed down to me when they were killed. And—"

His face clouded. The coffee made noises, and the liquid danced around in a little glass bulb on top. He took three cups and saucers from a cabinet and set them on a countertop near the stove. He opened the refrigerator and declared there was no cream. "Sorry. Sugar?"

She and Bess said "Yes, please." Even as the pot continued to perk, he poured the coffee. She wondered what he'd been about to say after *and*. He brought their coffee to the table and returned to the island. There were two chairs at the table. Who were they for?

He could have brought in one of the dining room chairs, but he seemed uncomfortable, as if he might run rather than sit. He began to talk about the lake house and mentioned his boat, which he liked to take out on the water to fish.

"You take fish out on the water?"

He laughed. "No. The fish are in the water. I catch them. Trick them into eating a worm and they're snagged."

"You caught the swordfish?"

"Yes." He grinned. "But not in that lake." He set his cup down. "Well, ladies, shall we take a look at the backyard?"

They went outside, and the first thing she noticed was a patch of weeds and vines that appeared to have taken over a perfect spot for a flower garden. But her gaze moved beyond it to the green lawn and the serene landscape.

She would love a home like this but couldn't allow it. "Armand, you've given up your apartment. Now you offer your home. There's no way I can accept."

Bess walked over to the weeds. Armand glanced at her and back at Caroline. "Tell me, Caroline. Why do you help the families of the *Titanic* victims? Why did you help those children you talked about? You mentioned an orphanage in London where you volunteered. Why?"

Her hand gestured. "You know why I help. They need someone."

"Exactly," he said.

She glanced at Bess, who pulled a weed and began tying the stem in knots, as if she were not listening. "So you'll do this because . . . because . . . " She scoffed, "Armand. I am not needy."

His slow, "I am," was almost imperceptible. His eyelids covered his brown eyes as his shoe scuffed at the ground. The silence grew. Neither had anything more to say.

He moved to the back door and held it open. Bess tossed away her knotted weed.

On the return trip she hardly knew what anyone talked about, including herself. Her thoughts were pressing. She helped the needy for two reasons. They needed her. She needed to be needed.

She understood the need to be needed.

But why would he need to do this?

Why and how did he need *her*?

His office was closed when they returned. He unlocked the door and went inside. At the top of the stairs, before he turned toward the rooms on the left, she said, "Armand."

He stopped, but his focus was on the floor. "I will rent the house on one condition."

His deep, sad eyes said he would suffer through whatever she had to say. "And that is?"

"I will let you become homeless only if the speed limit in that country place is at least fifteen miles per hour."

She didn't know the tune he was humming as he turned and walked to a room, but it sounded happy.

✿

"I can't go to that house with you," Bess said as soon as she closed the door of the apartment.

Caroline almost fell onto the couch. "What do you mean? Of course you can. I can't go alone."

Bess appeared to be in as much pain as Armand had before she said they would rent the house. He needed her? She needed Bess. "Can't we be friends, Bess?"

"You're not thinking straight, Caroline." She dropped to the edge of the opposite couch. "I need a job so I can support myself. Goodness knows, I'm not crossing that ocean again. And if I can't be your maid, I'll have to find employment." She sat at attention. "That's the truth of it."

Nobody was making any sense tonight. "Bess, you buy the groceries. Cook the meals."

Bess scoffed, "I have to eat. Now, we can be friends if that's what you want. But I can't let you pay me for that. I have to find real employment, not just take your money."

This was quite awkward. "Bess. I want to learn to take care of myself. Not have to depend on a maid, or anyone else."

"Begging your pardon, Caroline Chadwick." She became huffy. "We all depend on each other. But I don't take charity if I can help it."

Caroline had to admit she was not ready for independence. She could maybe cook coffee after having watched what Armand did. Bess remained quiet while Caroline thought. Then an idea dawned.

"Miss Hotchkins," she said in a formal tone, and Bess raised her brows.

289

"You've been in my employ for a number of years, but I no longer need a maid."

Bess folded her hands on her lap and lowered her gaze to them.

"However, I'm thinking of moving into a house where I need to employ a cook and housekeeper."

Shoulders often spoke volumes. "And someone who can weed flower beds." Bess now had her lower lip almost inside her mouth. "Do you know anyone who might be interested in that position?"

"Yes, Mrs. Chadwick, ma'am, I do." That woman could change moods like one turning a radio dial from a terrible report to sweet music. She had apparently acquired another dose of confidence, and looked Caroline straight in the eyes. "And when you decide you no longer want her in your employ and you can take care of yourself, just tell her so."

Caroline suspected that might take a while, perhaps the rest of her life. Bess said the hour was late and bid her good night. When Bess disappeared from the room, Caroline realized she'd never asked her why she hadn't married. Was it because she had to make a living?

She was rather surprised at her next thought. Armand Bettencourt was young, early thirties at the most. He was quite appealing in many ways. And why did a dark sadness sometimes creep into his eyes?

More than that, she needed to know why he said he was needy. How could she, who couldn't even take care of herself, be the kind of person Armand Bettencourt could depend on when he was the one helping her with her finances and a place to live?

Again she wondered, because she needed to be needed, why would he need . . . her?

## 52

*C*aroline felt content at the country home. Bess had no need to learn secretarial skills now. She stayed home to take care of the house and gardens.

Home. The thought felt nice.

A couple of days a week Caroline and Armand took the rented carriage to the station. She held the reins a few times, and Armand laughed. "Safer than in the McKay."

She punched his arm. He was quite muscular. He should be, spending as much time working on that lake house as he did in his office.

"And when do we get the car over here?"

"No, no. You said if the speed limit was fifteen, which it is. I made no car promise."

"But you smiled like it was the greatest idea ever." She squinted at him. "Like you're doing now."

He laughed. "Looks can be deceiving."

She didn't always care for obviously true statements, not when they made her think of herself. She was content, but always present was that threatening dark spot inside.

They took the Beaumont train into Halifax and talked as
friends, which they surely were, although the situation seemed
rather odd. He was in her employ, and yet she was dependent
on him for the rental house. If she were ever going to find
out what he needed from her, perhaps being a little personal
might be a good start.

The opportunity came the day the first burials took place.
William's was one of them. Armand went with her and Bess, as
did people from the surrounding area. They dressed in black.
She wore a new hat with a veil that shielded her eyes. She felt
Armand's eyes on her as if he thought she'd cry. She didn't.
Neither did Bess. But that little dark spot acted up, and for a
while she felt she was slipping into depression the same way
the *Titanic* had slipped into the ocean.

Armand must think her heartless. She would speak of
William. "We had a good marriage," she said one morning on
the train.

His head turned quickly toward her. "Good?" She saw the
reflection of his face when it turned toward the window. His
eyes were sad.

Maybe Armand was wondering what a good marriage was.
He hadn't opened up about his personal life, and she wouldn't
pry.

One day had been particularly depressing, understand-
ably so due to all the morbid things they were dealing with.
Friends and relatives came to the office, having been told they
could receive financial help throughout the city, including the
Bettencourt offices. There was talk of *Titanic* items being found
in the ocean or swept onto shore, including a deck chair. She
wondered who might have sat in it.

As if sensing her distress, Armand suggested they go for
a ride. He drove. She was startled when the car stopped. A
beagle came loping down the road, his legs bending like a

prancing show horse's. But his shrill yelping sounded painful. He stopped beside the car, whining.

Strips of hair were missing from his body and at one place across his head. "We must help him."

Armand said, "I'm sure you must."

She opened the door. The dog cowered, uncertain of her intentions. "Come, doggie. I'll help you."

He whined, stepped back, and yelped. All of a sudden, he jumped into the car.

"Bravo!" He licked her hand and settled on her feet while Armand gave her a wide-eyed look and then started the car.

Bess looked pleased when they brought the dog home in a big canvas bag with his raw feet bandaged. After a few days, Caroline realized how he soothed them just by needing them.

Several days later, Caroline sat on the porch in a rocking chair. As the beagle lazed near her, she saw a figure appear out of the fog from the direction of the lake house.

Bravo opened his big brown eyes and lifted his head. He whined, and Caroline laughed softly as the morning air filled with singing, as if all were well. She'd sung in church but never in the robust way he did.

He never came to his home, now hers temporarily, without a good reason or without being invited to supper by Bess, who usually took food down to him.

Bravo ambled off to meet him as Armand approached, singing "Down at the cross where my Savior died." She thought he might have chosen a better subject with which to greet her this fine morning.

But seeing the newspaper he held, she felt a warning rumble inside her. Maybe the song was meant to prepare her for something. She could tell him she was prepared. Nothing was certain.

He reached down and patted Bravo on the healthy side of his head. The beagle lowered his head as if he were in ecstasy and returned to his blanket beside Caroline's chair. Armand looked happy. "Thought you'd want to see the paper Willard brought this morning."

He leaned near, holding out the paper. He smelled like sawdust and paint and ordinary work. She liked that.

Her eyes devoured the picture. Dear Lydia and Craven, such a handsome couple, prominent in the picture, with others in the background. They stood smiling, looking like they belonged together. Caroline studied the full-length photo. Lydia's dress was lovely, but her jewels were more conservative than she would have expected.

She understood when she read the article. The focus was on their courage, which would make a display of wealth inappropriate.

After a period of seclusion, they met with a few friends to celebrate their marriage and the beginning a family, hoping their moving on with their lives would be an encouragement to others.

"Thank you for this." Caroline looked at Armand, sitting in the rocker on the other side of Bravo. "They're moving on with their lives. That's good." She meant that. She was glad for them. Her words should not have sounded forced.

He stood. "I'd better get back. I have to take advantage of the few hours Willard can give me."

Get on with your life? Why?

As he stepped out onto the lawn, she stood and moved to the banister. "Incidentally," she called, having no idea why, "are you taking me to your church in the morning?"

His brown eyes held the sun. "At fifteen miles per hour." Shortly afterward she heard *When Jesus shows his smi-i-li-ing face, there is sunshine in my soul.*

Well, at least that was a happier-sounding one. The fog had lifted. Her gaze moved to the sky, where the sun promised a shiny day.

He really did drive up to the house on Sunday morning in a car he must have rented at that place near the train station.

He introduced her and Bess to people who already knew about them and were friendly but not imposing. After seating them, he exited the sanctuary through a door near the stage.

He returned with the choir, which wore white robes with black lapels. Of course he'd be in the choir. He had a wonderful voice. He hadn't said anything. There were a lot of things neither of them had said.

The songs were nice, and she sang softly, "Sweet hour of prayer that calls me from a world of care." Bess did better, and Caroline wondered if and where her friend had ever attended church. Certainly not in the great cathedrals as she had. The choir sat, and she thought she was prepared for the preacher.

But Armand swung aside the half-door and walked out. The organ played. His voice filled the sanctuary.

*Our Father who art in heaven*

And she was back in the little boat.

Caroline's eyes moved toward Bess. They glanced at each other and quickly away. Caroline knew she was remembering that song being sung on the sea. A prayer.

Don't touch me, Caroline willed. Bess didn't but instead clasped her own hands on her lap.

*Give us this day our daily bread.*

They'd been hungry.

*For thine is the kingdom and the power and the glory forever.*

The A . . . *men* seemed to be strung out forever and she didn't know if she could stand it, but the people were saying amen and clapping. He sang extraordinarily well.

He returned to his seat as if he'd done nothing special and focused on the preaching. The pastor's topic was prayer. He reminded them to continue keeping the *Titanic* survivors in their prayers. All knew the Marstons, members of their congregation who had lost their lives. Shouldn't she feel peace and comfort instead of the rumble?

"And pray for the dog that Armand and his friends saved and are caring for." People chuckled at that. This was church? She looked at the mischievous expression on Armand's face. The remark took the tension from the focus on the tragedy. Armand would have known that. The pastor knew that. You can't keep talking about tragedy, thinking about it, without some kind of relief. Bravo! For the dog.

They had saved the dog.

Bess said Caroline had saved her life. Who had saved Caroline?

Out there, she'd seen hundreds and hundreds and hundreds calling on God and Jesus to save them. He didn't.

Out there, she knew she was going to live.

She didn't know why.

She was afraid of the *power* . . .

But she would like to meet the one who had saved her.

And ask why.

# 53

*C*aroline asked Armand about all that talk of being saved. She said she wasn't ignorant of God and Jesus and religion, but hadn't heard it as simply and plainly as the pastor had spoken it. "It sounds perfect, but if you have Jesus, whatever that means, why aren't people's lives happier, why—"

He interrupted. "Because," he said, "it doesn't make you less human. Just more divine."

"Divine?"

He was unwavering. "Yes. The Holy Spirit comes to dwell in you. You can cry and hurt and question, but it's like he puts his arm around your shoulder and says he'll get you through, and someday, maybe not in this world, you'll understand. No matter what, the soul is saved."

She shuddered, remembering he'd talked about the souls out there on the ocean. Had they been lost forever?

She'd been . . . saved.

But she was also twenty-six years old and felt . . . still adrift?

Yet, she began to go through the motions that these ordinary church people of varying means did. She attended Bible studies, and held them in her temporary home. She was supposed to serve the Lord. She was serving people. Surely that counted.

Weeks passed, and her life was full. She and Bess got into the habit of going to the lake house often, taking a lunch for Armand and Willard and watching the building's transformation into a quaint little cottage with two bedrooms and all the modern conveniences, and construction of the attached structure for boats.

Willard, being a fisherman by trade, although one would never know it considering the amount of time he was at the lake house, said they should learn to fish. Bess took to it right away and had no problem with putting a worm on a hook.

Caroline shrieked, but once she hooked a worm, after the lecture about that's what God made them for because fish had to eat and people had to eat fish, she had no problem. When she actually caught a fish, she screamed and carried on so much that Bravo whined and nudged the bucket as if to get rid of what had caused the tumult.

The next suggestion wasn't as well received. In fact it caused inner thunderclouds to act up. "You need to go out in the boat," Armand said.

"I did it," Bess said. "With Willard. We didn't go far."

She didn't even want to look at the boat. Armand had her touch it while he described it. He called it his sailing dory, made of Eastern white pine. The lines were simple, it had a flat bottom, and it was about twenty-three feet long. She liked the high sides, but that really made no difference. Boats could sink from the bottom. One just needed something to hold onto occasionally.

Fortunately, the next days were foggy. Then it rained. When a sunny day appeared, it was time. The four of them got into the boat and moved out onto the water. The clear sky matched the smoothness of the lake. She could see land all around. She could swim to land. But she wasn't really afraid the boat would leak, or capsize, or that she'd drown.

She straightened her shoulders, removed her hand from Armand's, and breathed in the scent of fish and water and cool air and sunshine. On shore again, she stood before Armand and grabbed his hands and thanked him. "That was a good thing," she said.

"I know it's not easy for you, Caroline. But you're doing remarkably well."

She was doing. That was something. "I'm getting attached to this place, the people, the church. But I should think about something more permanent. I can't stay in your house forever."

"Sure you can." His face colored as if he hadn't intended to say that. "To tell you the truth, I didn't know if I could bear having anyone live in the house. But that was something I needed. And I did it. Just like you got into the boat." He paced in a semi-circle, then returned. "While we're doing so well, what do you think of our going to some fancy restaurant for dinner? Some evening."

He must have seen her shock. "The four of us," he added quickly. "We're friends—of course."

Questions formed in her mind, but all that came from her mouth was, "Armand?" She looked into his face for a long time. His lips parted as if he needed to take in more air. His hair had tumbled over his forehead, so without really think-ing, she reached up and brushed it aside, which was fine for a friend to do, and realized their life vests were touching and she'd said his name and needed to follow it with something.

"Armand," she said again and smiled like a lady-friend would, trying to figure out what to say. Then she knew. "That's a delightful thought. But others might misinterpret. Even if it's the four of us."

He looked like he'd made the world's worst blunder. "You're right, of course. And it hasn't been that long." He was nodding.

Lest he think she didn't want to go with him, she tried to think of some way to dispel that idea. "Why don't I cook dinner for you? We'll eat at the house."

He rubbed his chin. "I thought you didn't cook."

"Bess has been teaching me."

"I accept." He looked intrigued. "Will it be the two, or four of us?"

"Four. Three." She shrugged. "I don't know. Does it matter?"

He grinned. "I was wondering if there's something I could get. If so, for how many?"

"Oh." She spread her hand. "I don't think so." Of course she didn't think so because she had no idea what she would cook.

"I can cook it for you," Bess offered when Caroline told her about her plans.

"I want to do it myself."

Bess's eyebrows did their thing. "Chicken. Baked chicken would be perfect."

"That's special?"

"In an ordinary way."

"Should I make those yeast rolls like you make?"

"Never! I mean, that takes too long," Bess said. "I know what. I have to go to the store anyway. If you don't mind, I'll pick up the groceries and you just get yourself ready."

She could do that. Wash her hair and pin it back in a roll. Maybe a little curl falling along the side of her face. No, not that. He might think she was trying to look like him. Searching the closet, she thought of all the clothes and jewels still in London and all of those lost on the ship.

But the ones she had bought in New York were sufficient. She wouldn't wear the suits she'd worn to church. Not the everyday skirts and blouses. Either the blue or green or, yes, the lavender. A sweet little silk dress with a darker sash and a mix of the two colors at the bodice. Too revealing? Well, no. Skin is skin, no matter where it's located.

The silver chain with a small diamond and matching earrings would do.

There. Not overdone or underdone at all.

When Bess returned, she asked her opinion. "Just right." The twinkle in her eye caused Caroline to believe it. "But you're not going to cook in it, are you?"

"Oh, well, no, of course not. Just making sure everything looks right."

She changed into cooking clothes and went down to see what Bess had bought. Cooking the dinner didn't seem too difficult. Just wash the chicken, put it in a pan, rub a little butter on it, stick it in the oven, turn on the heat, and take it out when it's done.

Anybody could make salad. Just cut up the ingredients Bess had bought. The rolls came from the bakery, already cooked. As Bess said, no need to make it look like she was going to a lot of trouble.

"Sure you don't need me?" Bess asked, and when she said no, Bess said she would be down at the lake house. She was going to try out the electric stove down there and make sure all was well. "You know there's a phone down there now."

Caroline nodded. "I have the number." Sometimes Bess behaved like she thought Caroline was a complete idiot. She did think, as the day wore on, she might use the dining room since the kitchen was heating up.

After she had made her preparations, gone upstairs, re-dressed, come down, and set the table, she heard the knock at the front door. So far, so good.

She opened the door and was aware that he looked very much the distinguished gentleman in his suit and white shirt and tie; perhaps his outfit was a tad more formal than the suits he wore to work. Since he had been working down at the lake house, he looked more rugged and sun-bronzed. She knew he was quite good looking but tried not to think of it much.

His mouth moved, but it said what she had: nothing. There was no reason to say you're handsome tonight, that would mean he usually wasn't, and if he said you're beautiful in that dress as William might have they'd both be complimenting the clothes, which both knew didn't make the person. But it sure could make you regard the person more closely, which you really shouldn't.

And he did seem to be regarding her rather closely. But she had reminded him she was a recent widow, so what was a man to do? She said, "Come on into the kitchen," and he did.

"Ah," he said, when they arrived, and he held out a bag. "For you. Us. Wine. With or after dinner." She took it and set it on the countertop near the sink.

Although she'd considered the dining room, she thought it safer to eat in the kitchen because she was serving and she really should have let Bess do this. Women didn't go around serving dinner while wearing silk dresses more suitable for dancing. Oh dear, no music. Not that she planned to dance.

Maybe she'd overdone it.

At least she didn't pull his chair out for him. He did it him-self. She already had the rolls and butter and bread plates on the table along with the glasses of water. She'd already perked the coffee, as he had that other day.

She took the salad, already in two bowls, to the table. There. Now, would he prefer the chicken with the salad or after? After. She'd make this a two-course meal. Three really. Bess had bought a cake. The candle. Where were the matches? My, he was quiet tonight. "Do you know where the matches are?"

"They used to be in the pantry."

"Oh, well." She gestured toward the window. "It's still day-light. We don't really need a candle."

"You're right," he said, and she sat. He asked if he might just thank the Lord for the food, and she said that would be nice, so he did. Then they smiled at each other and picked up their forks.

"So you got the stove put in," she said.

That started a good conversation about stoves, and there was much about stoves she hadn't been aware of. "I'm glad to have it," he said. "I love to catch a fish, come home, and cook it fresh. I enjoy cooking." He cleared his throat and added, "Too. The salad is good." He nodded and messed up his hair. "Very good."

It should be. Took her over an hour to cook it. Fix it.

"I made coffee too. Would you like it now or with the chicken?"

"With the chicken will be fine." He took a bite of a but-tered roll. Ate it all. And the salad. She had some left as her appetite wasn't the greatest at the moment. She'd just taken their salad bowls away and felt like taking a deep breath, but the air seemed different. She saw it then. Black smoke curling out of the top of the oven door.

By the time she screamed and jumped straight up, he was there, shutting the door, saying it was all right, just leave it in the oven. He turned it off, led her to the chair, and said these things happen all the time. He should have gotten a new stove for the house. That one was a few years old. They didn't need chicken anyway.

"The salad and rolls were perfect. Plenty." He got the wine. "Let's just laugh about the chicken and enjoy a glass of wine." He went into the pantry and returned with a corkscrew. Good. He kept talking, as if he knew he'd better. "I had Willard pick this up. Told him to get the best wine available."

He took glasses from the cabinet. He began to pour, then stopped and raised the bottle and read. "Dessert wine." He looked at her. "But there's nothing wrong with dessert wine," he explained, and she thought he thought she knew nothing at all about anything. "I think of it as a small amount after dinner to sip slowly. Some men like it with cigars. I don't smoke."

"The chi . . . chi . . . chi . . . ken did."

But neither of them laughed about the chicken. He said, "Why don't I just get rid of that for you?"

"No." He must have heard it. His face was as screwed up as hers felt.

She couldn't look at him. The only thing she could think of to say was, "I can't . . . c-c-cook."

"Here, I—" He touched her. Oh, he should not have laid a comfort-filled hand on her shoulder. It was too much. "Just go!"

She was wrong about the thunderclouds. The rumblings had been a warning of a volcano, and there was no way to prevent the eruption. It knocked the glass to the floor and her head to the table, and the lava, black and burning, flowed.

## 54

*A*rmand had driven the car. He'd thought they might go for a fast drive after dinner. But the entire evening had turned out to be disaster. But who knew what normalcy was anymore?

He had wondered if he could ever have a woman in Ami's house. In a personal way. But when Caroline had said she couldn't stay there forever, he said, "Yes, you can."

At first it had been because the two women had needed it. He was trying to be a good Christian and share what he had. He wanted to be helpful. But as time passed, he saw her there, working in the garden, exclaiming joyously, "I never got my hands so dirty before," and putting them right back into the dirt.

Little strands of wayward hair escaped from the roll, tightened with sweat, and she would laugh about it. She enjoyed making things grow.

He was a young man, and he enjoyed watching Caroline as she grew.

Now she cried.

He went into the lake house where Bess and Willard were having dinner. They looked at him and must have seen his distress. "What in the world?" Bess said, and Willard rose from the chair.

"Caroline is sobbing."

"What happened?"

"She burned the chicken, and I took the wrong kind of wine." He felt the heat on his face and in his eyes.

"She's crying about that?"

He moaned, "I don't think so."

Bess breathed a heavy sigh. "It's about time. I'll need to hurry. Will you drive me?"

"Willard can."

They left in a hurry.

When she said it, he knew what *It's about time* meant. How he'd sobbed about Ami, about the stillborn baby, and all the way back to his earliest memory of things not going the way he wanted them to, the way he thought God should handle this world and his life.

He felt like doing it again.

So he went off into the woods and fell on his knees and sobbed.

This time he sobbed about the same things with several additions. This time about disaster, and lost lives, and grieving people, and Caroline, and Ami again, and the stillborn baby, and all the earlier things not going his way. But it was different this time too. He knew he could blame and doubt and be angry and hurt and suffer and not understand, and God would pick him up and brush him off. The mud stains might stay on the knees of his pants, but God would wash away the hurt and bring that peace and love and assurance that passed understanding.

He knew because God had done it for him before. So it was all right to cry out. God could take it.

And when the ache eased, he would again mean what he'd said many times in the words of Job, *Though he slay me, I will serve Him.*

So he cried and moaned and groaned and hurt and let the pain leave him and travel to the throne of God.

When God would get around to taking it, looking at it, reviewing it, he would say *nothing happens that you can't bear and I'm with you always* and he would send his peace.

# 55

*B*ess told Willard he could leave. She encountered the putrid smell before entering the kitchen. She hurried to Caroline, slumped in a chair and her head on the table. A burnt chicken was in the sink, and its stink filled the air, mingled with the smell of wine. A broken glass lay shattered on the floor in a syrupy puddle of dark red liquid.

Caroline was making noises like some kind of machinery that was all choked up, trying to start, and just couldn't make it. Her chest was heaving, and she was banging the side of her fist on the table.

Bess took Caroline by the shoulders. "Let's go to the bedroom." Caroline let herself be led through the house, up the stairs, and into the bedroom. Bess didn't need to ask what was wrong. Her own eyes were tearing up. She mustn't let that happen. Caroline needed her for far more than she'd ever needed her for packing and unpacking her luggage, laying out clothes, dressing her hair, or even cooking her meals.

"Lie on the bed. Here, take this pillow and hammer into it, or hug it, or whatever you want to do. Just let it go."

"I try not—"

"Don't try not. Do it. Let it go."

Bess tried. Not to. But she did it. She let go. And began to choke and blubber and heave with sobs, and lay across the bed and banged both fists into it.

Caroline joined her. They cried and sobbed and wailed and made all the noise they could. And when they finished, they looked at each other and cried again. And when they finished, they forced more, made themselves cry it out. Unashamed. Deliberate. And the crying didn't hurt. It washed and cleansed.

They cried an ocean full.

But they didn't sink. They were in a little boat on top of the water.

Spent, they lay on their backs, breathing deeply, slowly, as if trying to get enough air after having run a race. Indeed, they had. She had the idea they had crossed the finish line. It didn't matter if you got there late, or were the last one to arrive. Just getting over was the important thing. Even if you had to crawl over.

When their breathing became more regulated, Caroline said, "That felt good."

"Shall we do it again?"

Caroline looked over at her. "I don't have a drop more."

Bess said, "Good. Because you look ugly."

Caroline gasped, but still smiled. Bess would never have said something like that before. Crying openly, brokenly, together, could work wonders. "You're no raving beauty, you know."

They laughed for a while, just because that felt good. "And we don't care how we look," Bess said.

"Exactly. And it's good just to breathe deeply."

"Yes, even if the air is filled with the smell of burnt, rotting chicken."

"Oh." Caroline sat up. "Let's go clean it up."

They did, and Caroline asked, "Where's Armand?"

"Oh," Bess said, "I think there was something he needed to do."

While they threw away the mess and cleaned up the kitchen, Caroline asked if Bess would tell her about her life.

Bess did so as they washed the dishes and dried them and put them away and cleaned the table and wiped the wine from the floor. Bess threw away the coffee, which was thicker than the wine, and made fresh.

She thought it time to be personal. Her life had been uneventful until she became a governess to a very wealthy family.

"I was foolish enough to fall in love—no, not love." She glanced at Caroline, who nodded. "I fell into obsession with the gentleman of the family. He represented all the world had to offer. I was stupid enough to believe I could step into his world. But I found out he could step into mine long enough to use me. And when the time came, when the young, pretty tutor came, he discarded me like a piece of trash."

Before long, with the kitchen decent again, they sat at the table, sipping coffee.

Bess thought she might as well tell it all. There was nothing you couldn't say once you've bared your tear-stained heart to another person. She took a good swallow of her sweetened coffee and set the cup in the saucer.

"I decided," she said, "I would learn all I could about that world. At another household with some older children, I sat in on the lessons. I read books and talked with the tutor. I determined to become like the mistress of the house."

She watched Caroline's eyes grow big. No way could she have known all that. But she encouraged Bess to go on. So she did.

"I was very frugal and saved my wages. Even asked for a raise in pay."

Caroline laughed. "Did you get it?"

"Oh, yes. I was invaluable." She chuckled. "I thought someday I would buy clothes like you bought me in New York, and wear a hat and walk like a lady and meet a gentleman and lie about my upbringing and he'd never know the difference. I would get into that other world."

She paused. But she'd come this far, which was a point of no return.

"We maids and governesses and housekeepers talk, you know. And when I heard Sir Chadwick was looking for an employee, I applied because that was a step further up the ladder. If I could learn how to look and act like you, I could go beyond third class in society. I might even skip one."

"Oh, Bess," Caroline said. "I never suspected such a thing. You were . . . invaluable."

Bess saw the light of understanding spark Caroline's eyes. Bess had gone beyond being a servant. She had become invaluable. "You see, I didn't want to be a servant. I wanted to be a lady."

Now sympathy lay in Caroline's eyes. What a tragic figure Bess must seem. "You wanted to be like me?"

"I know, pathetic isn't it?"

When Caroline gasped, Bess said quickly, "Oh, I don't mean being like you is pathetic. I mean trying to be anyone but yourself is pathetic."

"Well, I'm glad you changed that. This coffee is still hot, and if I threw it on you, you'd burn like a chicken."

So far, they could still laugh. "Mine's cold." She knew Caroline's would be too. She poured more and stirred in a little more honey.

Caroline sipped, then said, "I guess you see now you don't want to be like me."

"Oh, I saw right away I was changing the way I thought. I didn't want to walk or talk like you. Or wear silk and jewels and hats like you."

She saw Caroline swallow, although her cup was in her saucer. She maybe thought that was an insult.

"You changed me," Bess said. "You were, are, the sweetest, kindest, most generous person I've ever known. You kept your place and I kept mine, but you never said a harsh word to me. I was a servant but you never let me feel I was beneath you. You built me up. I no longer wanted to be like a lady. I wanted to be good like you."

Seeing the trembling of Caroline's lips and feeling it in her own, she wondered if they would blubber again. She had to say it all. "You saved me by being a good person. And then, Caroline, you saved me again. By making me take off that cap. You thought I, a servant, was worth saving."

"I didn't do it because you were my servant."

"I know. And I didn't go because I was your servant. Soon after I came to you, I vowed in my heart I would become invaluable for my own good. You taught me how to be the best kind of servant, and in my heart I would be a friend to you, even if you never knew it."

"I felt that," Caroline said. "I didn't know how to define it. Thank you. But you don't have to agree with me on this," she laughed lightly, "I don't think I'm so good."

Bess smiled at her cup. That was part of why Bess admired and respected her so much.

She heard Caroline sigh. "I don't see how Armand and I can ever relate well again. I'm completely embarrassed. And I'm sure he thinks I don't have a decent brain in my head."

"I'll bet he liked the way you look in that dress."

"He didn't say so."

"That proves it. If he thought you just looked nice, he'd say 'You look nice, Caroline.'"

When they stopped laughing, Bess said, "I have an idea how you can get past this." Caroline's doubtful gaze rested on her. "You've already tried having a friendly dinner, and that didn't work. Next time," and Bess said it seriously, "Don't send him away. Cry with him. And let him cry with you."

# 56

*C*aroline knew what Bess meant when she said cry with Armand. That didn't necessarily mean shedding any tears. They could care and share and listen. Armand had helped her and Bess. She could at least let him know she was as near or as distant as he wanted.

She phoned him while the fog still obscured his cottage, hovering over the lake and wafting through the trees. He answered after the first ring.

"Morning," she said, not knowing yet if it were *good*, "I called to say I won't be going into town with you this morning."

He said he had been getting ready to call her, that he was on his way out. He had meant to tell her last night. A case in another part of the city would keep him tied up most of the day.

She hesitated, but glanced at Bess, who shot eye arrows of warning. "Um," she paced the few steps allowed by the cord. "I'd thought you might come for breakfast. For leftovers."

She heard his chuckle, and Bess put her fingers over her grin.

"Yes," she said after he spoke again. "Your rain check is for tomorrow morning."

They rang off, and she felt that it might be a good morning, rain or not. Another day might be better, anyway, to get the chicken mess behind them.

She took the cup of coffee Bess handed her. "How could he bear to even look at me after that fiasco?"

Bess shrugged. "Maybe he liked your dress."

After they enjoyed the moment, Caroline pointed her finger. "What I'd like is a report on this Willard thing you have going on." Bess joined her at the table and told her.

The next morning Caroline opened the front door to Armand. As soon as he stepped into the foyer, she said, "Do you know what I was crying about?"

His dark eyes probed hers. "Everything?"

She knew he understood, and when they sat at the table she told him about the volcano she had mistaken for thunderclouds, while Bess set coffee before them and cooked their breakfast. "I want to be available to listen to others who might have such feelings, because I can understand the need to let it erupt."

"You're inviting me to share if I'm so inclined," he said. "That exact subject has been on my mind."

From the direction of the island came the sound of cracking eggs.

She sipped her coffee. He stared at his. Then he lifted his gaze. "I don't have a volcano inside me."

She lowered her cup, and then spread her hand to accompany the thought, *well, that was that. She had offered but he was fine without her listening ear and that was fine because there were plenty of needy people out there and she would—*

"Mine erupted a few years ago. But I have the thunderclouds."

She heard the sausage sizzle in the pan. Her eyes met his quickly, and just as quickly she lowered her eyelids over them. She should not seem pleased about such a statement.

"I've learned that I can question and be afraid when thunder rolls and lightning strikes. My vision can be obscured in the midst of the fog and rain. But the storms can't defeat me. I have someone with me."

She heard her intake of breath and knew he did too. He had someone. She should say that was wonderful.

"That someone puts his arm around my shoulders and walks with me when I cry. He leads me out of the storms. The fog will dissipate. The rain will dry up. They're temporary. What remains is steadfast. The sky and the sun are still there. So is God."

"Up there," she said.

He touched his chest. "In here."

"You walk through the storms singing."

"Exactly. When I'm not crying."

"I don't sing well."

"Then do what you do."

Bess brought the plate over to the table, and Armand got a dining room chair for her. "Thanks, Bess," he said, "for the great meal you made for Willard the other night. I ate it for you."

"You could have put it in the refrigerator."

"Willard did. But you see, my dinner plans changed, and by the time I got to the lake house I was famished." Caroline and he seemed to think that was funny. "But," he promised. "I'll make up for it by cooking dinner one night for you ladies."

He would, would he? "I suppose Willard will join us too," Caroline said, feigning consternation.

Bess grinned. "If you insist."

"I certainly do. I've been kept in the dark too long, but I did notice we were eating a lot of fish lately."

Caroline felt a great burden had lifted. She had faced her fears, laughed about her limitations, and made new friends. And thinking of Armand's words, "Then do what you do," a new idea began to form.

She had delayed facing the inevitable, but doing so had had a freeing effect. Now, instead of trying to bury something that would not die, something that couldn't be forgotten, she could help it be remembered.

## 57

"Champagne bottles," Caroline grumbled, along with the sound of the train wheels returning her and Armand to Bedford after a long day in the office. "My goodness, you'd think all one was expected to do on that ship was imbibe."

"No," he said with a faint smile. "It's just that bottles float more easily than steel."

But she'd counted hundreds of bottles that the currents had washed up on the beaches of Nova Scotia. "I'm not complaining, just commenting."

"I should hope not," he reprimanded. "After I worked on that project for weeks."

She leaned back, letting her head rest against the back of the seat, and closed her eyes. She had him read the newspaper accounts of items from the *Titanic* being found on the ocean and in other places, including New York. Armand contacted Craven. Although Armand's expertise was unquestioned, she suspected Craven's influence might have something to do with the plan coming to fruition and the legal process begun for them to start collecting the items.

Mrs. Jessup moved her desk over and set Caroline's next to it. She had her own telephone and file cabinet. A bedroom upstairs became a storage room for items found in their area. Jarvis seemed to think he'd been given a promotion by lugging boxes up the stairs. Since this was not a full-time job, Caroline kept no certain hours, but worked as needed.

The train's coming to a stop roused her, and she realized she'd been dozing. She was wide-awake, however, as soon as Armand rented the car. "Don't mind if I drive, do you?" She opened the door to get behind the wheel.

"Not at all," he said. "It increases my prayer life."

After she had playfully hit him, she drove the speed limit and laughed all the way home while he prayed. Bess invited him in for supper. While Bess cleaned up afterward, Caroline and Armand sat at the table, and he had fun discussing her driving.

When they settled down from laughing at her expense, she said, "I've been thinking about something."

He leaned back and held up his hands. "You want me to get the speed limit increased."

"Now, that's better than the idea I had."

"Sorry. I can't do anything about that one."

"Perhaps you can with this one." She hardly knew how to speak of it. "I don't know how to analyze myself. But I know I've been trained to be proper all my life. And then, crossing that ocean changed everything. I've rebelled and tried to be an ordinary person. But I failed at that."

She couldn't go on if he didn't take this seriously, but his nod encouraged her to continue. "I thought I should observe a year's mourning period for William. But that wouldn't change what is or isn't in my heart. And I don't need to wonder what people think. I'd like to see a little more of the world. I'm going to start—" How should she phrase it? Yes, "Stepping out. I mean, I am not an aged woman. What do you think?"

He looked tense. "Well, being a man who isn't exactly aged either, I can understand what you're saying. And since you asked, I'll tell you what I've observed."

She nodded.

"You'll never be an ordinary woman. You're a tremendously wealthy woman. That's who you are. You can be an influence on women of means. The Lord has blessed you that way, so don't try to be like everyone else. You have beauty, and brains, and depth, and goodness. And—"

He sounded agitated and appeared rather disgusted.

Her jaw dropped, and she stared at him. He stared back and colored. "I've said too much. I should leave. Thanks for supper, Bess."

His shoes padded through the house. The front door opened and closed.

"What was that about?"

Bess sighed. "I've heard the way to a man's heart is through his stomach. Must be something I cooked."

Almost as soon as she heard the car door slam and thought he was leaving, the front door opened again. Then he stood over her, his unruly curls awry. "One more thing. Since you're working in my office and we're traveling together, but you'll be stepping out, might I ask—" He looked like a child asking for a cookie, "with whom?"

"Youm?"

And so they did. On some Saturdays. He showed her the city, and the bays; and the four of them visited Peggy's Cove, where Willard lived; fed worms to the fish from the boat; went to church on Sunday and he sang to the Lord. He cooked once a week and she ate, and they played cribbage or bridge or whist.

Stepping out was fun, and Caroline felt as though she'd begun to live again. Then, to top it off, the attorney in California reported all appeared well with Phoebe and Henry.

Caroline wrote to Phoebe. The day she got a letter from Phoebe, she thought her heart would burst. She rushed into Armand's office and told him about it.

"Phoebe says she likes it there. The Freemans are fun, and they're going to have a baby. School's starting back soon, and she's continuing her piano lessons." The next part hurt Caroline's heart. She read it the way Phoebe wrote it.

*Henry has nightmares. I hold him until he goes back to sleep. He's a little brat and won't let anyone play with his Meccano set. But I love him.*

Caroline dropped into the chair and held the letter to her heart. "I fell in love with those children." She almost said something about the wedding. But that was best forgotten. That was Lydia's life. No, her past. "Mary Freeman is going to have a baby. Lydia is going to have a baby. Seems the whole world is."

"I think that's the idea," he said. Then he straightened. "You love children so much. So I assume, if I'm not being too personal, either you or William were unable—"

"Why no." That surprised her. "Why did you think that?"

"Because you said you were married at age nineteen and—"

"Let's talk about it on the train." She wanted to be near home. On the train, along with the rumble and huffing and chugs and occasional whistles, she told him about her good marriage with William and the joy of pregnancy. "I never carried one to term. Three months was the longest."

"I'm so sorry." He told her about his marriage with Ami. His face darkened. "She had a terrible time. The baby was stillborn." She felt his suffering when he said, "It was torture for Ami emotionally and physically. She died two days later. Then, it was torture for me."

When they reached the station, she let him drive.

"Have you thought of adoption?" he asked.

She felt uneasy. "Yes, and particularly concerning Phoebe and Henry. But I would love to have children of my own."

"I couldn't bear to chance my wife going through what Ami did."

She felt a chill and hugged her arms. "I intend to try. I'm young."

His face looked like the foreboding cloud, coming closer. "I wouldn't mind adopting."

They were at a stalemate. She wanted children. He did not want to chance a wife dying in childbirth.

The car stopped in front of the house. Caroline looked at the clouds. Lightning could strike. The rain could pour. She must hurry inside. Or walk through it.

"Armand, are you sorry you had that short time with Ami?"

His answer was quick as a wink. "Of course not."

"You would do it again, knowing?"

His grip was tight on the steering wheel, and his face was set toward the clouds' teardrops on the windshield. He spoke as if to himself. "It's better to live a short while with someone you love than deny yourself because you fear the other person will suffer or die."

"Yes, as you taught me that I shouldn't fear getting into a boat just because a ship sank." She opened the car door. As if he had just noticed, he said, "It's raining."

She stepped out into it and bent to look at him. "Someone implied I should try walking through it."

She shut the door. And walked.

He didn't call that evening nor had they mentioned an outing for Saturday. She awoke early, saw the morning fog and thought she'd try it. The thicket of trees was barely visible but served as a landmark.

She thought she'd bumped into a tree but this was softer than a tree and the branches steadied her and there was no lifejacket between them. But the fog, like enveloping arms, held them fast and the voice in the trees whispered don't be afraid and the fingers like a caressing mist touched their faces and the warm breath hovered like a vapor. When their cold lips had been warmed, considerably so, the fog was dissipating.

They walked from the trees and into the sunlight and turned to each other. Caroline removed her hand from his just long enough to caress the curls over his forehead but did not push them aside. She liked them there.

He had gold in his gaze, and he said with a sense of wonder, "You have a hint of green in your eyes."

"Must be the reflection of the grass."

"Ahhh," he said, looking up into the sunshine as if the most wonderful, amazing thing was a speck of green.

Laughing, hand in hand, they advanced along the vast green lawn, and she joined him in his morning song.

Armand did not sing the solo on Sunday morning. After the choir sang, a prayer was said while they bowed their heads and closed their eyes. Caroline felt a nudge, and there he was without his robe and she scooted over. He sat beside her on the pew.

Everyone stood to sing the final hymn before the sermon. Armand had the songbook opened to the right spot before the choir director said, "Please turn to page 75," and the organist began. Caroline opened her mouth to sing, but it got stuck. Armand ran his finger along the bottom of the words, "I love thee, I love thee, I love thee" and covered up the words "my Lord."

She thought, my Lord, what's he doing? He kept on for all four verses. But he didn't finger-underline any words except the *I love thee* ones and the phrase *how much my actions will show*.

She didn't think that exactly proper and it certainly wasn't ordinary and it might even be blasphemous and what would people think? They sat and to keep him from doing anything like that again she held his hand between them. She didn't know what the sermon was about, but from the way she felt, it must have been divine.

# 58

$\mathcal{L}$ydia's getting a letter from Caroline was like getting a present on a special occasion. Oh, Caroline would laugh about that when she saw the present Lydia's father gave her and Craven. But his present satisfied the aesthetic senses, as Craven had said. The letter touched her heart in a way no residence could.

She'd reveled in the letter all morning. Following her afternoon nap, she began to write. Craven walked into her upstairs sitting room. She laid aside her Sheaffer pen and lifted her face to his. "Home already," she said. His first priority, after her, was his presence in the New York office while keeping abreast of happenings in London.

Other days and evenings were filled with discussion of plans for the house, the baby, going out, having friends in. She hardly had time to think.

"I was able to leave earlier than usual." He began caressing her shoulders. "How was your day?"

"Wonderful." She held the letter up to him.

"Ah, a letter from her always cheers you." He sat on the loveseat in front of the window to read. He chuckled. "Doesn't surprise me. I thought they might just hit it off."

"We're both reading between the lines," Lydia warned. "But with Caroline living in his house and working in his office, something's going on."

"Caroline's a special person," he mused. She was glad he liked her. "I suspect Armand is too, although I don't know a lot about his personal life. He had a rough time. His wife—" He seemed to lose his train of thought. "She died quite young."

"Caroline didn't mention that." Lydia was about to ask how she died, but Craven began to discuss Armand's father.

"His father came from a long line of shipping. Quite successful. After the accident that killed his parents, Armand sold the business and became an attorney. He's quite a wealthy man but lives modestly."

"Caroline invited us to visit."

"That's out of the question for now. I have to get Robertson settled into the London office. But after the first of the year, that changes."

Yes, it had been arranged so he would be in New York permanently since everyone, except her and the doctor, expected the baby to be born in mid-January.

He handed the letter back to her. "Continue your writing, and give her my regards. I want to arrange for a nurse to be with you while I'm gone. And you might consider a downstairs bedroom. Don't want you falling down the stairs."

"I manage the stairs just fine, thank you. And this baby is kicking up a storm, so why shouldn't I? Besides, anybody knows exercise is good for you."

"You had that light-headed spell in Long Island."

"That's early symptoms. Long gone."

"You will have a nurse. And you will obey me on this." His gaze was playful, but she knew he was serious.

"Don't I always obey you?"

"Yes." He lightly touched her lips. "You do." Sometimes she wondered if he ever thought about this not being the way he'd planned his life. It was active for them both, as was the little life inside her.

But that would end, he often said, after the first of the year.

She knew it would end before this year was out. Then he would be—out. But for now she had a letter to write. Eager to tell Caroline everything, she picked up the pen.

> My dearest Caroline,
>
> Your letter refreshed me so, better than these cool breezes we're experiencing now that fall rid us of those terribly hot summer days. The swimming pool has been a great relief. Thank you for the invitation, and we so regret not being able to visit anytime soon.

Lydia looked at the letter again. Caroline had asked about her father.

> The news of our marriage and his first grand-child so delighted my father he recovered enough to go to the office, conduct business, and give us a present of any house we desired to purchase. His recovery meant Craven remained in New York long enough for us to find a house. But the doctor informed Craven that father isn't as well as he thinks. The good news had stimulated him.

Lydia stopped the flow of the pen. She didn't need to write about Craven being concerned about her father not having the stamina he used to have and that his medication might be adversely affecting his decisions. She should write the good news.

She would tell her about the house. At least touch on the highlights.

> Upon walking into this house, we both knew right away it is perfect for now. We could readily see the truth of the realtor's praise for the outstanding architecture and genteel elegance of this mansion. It's located in the Upper East Side in the borough of Manhattan and is bounded by the East River and Fifth Avenue Central Park!
>
> The house came completely furnished and is quite suitable, but we plan to redecorate after the baby is born. The only room we're changing and furnishing now is the nursery.

She decided not to go into detail about that. Caroline would rejoice for her, but Lydia didn't want to rant on and on and make her sad.

> Why don't you and your, ahem, landlord visit with us? And Bess, of course. Either when Craven's here or away would be fine.

Yes, that would be perfect. Caroline could be there when the baby was born. She already knew Caroline was someone to cling to when her life fell apart.

For now, however, all was well, and she told Caroline so.

> We are well.
> Your loving friend,
> Lydia
> P. S. Craven sends his regards.

The following morning the nurse sent by her doctor arrived for the interview. Lydia had already decided if she were the one who had been in that little room during that first examination, she would simply kick her fanny out the door.

She was, however, a middle-aged, gray-haired widow with an attitude concerning her expectations of a mother-to-be. Myrna might be someone to quarrel with for a change, so she hired her. She would occupy the bedroom next to Lydia's.

One evening Craven came home to find her writing down possible baby names. He became interested and sat beside her. "Who gets to decide, me or you?"

"I'll decide the first name and you decide the middle name. And the last name is a given."

"I should hope." He laughed.

Oh my, her remark had gone right over her head until he said that. "And if I don't like the name you choose, I'll change it."

"Exactly," she said and grinned.

"Beatrice," he read. "Your mother's name."

"If she's a girl, we might name her Beatrice Beaumont Dowd."

"You didn't let me decide that middle name," he said playfully, then grinned. "But I like it."

She was well aware of that. "And I could add Bella to her name. Bella-Beatrice Beaumont Dowd. I can call her Bella."

They laughed together.

"And if he's a boy, his first name should be Beaumont—" She shrugged. "You choose the middle."

He didn't see any he liked. "What about Keefe after my father? Beaumont Keefe Dowd."

"I like it." She returned his smile. "I can call him Beau. Oh, that's beautiful."

"So say the French." He paused. "As you are, Lydia."

She cupped her stomach, not quite as large as those of some of her friends had been at this stage, but like a stuffed cushion. "Like this?"

"Yes. And it rather surprises me. I never thought I'd be fascinated by the look of a mother-to-be. You're as beautiful as ever. Perhaps more."

"Thank you." She had come to take his compliments for granted. But he said it in such a tender way. Perhaps he was beginning to feel like a father.

She had this life today, and it was good. Feeling a jolt, she grabbed her stomach. Craven acted as startled as she. "Just a hard kick," she assured him. And herself. She'd done all this for the baby. Caroline had lost three babies. She must not lose . . . her baby.

# 59

After Craven's trip with Robertson, neither Lydia nor Craven expected him to sail again to London. But on the same day she had an appointment with the doctor, they heard the news that her father had been taken to the hospital.

"He's going to ask if he should leave me," Lydia told the doctor. "If all is well with me and the baby, there should not be a reason he can't be with my father."

Sitting across from her and Craven in his office, the doctor gave his report. "Healthy mother. Healthy baby. Some babies come early, some late, but your wife should have a normal delivery. The only problem I've encountered," he said and laughed lightly, "is with the father."

Lydia felt her eyes widen at the doctor's quick glance at her. Oops! She might have just given him something else to think about. Of course he couldn't have meant anything by it, and Craven said, "I know. I'm overreacting."

In the car he said, "I've told your father I'm bringing him here for a visit and he's willing. The ship's hospital can handle this for a few days, and his own doctor may come."

She would like to see her father. She had pleased him. She'd settled down with the man of his choice, and he wanted to see his grandchild. The plan was for them to arrive a week or so before Christmas.

"I'll be back in time for this event."

No, he wouldn't.

And one night the cramping became so persistent that Lydia buzzed for Myrna, who said she wasn't going to lose her baby, she was going to have it.

Then she was glad Craven wasn't there because if he were and said, "You can handle it," she would kill him, if she survived. The doctor was obviously a sadist and kept saying the worst would soon be over. Finally, she heard a lusty cry and wanted to hold the miracle created by her and . . . the maker of toy trains.

When she held him in her arms, nothing else mattered. She fed him. He was her Beau. Her beau as in beautiful. Her beau as in boyfriend. She would not stand by and watch a nurse care for her baby. The nurse could stand by.

She'd gone into labor on the fifteenth and her little Beau came December sixteenth, nine months and two days after he was conceived. Her friends who came to congratulate and celebrate believed him to be a month early.

Craven set sail as soon as possible after being wired, and arrived on the twenty-second. She was sitting in a rocking chair holding Beau when Craven quietly slipped through the doorway. Myrna rose from her rocking chair and busied herself at the crib. Craven could handle a railroad company over two continents but appeared ill at ease in the nursery. Beau was asleep. She stopped rocking.

Craven kissed her forehead, then straightened. She watched his eyes studying the child. His gaze focused on the white fuzz on Beau's head. Did he suspect? No, of course not. John's hair was brown. Hers was blonde. Craven would want his son to have his dark hair, his perfect face.

His expression showed no joy. He said, "I'm sorry, Lydia." She caught her breath. Somehow he knew. And then suddenly she knew: this was about her father.

He spoke quickly, "Arrangements are being made for your father. You and I have something here we must concentrate on." He looked at Beau again. "He has your hair. Otherwise he looks like . . . a baby?"

Her laugh was nervous. But he was right. Who could tell at this age who he looked like? But she saw John. Craven put his finger in the palm of the baby's hand, and Beau's little hand grasped it. That's what John would do. Accept everyone.

"He's a good size," Craven said with a hint of pride.

"Healthy. The doctor says he's a wonder."

"Mmm. Wonder how many wonders he's delivered."

"All of them, I suppose."

"Quite true. With one difference. This is Beaumont Keefe Dowd." Yes, that would make him a wonder of the world. "I should hold him."

She thought that a good decision. He was careful about Myrna putting Beau in his arms. But he did well. And he smiled.

John would have cried.

Beau did not cry when he opened his eyes but studied this man right back, though he could not keep his eyes open very long. Craven sat in the other chair and rocked. "I think he likes me." He seemed fascinated watching the movement of little eyes covered by eyelids fringed by long lashes and the little mouth that puckered. "He's trying to talk." The baby's nostrils moved as he took in a deep breath, and then he settled back into a relaxed pose. "No, maybe he's just breathing."

After a long moment he said, "I won't be handing out cigars. In fact, I'll give them up. This child doesn't need to breathe something like that."

Lydia wondered where this person had come from. This was not the Craven she knew. He said then, "What a Christmas present." He looked over at her as if she'd done something marvelous. "A family Christmas."

She had thought her father might spend Christmas with them. He wouldn't. But the following day she was made aware that he had given them their presents. She inherited the business and although she doubted anyone questioned Craven's business acumen at Beaumont, his total control would be undisputed, he being the owner's husband.

He behaved as if he were a permanent fixture in their lives without any reason to be otherwise. Then, she supposed, he might as well stay around for a while.

At least until he noticed who her son really looked like.

# 60

$\mathcal{I}$f we were to get serious," Armand said, soon after his blasphemous display in church that thrilled her so, "would you prefer not to live in a house where another woman has lived?"

She felt at home in his house. "Our memories, Armand, are in our hearts, not in wood and fabric and gold." She held out her hand, exposing her rings. "The good ones should stay with us no matter where we are. This house, or another, won't determine what you and I are to each other."

"I thought you'd say that, but I needed to know. So, I have a proposition."

She tilted her head, waiting.

"We have long winters here and can be snowed in at times. Your work in the office has slowed, and I know you want to do things."

She couldn't imagine where this was headed.

"I'd like you to consider redecorating the house."

"Yes, I could do that for you."

"In your style. What you like. How you think the house should look."

He had told her much about Ami. She had been from a middle-class family. Caroline knew now it had been Ami, and not Armand, who had decorated in the middle-class style. Ami likely hadn't known a great deal about decorating. But they wouldn't have cared.

"Yes, I would love to do that." She wasn't sure if she should add, *for you, for me, for us*. But already the wheels of her mind were turning. She'd contact Lydia. They could discuss this together. She wouldn't achieve anything near what Lydia described as her home, but it would be the kind of place that reflected much of who she and Armand were. Not pretentious, but elegant and welcoming.

Winter came early in November, and snow lay on the ground at the beginning of December. This slowed down any furniture deliveries. Darkness came early, and she'd look out the window and see lights on in the lake house and smoke curling from the chimney.

Armand and Willard went out into the woods and brought a huge Christmas tree for the house and a smaller one for the lakeside cottage. There were two things she wanted to do before Christmas.

The first, she needed to do at the office. She made a list of items. Logged them into the ledger. Wrote the tribute she knew better than anyone else, in memory of William Chadwick, a fine man who lost his life in the tragedy. What's in the heart is what mattered, but the rings she wore represented William.

She took the rings off her finger and laid them in a little box. She had no one to pass them down to and if she ever had children, they would not be a part of William. These would be kept in the room reserved for items to be put in a museum. A memory. She sealed the box and marked the appropriate number on it.

"I'll take these up," she said to Jarvis. She needed to do it all. And while in the room, she shed a few tears. She could do that now. Not hold it in. Let go.

That done, she could focus on her second task. Armand sat in his office not looking at her. She marched right in, and he looked up, his eyes red-rimmed. "Guess what?"

He did not look at her bare finger on the hand holding the edge of the desk. He looked everywhere else. She didn't think he would say, *you took off your rings*. And he didn't. "I'm invit-ing you to Christmas dinner," she said. "I'm going to make Rappie Pie."

"Rappie Pie?" That opened his eyes. "That's harder to make than chi . . . chi . . ."

"Oh, you!"

The way he looked at her made her heart flutter. "I'll be there," he said.

He was the first to arrive on Christmas Eve for the drop-in after the service and play. It seemed the entire congrega-tion came. They drank the punch, and ate the sweets Bess prepared. But they had really dropped by to see the colorful electric lights on the tree, a sight like none had seen before. Caroline loved to see the eyes of the children open as wide as walnuts and shine bright as the lights.

She felt proud of her new living room, the only room she'd had time to redecorate. The old furniture had been donated.

After everyone left, even Bess and Willard, Caroline sat with Armand in the living room sipping Christmas punch and enjoying the lights. "I'd like to ask you something." He moved to the couch where she sat. "I never thought I could love again, Caroline. But now I know loving and losing just prepares the heart for a greater understanding and a deeper love. Will you marry me?"

Her heart filled with joy. "I really would like to do that." He took a jeweler's box from his pocket, removed the ring, and slipped it on her finger. She asked that he switch on the lamps so she could see it better. "It's perfect," she said, and he took her in his comforting, loving arms and they sealed the commitment with a lingering kiss.

He soon left and Bess returned. They admired the ring, a large diamond circled with smaller diamonds and emeralds set in white gold. The kind of ring a very wealthy woman, who knew style, could wear without pomp but with pride.

Christmas day dawned with the ground covered with a beautiful blanket of snow. Armand and Willard came early for the gift exchange. They had promised to be conservative. They each had already made a donation to the church fund for helping the needy and making sure all the children in the area got something for Christmas.

Bess gave Willard a tackle box he'd mentioned to Armand, and Armand had filled it with fishing needs. Bess and Caroline gave each other scarves and gloves they'd picked out together and pretended they'd never seen them before. Bess gave Armand an inspirational book. Caroline gave him phonograph records.

Just when everything was sailing along, happy and perfect, Caroline opened her gift from Armand. She gasped. It took her right back to the *Titanic* and the night of the tragedy.

## 61

*C*aroline had instructed Armand to sell the house and furnishings in London, including her clothes and jewels. The
best ones were at the bottom of the ocean. At first she told
him to get her books, particularly *Once Upon an English
Country Garden*, because of the connection with Phoebe and
Henry, then she changed her mind and said, no, she would
break from everything in the past.

Now she held in her hands a copy of *Once Upon*, and her
hands shook.

Armand apologized, "Should I not have done this?"

"This is the best present you could give me. No, next to the
best." She waved her ring-finger hand. "Negative memories of
losses washed over me. But that's gone." She looked at it lov-
ingly. "Now it brings the good ones. This is written by Phoebe
and Henry's father."

Of course he knew that. "I suppose his books are available
in America."

"No," he said. "The attorney in California said Phoebe's relatives had a few copies but wouldn't part with them. But with
a little effort, we managed to find a new copy in London."

"Thank you. I'll cherish this. I'd like you to read it. You can identify with S. J.'s story." She paused. "And his recovery."

That afternoon she hoped the Rappie Pie would turn out to be a good memory. Or at least a decent meal. Bess had heard about it from Willard, who said it had come from the French Acadian region in southwest Nova Scotia over 150 years ago. It was a delicacy people especially liked to make at Christmastime and Easter.

Preparation took time, being done in stages. The recipe called for chicken or beef, and Caroline chose beef. Bess cooked the beef in water with onions, chives, salt, and pepper.

Caroline grated potatoes and added butter, salt, and pepper. Figuring out the directions, she poured the broth in three stages over the mixture of potatoes. Bess read the instructions aloud while Caroline spread half the mixture into a greased pan, added chunks of meat evenly, covered the meat with the rest of the potatoes, set a timer, and stuck it in the oven to bake for three hours.

"To brown," she said to Bess, "not blacken."

They laughed and checked the pie periodically.

Caroline dressed in green silk. Armand seemed to have a liking for that color. "This time I brought champagne," he said. It bubbled merrily in the flutes.

They celebrated her, and Bess's, successful dinner, along with Christmas day, as the savior's entrance into this world.

When she and Armand were alone, Caroline told Armand, "In my marriage to William, I may have become obsessed with trying to have a child. I want to put you first in our marriage. I'm happy with only you right now, and believe I can be for the rest of our lives."

"I believe you," he said, looking into her eyes.

They chose not to marry until after the April 15 memorial service of the next year. Caroline decided May was an ideal time for a wedding, marked by new life springing up, green and lush, across the landscape. In the little church, after they were pronounced married, they knelt and faced the cross while Armand sang "The Lord's Prayer."

They honeymooned in Cape Breton, an island off the southern tip of Nova Scotia. They could have been ferried over, but Armand wanted to drive and show her Cabot's Trail, named for the explorer who founded Cape Breton. He pointed out Beinn Bhreagh, which meant "beautiful mountain," where Alexander Graham Bell resided part of the year. He had named it after his ancestral Scottish highlands. "We can thank him for our telephones," Armand said with pleasure.

They spent their nights in the resort area of Baddeck. One pleasant day they hired a boat for a sail on the lake. Along the way on their journey to historic sites, they visited the fortress of Louisberg, where the French and English had fought. "The English won," Armand said.

"That surprises you?"

"No," he said and kissed her. After they returned from their honeymoon, Bess and Willard married and lived in the lake house until he sold his Peggy's Cove house and they found a place not too far from the church. Willard became a part-time fisherman, carpenter, and caretaker of the grounds. Bess continued as Caroline and Armand's housekeeper and occasional cook. By the time the house was finally renovated to Caroline's liking, Bess was pregnant.

That old feeling welled up in Caroline, but she cried for joy with Bess and turned to Armand for love.

Bess and Willard's little Caroline Joy came screaming into the world in March the following year. By that time, Caroline suspected she might have her fourth miscarriage.

She decided not to worry Armand with her fears and hope. "Will you go with me?" she said to Armand when the preacher invited anyone with a commitment to come forward. Armand walked down the aisle with her. She asked to be baptized.

She wasn't afraid of the water, but afraid of what she might hear. The memory of people in the water, freezing, screaming for help, dying, voices fading.

Could she stand it? But the Lord was baptized. He said, *follow me*. She knew she had his spirit in her heart. But she wanted to walk through. Commit to this symbol of being raised to new life, a spiritual life, a new beginning.

Knowing her fears, Armand wanted to assist. She walked into the baptistery, and Armand stood behind her. The pastor said, "I baptize you in the name of the Father, Son, and Holy Ghost." He put the handkerchief over her mouth and nose and his hand on her back. She felt Armand's hands on her shoulders, letting her know he was there.

Completely submerged, she felt the letting go of anything to hold on to, but knew others were holding on to her. She came out of the water, stood on her own two feet, and felt the handkerchief being moved away from her face.

After a deep breath, she said, "You can let go."

Armand and the preacher moved their hands away. She stood, with no one holding her but the invisible arms around her shoulders.

She heard silence. She knew the big decision had been asking Jesus into her heart, but in that moment she felt as if all her sins had been washed away and she stood clean and perfect because Jesus had died for her. Whether she lived or died in this physical body, she was now alive forevermore. More alive than she'd ever been.

And whether or not she carried the baby to term, she dedicated that life inside her to the Lord.

*The child is yours, Lord.*

# 62

In early November, Caroline had a difficult delivery. Armand was on his knees praying when the baby came, crying as if he protested coming out of his warm cocoon and having to face whatever might be in store for him.

Caroline propped herself up, and the nurse placed the baby on her heart.

The nurse said that Armand had had a worse time during the delivery than Caroline had. "He's out there trembling, his knees like reeds swaying in the wind."

She'd already had a mirror held up so she could try and be presentable, but knew there were circles beneath her eyes, her face was pale, and her hair was a mess. Armand came in and said, "You're the most beautiful sight I've ever seen. Are you all right?"

"Armand. We have a son. Our David."

He touched the baby. He kissed her face, laid his hand on her and the baby, fell on his knees, and thanked the Lord.

The doctor told them she would not have more children.

But their son grew, handsome, strong, healthy, and a little rugged like his dad, and kind. A little David.

The following spring, Lydia, Craven, and Beau, nearly two-and-a-half years old, paid a visit. Caroline's country home was an elegant but cozy place to visit, the lawn ideal for Beau to torture Bravo, who had outgrown his fear and licked and pawed. Beau tried to ride him like a horse and ended up on his behind every time. While Beau chased Bravo, Joy chased Beau while taking steps and falling and crawling, and six-month-old David bounced in his stroller, observing and applauding.

Willard and Armand proclaimed the joys of fishing. When asked if he wanted to try it, Craven shook his head. "I believe you. I'll leave the catching up to you. But I'd like to see that lake house."

They spent a somber time when they left the children with Bess and Willard to visit the *Titanic* victims' cemetery. Afterward, Caroline showed them the room in Armand's office building that resembled the beginning of a museum, including the shelf lined with champagne bottles. She pointed out William's rings and her tribute.

Craven laid his hand on her shoulder for a moment. She looked up at him and nodded her thanks. She knew the observant Craven saw the wistful sadness on Lydia's face. No one wanted to do this. Each one needed to.

For the moment, the happiness of friends and family and little children was forgotten, and tragedy remembered, as the conversation turned to the war that the world was fighting.

But they moved on to see happier places and returned home to the laughter and enjoyment of their families and the demands of children. When the little ones became too rowdy, Armand sang silly songs, and they loved it. He took them to a place where he had learned to find peace.

Caroline thought Lydia and Craven might not want to be on the water after the memories they had faced that day. But

Lydia said, "We've spent time on yachts with friends." So they went out on the boat.

The lake was a peaceful place, being surrounded by land and trees and mountains. The sun painted a pastel sky while drifting toward the horizon. They listened to the silence. Beau sat between Craven's legs, wide-eyed as if memorizing the scene. David took a nap.

The feeling was of peace and security and safety. They could be thankful for all their blessings.

Right now, there was peace in their families, in that little boat, with nothing to fear.

But they wore their life vests.

# 63

*O*ccasionally, Lydia thought of the late summer evening when Craven had posed a surprising question. Being only a few months old, Beau was in bed for the night. They were sharing how their days had gone. Since Lydia insisted upon the full care of Beau then and in the future, he was her main topic of discussion.

"Do you want more children?"

What surprised her most was that the thought had never entered her mind. Her life was filled, complete with Beau. "Do you?"

"No, I have my heir."

She had never thought of Beau in that way. But of course, he was.

"If you do, that's fine. I can handle it."

Did she want more children? Lydia doubted she could give the love and attention another child would require. Beau had all of it. "I don't think so."

"Give it some thought," he said. "There are operations."

She gasped and almost came out of her chair. "I will not."

"I'm not talking about you, Lydia. I'm referring to myself."

"Oh. You?"

"I've looked into it. Like I said, I have my heir. But you're quite young. If anything should happen to me or Beau—"

She put her hand on his arm to stop his words. The thought was unbearable. There was no way she could ever replace Beau.

Craven took her hand and held it a moment. She could not make this decision for him. "I don't want more children, Craven. But whether or not you have the operation is entirely your decision."

He squeezed her hand. "Thank you."

The operation was successful.

As the days and years passed, seemingly all too quickly, Lydia was mesmerized with how Beau would see the most minute flower close to the ground that would have been trampled on by adults. He'd say, "Ooooh" and touch it ever so gently. She spread her hands and explained that buds would blossom out into flowers. When she opened her umbrella, he said it blossomed out. They would laugh and laugh and laugh.

Even when he was very young, she had read poetry to him when Craven wasn't home. She'd loved it when John had quoted or read poetry to her. She wished she had the poem he had written about her. The only words she recalled were "golden loveliness." She often thought about it when looking at her son.

He had inherited the typical Beaumont golden hair, his a little darker than hers except when highlighted by the sun. But John's son had his loveliness.

"There's no holding that boy back," Craven said one evening, watching Beau and his antics. He was a little performer, and they encouraged his active mind and inquisitive nature.

He ran off to the sunflowers at the far end of the garden. To keep him in sight, they followed. Craven thought the flowers unseemly, having grown so tall. But Beau loved them. He looked up and spied a huge bee on the brown center and reached for it. She and Craven gasped, ready to shout for him not to do it, but the bee simply flew to another sunflower and he was never able to catch it.

Oh, he laughed. He was happy.

Beau turned with his little hands on his hips and his lower lip stuck out, playing his pretend annoyed part. "What's wrong?" Craven said. "Beau couldn't catch a bee?"

Beau punished the sunflower stem with a little slap and was off to something else.

Although they liked visiting with Caroline and Armand, none of them felt it wise to travel. Soldiers seemed to be on every street corner, and they needed the trains. She and Caroline communicated often, writing long letters about their precious boys.

Then Lydia did not hear from Caroline for a long time, but she read about the Halifax explosion. She and Craven feared for their friends. Just as it had with the sinking of the *Titanic*, people throughout the world were shocked, but not in disbelief, because they already knew how quickly and unexpectedly devastation could occur.

# 64

On December 6, 1917, the French munitions ship *Mont Blanc* collided with a Belgian ship, the *Imo*, in Halifax Harbor. The *Mont Blanc* carried a deadly cargo of explosives: 35 tons of benzol, 300 rounds of ammunition, 10 tons of gun cotton, 2,300 tons of an acid used in explosives and 400,000 pounds of TNT.

The facts were slow in coming, as they had been about the *Titanic*. The *what*, however, was diminished when compared to the *who*, for eventually it was known that over 2,000 people died and 9,000 were injured. Many others were devastated by the emotional and physical impact of the tragedy.

The faces of people, and the landscape, changed considerably. Armand had been in his office building when it shook and the windows shattered. He and his co-workers rushed out and saw the menacing gray cloud rising into the sky.

While they were still trying to comprehend what had happened, a huge tidal wave sucked up water from the harbor, swept over the devastated area, and carried back anything in its path, including people. Then a second tidal wave struck. The north end was flattened. Fires broke out.

Armand had experienced personal disaster, witnessed his loved ones' anguish, but this was different, affecting his own city, towns, families, friends, and neighbors.

Their having dealt with the *Titanic* disaster was like preparation for their current response. Temporary hospitals were set up. Everyone who had space offered it. Armand nailed boards over his office windows to keep out the cold and weather.

They'd been affected by the world war, but this was another kind of war. Soldiers and rescue workers rushed to dig through the rubble, hoping to find survivors. They welcomed the U. S. and British military who were in port and joined in the efforts.

The day following the explosion, a blizzard covered the eastern seaboard, and rescue work ceased, as did electric and telephone service. Armand was thankful that at least some would be warmed by the stoves and fireplaces in his office building and would have a place to sleep.

Some asked why God had let it happen and why didn't God do something, as they had about the *Titanic* sinking, and the war.

Armand said, "God didn't tell me that, but he seems to be saying that's why he left me here. To do something."

When he was able to get home, he and Caroline found solace in the arms of each other. Slowly, life returned to a semblance of normalcy. Caroline returned to the office. She recorded museum items brought in from the explosion, to join those from the *Titanic*.

✐❤

By 1918, peace came, to a certain extent. Caroline received the traditional Christmas card from Phoebe, now sixteen.

Bobby Freeman had died in the war. Everyone was sad. Phoebe did not describe Henry as a brat.

"He's a holy terror," she wrote.

Caroline hoped that was an exaggeration. Phoebe still played the piano and looked forward to graduating from high school next year. Maybe she could visit some time.

That thrilled Caroline. She wrote back and told her about David.

A card and letter came from Lydia. She wrote that they could visit in the spring after Beau's school term ended. David's would end three days later, but they'd work around that.

When Lydia arrived, the two friends picked right up where they'd left off.

Lydia told Caroline all about a new craze. There seemed to be plenty of those nowadays, but Caroline considered herself and Armand homebodies, although they socialized some.

Lydia had a friend who had returned from South Carolina, where she'd learned a dance called the Charleston. Lydia taught it to Caroline. "The world has discovered we have legs," Lydia said. "We might as well show ours."

They went shopping, bought short dresses and long necklaces, and later took their husbands to a club. They talked to the bandleader and danced the Charleston while onlookers stood around the sides cheering. The spectacle they made of themselves thrilled their husbands to pieces.

David was nearing six years old that summer. He'd already walked to the front of the church to give his heart to Jesus. Baptism was set for that Sunday, so they all went. Lydia had never seen a baptism. Neither had Beau. Craven didn't say.

In the baptistery, David stood in front of the pastor on a box so the congregation could see him. He looked adorable, his dark curls spilling over his forehead. He didn't need anyone else with him. When the pastor brought him out of the water, David swam out, to laughter and applause.

Afterward, David asked why they had laughed.

"Because you swam out of the water. Most people walk."

"My feet don't touch the bottom," he said.

"That's the thing to do, Son," Armand said. "Whenever you can't touch bottom, start swimming."

Because Beau wanted to see David's classroom, they all went to school the following morning. The last days were for show and tell. Parents were invited. David wouldn't say what his item would be. They suspected it was his friends from New York, or whatever was in the paper bag he held.

He stood before the class and said, "Some of you won't understand this, but . . ." Then, with all sincerity and confidence, he proceeded to tell them that Jesus had come into his heart. He told them how Jesus could come into their hearts too.

"That's my tell," he said. "Now I have to show it in my life."

He opened the paper bag and went around giving each child a piece of hard candy. Beau looked at his dad for permission, and Craven nodded. Candy normally wouldn't be allowed in the classroom, and Beau likely could not have it except at special times. Neither could David. But of course, he would have asked Bess for help, and she likely got the teacher's permission for David to show he wasn't all talk and no action.

Beau wanted to stay until the school day ended. Armand took Craven out on the lake in the boat. Caroline and Lydia saw that Craven held a fishing rod and Armand was demonstrating with his.

Lydia mentioned that Caroline and Armand's church was quaint, and had quaint ways.

"It's not high church," Caroline said, and they smiled.

"Time flies," Lydia said. "I can't believe Beau will be seven this year."

"This year?" Caroline had assumed Beau was born in January. That was when she heard about the birth from Lydia. However, a date hadn't been mentioned. But so what? It was just that everything that happened was often remembered and spoken of as before or after the sinking, and later, before and after the explosion.

"December 16," Lydia said.

Caroline did not welcome the pictures flashing in her mind. "David's is November 5. Would you like tea?"

"I'd love it."

"We're so blessed." Caroline busied herself with the tea, hoping they would move on to something else. Neither seemed to think of anything.

But that was fine. Friends don't have to fill every moment with talk.

And soon, the teakettle whistled.

# 65

*L*ydia remembered when Craven had laughed and said Beau couldn't catch a bee. But he didn't laugh as the years passed and Beau couldn't catch a ball. Not often. Not well. And the confidence of the child began to fade as he felt Craven's disfavor.

Lydia instructed the nanny and the tutors to praise him. They assured her he had no problem learning, he simply didn't want to waste his time on things that didn't matter to him. He liked history. That was encouraging. He loved flowers and helped the gardener.

Mickey Mouse and *The Adventures of Felix* cartoon hypnotized him. He devoured every comic book they could find, and he read the comics in the newspapers the way Craven read the *Wall Street Journal.*

Even the adults were fascinated by the first color cartoon, *The Debut of Thomas Cat*. Their friends tried to convince Craven that a child would naturally be more interested in an animated cat than a railroad company.

Craven had to agree. It would pass. But still, as Beau continued to age and grow, he had the build and stamina for sports and liked squash, playing tennis, swimming, running, and bicycling, but could never outdo Craven, who tried to teach him to compete. Beau would rather do those things for enjoyment. Craven wanted him to excel.

She couldn't say Craven didn't try. Wanting to expose him to the arts, they took him to the opera when he was sixteen. He loved it. He discussed the music, the story, the setting, the costumes, the makeup, and even a scene that could have been done better.

"That's encouraging," Craven said later, "he's thinking."

"He's just a boy," she reminded him. "And a teenager."

"He's a young man. After high school graduation he will work in the office and learn about the business."

Craven looked forward to it. Beau dreaded it and scoffed, "I can't imagine spending my life in an office."

Craven was taken aback. "We live a pretty good life because of that office, Beau. Are you aware of your advantages and opportunities? You have a company ready to be handed to you. And it's nothing to sneeze at."

"I'm sorry, sir." Beau backed down immediately. He didn't like disappointing Craven. "I do know all that. I do." He was nodding. Craven breathed easier.

That was settled. Beau would work in the office after graduation. He would start college in the fall.

Lydia had feared that her earlier years of reading poetry to him might influence him to try his hand at poetry. But she didn't know that he ever had.

At times she thought she saw John in him. He was handsome, as the Beaumonts were known to be. But she saw John in his manner. A certain gleam in his eyes, a light that came into them as if he had thought of something for the first time, his delight in everything about him, the good he saw in people and in life. He didn't need things and money to make him happy.

Craven couldn't understand that. Beau was his heir. He wanted him to work with him. So, though he wasn't competitive, he could at least be business conscious.

But he wasn't.

He dearly loved movies. He and his friends saw shows over and over, and he'd always share something new he had learned or heard.

That irritated Craven to no end.

One evening after she and Craven attended a formal dinner party, they returned late and went immediately to the master bedroom. Myrna came with a note and then was dismissed for the night.

Craven removed his dinner jacket and hung it in the closet.

She read the note, "Beau is off to the movies with his friends."

"Again?" Craven scoffed. He shook his head, then lifted his chin as his hands moved to his bow tie. He said in an off-hand way, "Sometimes I think that boy is no part of me."

Lydia knew she should say something like *or me either* and laugh, but something about the way Craven looked even as the words left his mouth turned her to stone.

And him.

He stared.

She stared.

Their eyes locked in the mirror's reflection.

She saw it happening in that eternal second. There wasn't time to make a joke or make a sound or get busy with something else. He spoke it. And it became fact.

She saw the accumulation of years become a single truth.

Not jumbled. But clear. Obvious.

Her insistence upon sailing to America for business reasons but never showing an interest in the business afterward.

The mild seasickness.

The association with John although he was not of their class.

The hurried marriage just to walk down a grand staircase.

The nausea at Long Island like that she'd had on the ship.

The baby born early.

Beau being nothing like him.

He had no heir.

He did not blink. He did not move. "Holy God," he breathed, and it sounded like a whispered scream.

She knew it was not profanity.

Of course, he never needed to use unseemly words. He was like a Roman emperor. Thumbs up. Thumbs down. It's done.

Nor was it the misuse of God's name. Craven made it clear he wouldn't tolerate ignorant, uncouth expressions from anyone with whom he did business or socialized.

Many times she had dreamed, had thought about those who went down in that freezing water, breathing for the last time, taking one last breath, choking with pain.

That was happening now. On dry land. Her life. Her marriage. Her son. Her husband. Going . . . sliding down . . . gone . . . never to have life again.

The *Titanic* had taken two and a half hours to sink.

The life they'd built together was taking a fraction of a second.

He looked as if his lifelong motto of "I can handle it" had been violated and confiscated.

Since he was immobile, she managed to tear her eyes from his, turn, and leave the room.

# 66

*L*ydia sat in the library below the staircase, with the door open to see if he came down the stairs. Suppose he didn't. Suppose he went to bed. Then what would she do? Go into another bedroom. Or, suppose this was the one thing he couldn't handle. Would he do something drastic?

Just when her fear rose to the point she thought of returning upstairs, he descended the staircase. He carried a suitcase. He did not look her way. His heavy footsteps crossed the foyer. The front door opened. It closed.

What now? What was he going to do?

Would he have a one-night fling to punish her? Stay with her and take a mistress?

He'd know that would lead to divorce. Never would she live with a man, him in another bedroom, and have a mistress somewhere. And divorce would involve money. Oh, he had his own, to be sure. He controlled the purse. But she, being owner of Beaumont Railroad Company, had the purse strings. She could pull them at any time, leaving him only a small fortune.

And the great Craven Dowd ask for alimony?

Never. That would be below his dignity.

If he decided on divorce, what would he tell his friends? What would the headlines, not just on the society page, tell the world? That he couldn't hold on to a woman, acclaimed by others to be very beautiful, and that he was so obtuse as to lose the lifestyle bought him by the Beaumont fortune?

She didn't intend to file for divorce and be put into a position to answer why.

So, *what was he going to do?* was far from a trite question.

He called four days later and said he would be home for dinner at seven o'clock. Please inform the cook to prepare his favorite meal. Please have Beau spend the night with a friend.

Could he not even bear to look at Beau?

Lydia tried to prepare herself for the inevitable, but she had no idea what it would be. She took a long, relaxing bubble bath; washed her hair and let the curls do as they pleased styling her hair the way he liked it; and wore a blue—his favorite color—cocktail dress he'd picked out for her at a fashion show. If he'd taken a mistress, he could see what he would be losing.

When he came home around six, he went straight upstairs, not even looking toward the library, where she sat with a book on her lap.

Was he packing?

Thirty minutes later, he came down the stairs and headed toward the kitchen. She went out the French side doors and walked around looking at, but not really seeing, the blooms in the flowerbeds.

What was he doing in the kitchen? Maybe he was putting poison in the food and would declare he wasn't hungry.

She walked along the path to the back of the house. How anyone knew where she was, she didn't know, but the cook came to the door and said dinner was ready.

For the end to an eighteen-year journey they would dine in the formal dining room.

Normally, she would not sit at the far end. Tonight she opted for that. Why not do it the way it was done in the movies Beau watched? Neither of them spoke, but he pulled out the chair for her. She sat, and he strolled to the opposite end of the long table.

The cook brought coffee.

Coffee?

Wine was a staple at dinner, whether or not anyone wanted it. He would have requested coffee.

Tonight wasn't even worth a glass of wine?

Might they not toast the demise of their marriage?

Perhaps the poison was in her coffee.

That's what she was thinking when the cook said, "Ma'am," and set her plate in front of her.

Perfect. Delectable. He could eat? Well, she could eat.

The longer they sat there, eating as if nothing was wrong, the more heated she became and partly because he looked so cool.

What did he think? Go away for four days and come home as though nothing had happened?

Then it occurred to her. He might have manipulated things and placed everything in his name and would leave her with nothing. He knew how to get things done.

She would not live in silence, pretending. This could have been talked over days ago.

She looked over at him, distinguished, calm, as if all were well with the world.

She made sure her voice sounded bland. "What are you . . . we . . . going to do?"

Without a moment's hesitation he said, "What husbands and wives do."

He was cutting his meat with a sharp knife. Was he thinking of her throat?

She wondered what that meant.

Perhaps just live together, go through the motions. She knew many who did, in spite of affairs, family problems, incompatibility.

Did he for a moment think they'd live in the same house but not share the same bedroom? Go through the motions of marriage, pretend for the world?

If so, he could think again.

Champagne was brought in and poured into flutes, reminding her of Long Island and the night he proposed and gave her the engagement ring. So they would toast to the farewell, as they had toasted to their beginning.

He lifted his glass.

She did not, but said, "No dessert?"

Expressionless, his long-lashed, steely gray eyes bore into hers.

Oh.

She drank her champagne.

# 67

All the way upstairs, she told herself she would endure whatever. She deserved some kind of punishment for taking away his pride, his son. But he'd punish her with his own body? How could any man use his body as a weapon?

But if that was his intention, she would endure it.

He removed her clothing, one piece at a time, slowly, not even touching her skin. What kind of preliminary to punishment was this? To humiliate her? Her body did not humiliate her. And he was well aware of how she looked.

He led her to the bed, and she lay as if out by the pool, lazing on a summer's day. Forced herself to think. She would endure.

She was a survivor.

Even if it were some brutal attack, she would live through it. He was not a stranger. He was her husband of eighteen years.

She closed her eyes and heard the music in the background. They'd had champagne. They must have music. Wasn't that the way to celebrate any event, beginnings and endings?

So, he would not apply for divorce but give her a reason to do so.

Force.

And what court would ever believe that a husband of eighteen years had forced his wife? Even servants could testify they'd had a lovely dinner together with champagne and music.

And she could never live with a man who forced her.

Was this just his way of saying a final farewell?

Yes, she would endure.

And she would survive.

And she would divorce him.

First thing in the morning she would contact an attorney. Not his. Not theirs. She would find her own. In the meantime . . .

She . . . endured.

The following morning she felt him slip out of bed. She waited, still, until a light tap sounded on the door. She drew in a breath but didn't answer.

"Ma'am," Myrna said tentatively, and she turned in bed, expelling a breath of relief. She did not want to face Craven.

"Sorry if I woke you."

"No, no. That's fine." It really was. She propped herself up in bed.

"Mr. Dowd had to leave early. He said you might like juice and coffee before you came down for breakfast."

Yes, she did.

What was he up to? Seeing the attorney already? Having had his goodbye celebration with a satisfying of his culinary and physical appetites, he would leave her with her thoughts.

Her thoughts were jumbled. She reached for the glass and drank. The fresh orange juice felt good and cool and refreshing in her mouth and sliding down her throat. She leaned back and closed her eyes, savoring the feeling.

She might have even slept longer were it not for having to make such vital decisions.

Sipping the coffee, she thought of what he'd done and not done.

She had no grounds for divorce. He had not forced her. He had no intention of getting a divorce. Why should he? He had his young wife and he had the Beaumont fortune. So what if he didn't have a son? He had never really liked him very well anyway.

And she?

Why put herself through such a thing? Or Beau? Dear Beau. Yes, Craven knew that too. If Beau were to ask Craven why they were divorcing, Craven only had to say, "Ask your mother. I don't want a divorce."

And what could she say? *We're getting a divorce because he didn't force me?*

If there were to be a villain in this, it would be she.

She showered away the remains of last evening. Craven's scent. The perfume she wore. Even, as she washed her hair, the feel of fingers in her tangled curls.

Mid-morning had come by the time she dressed in slacks and a short-sleeved top and went down for breakfast. Her eyes moved to the telephone. While possibilities and questions continued to muddle her mind, the telephone rang.

The maid answered and brought it to the table.

What now?

Lydia sounded a tentative, "Hello."

"Caroline?" Oh, there was no voice she'd rather hear at this time. She had a friend who would listen, advise, just be there for her and not condemn.

Before she could say anything, however, Caroline said, "I've so looked forward to this. Craven said I could break the news.

He said you'd never believe it if he told you." She laughed delightedly.

"I have no idea what you're talking about."

"Well, you know Craven came to visit with Armand. And you'll never guess what your husband bought for you."

No, she couldn't. Maybe a house so she would move to Nova Scotia and he would keep the Upper East Side one?

"Prepare yourself."

She'd heard that before.

"A yacht."

"A what?"

"Yes. A yacht."

As Caroline talked, Lydia realized Craven had taken the private plane and flown to Halifax. He'd spent time with Armand. "Even becoming quite a fisherman," Caroline said.

"When did he leave there?"

"After lunch yesterday. Now you'll have to come and spend time with us."

"Yes, yes, we will."

Reality was pressing hard on her mind, but it wasn't easy to grasp.

Was he planning to drown her?

She had taken away Craven's heir. She had lied to him from the beginning.

He had reciprocated by buying her a yacht.

Of course.

He had proof there was no affair. No mistress. Armand and Caroline could witness to that.

Even when she was enduring, they simply did what husbands and wives do.

And afterward, like he'd done on their wedding night, he'd held her gently while she softly cried.

There would be no divorce. Craven didn't want one. It would be much too messy for her and would affect her dear son. She couldn't have that.

Beau was home for dinner that night. Craven sat at the end. Lydia and Beau sat opposite each other, next to him.

A very nice evening. Just a family night. In her lovely home. Amid her lovely life.

She could endure this.

And later Craven said, "Have you nothing to say about the yacht?"

"No."

His nostrils flared ever so slightly.

She gave a little shrug. "I don't know what to say. I haven't seen it yet."

As if a grin were inclined to show itself, a minute tug appeared at the corner of his mouth.

# 68

*C*raven remained quiet while three families quarreled about what to name the yacht, since Lydia didn't want it named for her. The frustrated crowd gave up.

Craven said, "Bravo!"

While Lydia looked at everything but him, they all agreed he was so thoughtful to think of Caroline and Armand's departed beagle, who had given many hours of joy, particularly to the children.

No surprise to her. Craven had a way of doing everything well.

They christened the yacht, a perfect size for a few intimate friends, and sailed farther out on the water than they'd gone in Armand's dory.

Craven, Armand, and Willard competed fiercely for fish on one side of the boat while the teenagers, Beau, David, and Joy, rejoiced and cooperated on the other. Lydia, Caroline, and Bess lolled in their shorts, rolled their eyes, and discussed their banes and blessings.

They returned to New York for Beau's graduation and the celebration after. Before the guests arrived, Craven invited them into the library. Lydia and Beau sat across from Craven.

He began with what sounded like another lecture on responsibility. "You'll soon be eighteen and off to college. Do you have any idea what you want to do with your life?"

Lydia closed her eyes, wanting to object. They opened wide when Beau said, "Make movies."

"All right. You have my blessing and support for what this entails."

She heard Beau's intake of breath.

"We'll search this out together."

Beau was on the edge of the seat. Craven held up his hand. "This does not mean I'm buying you some company so you can play around. I can put you into this. And I can take you out."

Beau would believe that.

"Remember who you are. You have a name and reputation," Craven said. "You will not be allowed to dishonor that."

"I won't, sir."

That was a big order for a seventeen-year-old. And yet, glancing at him and seeing the jubilation on his face, Lydia remembered that anyone that young believed he could conquer the world.

Beau was overwhelmed. "Dad. This is unbelievable."

"Believe it. All of it."

Beau went over to Craven. His voice shaky, he said, "You sure know how to surprise a fellow."

"Runs in the family."

Lydia knew what Craven meant. But she smiled. Her son was embracing Craven, saying, "Thank you. Thank you."

Craven patted Beau's back. "You're welcome."

Even if Craven was giving him up, her son would have what he wanted.

Beau stepped back, his eyes tearful. "But I will work in the office this summer."

"I know you will," Craven replied.

Yes, that would be right and good. Craven couldn't exactly disown a boy who would someday own Beaumont Enterprises, and be Craven's boss, even if only on paper.

They were a family. Beau had what he had always wanted from Craven, his blessing and support. Beau need never know about that past life.

The secret was safe.

☙

Beau began discovering the world and its possibilities. When he came home from film school, and then his apprenticeship with a Hollywood production company who acknowledged his innovative ideas, the three of them had wonderful conversations.

Now that Craven didn't have to accept Beau, they got along fine. Beau began making a name for himself. He planned a documentary about the *Titanic*.

Now that Beau was an adult, Lydia and Craven had no reason to withhold information about the *Titanic* tragedy from him. "I wonder if the public has lost interest by now," Craven said. "There have been other tragedies, wars, and the stock market crash."

However, she and Craven gave him every opportunity and the means to form his own company. While gathering material for his documentary, he made a couple of movies that gained recognition, but he said acceptance in Hollywood did not come easy. The documentary, primarily about the making of the ship and the mechanical reasons it sank, was a surprising success.

Beau and his colleagues tested the public's continued interest by making another documentary, featuring survivors. He had ready-made material in her, Craven, Caroline, and Bess.

They said nothing to imply Lydia had married on the ship. Anyway, Beau was seeking material about the sinking and how they survived, not who might have walked down a staircase in a wedding dress.

Phoebe was not mentioned. The documentary featured mainly older people who had survived, including third-class passengers telling the horror of even women and children being trapped below. By the time some arrived topside, all the lifeboats, not even filled, were gone. He featured the terror, the horror, the injustice, the carelessness, the class distinctions as if he were not upper class, and Lydia was proud.

The documentary's great success shocked even Beau, the dreamer-producer. He'd tested the waters, and now he had greater plans. He wanted to make a major motion picture but knew that could take years. There were sets to build, actors to acquire, and other movies to keep his company financially secure without his parents' handout.

Somewhere along the line he found time to fall in love with an aspiring actress named Angelina who had trained in fashion design and worked in the costume department. Lydia had heard the remark that no girl was good enough for a mother's son. Whoever said it was right.

There wasn't anything particularly wrong with her. Everything seemed to be in the right places, and she was pretty. More than pretty, to be honest. But they couldn't very well talk about design because Lydia's home was furnished with the best and the latest and it had come from many places in the world.

The girl had traveled some with Beau's company, but she would have been on the set and not out touring the great palaces and learning about period furniture and such.

Beau shortened Angelina's name to Angel, which irritated Lydia to no end. "That sounds a little too heavenly for a common girl," she said to Craven.

But they had a lovely church wedding in California, followed by a reception, sponsored by the groom's parents, at the surprisingly acceptable place Angelina's parents had in Malibu. Craven had sent the private plane for the Bettencourts and the Oaks. David was a groomsman.

Craven had stood as best man for John.

He stood as best man for John's son.

She remembered he'd said for her, he was the better man.

Caroline said the unpardonable, "One of these days we'll be grandparents."

Lydia gasped. "I will never be anything that sounds like a . . ." she cleared her throat, "granny." They laughed. "Nor a baby sitter."

Caroline just smiled and said, "I've heard that before," as if this were a matter of a woman's prerogative to change her mind.

After the couple left for their honeymoon on the islands of Hawaii, David had his own announcement. His dad had taught him to catch fish. God would teach him to be a fisher of men.

In a private conversation Caroline told Lydia that David and Joy were together constantly when David came home from the university, and Joy had a break from her nursing studies. She believed they would marry.

"Are you pleased?" Lydia asked.

Caroline smiled. "That's what Bess asked me and I told her extremely so."

Bess had become a welcome part of their lives, and Lydia understood Caroline's reasoning even better as she explained.

"In addition to their being in love, Joy comes from a mom who knows how the upper class lives, and how to serve others with grace and humility. Willard is a conscientious, hard-working man. Joy has been influenced by those qualities," she said. "She's a bit sassy like her mom can be, but she's a sweet girl. A supportive type who will make a good pastor's wife."

Lydia marveled at Caroline's attitude. Maybe she should try to see the good qualities in Angelina.

Their children were making mature decisions, and there seemed nothing on the horizon to mar those ambitions of theirs. For the time being, all was smooth sailing.

# 69

The Second World War slowed Beau's dreams. He had White Star Line's list of *Titanic* survivors and had begun contacting more of them than he had when he'd made the documentaries. He'd sent out notices in the media for anyone with information or memorabilia to contact him or send items to the Beaumont office, where a room was set aside for such.

He wouldn't be available to receive the information, however. He joined the Navy and was assigned to the base at Pearl Harbor. Angelina and his production crew agreed that would be a wonderful setting for a movie with a love story theme.

Japan had a different idea. The shock of the bombing and fear drove Lydia to her knees. She and Caroline stayed in constant contact. David's experience was harrowing from the beginning. When the war broke out, the West Nova Scotia Regiment was mobilized as an active service force battalion. David was often in the midst of the fighting, serving as chaplain.

David returned home battle scarred, but not as one of the 352 Nova Scotians who lost their lives nor the more than one thousand who were wounded or missing. Beau's and Angelina's lives were spared. He served in Hawaii for the duration of the war and filmed the horror, but he also included love stories.

Lydia's arms ached to embrace her son, but after the war ended, he remained in Hawaii to film, promising to return soon. He asked if anything to do with the *Titanic* had materialized.

"A few survivors contacted the office," Lydia said, then added, thinking it would make him smile, "And a new case of champagne bottles arrived. Most wine bottles come empty, but the champagne is intact."

"I saw a report on that," he said. "The corks on champagne don't implode like those in the wine. I want them. When I make the movie, they'll come in handy. But," he went on, "the public may now be more interested in war stories than *Titanic* stories. Still, I might find something to regain their interest."

Lydia relayed the message to Craven, who said the same thing about waning interest. "But Beau thinks he might find something."

"He just might," Craven said, and it sounded like a warning. "He's relentless in his search."

A gnawing concern stirred. "Would you ever tell him?" She could imagine that if Beau found something to cause him to ask personal questions, Craven might say, *No. I'm not your dad. I make real trains. You come from a fellow who made toys.*

Her hand was on her heart when Craven said, "I, tell him? Break his heart? Leave him fatherless? When he questions me, I will say *ask your mother.*"

Craven said *when*. But it was an *if*. More likely a *never*. After all this time. Anything that came up would have to be from a survivor like Phoebe, who had been a flower girl. Caroline had kept in touch with her over the years.

But she wouldn't be concerned. So much had changed through the years. She looked at Craven. Except him. How could a man his age have no wrinkles, only a few lines and hair that had turned, not gray, but silver? She realized she was smiling, and he was watching her. Then he winked.

But she had another idea. "I'd like to go to Beau's office tomorrow. His former office workers might not be available when he returns."

The next day Craven left his office in the afternoon and came into Beau's. She looked at her watch. "I didn't realize it was so late. Let me file some of this, and then we can go."

"May I help?"

"There's a crate over there. Open that while I finish here. And if it's champagne, just stack the bottles on the shelf in the storage closet. Should be a tool in there you can use."

He tore off the envelope attached to the crate and read the letter inside. "Interesting," he mused. "These were found by a fisherman off the Newfoundland coast before the war, along with other *Titanic* items. Seems some deep-sea divers dislodged them, or something broke loose from the ship."

He read more. "Southampton kept the items but didn't remove these after seeing what they were. Of course, they've known of Beau's movie projects for years, and thought he might use them."

He opened the crate while she complained. "I don't know why people claim to have been on the *Titanic* when they're not on the passenger list."

"They want to be in a movie."

She supposed so.

"More bottles." He took the wrapping off the bottles and lined them up on the desk. Some were empty, most were still intact.

He was trying to remove a cork, and finally succeeded, then took a piece of paper from the bottle.

"What's that?"

"I'm reading it."

She was only trying to make conversation. He was taking his time.

Finally he said, "It's a note from someone who sent the bottle."

"Someone else wanting a part in the movie?"

"That could happen. Looks more like . . . utter nonsense."

Seeing his hand tighten, she thought he was about to wad it up and toss it into the trash. Beau would need extras, representing over 2,500 passengers, plus the crew. "Craven, why don't you leave the note in the bottle? Beau can sort out what's utter nonsense or not."

"You're right." He rolled the note and returned it to the bottle. "It's his movie. Let Beau sort it out."

*

Beau and Angelina returned from Hawaii the following week. Angelina looked pregnant, and her son was lovely as ever. Their time together was nothing short of wonderful. But he needed to get back to his studio in California. He sorted through what he had in his *Titanic* office. He and Craven decided a secretary at Beaumont could keep him informed about any information or material.

The visit was quite satisfying, although Lydia hated to see him leave. She and Craven spent more time at home nowadays, maybe because they were getting old or something. She was looking forward to a restful evening.

But that afternoon Myrna said the Grahams were downstairs. They weren't expected. Walking down the stairs, she saw Jean and Hoyt in the foyer, their faces stark. What could have happened to them?

Jean caught her hands. "Oh, Lydia. I'm so sorry, but—"

Lydia knew the something had not happened to the Grahams, but to her.

## 70

*A* heart attack, they said.

Craven had experienced chest pains after returning to the office following lunch with Hoyt.

They thought it might be something he ate. But he had another attack at the hospital and could not be revived.

The funeral was delayed to give guests time to travel from abroad. Board members, employees, and friends would eulogize him in the great church, which was worthy of the tribute to such a successful man.

She dressed in traditional black and wore a hat with a black veil that covered her eyes. The beautiful casket at the front of the church was surrounded by so many flowers the air was hard to breathe. The eulogy was one of praise for the respectable life Craven had lived, the good work he had done, the charities he had supported, and the fine family he had had. They were all blessed by the life he had lived.

Their life together for over three decades was summed up in one afternoon.

The congregation rose while the coffin—she thought John had been sent home in a wooden box—was rolled down the aisle, and she thought of another aisle, on a ship that sank.

"Mom," Beau prompted. She moved out of the pew. Her son held her arm. She walked down the aisle and out of the church. They rode in a black Cadillac to the cemetery, where a huge tombstone, befitting a great man, would later be placed.

But first, she and her son watched Craven Dowd's casket, just like that mighty ship, be lowered into the ground, along with her secrets.

The cards, the condolences, the visits, the calls were endless. People caring. Wishing her well. After two weeks, she insisted Caroline return to Nova Scotia. She hurt most when Beau left. But he said he was as close as the telephone.

One morning, their attorney paid a visit. He gave her a safety deposit box. Craven had willed that it be given to her two days after he was buried. Lydia took it, but had no desire to see anything financial. She was Craven's beneficiary, and the will held nothing to question.

But in a lonely moment she became curious. All business matters had been taken care of. Maybe the box held a present for her. His going-away gift? That would not thrill her. He was not here to tell her how beautiful she made a piece of jewelry look.

She took it to the library and opened the top. Surely there was some mistake. Craven left her *this?* She pulled out the blue garter John had taken from her leg and Craven had caught. And kept.

And a bottle? But without a cork. And without champagne. Picking it up, she saw a sheet of blue paper rolled up in it. She remembered Craven holding a piece of blue paper, then rolling it and saying, what? Oh, yes—utter nonsense.

She turned up the bottle, slapped its bottom, and caught the edge of the paper with her finger and pulled it out. She unrolled it and began to read the words written on *Titanic* stationery.

The . . . utter nonsense.

She screamed.

Servants came running. It took a while to convince them she only needed water, despite her thinking she might need an ambulance. They obeyed when she dismissed them but did not close the library door upon leaving.

She began to read the utter nonsense.

> *As sunflowers turn to contemplate the sun,*
> *I turned to view your golden loveliness*
> *And loved, desired to care for, not possess:*
> *To cherish till our earthly days are done.*
>
> *But then desire for pleasure we should shun*
> *Crept in: Brief bliss brought shame with each caress.*
> *Though we have sinned, I love you none the less,*
> *But more, yet more, 'til life's last thread is spun.*
>
> *That life is now too short. My child-to-be,*
> *Through these last hours I pray that you may grow*
> *In faith as well as form, that you shall know*
> *My love sent from my grave beneath the sea.*
> *Heaven grant that you may always feel this bond*
> *Of love until we meet in worlds beyond.*
> *John*
> *—Psalm 23*

She started to read the poem again and realized that this was John's name, his handwriting, his pen and ink—he had held this paper. She touched it to her cheek, to her heart, loved it with her hand. John's words had come from the depth of that ocean, and it had taken him more than three decades to find her. But he'd done it.

*My love sent from my grave beneath the sea.*

He wrote this while knowing those were the last moments of his life.

*I pray . . .*

He prayed for his son. She did not readily understand poetry and read it over and over. John wanted him to *grow in faith, in form, know his love, meet him beyond.*

Was this what Beau was searching for? Why he could never get enough information about the *Titanic?* Was John's prayer being answered? But what was it John prayed for? *To know his love. Feel the bond. Meet him.*

She read Psalm 23. John wanted them to dwell in the house of the Lord . . . what was it he'd said? You'll be in my heart . . . forever.

John's son had been on that ship, with his dad. Beau was saved from that disaster on the sea.

She reached for the phone. "Beau. I need you to come home. Why? Because I have everything you need for your *Titanic* movie, right here in my hands." She added silently, and in my heart.

She might lose her son's respect, but he would know his father's last thoughts were of him, for him. He would know his father's words had traveled from a cold, watery grave over three decades to tell him of the love that would be in his heart . . . forever.

## 71

*B*eau arrived late. "Get a good night's sleep," Lydia said. "We'll talk in the morning." After breakfast they sat across from each other in the library. He read the poem. Studied it a moment. Held it out to her.

"Put it on the side table. You may want to read it again after you hear my story."

"Mom." He leaned forward. "You've already told me your story."

"Not this one. Please don't say anything until I'm finished."

A furrow appeared between his brows, but he leaned back.

"Beau, you were on that ship."

She felt his stare, but she stared into the past. In her father's office John had displayed his toy train, huffing and puffing around its track. Why she happened to be there she didn't remember, but her father, and Craven, and the others were all laughing. She had looked up and into John's eyes. That was the beginning of forever.

She talked to Beau all day, pausing only for mid-morning coffee together, lunch apart, afternoon tea together, dinner apart, an evening glass of wine. She had picked at meals in her sitting room. At lunchtime, she looked out the window and saw him in the backyard, walking while he ate. She didn't know where he ate dinner. But she could not sit across from him and look into his eyes as if she were his mother.

She was giving her life. He was losing his. He obeyed her and said not a word.

She talked as the room grew dim, then dark.

"Are we finished?" he finally said.

Possibly.

She said, "Yes."

He switched on the light, and she shielded her eyes for a moment. They hurt. They were dry. She would like the comfort of tears. They didn't come. All she had was an ache.

She knew he was staring at her, but she could not meet his gaze. "He wanted you to know—"

"I can read," he said. "May I take it with me?"

She nodded. "Be careful. It's old." For the first time, she felt old.

He stood. "I'll leave now."

She looked at him then. When had he developed Craven's blank gaze, his unreadable expression, his bland tone?

Just as quickly, he changed. "You're right," he said. "I could make a movie of this. Call it *My Two Dads*. Or *The Boat With No Sail*. No, not creative enough." He scoffed as if he hadn't intended to say that. "I have to give this some thought. Excuse me." He left the room. He left the house.

He left this stranger.

# 72

From the time Beau began to grow inside her, Lydia had kept him safe with lies. Now she'd lost him with truth. She'd tried to give him his natural dad but took away the only one he ever knew.

Two weeks later, he appeared at her door. They shared no smile, no embrace. He suggested they go into the library.

Neither were comfortable. She saw it in his face. Heard it in his voice when he admitted it. "I've tried to absorb what you told me, and give some kind of response." He lifted his hand helplessly. "I can see a script, hear the lines, even know what they should be, but when it comes to talking about my own feelings, it comes out jumbled."

She smiled then. "John was like that. The more meaningful something was, the fewer words he could speak. He had to write them."

"That's the way of the writers I work with."

"Maybe I can make it easier. I'm not the mom you knew. I'm a stranger."

"Oh, far from a stranger. You told me everything."

Yes, and she would take whatever criticism he needed to fling at her. "Go on," she whispered.

"When I left here, I didn't know what to say, what to feel. At first I felt I had no dad. But I did, and do. I loved and respected Dad. And he seemed to be a good husband to you."

She couldn't know if Craven were the better man, but she could say, "The best."

He acknowledged that with a nod. "Then I realized I have two dads. But that flippant remark I made lodged in my mind. A boat with no sail." He scoffed self-consciously. "It's true."

She clasped her hands on her lap.

"I went out on a boat." He added quickly, "with a sail." The tension in his face eased. "I thought about Dad demanding I remember who I am. Could we have coffee?"

She nodded. He went over to the intercom and asked the maid to bring it. He returned to his seat. "David knew who he was at age six. He knew when your feet don't touch bottom, swim. I thought of all that." He grinned. "You can't be around the Bettencourts without having to think, beneath the surface."

That truth made her smile again.

"I never had to rebel against you."

*Until now.*

"You loved me every moment of my life. Never did I doubt."

*Oh, I do. Can you love me?*

"You were the perfect mother. And at the same time, the most beautiful woman in the world, who knows all the right things to do and say, to live the good life and be married to a successful, revered man." He heaved a deep breath. "I lived with that. My life and opportunities have been amazing. There's been no reason I shouldn't succeed."

She thought he was doing quite well for one who couldn't speak his mind.

"And then, as you talked to me that day, Mom began to fade like a scene in a movie when the camera moves away."

She was going to break her hands if she didn't unclasp them. No, that was all right. They would match her heart. Fortunately, Myrna entered then with a tray and set it on the coffee table. She couldn't reach for hers with numb fingers.

Beau picked up his cup and drank from it.

She waited for the final blow. He was dismissing her. He was a grown man, but he was her child, her baby. She sealed her lips as best she could and swallowed the scream threatening her throat.

He put his cup down. "You were no longer Mom. That's a label. Like Beaumont and Dowd. Good ones, mind you. And you'll always have that label. But, like you said, you were a stranger. A woman. A person. A flesh-and-blood human being. A scared little girl."

She wasn't sure . . .

"I didn't like it. I saw me as a scared little boy. Maybe that's why we're called children of God, no matter our age."

Now he sounded like David. But as he'd said, you can't be around them . . .

"I'm a grown man, have a wife expecting a child, have every opportunity at my fingertips. But I'm a scared little boy. I could not admit that to anyone but you, because that day you held nothing back, and became no longer just Mom. You're someone I want, and need, as a friend."

Like . . . Caroline was to her?

"I know," he said, "everyone else in this world could abandon me, by their own choice or by my stupidity, and you may not believe this, but I'm not perfect. But I know you will always stand by me, loving me."

She started to come out of her chair, but he halted her, perhaps aware her insides were doing the Charleston and her fingers were nearly broken. He took a sheet of paper from his shirt pocket. "Like it or not, want it or not, I have another dad. And he has reached out to me from the grave."

A tremble of her lips replaced what she intended as a smile.

He pointed to the paper. "In this, I was trying to make some connection with him and who I am and what I am."

She reached for the paper, unfolded it, and read.

*Life as a Boat*

*a tiny white speck*
*adrift in the sea*
*I loosened the knot*
*and set myself free*
*one little vessel*
*no rudders, no oars*
*so without care*
*with no confinement of shores*

*I thought what I thought*
*and did what I pleased*
*or so it would seem*
*to the boat that was me*
*the clouds and the sky*
*and the birds and the breeze*
*all beguiling and tempting*
*my new liberty*

*singing soft songs*
*and spinning great tales*
*of exotic new cultures*
*and swimming with whales*

I rocked and I listened
and I soaked it all in
skimming the ocean
with a proud little grin

life was so new,
so adventurous, so splendid
but on the horizon
was a scare that could end it
an inky gray spilled
into my sky of lush blue
and the wind and the waves
were confirming bad news

the blue now all gone
and the clouds began crying
the waves, once so gentle
now quarrelsome and fighting
and me just a boat
who had longed to be free
now caught in the fray
of a battle at sea

the wind that once whispered
now came in great puffs
whipping across me
and roughing me up
and the sea that once rocked me
now leapt in my hull
making me heavy,
uncertain and full

and now I could see
the glory of shores
the need for my rudder

*and the need of my oars*
*what once held me captive*
*and held me in place*
*was not done in spite*
*but to keep me all safe*

*the fates it seemed*
*had a lesson for me*
*a headstrong little boat*
*who had set himself free*
*I need ropes, and shores*
*to hold me in place*
*I need anchors and piers*
*and a good dose of grace*

*and wants with no thought*
*that consume me each day*
*can make me unhappy*
*and make me their slave*
*so seek anchors and make peace*
*in that place that you float*
*and that is the story*
*of my life as a boat*

Her son. The poet.

As if reading her mind, he said, "I'm not a poet. But I wanted to speak to my dad in a language he could understand. I've had a few classes in poetry and I know the one he wrote has form, but I don't understand much about it. Mine is, I suppose," he shrugged, "free verse maybe."

"It's the meaning that counts."

"Mom," he said softly.

She looked at him then. His eyes were kind. "You've bared your soul to me. I know it was hard. I don't share my deepest feelings, not even with Angel."

He gazed beyond her, as she'd seen John do when new thoughts came to him. "No one has ever said they want to meet me in the world beyond, in the other life, live with me forever. He wrote that in his dying moments. I was real to him. He loved me before I could do anything to deserve it."

His gaze met hers then. That sounded like church words. And if it was or wasn't, that was fine. He could say anything. They were friends.

"To become what he wished for me, what and who I should be, I need sails, and ropes, and anchors, and shores, and piers." He breathed deeply. She thought he could sometimes be as talkative as his mom, his friend, had been.

"Speaking of boats," he said, "I'd like to take Angel to visit with David and Joy. Will you go with us? Although I expect you'd prefer to stay with Caroline."

"But suppose Angelina goes into labor?"

"She doesn't let anything hold her back. Besides, Joy's a nurse. Hospitals are nearby. If the baby comes early, I'll say what Dad always said."

They said in unison, "We can handle it."

They laughed together. "I'd like to go. Enjoy my friends." Maybe it was time to let go of her smother love. "Get to know . . . Angel better."

## 73

After talking it over, Lydia and Beau sold their holdings in the Beaumont Company. He'd rather invest in movie production and be able to survive any box office failure. However, his successes increased. Craven would have been proud of Beau's becoming known as a major filmmaker in Hollywood.

Armand was one of the attorneys who handled the negotiations, and Beau carefully reviewed them.

"Mom," he said, "a year after John Ancell's death, his company was sold by his beneficiaries, his parents." Beau looked at her. "Sold to Beaumont Company for a considerable sum. The Ancells benefited more than if they'd kept the company. Later, the company was dissolved."

She drew in a sharp breath. In the 1920s Beaumont Railroad introduced their unique train design, which was far beyond the designs of any other company, and one of the reasons Beaumont continued to thrive during the Depression.

She must have said some of those words aloud.

"I suppose you might say that both my dads contributed financially, making possible what I've been able to do."

She returned his warm smile. A mischievous glint sparked his eyes. "How would you like to visit London?"

After all these years? While the idea was taking shape, he told her of his plans. "I'm considering making a movie of Stanton-Jones's novel. I'd like to check out the setting. You'd be an invaluable source, that having been back in your day—"

"My day? I beg your pardon. I happen to be sitting right here. This is my day."

They laughed. "Your . . . younger days?"

"Mmmm." She felt the excitement. "Maybe Caroline would go. Oh. And Joanna. This would be the trip of a lifetime for her. I think she knows every word of *Once Upon* by heart."

He agreed. "And Bess," he said. "I'm still gathering information for the *Titanic* movie."

She was doubtful, like before. "You think anyone is interested now?"

"Many lessons should have been learned from that tragedy. If I film *Once Upon*, written by a *Titanic* victim, that will reawaken interest."

She was nodding and thinking about who might like to take the trip with them.

Caroline hesitated at first and so did Bess, both being uncertain about visiting the past. Armand had retired and after a bout with cancer, was declared free of the disease. His favorite pastime was fishing and Caroline's was the grandchildren, the oldest being David and Joy's daughter, Joanna, now sixteen.

Joanna read *Once Upon* when she was only twelve and insisted Beau make a movie of it. He finally considered doing it. "You know I would be invaluable to you on this trip," she reminded Beau. "I know every detail of that book."

"I wouldn't dare film a scene without your direction." Beau grinned.

Lydia had watched the close bond develop between these two through the years and thought it lovely. In her teen years Joanna had reminded Lydia of Caroline when they first met.

Willard had no interest in leaving his part of the world. Joy and David would stay behind to check on Armand.

Caroline had lost contact with Phoebe several years ago, but Beau located her. She didn't want to make the trip, but said she'd love to visit with them in Nova Scotia some day. She had lost track of her own brother a long time ago.

Several months later, Lydia thought of the saying that time flies when you're getting older.

Well, so did she. Fly, that is.

She flew to London with Beau, Angel, their daughter, Missy, and the two-month-old Simon in Beau's private plane, along with Caroline, Bess, Joanna, and members of the film crew.

Some places in London presented a war-torn scene, but for the most part the women—no longer an heiress, a lady, and a servant—toured their past as equals, thrilling Angel and Joanna with their stories, which to the young women seemed like ancient history coming excitingly alive.

The highlight for Joanna was visiting where Stanton-Jones had lived with his beloved. She cried, standing at *Once Upon*'s actual country garden.

Beau filmed her, saying this would be a perfect scene for an actress he had in mind. This was a speculative trip, but Lydia had a feeling the *Once Upon* movie had become a sure thing.

At dinner Joanna couldn't contain her excitement and her descriptions of what she had experienced made it all come alive for Beau. "You know that would be one of the greatest movies ever."

"Sure," Beau replied. "But we haven't been able to locate Stanton-Jones' son, little Henry. We need him for permission, if he's alive. We can't just take someone's book and make a movie. The heirs and beneficiaries and relatives have to be considered. Otherwise we open ourselves up to lawsuits."

"But if nobody knows . . ."

His gaze reprimanded her. "We know."

She grimaced, well scolded.

"So we will not proceed with filming until we know if he's alive or dead. But we'll keep searching."

Joanna held up crossed fingers. "You have to find him. His daddy has one of the two most beautiful love stories in the world."

Lydia knew the other one was her and John's love story. The girl must have a penchant for unhappy endings. On the other hand, maybe that romanticism was about love that hadn't had time for any unhappiness to mar it, but was in the heart always as perfect and lovely. A fairy tale?

Was that why Stanton-Jones titled his book *Once Upon?*

Regardless, her heart skipped a beat when in a private moment Beau said, "Mom" in a tone that caught her attention. "I plan to locate my ancestors."

She didn't think he meant the Dowds.

"I want to know his background. But I will approach his relatives as a movie producer seeking information for the *Titanic* movie."

He assured her that this was not deceptive since John would be a vital part of the movie. Besides, John Ancell was his dad. But they need not reveal that.

"Would you like to accompany me?"

She would.

Later, they visited his grave: JOHN ANCELL, TITANIC VICTIM, 1887–1912.

His relatives, who were pleasant, hard-working middle-class people, were eager to give any information that would honor John. She and Beau laughed with them, hearing of his childhood. His siblings were proud of John, who had shown a special creative aptitude. He'd lived a happy life. Lydia thought he was happy now, looking down upon his lovely son. John's relatives gave legal permission for any information to be used as the movie producer saw fit.

They didn't suspect John had loved her and had loved Beau.

But she knew. And Beau knew.

## 74

"He's started talking mushy," Joanna complained at dinnertime after Armand said the blessing and they began to eat his delicious roast.

Armand reached for her plate. "No dinner for you, young lady. Calling my blessing 'mushy.'"

"I'm talking about Michael." Grinning, she held tightly to her plate. He knew good and well who she meant.

So did Caroline. "How mushy is his mushy?"

Joanna loved these dinner talks. She could be open with her grandparents. Her parents said she could tell them anything, but she was more comfortable confiding in Caroline and Armand. They weren't just grandparents. They were confidants and friends.

She'd learned the difference from Beau. She asked him about referring to Lydia by her name sometimes. He explained it depended upon the situation. He revered his mom. Sometimes she was a friend, like people who aren't related.

She found that fascinating and asked Caroline and Armand if they could be friends like that. They liked the idea. She began to understand the difference. When she had a cold or flu she'd moan "Grandmooootheeeer," and accept Caroline's loving comfort. When Armand had cancer, she called him Grandfather and read to him. Other times they were Caroline and Armand.

"Well," she said, "Michael and I went to a movie and then to get a burger. I wanted to talk about romantic things."

"Hold it," Armand said. "What kind of romantic things?"

She batted her eyes innocently. "*English Country Garden* things."

He nodded. She rolled her eyes and continued, "Michael reads mainly inspirational books." She expected another question, but Armand kept eating. "So then he starts asking how many children I want when I get married. I told him I wanted three before and five afterward. Don't look that way—I didn't. Just wanted to know if you were listening."

"I'm listening."

She and Caroline grinned at each other.

"Then he asked what kind of house I wanted. And this is the truth, I said I like where I'm living, with Armand and Caroline."

"Oh, boy," Armand said. "How long do I have to put up with a sassy ol' woman?"

Joanna quipped, "Until she leaves you."

"Ohhh." He got up and went over to Caroline and kissed her. "I'm not talking about this one. She's my sweetheart."

On the way back to his chair he grasped Joanna's shoulder. "You're all right too."

Joanna knew that. She'd come to live with them when she started to college since they lived close to the university she wanted to attend. After her dad retired and started preaching at the Peggy Cove church, she preferred staying here.

"Joanna, if you don't care for Michael, why do you date him?" Caroline asked.

"Because he's a good Christian man, a youth director even. He's everything a girl should want. Maybe I've been overexposed to great, fantastic, sweep-you-off-your-feet kind of love stories. Some of my friends say I've seen too many movies." She sighed. "Maybe I'm destined to live a life of books and Beau's movies."

Caroline touched her hand. "There are all kinds and many degrees of love. If you marry someone, it should be your decision, not what others think is best."

Joanna nodded. She knew her grandparents' stories. But even the first one Caroline settled for didn't sound all that boring. After all, they had traveled first class on the *Titanic*.

"Let's pray about it." Armand held her hand and asked for the Lord's leading.

"Thanks," she said after the "amen." "I have a man right here whose love fills my heart."

They all smiled at each other. She certainly didn't want to settle down with someone without the Lord's leading.

The mood passed. She basically liked her life. After graduating with a degree in English, she started working at the museum in Halifax. Caroline and Armand had been great contributors through the years, with items Caroline had collected, her volunteering, and their financial support. Many people were saddened when they visited the museum. Joanna was sorry so much grief came from that disaster, but she thought of the items as representing people and wondered about their lives and liked having them remembered.

She wondered if Beau would ever get around to a *Titanic* movie. And the *Once Upon* might have to be forgotten too. Maybe some of her novel ideas wouldn't come to fruition either.

Well, maybe hope did spring eternal, she thought when she got a letter from Beau.

She read the information.

> Henry George Stanton-Jones
> Adopted by Mary and Bobby Freeman – name changed to Henry Jones Freeman
> Bobby Freeman—deceased—WWI
> Mary Freeman married Frank Morris—owned small business in California
> Frank Morris adopted Henry Freeman—changed name to Henry Jones Morris
> Henry Jones Morris marries Betty Lou Holcombe
> Henry and Betty Lou Morris have one child:
> Alan Freeman Morris
> Betty Lou (high school teacher) and parents (Holcombes) died in house fire (child saved by Henry)
> Henry Jones Morris occupation: US Army 8 years, handyman/janitor (cause of death: alcoholic cirrhosis)
> Living son of Henry and Betty Lou Morris:
> Alan Freeman Morris
> Military Service: Korean Conflict
> Education: GI Bill, Journalism
> Occupation: Freelance writer, tabloid reporter
> Residence: New York suburb
> Father: Henry Jones Morris, deceased
> Mother: Betty Lou (Holcombe) Morris, deceased, child Alan witnessed burning house with father

Joanna sat and cried at the sadness. The *Titanic* first-class little boy she'd heard so much about had had such a sad, unsettled life. He had experienced two horrible events, losing his dad and grandmother the night of the *Titanic* sinking, and then watching his wife and her parents burn in a house fire. The reason for alcoholism seemed obvious.

His little boy had watched a house burn with his mother and grandparents inside. He might have turned to the bottle too, like little Henry. She cried for them all.

Finally she dried her eyes and resumed her work but shook her head looking at the report. Amazing, how a life could be reduced to one page. A brief description, a bit of history, sometimes a comment by a loved one.

Then she read the rest of Beau's letter. There being so many people with the same name was one reason they hadn't tracked him down sooner. But this one seemed likely. Beau was busy on a project, but Joanna could contact Alan Morris.

One of her duties at the museum was to contact anyone related to the sinking. The fiftieth anniversary memorial would be held in less than two years. The plans for that were already under way.

Joanna had been in love with the book and the possibility of a movie. She'd visualized their finding little Henry, now a grown man, and hearing his story. She thought he'd be proud of his dad for writing such a wonderful book. Now she learned he died an alcoholic.

Beau's letter said she shouldn't mention the movie. He likely felt as she did, that he might not be the kind of person with whom he wanted to conduct business. She would just try to find out if Alan Morris's dad was Henry Stanton-Jones, but the thrill of it wasn't there now.

# 75

Alan Morris had accomplished one major feat in twenty-seven years. He'd become a failure. Although sobriety wasn't doing much for him, at least he hadn't followed in his dad's footsteps. He added *yet* to that thought.

His dad died of alcoholic cirrhosis that had led to kidney failure. He left nothing of value. Alan couldn't criticize though, because he was nowhere. He'd tried his hand at writing the great American novel and had visited a couple of major publishing houses in New York. He took editors to lunch and established a short-lived relationship with a first reader, but still got rejected—by the editors and the first reader.

Newspaper reporting for a small town suburb of New York City and an occasional article in a magazine about subjects that didn't interest him weren't exactly his idea of success.

Besides that, the actress he'd met after the first reader also broke his heart when she jilted him.

He had friends he invited over to watch football, or he went to games and vented by yelling at the players and referees. And sometimes at the crowd. The bigger the crowd, the better.

Sometimes his buddies talked about when they were kids and their dads took them to ballgames. His never had. Said he couldn't stand the noise and yelling. Then he'd drink himself silly and fall asleep and later wake up the entire household, yelling "Feeb! Feeb! Feeb!" because of a nightmare and didn't know what it meant.

Afterward, those buddies went home to wives and children. He went home to a lonely apartment, where a typewriter sat on the kitchen table sporting a blank sheet of paper, and a refrigerator stood empty, begging for food.

Today was no different. Same old routine. Report what's going on in the suburbs. Don't think about bigger papers. They have their city reporters, and the suburbs can't compete. The murders aren't as drastic, the fires are not as big, and the high school football games are not as impressive as the pro games. He'd given up looking for the big story. When his dad gave up, he'd turned to the bottle. Alan had hated that. Now he began to understand.

He trudged up four flights of stairs, weary from chasing a false lead for half a day, and threw the mail on the kitchen countertop. While the coffee perked, he tore open the envelopes with his finger. Bills! Junk mail.

He came to one from an unfamiliar address. A museum? Nova Scotia? He laughed and ripped open the envelope. "Want a donation, huh? I could use what you spent on that stamp." The aroma of the coffee livened his senses, so he poured a cup. After an ample gulp, he unfolded the letter and read.

> Dear Mr. Morris:
>
> Due to previously undisclosed information about the sunken *Titanic*, and after intensive investigations, we have reason to believe you may be a descendant of a victim of the disaster.

We have important material that should interest you. Please contact us at your earliest convenience.

Plans are currently under way for the Fiftieth Anniversary Memorial of the sinking of the *Titanic*. Relatives of victims and survivors will be recognized in special ceremonies. We would appreciate knowing of your intentions so we might prepare properly.

Sincerely yours,
Joanna Bettencourt
Assistant to the Director

If he'd had a mouthful of coffee, he surely would have spewed it across the room. What kind of farce was this? Organizations offered to include your name for a price. Was this something like that? Besides, so what if he was a descendant of a *Titanic* victim?

Turning toward the trash can with the letter, he laughed aloud. Now, if whomever had left him a bundle of money . . .

Whoa!

A lot of rich people died when the *Titanic* sank. He took another look at the letter. Information. Investigation.

There had to be a catch here somewhere. But, looking toward the blank paper in the typewriter, he reminded himself he was supposed to be a reporter. Maybe he could get some kind of story out of this. A lot of people brought up the *Titanic* almost as often as they did World War II, their surgeries, and the weather.

He studied the letterhead. Halifax Museum, Nova Scotia. Couldn't afford to go there.

Tomorrow, he'd call and check it out. Maybe.

When tomorrow came, however, he was reminded that it never really came. It was today again, and he was still in the same rut. Some of the old stirrings started. Like someday that big story would fall from the sky. But only the rain kept falling.

He might get some mileage out of this.

He'd put a little mileage on that rattletrap of his and see what awaited him at the museum.

So this is what it had come to. If you can't write the great American novel, go to a place that commemorates times and people long gone.

They could put him on display.

That would be fine, as long as they fed him.

# 76

Joanna was sitting at the desk in the entry of the museum when the door swung open. In her peripheral vision she glimpsed casual pants and a knit shirt. She lifted her index finger to indicate she would be right with him. "Yes," she said into the phone, "I will send official confirmation. Thank you. Goodbye."

Just as her left hand meant to hang up and her right hand meant to come down out of the air, she looked up. The receiver banged to the desk, the finger pointed at him, and her mouth opened to say, "May I help . . . ?"

But her eyes stuck. Her words stuck. Her entire being shouted, "Help me!"

Oh, this should not happen.

He should not be in her dream this way. He should be with his wife in that country garden. She obviously had read the book too many times, had obsessed about that movie too much.

*Go away.*

But the phone was urnt-urnt-urnt-urnt-urnt-urnt-urnt-urnt-urnting until he picked it up and casually placed it on its base and it stopped and she wondered if he had a magic formula to stop it in her heart.

He'd walked off the back of the book and stood there now, right in front of her, embodying the description she'd heard many times. Tall, dark, extremely good-looking.

"Joanna Bettencourt," rolled off his silver tongue, and she almost rolled off her chair when he said, "I believe you summoned me."

That proved it was a dream. Or worse, an apparition.

"I-I didn't summon anything—anybody."

"There's another Joanna here?"

The apparition gestured to her shoulder. She threw her hand up, and it landed on her name tag.

"Alan Morris," he said.

He didn't offer his hand. Maybe he knew a woman should be the first to offer—or did he know she'd not just lose her cool but would completely melt?

And he wasn't the picture on the book cover.

He wasn't in black and white.

This one showed up in living color.

"I believe you wrote that we might have a little business to conduct." A jaunty grin displayed his dimples. A touch of silver gleamed in his deep blue eyes. "I'm all yours."

Everything in her struggled against saying, "Thank you."

But why shouldn't she? He'd come in response to her letter.

Maybe he'd come as an answer to Armand's prayer. To her longing for someone able to sweep her off her feet. Someone to give her a great love story to tell over the years, to cherish for decades like Armand and Caroline, like Lydia and John, and Lydia and Craven.

The grandson of the novelist who wrote about the *English Country Garden*.

Perfect!

She showed him the stateroom keys that had been found in Stanton-Jones's and Lady Lavinia's clothing.

"What's—" he questioned, "that got to do with anything. Those names? Lady? The double name?"

He knew nothing of them. "That's it?" Disappointment shrouded his face. "You have the wrong person."

"You'll know when I show you something else."

He followed her home in his car.

When Caroline saw him, she grew emotional and wanted to hug him. She did. They sat at the kitchen table. Caroline handed him *Once Upon*. He looked blandly at the cover and turned it over.

He was startled. "My dad resembled him."

Caroline told him about Stanton-Jones on the *Titanic*, and little Henry on the *Carpathia*, the birthday party, the package he'd held onto, the Meccano set.

"I have that set," he said with wonder. "Everything in the house burned. Dad kept the set in the trunk of his car. Said he'd had it since he was a child."

Caroline told him what his sister had written. "Mary and Bobby Freeman forbade her to mention the disaster, said Henry was too young to remember and if she told him it would warp her brother's mind. He had nightmares," Caroline said. "He would call for Phoebe and—"

"Wait," Alan interrupted. "He'd call for what?"

"Phoebe. His sister."

"Phoe-be," he said slowly. "Dad had nightmares and would scream out something like 'feeb.' I thought it had no meaning." Alan raised his hand to his hair and clenched it, as if this were all a wad of something difficult to untangle.

"He never mentioned a sister. But he often said he had nothing." Alan spoke the words self-consciously, as if he hadn't meant to imply his dad considered him nothing.

Armand spoke wisely, "Childhood trauma, it sounds like. Maybe he didn't remember the tragedy, but he experienced it. It was in there."

Joanna wondered if Alan was living with childhood trauma. She shared the information Beau had sent. "That had to be horrible, your watching that fire."

Alan shook his head. "Dad didn't let me watch the burning. I just saw the ashes."

That held the sound of a double meaning.

"Dad was in the yard. I'd just gone inside when it happened. The boom. The flash. He rushed for me. By the time he got me to safety, the house was engulfed. He held my face to his chest and kept murmuring that he was there, to listen to his heart and I'd know everything would be all right."

Caroline wept. When she was able to speak, she told him about being in the boat. Told him how she held Henry, what she told him, and that Phoebe kept saying she was there.

Alan's voice trembled, "If either of us had known, things might have been different."

Armand touched Alan's arm. "We can't do anything about the *if*'s. We deal with what is."

Alan nodded. "I learned about that in the war. Fight and survive."

They agreed, and because Lydia's secrets were known now, Caroline began to tell about precious little Henry as a ring bearer. They all laughed and delighted in the memories. She told Alan about Lady Lavinia. Through the day, through dinner, into the evening.

Finally, they decided there were so many stories, so much to talk about, they'd invite others to tell him more. In the meantime, he could stay at the lake house.

Caroline had a good feeling about him, and Armand gave Joanna a knowing glance before taking Alan to the lake house.

Joanna hoped Alan would get busy with his broom, because her feet were ripe for the sweeping.

# 77

$\mathcal{A}$lan thought he'd found a gold mine in meeting the beautiful Joanna but realized she wasn't someone to toy with, but a girl a guy might take seriously, something he hadn't considered before. Not that he'd had much opportunity in the past few years, having been on the front lines with a weapon in his hands.

He was fascinated that she held in her hazel eyes the green secret Armand told him about, inherited from her grandmother. Joanna cooked a dinner for him in the lake house. They walked along the lake, watched the sunset, embraced in the twilight, kissed in the dark, and returned to the lake house, where she walked right past as if without a thought of going inside. She took him to church on Sunday. He hadn't done that since his childhood, with two parents, a lifetime ago.

Joanna called Phoebe, and Alan talked to her. Phoebe cried. He had an aunt. His dad's sister.

He had friends and family and a girlfriend who were beyond anything he could have imagined, and he was an imaginative fellow. He'd never known family life could be like this. He met Caroline's family and Bess's family and heard their stories.

He said he'd send for the Meccano set, but they didn't want to chance it being lost in the mail. His landlord would be notified, a servant . . .

*Servant?*

. . . would be sent to get it, and Lydia Dowd would fly in with it.

Lydia Dowd. Beautiful older woman with hair like snow. Eyes like sapphires. Money written all over her, and around her neck and on her fingers, looking like a jewel herself. With some people you just knew. Anybody in New York knew the name.

Lydia, as she insisted he call her, told him a shortened version of her story. Even so, it sounded like a best-seller to him. Alan's dad had been a ring bearer in her wedding on the *Titanic*.

Who wouldn't sit—stand up and listen to that?

He remained sitting, but it wasn't easy. Stanton-Jones, his grandfather, had become John's best friend on the *Titanic*. These people had been first-class passengers on the *Titanic*. They treated him, one who struggled to pay rent, like a first-class person.

Their stories, his story, became bigger than life. But he could get it on paper, and it would be his life.

Each night before turning out the lamp, he stared at *Once Upon* on the bedside table. He hadn't read it. Just reading the author's name was enough.

Henry George Stanton-Jones, II.

What a name.

So Alan Freeman Morris's dad was really Henry George Stanton-Jones, III.

Or, Henry George Freeman Morris Stanton-Jones, III.

Alan was, if he took his dad's name, Alan Freeman Morris Henry George Stanton-Jones, IV.

That wouldn't even fit on a book. He could use it and take up two lines or shorten it to Alan Stanton-Jones, IV.

He could write the *Titanic* book in time for the fiftieth memorial. It would be celebrated all over, even in England and Ireland.

At last, the great American novel was laid in his lap, meant to be. His time had come.

They all acted like he was somebody. Well, his grandfather was a famous novelist. His great-grandmother and great-grandfather were royalty.

As if that was not enough, they all became ecstatic about Lydia's son arriving.

Beau Dowd!

No. Couldn't be that one. The biggest movie producer in Hollywood?

But he was.

And he moved into the lake house with Alan. He wanted to get to know him.

This slowed down Alan's interaction with Joanna.

After all, he had to make a living. No, make that a mint.

Beau talked to him like he was just another guy, so Alan reciprocated. He was a descendant of royalty, after all. He finally mentioned he might write a book about the *Titanic* and discovered what he should have known all along. Beau had the rights to everyone's stories. Legal right. Contracts.

Alan had nothing.

Until he learned that Beau Dowd needed Alan Morris's legal permission, his being Stanton-Jones' heir, to make a movie of *Once Upon*.

Alan stared at the contract. The advance would enable him to give up the rinky-dink apartment, be financially secure for longer than he could estimate. And he wouldn't need additional work anyway since he'd be consulting on the filming of the movie.

Considering his newly-acquired background and the association with Beau Dowd, he could almost see the greenbacks covering his life like springtime across a meadow.

Several weeks later he strolled along the path by the lake while the sun dropped into the horizon and the sky turned dark and he found himself alone.

Lately, he hadn't given much thought to eye color.

## 78

*J*oanna had grown up with family and friends who shared their confidences, admitted their weaknesses, and prayed together. She didn't feel the time had come for her to share just yet. She knew Alan needed the acceptance they offered. He had family now. He had friends.

Having spent a restless night and awakened early, she made coffee, filled her cup, and went out back. Fog lay across the landscape like the mist that lay over her mind.

"May I join you?" she heard as she stood staring into visibility obscured.

"Any time." She recognized the voice of Beau, with whom she'd had a special bond since she was twelve and approached him about *Once Upon*. They'd discussed it as if he valued her opinion.

Since then, she valued his opinions in particular. In silence she finished her coffee, set the cup on a table, and walked with him through the English gardens Caroline loved to tend. They looked like they belonged in an impressionistic painting.

"Why did it change, Joanna?" Beau asked.

"He changed."

"How?"

"When I first saw him, I knew my fantasy of a love story like the *English Country Garden* had arrived," she said. "He could, and did, sweep me off my feet. I fell in love with the good qualities in him." She sighed. "Maybe I thought something was there that wasn't."

"What did you think you saw?"

"A vulnerability."

"Like inside him is an insecure little boy? Wanting his daddy's love? Wanting to be something, somebody, and beginning to think money could buy it?"

"Exactly what I was thinking." She laughed lightly. "At least, something like that. He's become a different person."

"You're right. He is a different person. You expect humility?"

His question held the answer to that. They walked beside drystone walls lined with trees standing like gray sentinels.

"So. He changed from a fantasy to a real person. Tell me, if you had to choose, what would it be, Alan or the movie?"

She turned quickly. "You wouldn't take the movie from him, would you?"

"I could. He'd keep the advance, but there'd be no movie, no fame, and he'd become his old, charming self. Is that what you want?"

She felt foolish. "I want it all."

"And what is 'all'?"

She scoffed. "Why didn't you become a psychiatrist instead of a movie guru?"

He shrugged. "I seem to be doing all right." He laughed lightly, then grew serious again. "Alan's bright. Maybe he'll have a quick recovery. When he learns he's a boat adrift, he'll come around. You and I have been blessed by people around us who have learned the difference between illusion and the real thing."

"You like him." Oh, she hoped he did.

"Yes. I see his potential. I see his need. His grandfather and my dad became friends on that boat, not because they were first-class, but because they had two things in common. Their creativity and their faith."

She nodded. "When you asked what I wanted most for him, I almost said 'me.' But 'me' is not enough."

"And he's not enough for you."

"I know. I've already pulled away. Just not in my heart."

"You know how Caroline says people react differently. Some come around quickly, some slowly. Maybe I can speed things up a little. Trust me."

She had no idea what he meant, but as they walked back toward the house, over the open fields spread out before them, the mist had risen.

# 79

Alan thought Beau might give him some advice. "I've messed up with Joanna. We were doing fine. She was delighted about the movie. Now it seems everything connected with it puts distance between us."

"Would you give up the movie to get back your relationship with her?"

"You're not serious?"

"If Joanna wants you and you want her and you'd be happier without the movie deal and all that's going on with it, I'll tear up the contract. You get to keep the advance."

Beau turned and left the room.

*Would I really?* Alan wondered.

Beau returned with the contract, which represented fame and fortune. Which was more important? That or Joanna?

Could he give up . . . his dream?

Not a chance. He said with confidence, "Tear it up."

Beau tore, saying, "This is the original. And I will throw it in the trash. You want to see?"

Alan didn't need to. Beau wouldn't mess around with him. The whole clan was probably fed up, and Beau wouldn't want the likes of him on a movie set. These were open, honest people. He might try it. "I've been a jerk most of my life. I don't deserve her." He shrugged, talking to himself really. "Now what do I do?"

"I can't tell you that. Have you read *Once Upon?*"

Alan shook his head. He was supposed to consult on a book, and he hadn't even read it. He'd been thinking fame and fortune.

"Try it," Beau said. "Your Grandfather might have words of wisdom for you."

That night, Alan propped himself up in bed. Great job! He'd just given up the chance of his life with no greater chance of renewing the relationship with Joanna.

But he started reading. *Once Upon an English Country Garden—a love story.*

A romance?

Henry George Stanton-Jones II wrote a romance?

The book became a best-seller in all Europe. All right. So his famous grandfather wrote a romance. He began to read.

> Sensing my presence, she turned, the breeze teasing the bottom of her skirt, swirling it lightly around her ankles. Her gloved hand reached up to steady the straw hat on her black hair. I could feel her gaze but couldn't make out the eye color. She was all in white, standing with a background of the English Country Garden where colorful flowers swayed and danced and were as high and higher than she. She was so fair, and seemed to be a wisp of a girl. The white against the color made her all the more outstanding.

> I had felt every emotion I'd ever heard of. But I never before felt what I did that day and knew it must be love.
>
> I knew it was that indescribable word *love* so lightly tossed about.
>
> I loved her.
>
> She smiled faintly. And I knew she loved me too.
>
> I couldn't speak. Could only offer my arm. She took it and we strolled along the garden path. Enjoying the beauty. Not the scenery so much as the knowing, the feeling, the absorbing the power of love.

Alan sighed. Well, his grandfather had known how to write a sweet little love story that appealed to the general population. Alan figured he could do better. Not on a love story, but something with action and drama. His life certainly had drama.

Then his eyes fell on the next line.

> I should have known anything so beautiful, so perfect, so overwhelming, all-enveloping was simply too good to last.

That line kept him reading. Yes, it was the story of romance and love, but its being too good to last haunted every line after that.

Alan became engrossed with the character, and analyzed what he felt. The character hated God for letting her suffer. But he stifled his anger and hurt because her faith in God gave her strength, peace, a greater love of life, and an acceptance of leaving them all.

It was not until after her death that he called on that God in earnest. He'd felt her bearing children had weakened her further, but she left him with parts of herself. That faith, that knowledge gave him the will to live, to eventually write again.

Alan laid the book aside. No, the book wasn't about romance, but about the deepest emotions one can feel. About life, and love, and disappointment, and hating God, and learning to accept. His grandfather had learned hard lessons.

Alan looked at the title *Once Upon*.

It started as a fairy tale.

Was the ending a fairy tale too?

Could one really—really and truly—know God's presence like his grandfather claimed? Was there a greater love than what human beings could give each other?

Alan read the author's note. Writing the story had given Stanton-Jones clarity. As he poured out his heart on paper, healing began. As he searched for God's answer when there seemed to be none, he began to experience that reaching for God, and putting the story down brought him relief.

No human could heal Stanton-Jones. Not his mother. Not his children.

But God's presence did.

It did not take away his grief and longing for her.

It gave him a reason to live, a reason beyond what anything on earth could give, beyond what any human could give.

"I've been a jerk," Alan admitted again to Beau the next morning. "I've been overwhelmed, to say the least." He laughed at himself. "But I don't how to find what your family has. What my grandfather had."

"Alan, they didn't come by it easily. You've heard their stories."

"I guess that's it," Alan realized. "Their struggles sound like stories that can be put in a book. But they are content. I don't really know how to go about having that in my life."

"Go fishing," Beau said. "With Armand and David."

Alan didn't know if he'd ever be a fisherman, but Armand and David sure were. Alan knew he was in shallow water right now. Maybe someday he'd be able to go deeper. Now he needed to do what he feared, learning to be honest about who he was. He had no idea. He'd thought he was the son of an alcoholic. A soldier with a gun. A writer with no career. A descendant of royalty. None of that had brought him anything but grief. The fishermen said God would show him what he had in mind. That was rather daunting.

These people, who'd been through more trials than he could imagine, wanted to help. He thought about talking privately with Beau, but he knew that wouldn't work. These people were family. This wasn't about impressing Beau, or Joanna. And being honest would drive her further away, not endear him to her.

Something deep inside stirred, as it had done in church when he was just a boy, as David said it had done for him. Instinct said this was not about getting a girl, or getting a movie.

Joanna, Beau, Caroline, Armand, and he gathered around the kitchen table. Honesty would be accompanied by cookies and coffee.

Alan opened his heart to them. Exposed his limitations, his doubts, his fears, his aspirations. "I'm not taking that advance for something I'm not doing. I'll find a job."

"You have writing experience," Beau said. "Think you could evaluate and edit scripts, and read novels and review them for movies?"

"I'd sure like to try."

"Doesn't pay much."

"Some is better than none. And I've supported myself." Be honest. "Barely."

"Fine. We'll try it for a while and see how it works out."

Armand spoke up, "And you're welcome to stay in the lake house during this trial period."

Alan knew they were giving him the chance to prove himself. "I don't want—" His words stopped when he looked at Caroline, who had told her story about the need to, and joy of, helping others. He cleared his throat. "Thank you." He needed these people.

"I'd like to know all you can tell me about—" He almost couldn't say it. "My relatives. And especially little Henry." He didn't mean their prestige or money.

They seemed to like that.

"And Alan," Beau said, "before you're too hard on yourself, know that my aspirations have always been fame and fortune. It's one reward of doing something well. We just need to get it in perspective."

Alan was too tough to cry.

So he didn't know why his face was wet.

But so was Joanna's. And Beau seemed to have something in his eye.

Joanna admitted to Beau she had some soul-searching to do too. "You know why he swept me off my feet?"

Some of Craven's mannerisms must have been passed down to Beau, who could answer a question with a minute shift of his eyes. Beau did that, and then he grinned.

She might as well admit it out loud. "It was part of the fantasy. And his relationship to Stanton-Jones and his love story and the *English Country Garden*. But I'll bet you knew that."

"I've known how much you love that book since you were twelve."

"And I'll bet you're trying to teach me a lesson too, by not making that movie."

"You still have a few things to learn."

Yes, she did. Like who and what Alan Morris was.

"How do you feel about him now that he's not a concept?"

"Well, he is gorgeous." She laughed at his warning look. "But there's nothing more appealing than a man who really wants to learn why God put him here. I mean, look at you, God's done a fair job with you."

"Ah." He frowned. Then they hugged.

After a few weeks, Beau said, "Alan is doing an excellent job. He has more creativity and expertise than this job requires."

Joanna knew that meant career possibilities for Alan. If he didn't break the heart of Beau's niece.

Joanna knew she had to learn who and what Alan was, the same as he did. They often sat in the kitchen and collaborated on some of the more difficult scripts or novels. They discussed, and talked, and walked, and sat on the patio and learned about each other.

It didn't take long for her to realize Alan's wonderful qualities. Like her family and friends, he too was a survivor. He'd survived the loss of his mom, the tragedy of his dad's inability to cope, a war, and his own humiliation of false pride.

One evening she walked down along the lake. He came out to join her. After one of their honest talks he said, "I would like to offer you the world, Joanna, but I have nothing to offer."

"What do you think I want?"

He sighed. "I think we want the same thing, what Caroline and Armand have."

She nodded.

"But I can never live up to your standards," he said.

"Neither can I," she replied softly.

He knew what that meant. No one was strong enough, good enough. They needed the Lord's help. "Perhaps," he said, "we could learn together."

They might start with a kiss, and she raised her face to his. The kiss began as the sun sank into the horizon. By the time they finished, the surroundings were dark, but she felt rather light-headed. His smile dimpled his gorgeous face. She had to warn herself about that broom sweeping.

# 80

$\mathcal{L}$ydia came to the country house two weeks before the wedding date. They'd been friends for almost fifty years, but on this matter Caroline couldn't be sure of Lydia's reaction.

"Let's have our tea outside," Caroline suggested that lovely spring afternoon. They picked up their cups.

Lydia looked toward the hallway. "Aren't Bess and Joanna joining us?"

"Oh, they'll be along." That's what concerned Caroline.

They sat a small table near the flower bed next to the house. Caroline needed to get some unpleasant news out of the way. "Lydia," she said softly, "Armand's cancer has returned. He doesn't have much longer."

"I'm so sorry."

Caroline nodded. "We've had a good life. No," she corrected, "it's been exciting and fulfilling."

"I know," Lydia said. Of course she did. "I will be here whenever you want me, need me."

Now she would bring up a proposition she'd had in mind. "Why don't you move out here with me? Joanna will be gone, and you know we have plenty of room."

"Be careful what you ask for. That has crossed my mind. Children and grandchildren are going their own ways. I'm just rambling around in that big place." She laughed. "You and me and Bess. Wouldn't we have a time?"

"Haven't we already!"

"We've survived . . . a lot."

"And become the best of friends through it all."

As if on cue, Bess came to the back door. "It's time."

Yes, time to find out if their friendship would survive this. Would this devastate Lydia? There was only one way to find out.

"What's going on?" Lydia demanded.

"You'll see."

They led her into the living room. Joanna, wearing Harriett Sylverson's unique creation, looked as skeptical as Caroline felt. When Lydia stepped into the room, a cry escaped her throat, and her hand covered her mouth. Tears streamed down her face. "How is this possible?"

"In the Waldorf Astoria, you handed it to me in a paper bag and said do whatever I wanted with it."

"And you kept it for almost fifty years?" she whispered.

"Until the time seemed right to let you know. Is this right? Or wrong?"

"It's . . . it's perfect. I've never seen anything so beautiful." She touched the wedding dress she'd worn when she married John and walked down that grand staircase. The past had come alive for her.

"Are you going to be married in this?"

"That's your decision," Joanna said.

"I would love for you to wear it."

Caroline wiped at her tears, seeing that the surprise had not brought a sense of devastation but lovely memories.

Two weeks later Caroline's granddaughter and Henry George Stanton-Jones's grandson would take their vows. At another wedding Caroline had been matron-of-honor for a fairy-tale wedding on a ship of dreams. That's when she'd vowed to love William, though never got the chance.

But she got a chance to love Armand. And now their granddaughter, the beautiful girl in her white gown, was escorted down the aisle by her father, who would also perform the ceremony. The handsome man at the front of the church watched her with love in his eyes and with a smile that dimpled his cheeks. When she came up to him, his hand reached for hers and they turned toward David and the cross.

As long as they kept facing the cross, they'd make it.

They said their vows.

Armand's voice wasn't as bold as it used to be, but the heartfelt words were touching, reverent.

> *Our Father*
> *Who art in heaven*
> *Hallowed be thy name*
> Quiet, beautiful.
> From the heart.
> *Thine be the kingdom, and the power, and the glory*

Caroline felt a nudge and looked down, and Lydia handed her a tissue for her tears. She wiped her eyes as Armand held the note *forever . . .* forever.

Lydia wasn't sure what emotions might well up inside her. Her friends knew that. Beau knew that, and he stayed beside her. They watched as the bride and groom danced the first dance in the fellowship hall while guests observed and applauded, and then joined them.

"Amazing," Lydia said to Beau. "You and I were on that ship with your dad, Joanna's grandmother, and Alan's grandfather."

He blew a quick breath. "Now that's movie material."

"It's life," she said and he nodded.

"Speaking of movie material," Beau said, "my wedding gift is a new contract for Alan to sign. No reason why we shouldn't begin filming *Once Upon*, even while they're on that honeymoon."

Before the couple left for London, there was one more planned activity for the *Titanic* survivors and the descendants of victims.

They went out in the yacht with carnations that they would toss into the water that would be taken out to sea. This was a symbol of what the ocean's depth took from them, and what it brought to them.

Beau threw his. Lydia thought he threw it in memory of his dad who survived the *Titanic*'s sinking, and the one who didn't.

She thought of both. Craven had been best man at two weddings. Without him, life would have been . . . worse.

At the end of John's poem, the last thing he'd written was *Psalm 23*.

They quoted the psalm.

> *Though I walk through the valley of the shadow of death,*
> *I will fear no evil.*
> *I will dwell in the house of the Lord . . . forever.*

Lydia threw her carnation. It danced and swayed as it caressed the surface of the water. "John," she whispered.

Her love for him had survived.

As if in reply, her son, John's son, slipped his arm around her shoulders. And she knew John was holding her, as she was him.

In their hearts . . . forever.

# Epilogue

God brings men into deep waters
not to drown them but to cleanse them.
*John H. Aughey*

"Peace I leave with you, my peace I give unto you: not as the world giveth, give I unto you. Let not your heart be troubled, neither let it be afraid."

*Jesus (John 14:27)*

# Discussion Questions

1. Do you think the sinking of *Titanic* was an act of God or of man? Why?

2. One intelligent, logical character describes another as a dream, as if that were a failing. Which is of greater importance in the world in which we live? Are they of equal importance?

3. A character concluded that he must not only avow his love but also show it. Do you find that essential to a relationship? How does one show what he/she avows?

4. John asked forgiveness for himself and Lydia. He professes to be a Christian. She doesn't. Is she forgiven? Can someone be forgiven for their personal sins if they ask but are not a Christian?

5. Do you think Lydia's and John's sense of guilt for having been intimate before marriage is because they felt it was against God's commands, against the culture of the day, or because her pregnancy would be a sign of what they'd done? At what point do most people feel guilty? After doing wrong or after being caught?

6. Could you ever lie to your husband about the fact that you were carrying another man's child? Or, have you ever raised your spouse's illegitimate child? Should you tell that child his true parentage?

7. How do you feel about Caroline wanting to be *ordinary*? What does *ordinary* mean? How does wealth affect who we are? Should it? If we are born to wealth, it does seem to have something to do with making us the person we are. Can/should we try to change that?

8. How does being involved in a national tragedy change the way a person grieves? Is there comfort in knowing you're not alone in your grief, or is it diluted because you are just one among many?

9. Have you ever been in a situation where your own grief (or another emotion) made you forget that someone else was suffering too, the way Caroline suddenly realized that Bess was also grieving?

10. People freezing and dying in the ocean were calling out for God and Jesus to save them. Do you think Jesus would say to them, as he said to the thief on the cross, "Today you will be with me in Paradise"? Would this be like a deathbed conversion, or would it be too late for those who had previously not believed in God and Jesus?

11. The character, Craven Dowd, is an enigma. Do you think he is a believer in the Christian faith or not? Why or why not?

12. Culture gave the characters the status of first-, second-, and third-class passengers. Did the surviving characters in *Hearts That Survive* change their personal definition of class? How does today's culture define the status of people? How do you define a person's worth?

13. Bess had her own unique definition of friendship. What is yours? What should determine who we choose as a friend? Is friendship conditional?

14. When one of the characters is dying, he is described as one moment being plunged into painful darkness. The next instant he is in the presence of serene light. Do you believe that is the experience of death? What do you think the moment of death is like?

15. How do you feel about Lydia keeping secrets? Can we judge if she was right or wrong? Why?

16. Alan says he can't live up to JoAnna's standards. JoAnna replies, "Neither can I." What does she mean by that?

17. In 1912 men were expected to die for their wives, to give up their lives for the women and children. Do you think the same concept is alive and well today? Would men still abide by the "women and children first" unwritten rule? Would it be selfish for a woman to want men to sacrifice their lives for them?

18. Are we any safer with our feet on the ground than in a ship on the sea? Do you think people would change their way of living if they really thought they were subject to disaster at any time?

19. Can you identify with any of the characters? In what way are you most like one of the characters? most different?

20. Were the survivors of *Titanic* saved by chance or was it God-ordained? If you were one of few survivors of a tragedy such as the *Titanic* sinking would you think it was chance, coincidence, luck, or God-ordained?

Want to learn more about author
Yvonne Lehman and check out other great
fiction from Abingdon Press?

Sign up for our fiction newsletter at
www.AbingdonPress.com
to read interviews with your favorite authors, find tips
for starting a reading group, and stay posted on what
new titles are on the horizon. It's a place to connect
with other fiction readers or post a
comment about this book.

Be sure to visit Yvonne online!

www.yvonnelehman.com

Donn Taylor, who wrote the poem John composed for Lydia in
the novel, is a poet who holds a PhD in Renaissance literature and
has more than twenty years' experience teaching poetry. His poetry
has appeared in *Christianity and Literature*, *The Lamp-Post* (Journal
of the California C. S. Lewis Society), and other journals, as well
as general audience publications such as the *Presbyterian Record*
(Canada). His poetry collection, *Dust and Diamond: Poems of Earth
and Beyond*, was published in 2008. Donn is also a novelist, and
his fiction includes the suspense-filled *The Lazarus File* and a light-
hearted mystery, *Rhapsody in Red*. He has also published essays on
writing, literary criticism, ethical issues, and U. S. foreign policy. In
a prior incarnation, he served in two wars with the U. S. Army.